Aoife Macarthy

Justice or Revenge

Carolyn George

Remember Me when I am gone away,
Gone far away into the silent land;
When you can no more hold me by the hand,
Nor I half turn to go yet turning stay.
Remember me when no more day by day
You tell me of our future that you planned:
Only remember me; you understand
It will be late to counsel then or pray.
By Christina Rosetti

PROLOGUE

"Three weeks, four targets. We choreograph every move. We plan every conversation." She was excited but trying her best to appear calm. The group in front of her were angry and scared, volatile and withdrawn. A dangerous mix and no one could blame them.

"And anyone who wants to walk away can. No recriminations, no judgement. We've all been through enough shit."

The poorly lit basement room didn't allow for close scrutinization of faces; one of the reasons that this particular meeting place was so popular, but the energy from the twenty or so participants was palpable.

The tall, well-built young man next to the speaker joined in. "We'll split into groups. Those who are willing to get revenge in a more physical way, others who do research and surveillance, and those who talk to the media."

The room became quiet; pensive. The likelihood of the police listening to them and be willing to go up against a group of men that had at one time wielded power within the church, the council and the police force was limited.

The group around him were a straggly collection. He looked at their solemn faces. Most of those who were here had managed to pull their lives together and were in decent jobs or training for careers that would provide a steady income. More than half of them had been in trouble with the police at some point. There were others who had never made it out of the barricades. Broken minds and even bodies, suffering from chronic anxiety, eating dis-orders and other issues.

"OK. It sounds like we have the start of a plan," said the

woman.

"If we start this, we've got to stick together. We can't backout." Said a slender woman in her mid-twenties who had been standing to one side, scanning the faces.

The well-built young man stood up. "Who's in?"

Everyone put their hands up.

CHAPTER 1.

DURDHAM DOWNS

Aoife walked briskly across the grass of Clifton downs. Despite having given herself permission to take a break, Aoife did not do 'sedate', she moved with purpose.

She had relocated to Bristol just ten days ago and was splitting her time between cleaning cupboards, painting her bedroom, unpacking boxes and exploring her new home city.

She had been born in Teddington, a suburban area of West London, to parents who had spent every holiday hiking through wild parts of the world. The only concession they had made when their children had arrived was to avoid the more dangerous areas. Aoife and her elder brother had both learned to climb and sail as soon as they could grip a rope, and very little allowance was made for having small legs when walking in relatively tame areas like the Lake District or Scottish Highlands.

Aoife had maintained the lifestyle, spending as much of her free time as possible in open spaces throughout her years at Bristol University and the following years based back in London. Recently the excitement and sparkle of living in London had worn off and she could no longer ignore the dirt, pollution and sheer number of people that filled every space in the city.

The very public end to her relationship with lead guitarist Cameron Connery, had been the catalyst that pushed her to search out a place that suited her chosen lifestyle. She needed somewhere that provided the potential for both work and her need for emotional and physical space. Tempting as it was, she didn't want to hide away in one of the furthest corners of the British Isles. As a journalist she needed to be in touch with events and have a decent transport system nearby to get her there. Bristol fitted the bill perfectly.

Leaving the Suspension Bridge, Giants Cave and eighteenth-century observatory behind her she headed through the woods in search of Peregrine Watch. Aoife had read that Peregrine Falcons had nested in the Avon Gorge since 1990 and March was the time to see their aerial courting displays – if you were lucky. She hadn't brought her binoculars with her but trusted that her keen eyes would pick something up if it was there to be seen. She wandered along the twisting, muddy paths pleased she had thought to wear walking boots. The cool blue sky with just a few grey clouds creeping in from the west did not worry her. She'd placed a waterproof jacket in her backpack, and she could always fall back on catching the bus that went past the Downs and would drop her within a hundred metres of her front door.

Aoife scanned the open spaces over the Gorge just visible between the trees, marvelling at how few people were nearby. She let her fingers drift over the rough trunk of a large beech tree taking in the earthy smell of damp leaves and tree bark. Turning back toward the small lane a sudden movement caught the edge of her gaze. She turned her head sharply but saw nothing unusual. A man in his forties was carrying his young son in his arms, probably too tired to make it back to the car after walking up the steep hill. As she glanced over, she saw that the child was crying and flailing his little arms against the man's strong shoulders and neck. The man barked something only causing the boy to shout louder.

"No. No. I don't want to!"

For a few seconds the sun came from behind the clouds making it difficult from Aoife's position to see into the darker woods. As she squinted toward them the man upped his speed and started to trot. An uncomfortable feeling ran through

Aoife's body as she marched along behind and a little to one side.

"I want mummy. Where's mummy?" The boy cried.

Unaware he was being watched the man held the boy away from his chest and shook him, making the child's head rock awkwardly back and forwards.

"Shut up!" The man pulled keys from his pocket and pointed them at a nearby sea-green car parked thirty feet away on the road. The lights flashed signalling that the doors were open.

Aoife started running toward them.

Fearing he was going to make it to the car before she caught up with them, she yelled hoping she would slow him down and get his attention. She certainly had that.

Jerking his head to her direction a moment's look of irritation crossed over his face as he picked up his pace. He was watching her with a mixture of anger and fear. She placed herself between the man and the car as she pushed away the small niggle in the back of her mind that this might just be a fraught dad overreacting with his stroppy toddler, and she was about to make a bad morning worse.

"Hey." She said in as friendly a manner as she could manage.

"What do you want?" The man was trying to play calm but failed. His breathing was hard, his face flushed with exertion and angry shadows had formed under his eyes.

"I couldn't help noticing the way you shook this boy. He seems very upset."

"Well, kids, they never know when it's time to go home." His face flicked emotions as he glanced side to side to see if their interaction was being observed.

"I don't think shaking them until their brains rattle helps."

"I need to get him home. His mum will wonder where we are. Excuse me." He went to open the back door of the Peugeot, but Aoife stepped in front of him.

"Could I talk to your son please?"

"Out of my way. As I said, we're already late."

The boy's big blue eyes were staring at her. Probably four

years old Aoife thought.

"Is this your daddy?"

The boy shook his head.

"Don't be silly, of course I am."

"No!" cried the boy as he pushed at the man's face.

"I know you're in a hurry, but I'm sure as a parent you understand. Would you mind showing me some identity?"

"Fuck off. Who do you think you are? A cop or something." With the boy in his right arm, he tried to push Aoife roughly out of the way with his left. She grabbed his wrist and elbow and with one step forward and to the side twisted his arm behind his back. As long as he was holding on to the child, she could do no more without risking hurting anyone.

"Calm down. I only want to make sure the boy is okay."

"You crazy bitch. Let go."

"Put the child down."

Too[swept up in the moment and worried for the child's safety to be scared, her voice was steady and reasoning. To her amazement he did as he was told and to her relief she noticed another car pull up behind the Peugeot.

Not wanting to lose concentration she could only see in the corner of her eye a male shape gets out of his car as he called "Is everything OK there?"

"Get back little one." She said quietly but firmly to the boy who was staring open mouthed at the antics of the adults. Then in one movement she let go of the man's arm and jumped back herself, just out of his reach in case he decided to lash out.

To her surprise instead of coming after her or the boy he yanked the driver's door open and jumped in. This resistance and adult intervention were obviously not what he had bargained for, especially as they now had an audience. As she turned to look at the child, she became more aware of the middle-aged man standing nearby.

"You okay luv?" he asked.

Aoife ignored him, pulled her telephone from her hip pocket, pointed it at the driver's side window and snapped off a couple of photos. As the engine of the Peugeot SUV roared into life and the car moved away she managed to get a couple more pictures to include the registration number.

"I'm fine." She said belatedly. Looking at the kid she stooped down in front of him and held out a hand. "Hey little one, do you know where your mummy is?" The boy, whose fear was pushed to one side for the moment, shook his head. Then he looked over his shoulder and pointed in the general direction of the trees.

Aoife took a moment to steady herself before she looked up at the middle-aged man. "I think that guy was trying to abduct this little chap."

Five minutes later the flashing lights of two squad cars and an ambulance broke the calm ambiance of the spring morning, and Aoife was sending the photos from her phone to the number the police officer had given her. A distraught young woman with shoulder length, sandy coloured hair dressed in jeans, trainers and waterproof jacket was hugging her son while wiping tears from her eyes.

CHAPTER 2

FRIDAY

Within the first week of arriving in Bristol Aoife had walked considerably more than one hundred kilometres according to her fitness tracker. Despite having given herself permission to take two weeks off work to discover the delights and layout of her new surroundings, she had still set herself a packed regime.

Rising early was not a problem so by ten o'clock each morning she had breakfasted, unpacked, and put away the contents of at least four boxes. By the end of the week bookcases were fixed firmly to the walls, and the second-floor loft room, with its stunning views overlooking the city and the suspension bridge beyond, looked like an inspiring and comfortable place to work.

By eleven o'clock each day she had showered and dressed in sensible shoes for exploring her new hometown. Setting off on a different route each day, she made a mental note of bars and restaurants worthy of a visit at a later date.

She had walked across the Clifton Suspension Bridge, ridden the ferry boats along the Avon through the centre of Bristol, from the quay behind Temple Mead Station, and caught the open topped tourist bus, learning facts and history that gave Bristol its reputation.

The balcony overlooking the harbour at the Watershed Café, was a perfect spot to relax, make notes and drink coffee. While the several markets, antique shops, and the more interesting and quirky boutique shops, had supplied her with ideas as well as groceries.

Halfway through the second week, her curiosity temporarily satisfied, she had begun to feel the familiar itch to work.

There were always stories that needed to be written. Since

her investigative skills had started to be noticed in the last couple of years, and she had been named *as "one to watch"*, work had come her way, enabling some choice in the projects she immersed herself in. She had a nose for an interesting and worthwhile story, and the ability to produce words that painted clear pictures in the imaginations of her readers. A few offers of collaboration were already available, but nothing that excited her, and she felt she was best suited to working alone for a while.

The second Friday in her new house, was spent sitting on the floor of her office at the top of the house, sifting through the boxes she used to store clippings, photos and general research. Over the years she had travelled a great deal. Airports excited her, but she loved trains more and there was nothing like getting in her car and heading off on an open road. For the moment though, she wanted to stay put for a while, or at least, find something that could keep her based in the west country and was an easy journey home most nights.

By lunch time she had whittled the piles of paper and notes down to just three folders.

Tonight, her friend Leigh was leaving work early and arriving at Bristol Temple Meads Station at just after 5pm for the weekend. This would be the first visitor to Aoife's new home, and she wanted to leave herself time to make sure a bed was made up, the house was neat enough, and she was relaxed and ready to welcome her friend. She gave herself three hours before she had to put work to one side and allow the weekend to begin. With a sandwich by her side, Aoife settled down at the large wooden kitchen table with her laptop, a notebook and a pencil.

The phone rang.

"Hi, you probably don't remember me. My names Christian Bailey. I'm a sportswriter at the Guardian."

"Hi Christian. What can I do for you?"

"You've just moved to Bristol haven't you?"

"Yes."

"This is not my field, but I've got something I think you could be interested in. A story I mean. Nothing to do with sport. I've been contacted by someone looking for a journalist who might be interested in a number of similar deaths in Bristol over the past decade. The police have dismissed them as accidental deaths. All young people mostly by drowning. All passed off as misadventure."

"And you think there's a story in kids who get shitfaced and then fall in the water?" Aoife shook her head in disbelief.

"Not when you say it like that. Apparently several of the victims didn't drink and never took drugs but that was not mentioned in any police report. And not just teenagers."

"And you thought of me?"

"I would have thought of you anyway of course, but they asked for you by name. Apparently you're already a legend in the Southwest."

Aoife sighed. "Oh shit. It's going to be like that is it?"

"Don't knock it, It's seriously good PR. I looked up the story. You kicked ass! Saved a kid and became a hero. It might have landed you you're first hometown story. I wondered if I could give them your number?"

CHAPTER 3.

GIRLS NIGHT OUT

Aoife had always been a pub girl. Hiking through the British countryside with her family had involved many pub gardens eating lunch, or quiet corners of the lounge bar if the weather was bad. A decent British pub was becoming a rare phenomenon, and she had been pleased to find The Shakespeare just a few roads along the brow of the hill from her new home. She had chosen to start Leigh's introductory whistle stop tour of Bristol at the pub before heading down to the trendier venues by the river.

Leigh was sceptical about her friend's move, so that evening, as they settled at a corner table, gin and tonics in hand, Leigh had again made her feelings clear.

"You're a journalist! And not just any journalist. A prize-winning investigative journalist at the tipping point of a brilliant career." she protested.

"I've moved house. I haven't stopped writing."

"You've moved a hundred miles away!"

"Ninety minutes on the train."

"Exactly! That's a long way to pop round for a cup of coffee."

"When was the last time you popped around for coffee?"

Leigh ignored the question. Aoife recognised her friend's approach to any argument. If the point did not support her case then it got swept aside. "It might be cheaper here than London, but you haven't got enough money to retire. What about your work?"

"It's not just London that has high speed internet you know.

And this is Bristol. Hardly the back of beyond."

"But your contacts are all in London. I don't think anyone here will even recognise you, let alone give you a job or a tip off."

"And that's one of the reasons I like it." Aoife smiled. "That and the river down the road. The open countryside nearby, Porthcawl an easy hop away."

"I thought you thrived on the tip offs and gossip."

"I can work anywhere. Anyway, it turns out I am well known in Bristol." She tapped on her mobile "Got my first lead off the back of this." She passed Leigh her telephone, then laughed at her friends open mouth and wide eyes.

"How the hell did this happen? Aoife did you really tackle a man on your own?"

"Didn't plan to. Just happened to be in the right place at the right time."

"Less than two weeks and they're already calling you a local hero."

"Well, I wouldn't say that exactly, but it did mean someone tracked me down and has asked if I'm interested in following a story. Even if this one doesn't work out, most of what I do means travelling anyway. It takes me fifteen minutes to walk to Temple Meads! When did you last walk to a major train station?"

Feeling on the losing end of the argument Leigh looked around at the crowded bar. There was a mixed bag of customers. A few could be locals born and bred. Totterdown with its multi-coloured houses and design graffiti, narrow streets, urban village atmosphere and artistic background, attracted a lot of young people too. Loud chatter and the occasional high-pitched laughter drifted through from the crowded garden. The bar was propping up all male groups; there were a couple of tables of mixed sex gatherings, but Leigh and Aoife were the only women without a man by their side.

"I thought you liked the theatre and the art galleries." Said Leigh.

"I do like the theatre, and there are three in walking distance from my house. If I feel a need for a West End fix I can jump on a train and stay with you for the weekend. It's easier than dragging the surfboard out of London or hacking down the M4 for hours to The Forest of Dean."

Leigh looked perplexed. She had stuck around Aoife since they had shared a cheap house in London when they were fresh out of university. They had both bought their own homes since then. Their lives had moved on and pulled them in different directions, but they stayed in contact. Sometimes Aoife wondered how they had remained friends when they met up so rarely. The truth was they knew each other too well and it was no surprise that Leigh Truelove had been the first of her acquaintances to insist on making the journey to the west of England to visit and celebrate the next step of Aoife's life. Right now though, it didn't seem much of a celebration, more of a reprimand with the potential to turn into an all-out haranguing as the gin and tonics were replenished.

"You are the most interesting woman in the pub though." Leigh raised her eyebrows, a grin on her lips as she took a sip from her glass.

"Oh, yeah, course I am. You know me. That's obviously the reason I moved here." Aoife shook her head and grinned.

"And I'm not the only one who's noticed." Leigh winked. This was her attempt to move the conversation in a more light-hearted direction. Aoife's emotions were still too raw to even contemplate a romantic relationship or talk about one. She hoped her friend was sensitive enough to pick up on this.

The professional side of Aoife rarely shied away from an argument. Her quick mind and dogged intent to discover the truth all helped to earn her reputation as a journalist with unwavering determination. At home and with close acquaintances she was quiet, mostly affable, and unlike some of her friends, good at keeping her emotions under control. Now she realised the onus was on her, not Leigh, to drive the direction of their conversation and that action needed to be taken if the evening was not to collapse in a disgruntled failure.

"Let's move down to the Harbour side. There's a tapas bar if you're hungry. Or a few half decent restaurants."

"Won't it be full by the river on a Friday night?"

"Dunno. It's still early and it's out of season. We'll find somewhere. It's a nice walk anyway."

Aoife picked up her shoulder bag, which Leigh guessed, carried a notepad an assortment of pencils a wallet and probably no makeup. Leaning on the table in front of her as she unfolded her long legs, Aoife used the opportunity to whisper in her friend's ear.

"I think you've got an admirer. Dark hair, blue shirt, good looking, leaning against the bar with two other guys." Aoife smiled as she noticed Leigh's cheeks turn pink. That should distract Leigh from berating her for a while and take her mind off to a more sociable direction.

"Have a nice evening ladies." One of the guys by the bar said as they walked past. The blue shirt man who had been looking their way earlier smiled and raised his glass as they passed by.

Aoife gave her friend a little nudge as they walked out into the clear night air and they both chuckled.

"Nice." Said Leigh admiringly.

"Not bad." Said Aoife. "You can still turn heads." Leigh was a good five inches shorter than Aoife. Dark haired and petite with large brown eyes and curves in the right places. She had always seemed to bring the nurturing side out in men. Unlike Aoife, who being much taller and rangy in build and looking like she could care for herself, seemed to be more of an acquired taste.

"Thanks, but I'm not sure it was me he was interested in." said Leigh.

"Ha!"

"When are you gonna realise lady?"

"Oh, I have no illusions."

"You're perfect"

"No I am not." Aoife's voice was calm and firm.

"No, you're not…. But you are fascinating."

"Formidable. Last time I had this conversation with a man he said I was formidable." They both laughed.

"Well yes. Bloody scary sometimes. But some men find that appealing. Maggie Thatcher was considered pretty hot stuff by her cabinet."

"Oh yes, that's me. The middle-aged stuffed shirt's pinup girl. I wonder how many thirty-four-year-old women nurture that ambition." She punched her friend's arm playfully and both women chuckled.

They walked down the hill and over the Banana Bridge toward the centre chatting companionably. The underlying animosity from earlier put away for now. It was a warm enough evening for early spring to have encouraged people out onto the street. Families were making their way home armed with fish and chip suppers. A group of teenagers ran past laughing and shouting as they rushed to catch the bus to the more fashionable Gloucester Road. As they crossed the Bascule bridge and turned into Queens Square, now restored to its charming 1817 layout, Aoife could tell that Leigh was impressed.

"How many rivers does Bristol have?" Leigh asked as they started to cross their third bridge.

"Just the two. In fact one really. It splits to form an island. This was the old Harbour. It stops just up there." Aoife pointed to the water running over ornamental steps a hundred or so metres to their right. They paused for a moment on Pero's Bridge to take in the view of the bars, restaurants and clubs. Their coloured lights reflecting off the water gave a magical feel.

Leigh walked to the far bank, resting her arms on the metal railings that overlooked the river. "Maybe I can see why you like it here," she said. It was still early evening. The area was busy but not packed. Students and late night revellers hadn't yet arrived in force.

"I've always loved the Thames and London South bank at night." Aoife joined her friend. "This isn't quite the same, but I think in lots of ways its prettier. More charming. Makes me feel like I'm on holiday,"

"Not to mention the cute men in the bars." She returned the glances of two men who passed them before disappearing through the doors to the Piano Bar.

"Yeah. Except I don't spend a lot of time in bars on my own." Aoife laughed.

"You'll find friends. You're far too attractive to be on your own for long."

"We'll see."

While Leigh went inside to buy drinks and ogle men. Aoife sat at one of the tables along the bank. Her eye was drawn to a small group of young people in theatrical outfits with beautifully painted faces. A tall lean man with dark skin tone wore brocade tunic and burgundy wide leg trousers. His face was painted in sweeping colours to match, and his soft brown eyes were emphasised with electric blue shadows and long eyelashes. Two of the girls had artistically drawn birds perched on naked branches painted on a background of chalk white faces. At the back of the group a matching couple of Pierrots walked arm in arm, heads close together. Others wore head bands, feathers, and different designs painted on their faces. All looked exotic and happy and comfortable in each other's company. For a moment Aoife felt a slight pang for a life she once had but was now forever out of reach.

Leigh sat down and placed their drinks on the table. She caught the tail end of the outlandish young group and smiled.

"I'm going to miss you being close by, but you don't change the world by looking at it, and you're determined to leave your mark. So, here's to change!" She raised her glass. Aoife followed suit. "Perhaps I should visit more often and escort you to the social whirl that is Bristol." Leigh smiled.

Aoife slipped her arm through her friend's and gave her a squeeze. "We don't see that much of each other anymore. Even when I was in London. And now you've got a free holiday destination whenever you want it. Long walks in stunning countryside. We can get to the seaside in forty minutes. And I can still come and visit to get my hit of culture."

"The best of both worlds." Leigh said quietly.

"Exactly. The best of both worlds." Aoife said raising her glass.

CHAPTER 4

KEELEY

Aoife was sitting in the café in Waterstones book shop on Union Street waiting for Christian Bailey's referral to show up.

She didn't have high hopes for this one. However, she had done some research on the drownings and there were an above average number of deaths. That didn't necessarily mean anything. Bristol was a university city with a river running through the middle.

Having waved goodbye to her friend the previous night, Aoife had felt her phone vibrate. Expecting it to be Leigh either exclaiming that she had left something behind or that she'd spotted a drop-dead gorgeous man on the train, Aoife picked up with a smile on her face.

"Hi."

"Is that Aoife Macarthy?"

Aoife snatched the phone from her ear and looked at the caller ID. She didn't recognise it. "Yes."

"I was hoping we could meet up." It was a girl's voice.

"Who am I speaking to?"

"Keeley Tomlin."

Aoife agreed to meet. She wouldn't normally accept an approach like this without serious background work, but a phone call had endorsed Christian Bailey's account. Google search produced stories of missing and dead teenagers in the area. And as Leigh said, she needed to work on creating her local network.

Well populated, public places when meeting a stranger was mandatory. She was, drinking coffee opposite an attractive somewhat earnest looking woman. Young, but older than her voice had suggested.

"How did you get in touch with Christian Bailey?"

"A bit of investigative research." Grinned the girl. Aoife didn't look amused. She handed a lot of cards out to contacts, some of whom were dubious characters, but it came with the job. However, she'd been surprised to get her first lead so quickly. Keeley had asked if they could meetup the next day.

"I saw your name in the news after you saved that kid on the Downs. It said you were a famous journalist. My brother-in-law has a brother who works for The Guardian Newspaper. He put us onto you when we told him we had a story. He agreed it might be the sort of thing you'd be interested in. He also said you were the best and we could trust you."

Aoife leaned back in her chair "Wow!"

"He said you were brave, but I knew that anyway. Tackling that perv like you did."

"I'll have to consider hiring Christian Bailey as my publicist."

"What's that thing they say? Six connections away from anyone in the world?"

"Six degrees of separation. Seems it might be true," acknowledged Aoife dryly. "So, what is this story that needs to be given the light of day."

"You might have read in the local news about my brother Harrison Tomlin?"

Aoife shook her head. "I've only been in the area a few weeks. Not up to speed on local matters unless it's in the headlines."

"It should be headline news. That's the point. Police corruption. This is huge, and not just locally. If you help us, it will make the national news and the cops will have to do something about it."

Shocked at the bitterness in the girl's voice, Aoife kept her emotions masked. Everyone thought that their case was important.

Keeley continued. "There's a conspiracy I'm sure there is. It involves at least one doctor, businessmen and some councillors."

"You've taken this to the police?"

"Aren't you listening? We don't trust any of them. They're rotten through and through. We know for a fact there's at least one high ranking police officer involved." She saw Aoife frown and reined herself back "Anyway, they haven't joined the dots yet. I mean they're always overworked, the police, aren't they? And their priority is the big drugs gangs what with county lines and all that. They just see me as a silly little kid.

Aoife looked at the young woman opposite her. She may have a young sounding voice, but she certainly didn't look like a child to Aoife. She was not classically beautiful, but she was well developed in ways she knew most men would find attractive. Her clothes were off the peg from mainline chain stores but well chosen. The overall effect was put together in a style that enhanced her natural assets. If you like the sexy, dusky brunette look.

So far, despite the intense manner, she came across well. Certainly not stupid nor a little girl.

"OK. Well, we're here. What do you want to tell me?"

Keeley took a deep breath. "My brother, Harrison, was engaged to marry Iqra, a special girl. Their wedding was arranged for next month."

"And before you start, I don't do family feuds or local rivalries." Aoife interrupted.

"Nor do I!" Keeley looked irritated, took a slightly smaller breath and continued "Iqra disappeared just after Christmas. She had no reason to leave. She was killed. Murdered."

"Are the police treating it as murder?"

"No. They insist she has run off somewhere. But she had no

21

reason."

Aoife was never sure what to say about the death of a loved one to someone she didn't know. As far as stories go this was a better start than she had expected but "sounds good" probably wasn't appropriate. She mumbled "I'm sorry. That must have been a shock for the whole family."

"It was." Keeley drew another deep breath and with renewed determination she placed the palms of her hands on the table in front of her, sat up straight and began her story.

"Iqra, Harrison's fiancé, was from a reasonably wealthy Pakistani family. Muslim. My brother is an Anglo-Saxon atheist. Or perhaps Agnostic would be closer to the truth."

"And that caused problems?"

"Not with Iqra's family. At least I didn't think so. They invited Harrison into their home and celebrated their daughter's good fortune. My brother is educated and although we are a very ordinary working-class family, he studied law in London. He recently joined a top firm in Bristol. My parents are both super proud of him and I think Iqra's father was thrilled to have a lawyer in the family. Harrison is very easy to get along with. Not at all up himself or anything." Keeley looked up at Aoife to check she was following, or perhaps looking for approval.

Aoife tried to keep her features as neutral as possible whilst still looking interested. She had to admit, she wanted to know where this was going. The best plan was to stay quiet and let the girl continue at her own pace.

"My family on the other hand, well the audience was split. My sister and I went to school with children who were black, Asian, Eastern European, Muslim, Christian, Hindu. A real mix 'n match. To us Iqra was just a really pretty, fun, intelligent girl." Keeley looked down at her nails for a moment. "I think mum liked her too, at least to start."

"And your dad?"

"My sister and I had met Iqra a few times, but she'd never been to mum and dad's house before. I thought it was a bit strange. Iqra was worried they wouldn't like her. Perhaps

Harrison knew something we didn't.

"Dad took against her from the moment she walked through the door. I've never seen him like that before. Harrison got very upset. Dad said he didn't want Iqra in his house again. He and Harrison really fell out about her."

Tears formed in the girl's eyes and Aoife could tell that whatever was coming next was the crux of the matter and stressful, at least to Keeley.

"Six weeks later Iqra was gone. The police investigated but within a couple of weeks they had Jamal, Iqra's brother in a cell. Said it was obviously an honour killing. Good Pakistani Muslim girl marrying outside the community. But there's no body so they can't charge him."

"No alternative reasons came up?"

"The police took the easy option. Jamal had been in trouble a couple of times as a kid. He stole a car once. Got into some sort of fight at school protecting his sister from bullies. Gave them a black eye and one of the boys was kept in hospital in case of concussion. But that was years ago. He's twenty-eight years old now. Mahira, his wife, had given Jamal an alibi. The police dismissed it as a wife protecting her husband. Apparently he'd been seen out of the house earlier that evening." As I said, they just see me as a silly little girl and when I told them how happy the Aziz family seemed to be and how close, they pretty much ignored me."

"Jamal is the brother. Had you met him before all this happened?"

"Yes of course. He would have been Harrison's brother-in-law. My sister, mum and me went to Iqra's family house the week following the dinner at ours, to meet them all. And before you ask, Jamal seemed really pleased for his sister. He chatted quite a bit with Harrison."

"Your father didn't go?"

"No."

Throughout their encounter Keeley had looked strained.

There had been moments when her voice became tight, and Aoife thought the girl might cry. Each time she had swallowed hard and fought back her emotions. Now, as Aoife watched her struggle once more, she noticed that underneath her makeup, the blood had drained from her cheeks. The fingers, that had rested on the table during her monologue, were trembling.

Aoife reached forward to lay her warm palm over the girl's arm. "They have really nice Danish pastry in here. Shall I get us one each?"

Keeley shook her head then looked up "Cappuccino would be nice though."

While Aoife waited at the counter she tried to resist the temptation to stare back to check that Keeley wasn't out the door and halfway down the street.

Aoife didn't know if there was anything of relevance to her in this girl's story, though her gut was telling her there was. And she trusted her gut. She got the feeling that, despite the outward bravado, this young woman had dug deep to find every ounce of courage available to her to walk through that glass door and sit down opposite a journalist. Aoife had seen girls reach out to her before. They believed that a writer would be more likely to listen to them sympathetically than a police officer. Or perhaps it was because she was relatively young herself, and being female helped.

She picked up the tray and, looking over her shoulder, was pleased to see Keeley had regained a little of her composure.

"What happened next?" The cups in front of them, the courtesies articulated Aoife sipped her coffee and waited.

"That's the sort of end. I don't know where to start with the rest." Keeley looked over to the bookshelves and watched a father helping his young daughter to choose a book.

"Well, personally I think starting at the beginning is overrated. The middle is just as good. Or the end. Whichever comes easiest."

The girl gave a weak smile. "When Harrison first brought Iqra to our parent's house for lunch Ma was very excited. She had cooked a real feast. She'd checked with Harrison what food his fiancée liked and had included as much as she could. Roast chicken with all the trimmings but no bacon and made an amazing meringue and fruit dessert. She doesn't really like cooking.

As a child I remember food was anything quick and simple. Mum works long hours at an old people's nursing home and food's never been a priority. So this was a big deal. Dad had bought a couple of bottles of champagne, and we were all invited. Me, my sister Petra and her husband Freddie, and their kids. It was a real party atmosphere.

When Harrison and Iqra arrived, mum went straight up and kissed Harrison and gave Iqra a long hug. My sister and I did the same, the kids were excited, and it was all a bit of a bustle and very noisy in the hallway, but then I looked up and I noticed… I… I think I noticed, a look of horror cross Iqra's face. Just for the briefest moment because then she turned and handed my mother a present. But I'm sure I'm not mistaken because as I turned to walk into the kitchen, I saw my father standing in the doorway. He had a look I hadn't seen on his face before, and I felt a chill run through me."

"What sort of look? It must have been really something if it disturbed you?" Aoife prompted.

"He looked scared. I mean his eyes were huge and he looked like he might fall backwards. Really terrified."

"Your father looked scared?"

"Yes."

"Do you mind if I take notes?" Aoife reached for her pencil and notebook, "It helps to keep everything straight in my head."

"Sure."

"What did you do?"

"Nothing. I just froze for a second. Everyone else was busy hanging up coats and introducing the children. No one else noticed. I followed dad into the kitchen, but he wasn't there.

When I went into the dining room with plates of food five minutes later everyone was there including my father."

"And...?"

"Nothing. That was it. Dad was quieter than usual, but no one else seemed to notice. When mum brought the pudding through my sister got the champagne from the fridge and Freddie opened it and filled everyone's glass, which was odd because it should have been dad's job surely? Freddie did a toast and we all said congratulations to the happy couple and that was it."

"And your mum didn't comment on your dad's handing over the reins?"

"Dad doesn't do speeches so perhaps she thought it was pre-arranged like that. But no. No one said anything it would have been too awkward. But I could see that Harrison was... I don't know. He kept giving dad sideways looks. Not nice ones."

"OK." Aoife leaned back in her chair once more and sipped her coffee. "And you didn't think any more about it until now?"

"No, I did. I thought about it a lot, but I persuaded myself I was mistaken."

"And this was when roughly?"

"Five weeks before Christmas. I share a flat in the city here. It was Christmas parties at work and drinks with friends and I had no reason to go home or talk to anyone. Not until December nineteenth. Petra, my sister, was going to her husband's family for Christmas, so she arranged for Harrison and me to meet her for drinks after work and swap presents."

"Not at your parent's house."

"No. Petra and my dad have a history. They never saw eye to eye since Petra was at senior school. Since she left home she rarely goes back to the house. Never if dad's there. The party for Harrison and Iqra was an exception."

Aoife made a note to ask about this later. "And what happened when you met up for drinks?"

"Harrison told us he and dad had met up and had a stinking

row. Dad didn't like the idea of him and Iqra getting married. Apparently it got very heated, and dad said he didn't want Iqra in his house."

"And your mother?"

"Harrison said mum was crying but basically stuck by dad and said she thought it was for the best. I called dad and asked what the hell was going on. He said it was nothing to do with me. The subject was closed.

I had already made arrangements to spend Christmas away with friends. We'd rented a cottage in the Lake District, so my parents were alone Christmas day. Five days after I got back Petra rang, told me to get to her house straight away. Harrison was there. I could tell he'd been crying. It's weird seeing your grown brother cry. He said Iqra had gone. Not been seen since she left her friend's house. He is sure something awful has happened to her."

Many thoughts had been running through Aoife's mind as the story had unfolded. She had a dozen questions she wanted to ask, but she held back. Keeley had been getting more and more uneasy as the story went on and her initial confident manner had diminished. Neither wanting to scare the girl away nor risk putting thoughts into her head Aoife chose her words carefully. Although she thought she knew; she still wasn't sure why Keeley had come to her.

"Do you know why your dad felt so strongly about Iqra?"

Keeley shook her head. "No."

"Had he criticised people of colour or different religions?"

"That was the weird thing. I mean, I don't think he has any close Asian friends, but he chatted to kids we brought home for tea. Told stupid dad jokes. Treated them just the same as the white kids."

"Are your parents religious?"

Keeley snorted. "I don't think Dad's set foot in a church since he was christened."

"Have you heard him deprecate, or belittle Muslims? Or any

religion?"

"Not that I can remember, no. I went through a phase of reading the bible and wanting to go to Sunday School when I was little. Mainly because my best friend went. Her parents were Methodists. I nagged. Dad's response was to take me swimming on Sunday mornings to distract me. I remember he introduced me to the library too. We went on Saturdays. He helped me choose three books I'd like to read. All non-religious." She smiled. "And that was it."

"When there's a programme on television or maybe an article on the news about children from other countries starving or having a tough time, does he comment?"

"Well yes, but in a good way. He's given money to charities that help kids in Asia and Africa."

Aoife rested her chin on her hands "So an interesting account of your recent family history but not the reason you've spent time searching me out."

Keeley turned to look over at the shop and bookshelves again as she spoke. "Because it doesn't make sense. Jamal loved his sister. The family were excited about Iqra marrying Harrison." She hesitated, looked Aoife straight in the eye and said. "And because it's not the first death or disappearance like that."

And Bam! That was it. Here comes the real report Aoife thought. "Like what exactly?"

"People who do not drink, do not take drugs, suddenly found with puncture marks in their arms or stomachs full of gin, and fall in the water, or disappear."

Aoife took a few seconds to digest everything she had heard and decided to put the last sentence to one side for the moment. "Tell me Keeley, you've obviously given this some thought, why do you think your father felt so uncomfortable around his future daughter-in-law?"

The girl did a reasonable impression of a fish out of water. Her mouth opened and closed several times as she squirmed awkwardly in her chair but said nothing.

"O.K. Let's put all the clues together as you have told me." Aoife pulled her notebook and a pencil in front of her and started to write.

1. Neither of your parents claim to be racist.
2. No one in your family had anything against Harrison marrying an Asian Muslim girl.
3. You thought Iqra was clever and charming.
4. Your parents had gone to a lot of trouble to prepare a celebratory meal to welcome Iqra into the family.
5. Iqra had a look of horror on her face when she saw your father.
6. The look on your father's face when Iqra walked in with your brother sent a chill through you.
7. During the meal your father appeared to have second thoughts about the marriage. To the point that he didn't open the champagne he had bought and cooled especially for the occasion.

"That's not true. We drank the champagne."

"But who brought the glasses to the table. Who opened the bottle? Who gave the toast?"

"Petra. Freddie." Keeley looked glum.

"It was when your father met Iqra that he turned hostile. And yet you, Petra and Freddie all thought she was charming."

There was a long silence as both women stared at the words on the paper.

Eventually Aoife asked, "What do you make of it?" The answer was staring them in the face, but she needed Keeley to be the one to say the words.

"I don't know. I mean, yes, dad decided against her which is odd when he was so happy for Harrison initially, until he actually met Iqra. But I really can't think why."

"Do you want to know what I think?"

Keeley's hand started to tremble, fear flashed in her eyes, obviously worried about what the journalist was going to say, but she nodded anyway.

"I think Iqra reminded your father of someone. Perhaps she looks like her mother or an aunt who he had met in the past. Or...." Aoife paused and watched the girls face closely "and this seems more likely from Iqra's reaction, your father and Iqra already knew each other. They'd met before the day of the party." Aoife was convinced that Keeley had drawn the same conclusion but didn't want to put her suspicions about her father into words.

"But they didn't say anything."

"Perhaps they didn't want anyone to know."

"But why not."

Aoife raised an eyebrow in a *"You've gotta be kidding me"* kind of look, "They felt guilty. Perhaps they were ashamed." She suggested.

"You mean they'd had an affair? That's ridiculous. My dad is sixty-two. Iqra is only twenty-four."

"I'm not saying that is the case. I'm just stating the facts as you've presented them. They are hiding something. Have I missed anything out?

"No."

"Tell me Keeley. Why did you ask to meet me?"

"I think ...." She looked at Aoife for a moment trying to assess how her next suggestion would go down. "Look, I know you may think I'm stupid with an overactive imagination just like the police did."

"I don't think you're stupid Keeley. Go on. What do you think?"

"I think it's very strange that Jamal should kill his sister.

30

There's no way Iqra would commit suicide either, which has also been suggested. And why would she run away, when just a few days before she was telling me how excited she was and how perfect her life was going to be."

There was another silence which Aoife refused to fill while Keely clenched her fists on the table.

"A few weeks before Iqra disappeared, Anwar, a friend of Iqra's, a boy who is tea-total and completely anti-drugs, was dragged from the river with a skin full of whisky and heroin pumping through his veins."

Aoife realised just in time what bad taste it would be to point out that Anwar's veins or, heart, would not have been pumping anything by the time he was dragged from the river.

"I can see that it doesn't seem straight forward, and I understand why you're upset. Before we get into Anwar's story, you still haven't told me why you think I might be interested."

"Because when I sat down and thought about Iqra and Anwar something started to niggle in the back of my mind." She wiped her spoon around her cup and licked the cappuccino froth from it. "This is where you really are probably going to think I am being silly. The police did."

"Try me."

"They may not be the only two."

"What do you mean?"

"There have been others who died in the same way in the last couple of years and, according to a friend of mine, before that too. The police have dismissed them as random druggies who have OD'd."

"And you're saying the police have not made the connection or that they ignored it?"

"Back then, the police didn't want to know. Still don't. They said it was troubled young people, or kids mucking around too close to the water. You should speak to my friend Daisy. Her best mate Cara died in the same way."

Aoife made another note. "Hang on, back-up. You haven't

told me about Anwar."

"No. I never really knew him. Just by reputation and I saw him around, but that was all. As a child Anwar had always lived in his own world inside his head. He played weird games and talked to himself. Sort of built barricades around his thoughts and emotions. Never seemed too upset when others tried to bully him. By the time he reached middle school we all knew his father was unpredictable and he didn't want anyone in his house, so Anwar didn't accept invitations either."

"So how did he and Iqra become friends?"

"Iqra said they had found each other in year ten, when being the only pupils without a partner, they were put together to complete a science project. Neither were put off by the other's reticence, speaking only when necessary. Iqra found his careful manner and long silences peaceful, and Anwar's attitude became less obstructive."

"Do you know any of his other friends?"

"If you speak to Mahira, Jamal's wife, you should ask her. They were friends. She knows I got in touch with you."

"OK. Is there anything else?"

"Yes. As I said you need to speak to Daisy Marston. She knows lots more than I do. She was best mates with Cara Felton. She's dead too now. Another so called suicide, but she had a kid and a great man in Chris Wakefield. A real keeper. She'd turned her life around. Daisy knows something's wrong. She wasn't sure about speaking to the press. Thought she might end up dead too. I think she'll speak to you though. She was well impressed with you saving that kid. Did you get a good look at him? The perv?"

"I got photos and his car registration."

"They won't find the car; or if they do it will be stolen. I bet as much as you like he works for Harvey."
"Who's Harvey?"

"Michael Harvey. He owns a load of businesses. And half of them are bent. Not the sort for reporting taxes."

"How do you know him?"

"He's a perv just like the rest of them. And a pimp. General scumbag. No one ever gets anything on him. He always keeps in the shadows, gets others to do the dirty work. Not sure who can give you the dirt on him. I'll get Daisy to contact you."

CHAPTER 5

TUESDAY EVENING

T his had been the eighth week the team had followed Habib Patel and written his activity and timings in their report; the third turn Gina had been allotted to monitor his movements alone. To watch him disappear through the white doors and into the community hall at seven o'clock. She knew what the sign on the door said but now she needed to write up a full report for the group so that they could discuss the best plan of action and work out the fine details. She walked the few steps from the pavements up to the door and took a photograph on her mobile phone.

7.30-10:30pm, £25 annual membership (first three sessions free)

Looking for something a little different on a Tuesday evening? The Webster & Jay Board game Circle just might be for you. With over 200 games and friendly, knowledgeable volunteers to help you learn them, whether you're after the latest board games or some old-school classics we've got you covered.

You can enjoy playing with your friends or meeting new people.

Tea, coffee and snacks available.

"Hey love." A deep, gentle voice said from behind her.

Gina felt her heart thump as she turned sharply around to see an old man, no taller than her, with a broad smile, red woollen scarf and cheeks to match, probably in his seventies, standing behind her. He looked kind, like he could be someone's favourite grandad.

"You thinking of joining us?"

"No. It's not for me."

"Play a few games. No obligation to join. It's not all old fossils like me. Couple of nice looking young men too." he winked.

"Thank you. It's for my dad. I'll let him know." She gave her sweetest smile "Maybe not about the young men bit." And walked back down the path wiggling her fingers in a little wave.

It was a nineteen-minute walk along the path between the woods and back gardens from Habib's house in Sully Road where he lived with his wife and aging mother, to the community hall. He had arrived as the doors opened and stayed to the end regular as clockwork every week for the last two months. The predictable routine would make their task a lot easier.

She watched as the target, a short, middle-aged man, walked along the road toward her. His belly pushed through the front of his jacket and covered the top of his trousers. His thinning hair was grey, his brown skin dotted with dark patches and his teeth crooked. A far cry from the athletic young man who had preened and strutted on the football pitch in his youth. Now he swaggered his bulk around as the local councillor. He passed by her on the other side of the road with just a cursory glance. He did not know her. They had never met. The reconnaissance team was always made up of people that could not trigger memories on either side. It was safer that way.

Being a spy came naturally to Gina. She wondered if the other's felt the same. As a child she had spent evenings, sometimes whole weekends, staying very still, not daring to move or even breath out loud. Listening. Keeping invisible.

Eavesdropping on the others behind doors. At bedtime, heeding every movement, observing gestures and changes in the moods of the grown-ups. Hoping for the best, fearing the worst.

As a teenager Gina had known the habits of her whole family and could have written their diaries from memory. When her mother went out, when her uncle and his friends arrived. The nervous glint of anticipation in her father's eyes and the way their voices changed. Louder and somehow sticky. She noticed everything about everyone who passed through their small, terraced house.

The big difference now was that she did not feel as alone as she had as a child. She reported back to the others who made their own notes of her findings. That and the fact that she wasn't the prey this time around. And it was nice to feel in control. To be the person with the power who knew what the next move would be. And it wouldn't be anything for her to fear.

She wondered if she should take it up as a career. Join GCHQ and get rewarded financially for her ability to listen and remember, gather sensitive intel. She knew she was good at it. It had to pay more than she got on the tills in the local Asda. And with the training she'd receive she would be able to kick ass. That appealed. Perhaps she should learn karate or kung foo. There was a Martial Arts Academy nearby. She would never have to live in fear again.

It was three hours before her target appeared again, as she knew it would be. The sky was dark. This time he was leaving the hall to walk home. The streetlamps were making the road shine slickly in the drizzling rain. Gina had slipped a woolly hat on over her pale hair, and now wore a green parka. Not that Mr Patel could see her where she sat in her car a few yards back from the club. She waited for a minute before she got out and closed the door quietly behind her. She followed at a distance and watched as Habib turned left onto the short cut through the hillside nature reserve that overlooked the River Avon. During the day the woodland with its wildlife and the open spaces with fantastic views of Bristol attracted dog walkers, families with picnic baskets and children flying their kites. At night it was quiet and deserted.

Gina looked at her watch and made a note of the time as she passed the first trees that formed the hillside woods, then paused at the edge of the park keeping her distance from the shadows, the girl watched Mr Patel until he entered his garden gate and was out of sight.

CHAPTER 6

DAISY

Aoife knew immediately that the thin, anxious looking girl dressed in a mixture of denim and bright cotton hovering in the doorway was the person she was here to meet.

She was very different to Keeley; petite and easily mistakable for a much younger girl, as she nervously looking around. Her DM boots looked the most substantial thing about her. Her otherwise loose, shaggy, dark hair had two thin, deep purple braids. Her eyes heavily outlined with black looked even darker against pale cheeks and her ears and nose carried an assortment of silver rings and studs. Aoife would put money on there being more metal inside her mouth too.

Aoife raised her hand and stood up as Daisy Marston approached.

"Hi Daisy. Thanks for coming."

The girl sat down quickly, and Aoife noticed that with her hunched back slightly lowered head and hands firmly clasped between her knees, she appeared to be attempting to take up as small a space as possible.

"Hi."

"Can I get you a coffee, tea, juice?"

"Tea please."

"I'm going to order a toasted teacake. Can I get you anything? Pastry or bun?" Before Daisy had arrived Aoife hadn't intended to eat anything, then, on seeing the skinny girl, some deep maternal instinct took over with the need to fatten the girl up a bit.

"Can I have the same as you please." The girl hadn't made eye contact yet, and her over politeness reminded Aoife of a young child doing as her mother had instructed.

When Aoife returned, drinks and snacks in place, her hand moved to pick up her pencil, as was her habit, ready to note everything of interest. At the last minute she decided against it. Experience told her that if she was going to get any information this morning she needed to put this girl at her ease first.

"So how do you know Keeley?" She kept her voice soft.

"We were at school together."

"Have you been friends all your life?"

Daisy looked shocked. "No, not really. Keeley's a really good musician. Did she tell you she sings?"

"No. I didn't know." This seemed a non-sequitur, but she was willing to wait it out.

"She sings and plays the piano. Never had lessons. Not formal ones any rate, but yeah, she's really good at the karaoke nights."

"Are you a musician too."

"Not really. I play guitar and trumpet. I'm pretty rubbish."

Aoife tried to picture the diminutive Daisy finding enough puff to play a trumpet and failed. "Do you go to karaoke?"

"Yeah. But I try to get on stage before Keeley then I don't sound so bad. No one wants to be the act that follows Keeley." A small smile fluttered on Daisy's lips.

"Is that how you know Keeley?"

Aoife felt a vibration running through the table as Daisy's right leg started tapping nervously up and down.

"No, Cara was my best mate. We started school at the same time. Hung out together. She didn't like singing that much but came to support me. She was another one that could pick up any instrument and play it though. She had a proper talent."

"So Cara and Keeley were friends?" If it took this many questions to get a simple answer out of this girl, Aoife thought, teacakes would just be the first of many courses. They would be here until dinner.

"Yeah. They weren't best mates or anything, but they did the music thing."

"It must have been a terrible shock then, when you heard that Cara was dead."

Daisy lifted the large mug of tea as if to drink it but pressed it against her forehead instead until she almost disappeared behind it. "Yeah."

Noticing that both their tea cakes were still sitting untouched Aoife spread butter and then a spoon of jam on hers giving Daisy time to control her emotions, fearing that she was crying. To her relief Daisy put her mug down and turned her attention to the pastry too. When she looked up there were no tears.

"She was murdered." It was such a simple statement. Not loaded with bitterness and pain.

"What makes you so sure that Cara didn't commit suicide?"

"Because she thought that to take your own life is a terrible sin. And because she loved her son and her husband. She would not leave them if she could help it. And especially not like that."

"Would you describe her as a religious person?"

"No. Spiritual maybe. She didn't go to church."

"How old was she when she died?"

"Twenty-three. Two years ago. They found her in the water by the tow path in Bath."

"So, if she didn't kill herself, then do you have any thoughts about why she died?"

Daisy lowered her eyes. Her fingers twisting the many bracelets that adorned her right arm causing them to catch the glow and sparkle from the coloured lights that hung around the window and along the wall at her side. Aoife gave the young woman space to speak at her own pace. If Daisy was right about Cara's spirituality and love of her family, perhaps there really was something bigger going on.

Eventually Daisy whispered, "I don't know." She lifted her chin to look directly into Aoife's eyes. "But I know she didn't kill herself."

It was Aoife's turn to pause now. She felt that Daisy knew more than she was saying. That with the right question Aoife might find the key to open this young women's thoughts. If she came on too strong and sounded as though she were interrogating her, she was sure Daisy would clam up. She just needed to find the right balance of words to prompt an unprejudiced answer.

"You know why I'm here? Why I'm asking these questions."

"Yeah. Keeley told me."

"Keeley asked me to look into why there has been so many similar deaths and if they're connected. She thinks there could be a story that needs telling."

Daisy gave a barely perceptible nod.

"Do you agree? Do you think there is something unexplained happening?"

"No. I don't." Daisy looked defiant.

Aoife sat back surprised. "You think there's nothing unusual in the deaths of your friends?"

"It's all perfectly simple. Everyone who has died was killed because they wouldn't stay quiet anymore, so they were bumped off."

Aoife watched the girls face for a moment, her eyes squinting in concentration. "You sound very sure."

"I am sure."

"And do you know who 'bumped' them off?"

The girl shook her head and looked down at her plate.

"Do you know if Cara was scared of anything? Did she seem nervous or maybe unhappy?"

"Everyone says she must have been really unhappy, but she wasn't. The day she had little Archie her life changed. She said it did, but I could see it too. She'd gone back to college did you know that?"

"What was she studying?"

"She went back and did her A levels, got better grades. She was accepted by UWE to do nursing." Bristol was well known for having two universities. The University of the West of England spread round the outskirts of the city, but the biggest campus is based around state-of-the-art buildings just off the M32.

"That's impressive with a baby in tow. What did her husband think about her going back to school?"

"Chris? He was right chuffed. So proud of her he told all his mates how smart his wife was. There's a nursery on campus. She'd arranged to have Archie there."

"Christopher Wakefield and Cara Felton." Aoife had dug their names out from the newspaper articles. "They weren't married were they?" She concentrated on keeping her voice light and non-judgemental.

"No." Daisy said defensively "But that didn't matter. You don't have to be married to look after each other. Chris adored her and Cara knew she was onto a good thing."

"Good thing? In what way?"

"He's a solid bloke. And gentle. After everything Cara wouldn't have most men near her." A look of horror came over Daisy's face and she immediately stuffed tea cake in her mouth as if to stop any more words coming out. Aoife thought it comical, almost like a cartoon character. She managed to turn her grin into what she hoped was a sympathetic smile.

Aoife decided against the direct question. "She sounds like a pretty amazing person. Getting her life sorted."

"She was. And she tried to help me too. Encouraged me to … you know."

"She helped you?"

"Yeah, I went on a training course too. Nothing like hers, just baking."

"Baking? I wish I could bake."

"Yeah. It's good. Bread mostly, but I can do cakes too." The young woman's face had lit up just talking about her passion.

"You think she was happy?"

"I know she was worried."

Aoife wanted to leap in with the next question already lined up in her mind, but she took a shallow breath instead and waited for two beats.

"Did she tell you what she was worried about?"

There was another barely perceptible nod. In the moments following her affirmation Aoife waited in expectant silence, wondering what Daisy planned to say, and how she expected Aoife might react, when she did.

Taking a deep breath, the girl sat up straight lowered her shoulders and looked out the window. As if in that moment she had made a decision she turned her back to the room. "Something happened at the care home. Years ago."

"Cara was in care?"

"Her dad had taken off when she was ten. Her mum died when she was thirteen."

"That's tough. Did you still see much of Cara when she was in care?"

"Yeah. I saw her all the time. She still came to school." Aoife noticed the sparkle that had been in Daisy's eyes when she was talking about baking had gone.

"She didn't miss school then?"

Daisy was no longer looking Aoife in the eye. "Some. It's why she had to redo her A levels."

"So she was there 'till she was eighteen?

"She was at a couple of foster homes. The last one she said was really good. When she eventually got in with Mr and Mrs Davies it was much better. She kept in touch with them. Went to their house for tea when she had the baby. They bought him a little outfit. Sort of dungarees and stripey jumper with a matching woolly hat. It looked pretty cool. Cara was right chuffed."

"Did you and Cara stay good mates?"

"Yeah. Yeah we did. She really helped me when I had to go into care for a while."

"You were in the home too?"

Another deep breath. "My dad died. Cancer. So, when my mum had an accident there was no one to look after me and my little brother."

"I'm so sorry. That must have been terribly hard on you and your brother."

"Yeah, but it wasn't so bad for us. We were allowed to go and see mum in hospital a couple of times a week. I snuck out of school to go and see her in my lunch break too. The nurses never told on me. She was in a weird contraption keeping her hip and leg straight. She'd been hit by a car that had been t-boned by another car coming out of a turning. It was awful but it could have been worse. She limps a bit now. Struggles with the stairs. But she got a decent pay out. That and my dad's life insurance got us a little house over in Southville. Suits mum down to the ground being an artist and all that. It's got an attic room with big windows."

Aoife realised Daisy was suddenly talking freely. She knew she had to try her best to keep the conversation flowing for a while. "So you weren't in the home for long?"

"No. Ten weeks. Then mum was allowed home. She had a nurse and a helper for a few weeks. Simon and me had to help too. I did the cooking." She said proudly and surprised Aoife with a cheeky grin. "I could cook pasta, make omelettes, bake cakes and Simon could walk up the chippies." She giggled at her own joke. "Mum doesn't like deep fat friers. They scare her. I even did a roast a couple of times. I think we all put on weight. That's what mum said anyway. But she was dead proud of me I could tell."

Aoife smiled back. "I could do with you at my house!" Which won a short chuckle from the girl.

"I was only fifteen. I could cook you a decent meal now though." She beamed proudly.

"And you kept in touch with Cara after you went back home."

"Yes. As I said, we were at the same school. We were good mates by then. I wanted mum to foster her, but I knew it couldn't happen."

"Why not?"

"Mum was poorly for about six months. Then when she did go back to work, she was still working two jobs. Even though we had the house by then. She has always tried the best for me and Simon. He's at uni now." She said proudly.

"What's he studying?"

"Computer tech at Bristol. He says he wants to work at GCHQ."

"That sounds good. So, what happened to Cara at the home?"

Daisy's face instantly became dull again. Her body seemed to deflate. Aoife stayed as still as she could.

"She started going out at night with some of the other kids from the home. Hanging around town. Outside bars. Did a few drugs. Just poppers, never anything serious."

"They weren't locked in at night?"

"No. And even if they had been it was easy to climb out the windows. None of them were locked."

"She must have met a lot of people. Young pretty girl like her."

"Yeah, she did."

"Not all of them nice." Aoife pushed.

Daisy sighed heavily, rubbed her forehead and looked Aoife straight in the eye. "She got into sex."

Aoife had been expecting this. It was a story she had heard too often. But it still felt like a blow that forced her to sit back in her chair as she braced herself for what she knew was coming next. For a moment she couldn't think what to say that didn't sound either trite or judgemental.

"With people who didn't treat her well?"

"They were pigs. I mean, Cara was only a kid. Fifteen years old. Several of the men were seriously old. In their forties or fifties. She tried to get away, stop going out, but they weren't having any of it. They made good money from the kids in care.

Once they got her name they threatened her. Said they had her on video. Said she'd get a name for herself as a slapper and a police record."

"You said 'them'. They made good money from 'them'. Were there other children from the home too?"

Daisy looked down. Aoife wondered if she was trying to decide how much to tell her.

"Yeah. And not just from the home."

"Did Cara tell anyone?"

Suddenly Daisy looked scared. Something had spooked her, and Aoife did a quick, discreet scan of the café and the street immediately outside. Nothing caught her eye.

"Look I gotta go. Pick up my kid from nursery." In one movement Daisy had collected up her phone, jacket and handbag and was standing up.

"Of course. Look can we meet again?" Aoife quickly fumbled in her wallet and pulled out a card with her telephone number. She placed it on the table and to her relief Daisy picked it up.

"I dunno. Ryan doesn't like me talking about it."

"Is Ryan your bloke?"

"My husband"

"You told him about Cara?"

"Not really. Just that I thought she knew some bad people, and something was wrong."

"Why doesn't Ryan want you to tell anyone?" Aoife felt alarm bells vibrating in her head.

"Says it's none of our business. Says it's dangerous."

"Who will know?"

"They know. They find out. I've got a good life now. A little house and a good husband." With that she turned to walk out.

"Thank you Daisy." Aoife called after her and was surprised to see the girl turn and walk back toward her.

"Remember, Cara was a good girl. No matter what you might think. She just had rotten luck. That doesn't make her a bad person." Tears were forming in her eyes and her voice sounded tight with emotion.

"I know. She was your friend. She must have been nice." That comment obviously wasn't what Daisy was expecting to hear and she frowned hard as if trying to get the measure of her interrogator. Then she turned and walked out of the café.

Aoife ordered herself another coffee and sat back at the table. She knew that children with a history of foster care and institutions were more likely to develop mental health issues or get into trouble. That's almost certainly how the police would have seen it even if they had tied the three deaths together. Although neither Iqra nor Anwar came from a broken home they knew each other. She couldn't help but wonder if there was another thread of some sort linking the deaths of these young people. Cara had been pushed into prostitution, perhaps the others had too.

Aoife would have to find out if either Anwar or Iqra had similar experiences. She was also confident that Daisy had more to tell. If that was the case, if there was a predator, then they had to be stopped and the only way for that to happen required people to speak out and the police to listen. For this young woman to tell her friends' story required courage. And Aoife was the person she had honoured with her trust.

It was time to talk to the police. Aoife had made a few friends in the Met while she worked stories in London. Perhaps she could find someone to recommend her to the Avon and Somerset Constabulary.

CHAPTER 7

DI COOPER

Detective Inspector Benedict Cooper's morning was not going well having just returned from court where he had hung around for ninety minutes waiting to be called only to have the case postponed. On his arrival back at his desk he was aware he was receiving curious looks from Sergeant Aida Goss who presently appeared in his doorway. He looked up enquiringly without speaking.

"How was your meeting with the journalist?" She asked.

DI Cooper usually found her broad Welsh accent attractive. At this moment with the strong hint of amusement in her voice it was extremely irritating.

"Fuck!"

"That bad?"

"No, I forgot" He threw an icy look at her "as you well know."

"She just called. She's still waiting in Mackenzie's down at the Harbourside. Apparently she's sitting there working so she's not too upset. Just wanted to make sure you hadn't forgotten." The sergeant's enjoyment was apparent as she leaned against the door frame.

"I don't suppose you'd like to go in my place?"

"No thank you sir. Anyway, she is the Super's pet project. Best left in your capable hands I think."

"Quit the sarcasm." Benedict snapped as he gathered his belongings back up.

"Why is Superintendent James so keen to have us cooperate with a journalist anyway? I know she saved that child in the wood, but really?"

"Because she worked with the Met on that fraud case last year." Ben flicked his eyes up and saw his sergeant waiting for more. "She not only dug up a lot of the leads she also knows a lot of people in high places."

Aida blew out sharply through pursed lips. "Ah. Better be on your best behaviour then sir."

"Take that silly grin from your face sergeant."

"Yes sir." Aida's smile broadened.

By the time he had rushed back down the stairs and hurried the half mile to the Harbourside café, DI Cooper's mood had deteriorated further. He walked swiftly along the covered walkway and turned through the glass doors of the big café/bar. To his relief it was almost empty. He spotted a woman in her early thirties, with short, spikey, almost black hair, who resembled the photograph that Aida Goss had supplied him with.

She was sitting at a table in the furthest corner tapping away on a laptop. As the police officer approached she looked up and her sparkling smile blew away a few wisps of the black cloud that were hanging over him.

"Aoife Macarthy?"

"Hi yes. You must be DI Cooper. Would you like a coffee? Or maybe a cold drink? You're looking a bit warm."

"Coffee, white please." While Aoife went to the bar he took a deep breath and tried to release the tension across his shoulders. He glanced across at the woman as she was tapping her credit card. She was younger than he had expected and dressed casually in an oversized sweater that covered her hips with jeans that hugged her slim legs. He had originally intended to look her up on the internet before they met but in the rush it had slipped his mind.

She returned with a tray that contained two large coffee cups a flapjack and a chocolate muffin.

"I thought if you'd been rushing around all morning you might be in need of some sugar. Not exactly healthy I'm afraid." Her smile was broad and appeared genuine and Benedict found his irritation at being sent to a meeting he didn't have time for, with a journalist he didn't know, just to please his boss's boss, dissolve a little more.

"Thank you. That's thoughtful."

"Your sergeant said you've been in court this morning."

"Yes." He looked at the two cakes and really wanted to pick up the chocolate muffin but went instead for the smaller of the two and bit into the flapjack. If Aoife was disappointed with his curt answer she didn't show it.

"I'm sorry if this isn't the most convenient of venues for you. I've only been in Bristol a couple of weeks and haven't sussed the place out yet."

"There are cafes closer to the station," he swallowed the large bite of flapjack and realised he was being rude. This young woman may be a journalist, but she had waited while he was forty-five minutes late. She hadn't complained or shown any sign of impatience and he was now stuffing his face with the cake she had bought for him.

"But it's nice to get further away sometimes." He added. "My boss said you had information that might be of interest pertaining to the disappearance of Iqra Aziz."

"Yes, thanks for coming. I do appreciate journalists have a reputation for sticking their noses in where they're not wanted. I try not to do that too often." She smiled. "Only when I think there could be something that might be useful."

"To you."

"I'd like to think in this case mutually beneficial."

"I've heard that one too many times."

"I'm sure you have. I have too. This might just be a case of bereaved friends and family looking for easier ways to explain their loved one's death."

He looked across the table at the woman with intelligent blue eyes and pale skin. Not classically pretty but there was something attractive about her.

"Talking to a journalist helps them give voice to their feelings."

"The good folks of Bristol seem a talkative bunch. It would make your life easier if they chose to sit in cafes and tell you their deepest anxieties?" Aoife kept her face straight, but Benedict noticed a mischievous light in her eye.

"Well, Bristolians are a very sociable bunch on the whole, but I would be suspicious of anyone who randomly sat down in front of me and confessed their crimes."

"I've been approached by a young woman who has information that might put a different slant on a situation your force has been looking into."

The detective instantly felt his hackles rise but tried to control his expression. "So why did she come to you?"

"Because she found out I was in Bristol and that I worked as an investigative journalist."

"How would she find that out?"

Aoife looked amused "I asked the same question. She saw the article about the young boy on Clifton Downs. And apparently her brother-in-law's brother works at the Guardian." She saw his confusion and laughed "Where I used to work."

"Which must be very flattering. And she hunted you down because?"

"I don't think it was me specifically she hunted down. it just happens that I have recently moved to the area. That, and the article. She is looking for someone to help her put the pieces together. Someone she can trust and who will listen to her and possibly her friends too."

Benedict couldn't help but note the implication. "I'm sorry to be tedious about this. If she has information which you think is important enough to discuss with the police, then why did she not miss out the middleman, or woman?" He picked up his coffee to cover some of his annoyance.

"Rather than waste time with the twenty questions, why don't I tell you what I know, then if you choose, we can discuss the motivation after?" There was a super sweet, smile masking her irritation, and a frown had formed on her brow. Benedict had to admit it gave him a tinge of pleasure.

"This girl is close friends of Jamal's family and ...." She began.

"And they claim that Jamal Aziz is innocent." DI Cooper interrupted. An unattractive smirk lifting one side of his mouth. "That is not news. It's also not surprising. Families often swear their loved ones couldn't hurt a fly."

"So you do know the case, but you didn't work on it?"

"I do, and no I didn't."

"I haven't spoken to Mr or Mrs Aziz. But those I have spoken to, think not only did Jamal have no reason to kill his sister, but there are others who seem to have a much greater motive."

"Look, the Aziz's have lost their daughter and now they worry they will lose their son. They will grasp at anything to help ease that pain."

"Did you talk to Harrison and his family?"

"You mean Iqra's fiancé?" The sarcasm was heavy. Aoife ignored it.

"Yes, and Jamal?"

"I've seen the tapes." He didn't add that Superintendent James suggested his team get up to date with the case only two days ago.

"And you think her brother did it?"

"In my opinion, if he was responsible then he really is in the wrong profession. He was distraught. I have seen a great many grieving families, and he was shattered by the news. And yes, of course we checked him out. His actions were suspicious, and his alibi was flaky. That's why we let him go but are keeping an eye on him."

"And there's the small matter of there being no body." Aoife tilted her head to one side and grinned. "It's not him that acted suspiciously according to my information not everyone welcomed Iqra into the Tomlin family."

"Who exactly."

"Harrison's father."

"Have you spoken to them?"

"No."

The detective sat forward. "So, you haven't spoken to Mr and Mrs Aziz or Mr and Mrs Tomlin?"

"Not yet. I came to you to find out if you suspected the Tomlins or dismissed them for a good reason. I'm not trying to make a story out of something that doesn't exist."

"Or you're fishing for information." He took a sip of his coffee, Aoife said nothing. "You say they have a motive. What might that be?"

"If you let me tell the story as I understand it you will find out."

"Why are you poking around in this case?"

"Oh, I'm not sure I am." Aoife smiled "I knew nothing about any of these deaths last week. However, three people apparently want to talk to me."

"Three people?"

"Mm hm." She decided not to give anything away unless DI Cooper decided to listen. Really listen.

"Again, why would they come to you? And what do they expect you to do about it?"

"I'm not sure. To be honest I asked them the same question. Look, we're going around in circles. Please stop trying to interrogate me. I have done very little so far with the information they gave me, and I'm not sure if there is anything in it, which is why I contacted you."

He raised his eyebrows. "And what do you expect me to do?"

She paused, to collect her thoughts, but it also gave Cooper a chance to control his own irritation and reflect on how much of a dick he was being. He attempted to sit back and relax.

"Well from the way you're behaving at the moment, sod all!" The smile was replaced with an icy stare. She got no reply. "Let me tell you the part of the story that I know. If it rings any bells or makes you feel uneasy in any way then you can look into it. If it's all stuff you know already and checked out at the time, then the coffee's been on me, we shake hands and go our separate ways."

D I Cooper looked weary but shrugged his shoulders "I have heard about you. Not just from what I've read in the media. My colleagues say you saved a child's life. That was brave." He sounded genuinely impressed.

Aoife felt the colour rise to her cheeks. She liked getting her articles in the media but didn't like being the subject of the stories herself. Cooper's sudden change of attitude took her by surprise though. "Yes, well, not really. The boy looked upset and instinct kicked in. I was lucky."

He looked at her appraisingly and his face softened. "OK. I'm here. You might as well tell me what you have."

Aoife recited the stories Keeley and Daisy had told her in as an abbreviated form as she could manage without leaving out any important details.

"The gist of it is that Cara had a husband who was a good bloke, a son she adored and a place at UWE to study nursing. She did not do drugs, rarely drank and she was happy." Aoife finished.

"How many friends and family of suicide victims have you seen reported as saying how shocked they were, they never saw it coming?"

"I thought you lot had it down as misadventure?"

"It was. I'm just pointing out that friends and family don't always notice what's under their noses."

"But it does sound as though she'd got her life in order. Despite a rough start she had the support of her foster parents, and a husband who was square in her corner. And no one saw her drinking that night."

"There's no proof that she didn't go on a private binge. The autopsy didn't come up with anything that looked like assault."

"But if no one was looking for foul play, could something have been missed? In the light of everything else is it worth looking into?"

54

Aoife had changed tactics and turned her thoughts into questions not directions. It didn't seem to have worked as she noticed the frustration in the detective's voice.

"The pathology report confirmed that she was high on crack. We know she had a difficult childhood and got into trouble with the wrong crowd as a teenager. We don't have sufficient evidence or resources to open every bloody misadventure and suicide case."

Aoife put her hand up to stop him before he got worked up. While she might not ever like DI Cooper, she did want to try for a decent working relationship. Police officers were useful to have on your side in her line of work.

"I realise that. If she was groomed and blackmailed as a kid, then turned her life around it's possible her past came back to grab her. Iqra, Cara and Anwar Patel all knew each other. I'm not asking you to risk anything. I was just wondering if there were similar cases. That's the story I'm interested in." She gave him a chance to mull it over before she continued.

"There is serious discord in the Tomlin Household. It was the first Christmas they hadn't spent as a family. Apparently this year mum Tomlin worked the Christmas day shift at the Nursing Home."

"That's her normal place of work?"

"Yes, but previous years she'd only done half a shift or had the whole of Christmas day off. I guess she felt it would have been a pretty quiet holiday at home without any of the children. She chose the company of the older folks."

"At the care home?" He looked surprised.

"A lot of inmates go to family for the holidays. Some of the staff bring their own family in for lunch. Having a mix of ages there makes it jolly for everyone." She watched the DI's expression show a hint of disbelief. "Old People not your idea of a jolly Christmas I take it."

"I have a grandmother who I enjoy spending time with." He said defensively. Aoife waited for him to elaborate. He didn't. "So, are Keeley and this Daisy looking for you to write up their story to win some sort of fame and possibly fortune?"

"Look I get it. You don't like hack journalists interfering and anyone who comes to me must be doing it for their fifteen minutes of fame." She sat forward "I don't have to tell the police anything. I am good at what I do. With a bit more research I'll have a story and you can wait to see if the police end up with mud on their collective face when you read about it with the rest of the world!" She gulped down her cold coffee and started scooping up her laptop and papers. Disappointed that this man refused to see that occasionally people spoke to journalists because the police had let them down.

DI Cooper looked on in silence. Irritated that he was here when he had a desk piled high with work. Irritated that he had wasted his time hanging around in court and pissed off that the public would rather go to the media than talk to the police. And now here she was being hysterical because he was doing his job and checking the authenticity of her story.

DS James would ask him how it went and would not be happy if a story appeared in the papers without warning. The Superintendent, who was normally no fan of journalists, thought Aoife Macarthy worth listening to. If it got back that, this woman had offered the police information, while he turned up late and had given her nothing but a hard time, any mud flying around would definitely find its way to his face.

He stood up so abruptly he made Aoife jump. "Can I get you another coffee?"

"Sorry?" She looked up confused, unsure what she'd missed.

"You may have something. If you can stay a little longer I'd appreciate it."

"Hm." She looked at her watch hesitating. DI Cooper had obviously missed out on the lesson in charm and charisma.

"Ten minutes?" He pushed.

"Sure." Aoife sat back in her chair and placed her notebook and a pencil back on the table.

As they settled back, sipping their fresh coffees Cooper made an effort to reorganise his attitude "Do you think Keeley and

Daisy have more to tell?"

"I know there's more. It's whether I want to continue with it or not. When I pointed out that what Keeley told me cast her father under suspicion, she was anxious but stuck to her guns. She had to have known how it made her father look, just didn't want to put it in words."

"Wouldn't be the first daughter with a grudge against her father."

"No. But she does come across as reliable. I got the impression they both had more than they were telling me. Probably just testing me out."

"Any thoughts as to what?"

"Possibly, but it's just a feeling. I trust my instincts, but I need to check a few facts first before I tell ..." A lopsided grin crept to her lips. "Before I tell the police."

"Ahh." There were several comments that sprung to his mind at this point, but he kept them to himself. "So why search you out, not the police?"

Aoife had the feeling he was looking down his nose at her. He'd repeated this question several times now. It obviously grated on his ego. "Perhaps she trusts me." She stared at him waiting for the other half of the calculation that she didn't put into words form in his mind. It did and he snapped his head away but not before she saw his mouth harden and the stony look form in his eyes once more.

"Trusts you to do what exactly?"

"I don't know. To listen? To keep an open mind. To dig a little deeper and see if I can find any facts that weren't uncovered in the original investigation. To do my job?"

"Are you implying that the police didn't do their job?"

She took a deep breath. She didn't think she liked this man very much, but she was used to dealing with despicable characters. The most important thing was to walk away with as many facts as possible that would help move her own investigation along. She thought DI Benedict Cooper probably wasn't despicable, just another overworked police officer who had learned to expect flak from all sides no matter how good a job he tried to do. She softened her face and attempted a smile.

"I think the police do the best they can under extremely trying circumstances." She could tell she'd failed to win him over, but there were signs she might have softened his attitude a little.

"Well, I'm not sure why you have come to me. What exactly do you, or these girls think is going to happen?"

Aoife bit back the first comment that came to mind. Then she swallowed the second. "I didn't come to you. You were sent to me by Detective Superintendent James." She tried hard to keep the edge from her voice but knew she was failing. "I thought it was polite and sensible to tell you that I am planning to look to see if there have been any similar deaths in recent years, particularly in Bristol. I am planning to speak to people who know the families involved. I will investigate the reports of several previously sober people suddenly behaving out of character and falling in the river." She smiled, "Apparently it's quite a common phenomenon around here. And then, I will consider if there is a story that would be worth pursuing."

"You mean you are threatening to write yet another article about how the officers have colluded with gangs and try to blacken the reputation of the police force."

"And have they?" Her tone was sharp her grey eyes stony. "Shit, you really do want to think the worst of me don't you!" She stared at him hard. "I mean I am letting you know that I will be digging into the facts behind the disappearance of Iqra Aziz, the death of her good friends Anwar Patel and Cara Felton. I was offering to share with you anything that might be useful."

"I've yet to come across a journalist that was working to make my life easier. It's all about a sensational headline regardless of the lives that are damaged on the way."

"I'm sorry you feel like that. I thought you might like to hear what I learned as I progressed. I mean, someone else doing some digging for you can't be all bad." He didn't look impressed. She decided to give up on the nice and say it like she felt it.

"And I promise you that if I were threatening anything you would certainly know!" She realised as soon as she stopped that the waiters were watching her. She hadn't perhaps phrased that last comment as well as she might, and her voice had carried across the room. She watched as he stood up slung his scarf around his neck and shrugged into his jacket.

"Thank you for the information. Ms Macarthy. And your time."

She was tempted to open her laptop and pretend to ignore his departure as if his comment and sharp tone meant nothing to her. But she wasn't that person, and she didn't want to be either. She stood up and, to DI Cooper's obvious surprise, with one step was by his side.

"Look, that came out wrong. I genuinely do want to pass on anything I discover that might be useful to your case. I have no wish to throw aspersions on the work the police do."

He took a moment to take in the words she offered. Her mind was obviously sharp. Her skin glowed and she looked fit and fresh faced in a way he envied. He looked at the shrewd expression, the bright eyes, firm mouth..

"Thank you." He paused for a second and then put his hand out. She took if in her own and they shook.

"So, if I do come across anything would you like me to contact you?" she offered.

He pulled out his wallet and removed a business card which he placed on the table. "Please. Keep in touch."

This wasn't an enthusiastic acceptance of help so much as wanting to keep tabs on her progress. Whatever she planned to write he could warn his bosses before it hit the headlines.

Aoife had had worse starts to a relationship with a potential source. Up to and including having the door slammed in her face and a punch on the nose. All in all, she thought as a smile formed on her lips, a promising start.

CHAPTER 8

MEETING

T he five men leant back in their chairs, legs loosely crossed, faces taught, drinks in hand. Each processing the news that Douglas Thornbeck had relayed from ex-superintendent Mewse.

"You say this journalist asked the police about Cara and Anwar? No other names?" asked Harvey.

"She mentioned Iqra Aziz too, but she knows it's an ongoing case." Said Thornbeck.

"I don't know why you were so worried about Iqra. You had her in a corner. She wouldn't have dared tell or it would have come out that she's a promiscuous little whore." Said Habib.

"You think that would be the headline in the newspapers? Fourteen-year-old whore found pleasure by having sex with groups of middle aged men. That will be the lead story?" Griff Tomlin snarled.

"There've been too many deaths. Someone is going to be rooting around in the muck. The others are going to get scared. If they think we're picking them off one by one they have nothing to lose by talking." Said Habib.

Thornbeck topped up his own glass then offered the bottle to his guests. glass "You should have made sure Iqra understood what was at stake. Convinced her that if she didn't want to ruin her wedding plans, she needed to keep her mouth shut. Her fiancé wouldn't be so keen to marry her if he knew she'd slept with his father." The others stared at their host.

"If she'd told him now or later my son would have killed me."

Growled Tomlin.

"Harrison is not like that. He is a good son." Father Rowan was rarely in Bristol anymore having moved to a Parish in the Cotswolds seven years ago. He had been summoned all the way to Weston-Super-Mare and Thornbeck's study, for this meeting and, for the most part, sat nervously swilling his whisky in its glass and saying little.

"He is a man. A good man who will never forgive his father for betraying his mother. Let alone with his future daughter-in-law. He is also a lawyer. He will want to know all the facts and the details." Tomlin glared back.

"That would be uncomfortable for sure, but it won't just be his old man he dumps in the shit. If someone starts poking around and any of the kids talk it would be all of us and a whole lot worse for everyone." Said Habib Patel.

"What were the odds of your son meeting the girl? I wouldn't have thought they mixed in the same circles. She had to be silenced." Michael Harvey's voice was cold and authoritative.

There was a moment where everyone stopped, features turned pale, and eyes flicked sneakily from face to face. No one in the group looked comfortable. A few of them looked sick and Michael Harvey worried that their hearts might not hold out as their minds pondered the consequences of their actions.

"You don't think …" Griff Tomlin was shaking.

"She knew Harrison was your son?" Thornbeck rubbed his brow "You mean it hadn't occurred to you?"

"I thought we had got rid of all this." Said Rowan

When it had all started over two decades ago, they were younger men full of swagger and married to women who cared more for their children than what their husbands might get up to when they left the house.

It was easy pickings. Most of the girls - and the boys - were in the state system. Cared for by nuns and monks who were more than happy to turn a blind eye for a few notes or a new roof on the church. Then the children's home had been taken over by the council and a new manager appointed.

Marion Newel had come in with good intentions. Long hours, lack of support and poor pay had all played their part in persuading her to turn a blind eye in return for enough money paid into an offshore account to set her up nicely when she retired.

The demand for young bodies had grown, bringing them a high return on their investment, and forcing them to spread their net. They discovered uncles, or even mothers, willing to hand over their children in return for cash or drugs, or to pay off a debt.

Griff had tried it on with his own daughter Petra for a while, threatening that if she told anyone then it would mean the dissolution of the family. Petra and her younger brother and sister would lose their home. But, unlike some, he had never made his own children available to others in the group. The thought of their disgusting sweaty bodies rubbing up against his little girl repulsed him. Several of the others did not suffer from the same qualms.

None of them had ever seriously considered what might happen in the future when these children grew up; became adults able to speak out if they chose. Times had also changed. Especially since Jimmy Savile's antics had made headline news for months.

People were being encouraged to not be ashamed of what had happened to them; told it was not their fault and to name the men who had taken pleasure from them as children. Even now Griff could not see it as abuse. In his mind children became sexually active from a much younger age than most people wanted to admit. And he had always rewarded well. Some of the kids in care were up for all sorts if the money was right.

The uproar about celebrities, faces that the public had loved and trusted, responsible for forcing vulnerable young people into acts against their will, had brought a stop to their circle. Michael Harvey had found other ways of supplementing his considerable income, the other's found pleasure elsewhere.

"Griff's right. If he goes down, we all do. We can't leave it to trust. We had to shut her up." The weather-beaten face of

Douglas Thornbeck was impassive.

"We have to make sure the others know that if they open their mouths there will be consequences." Added Tomlin.

Despite the strong words the mood of the group remained morose. Glasses were emptied and the group left.

CHAPTER 9

MAHIRA

Aoife pulled up alongside the pavement and switched off the engine. Opening her car door, she turned to look at the neat, modern semi-detached house that Mahira and Jamal Aziz had made their home. Freshly painted blue front door, symmetrically placed flowerpots stationed along the path and beautifully mown lawns either side. All in stark disparity with the chaos that was concealed within its walls.

She walked up the short path to the porch and rang the bell. Mahira had refused to meet in a café to discuss her family. She had arranged a time when she felt sure other family members were unlikely to drop in and disturb them.

Aoife made a concession. Instead, she had left a message with Leigh. It had included Mahira's address and DI Cooper's telephone number.

The door was opened by an attractive woman with her long, silky, black hair tied back in a thick rope braid that reached to her waist. She wore an ivory coloured top that hugged her slim body tucked into wide legged, dark pink linen trousers.

Mahira led her into the bright lounge that was also used as a dining room. "Please do sit down wherever you like. I've made coffee but you can have a cold drink if you prefer. Pineapple juice, diet cola or water?"

Aoife chose a comfortable looking chair that stood at right angles with the settee. "Coffee sounds good. Black no sugar."

Seconds later Mahira appeared with a tray that held two mugs and a mixture of fancy chocolate covered biscuits.

"Thank you for coming to see me. With your support, getting the story out will be much easier. Keeley has told me about what you do. She emailed me some of your work. The articles on FGM and those men who stole money from their customers."

Aoife smiled, taken aback slightly by the research these women had done. Not sure what to say, she took a biscuit and nibbled one edge, stalling for time. "You know that I'm not sure yet if I will be running with your story. To be honest, I'm not sure what the story is."

"I thought Keeley explained everything to you about Iqra and Harrison."

"She told me some things. Probably not everything." Aoife smiled "Each person has a fragment of a situation seen from just one point of view. Twenty people can witness the same scenario, and each come away with a version that differs. That's why I'm here."

"Of course." Mahira looked down at her hands, twisting her wedding band before saying "You know of course, that I am going to say there is no way my husband hurt Iqra. He loves his sister. That is my take on the situation."

"Before we go there, could we talk a bit about Iqra. Did you discuss her work for instance?"

"She didn't talk about her work so much. She loved her job and loved feeling that she was doing something worthwhile."

"And what was her job?"

"She worked at a refuge. A women's refuge."

"That can be a very demanding job."

"Yes, I think it was. Of course, she couldn't talk about the women, but at first she was full of the statistics. You know the number of women who are abused in the UK, how many of them die every year. She volunteered to go on every training course available and, although sometimes it made her sad, mostly she felt very honoured when women opened up to her. There was a light in her eye. She felt as though she was making a difference."

"It can be hard to hear some of their stories. She must have been a special woman."

"She was a strong lady. You know? Tough inside. Harrison was proud of her. So was Jamal. He adored her."

Aoife gave a grim smile "He wouldn't be the first person to kill someone he loved."

"He didn't kill her." She said firmly "They got on really well together. Not just brother and sister but friends too. When I first met Jamal, I was a little bit jealous of his relationship with Iqra. They seemed so close. I never had a connection with my family like that. I didn't understand it. They could banter and laugh and even argue but they never fell out for long."

"I'm sorry, but it still doesn't prove anything. A minor argument can get out of hand; one of them discovers something about the other that they find shameful. How many times do you read about a parent in the papers talking about how gentle and considerate their son is? Or a neighbour saying, "I can't believe it, he seemed such a nice guy and a great family man?"

Mahira was perched on the edge of the blue striped settee. Her face earnest. "The police were biased from the beginning. Iqra was going to marry a white non-Muslim. They were obsessed with that fact. It had to be a so called 'honour killing'. They tried to blame my father-in-law, Iqra's father, but he was away with his wife and family members in a restaurant at the time. They looked for uncles and grandparents. Then they turned their attention to Jamal and Eber her brothers, my husband and my brother-in-law."

"How did the family feel about mixed-race marriages?"

"When Iqra first told us she had found a man she would like to marry and that he was white there were a few comments and questions but only I think because her family cared for her. They worried about her future happiness."

"What sort of comments?"

"You know. Marriage is hard at the best of times, have you even considered the extra burden of mixed-race children? Have you talked together about religion? Will Harrison convert? Have you thought that not everyone will like the idea of him marrying an Asian girl?"

"All valid questions."

"And the only ones the police focused on." Her frustration suddenly bursting out, Mahira jumped up from her seat and strode past Aoife, her face contorted with pain and her fists forming tight balls. She stomped around and stood at the back of the settee. "We are not heartless. Our parents are Muslim yes, but they have brought their family up in the UK. They respect the British way of life. They have always wanted their children to be happy."

"And they all gave each other alibis?"

"Yes. And the restaurant staff. Customers saw them and they were picked up on CCTV as well. Even the police realised her father and uncles couldn't have been involved because they had all been seen eating together. The police seemed frustrated. Impetus had gone. Then someone said that Jamal had left football training early that evening and the police believed it. Jamal was working that night; he left training to have a shower before his shift started. A neighbour thinks they saw his car here; the police said she must have been mistaken. It didn't fit with their story. If he had come home to change, he wouldn't have had time to meet his sister by the river. Which is stupid anyway. Why would they go to the river?"

"Where does Jamal work?"

"At the port. He's a shift supervisor at a depot in Avonmouth."

"And that was the only thing they have against Jamal?"

"No." Mahira looked down, some of the fight left her. "They said footprints on the bank matched Jamal's football boots. If he had gone straight from football to the river and then on to work without showering, he had time. Jamal would never go to work without having a shower, and he wouldn't drive in his football boots."

"Who called the police when Iqra didn't come home?"

"Her parents were worried when they came back from the

restaurant. It was late and she wasn't home. Iqra had gone to her friend's house, but she left there at seven thirty. Eventually my father-in-law called the police. They told him not to worry. Said she had probably just met other friends and forgot the time." The young woman looked away while she mopped her eyes and attempted to control the tears.

"It does happen." Offered Aoife. "Did you know the young man who fell in the water a few weeks before, down by the Marina?"

"Yes. We were at the same school together. His name was Anwar. We lost touch though. I mean we were never close. I've seen him around town a few times. My dad knows the family, or at least he knows the boy's father from the Mosque." She frowned "Why?"

"I heard his family were surprised when the pathologist's reported back a substantial amount of cocaine in his blood."

"My dad said none of his friends had any idea that Anwar had ever taken drugs. But why do you want to know about him? He was walking home from an evening out with his friends when he fell in the river." She looked at Aoife questioningly.

Aoife ignored the question. "I'm led to believe that he and Iqra were close for a while."

"Yes," Her tone changed "At school. They were both quiet people and they just gravitated to each other. Apparently he did well at school. You know his eldest sister died when Anwar was young?"

Aoife nodded. "He was training to be a carpenter wasn't he?"

"He loved his job, and he was looking forward to getting married."

"To lose a wife and a son. Mr Patel, his father, must have been crushed."

"My father saw them at the Mosque. He never really liked Habib Patel, but he thought Anwar was a good boy. By the time he got to senior school my dad was worried about him, he was cutting himself off from the community, withdrew from everyone. Occasionally it made him a target for bullies, but his attitude mostly kept people at bay. The drugs thing didn't make sense."

"Circumstances change. People change. Anwar had gone back to college. He was being bullied. Families don't always know what's going on in each other's lives. Even close ones."

"I didn't know he was at college. I thought he was working as a builder."

"Carpenter. He was an apprentice, and it was a day release course." Aoife had done her research on all the young people who had been pulled from the river.

Mahira picked up a cushion from the settee and traced the pattern with her finger. "He would have liked that. He was good with his hands. Liked making things."

"That sounds as though you knew him well?"

"No not really. He drew as little attention to himself as possible. As I said he was Iqra's friend. The one person he trusted was Iqra. She had noticed him, which most girls didn't. She'd not shunned him nor forced her company on him. They are a couple of years younger than me. We used to chat sometimes. He used to go to Iqra's house after school, eat his tea there, that sort of thing. Jamal was there too of course." She looked confused. Aoife waited to see if Mahira was going to elaborate.

"We used to hang out together a bit as kids."

"Kids?"

"Yes. I was eleven, twelve, something like that. A bunch of us went to the park. We drifted apart. I didn't see him much during GCSEs." Aoife remained still. If Mahira was going to confide something important this was the moment.

"They weren't a close family. Anwar hated his father. He used to get in to trouble because he would go to friend's houses after school, he came to my house sometimes, as part of the group you know, when he was supposed to be at home."

"Did he say why he hated his father?"

Mahira blushed. "What does this have to do with Jamal being accused of killing Iqra? I don't see the connection."

"Nor do I. Not at the moment. Just curious. And it is amazing how webs are woven. Something you think is irrelevant can turn out to be the key that unlocks everything."

"I know his father was not a nice man and I know that Anwar was scared of him."

"Did he ever tell you why?"

"No. We were still babies back when I knew him." She looked up suddenly. "But I do know that Anwar and Iqra were close friends. They seemed to, I don't know, support each other."

"Thank you for your time Mahira. If you think of anything else, then let me know." Aoife stood to leave.

"Are you going to keep looking for more?"

"I know it's difficult to hear" Aoife continued, "but unless you have proof or a substantial reason for the police to take another look, the case won't be re-opened and It's not a story the papers will be interested in."

"I know the police didn't want to know what really happened. They have closed their minds. They want to blame Jamal but without a body they can't. She's just another missing person. And they don't care. They have someone in their sights, and it doesn't matter to them if it's the wrong person. A young man like Anwar doesn't just throw his life away like that. And a brother doesn't murder the sister he loves." She turned and stared accusingly at Aoife. "But I thought you would understand." Mahira had raised her voice.

Aoife kept her speech soft and calm, her tone reassuring, and her words were measured. She was pretty sure that this outburst was not aimed purely at her and was more to do with general frustration and the dark cloud that hung over the family.

"It doesn't work that way. I look at the facts and the evidence. I look at Iqra and consider any reason that she might attract ill will or an outside antagonist, and then I look for motivation. If there is someone who thinks they might benefit from your sister-in-law's death. Just as the police will have done."

"They didn't. The police did not investigate, they jumped to conclusions."

Aoife decided not to get into that conversation.

"Do you believe me?" It was a clear challenge.

Aoife side stepped the question by asking one of her own.

"Tell me Mahira, why did you want to talk to me? What do you expect me to do?"

"Keeley spoke to me. She said she had read your work and met with you. She said we could trust you. You have proved that you care about the truth. We need someone we can trust. My husband has been accused of murdering his sister. It's only the lack of a body keeping him from prison. I know it was not him, but I have nothing new. You have found evidence for women who could not speak up before when the police weren't interested."

"Not in this sort of situation. Fraud and FGM are both different to an alleged murder." Aoife knew Mahira was referring to the work she did helping to expose the extent and spread of Female genital mutilation in the UK.

Aoife had momentarily become well known in journalistic circles and had won a minor award for investigative journalism after working on the story for over two years. She had also suffered the backlash in the form of threats from a small section of the community who believed it was their right to damage their children. To cause pain and suffering to young girls. Many of whom were teenagers looking forward to a trip of a lifetime to see where their parents had grown up only to be betrayed. Some still at primary school. All came back traumatised.

"That project had involved a widespread conspiracy with a lot of potential threads and discomfort to work with. We knew it was happening, we just had to find out who was involved."

"This is exactly the same. Yes. A widespread conspiracy. So why are you here if you're not interested." She spat the words as her anguish started to get the better of her.

"I didn't say I wasn't interested. I can't work miracles. If the police have found nothing, your family have no evidence to

71

prove your husband's innocence, and there is no other motive for someone wanting her dead, the chance of me finding anything is, well.... slim." She looked at the woman whose disappointment was written all over her face.

Aoife still had the feeling that there was something she was not being told. She had her suspicions, but she couldn't put suggestions into this woman's head. Mahira had to be the one to speak first. Aoife wondered if Keeley or Daisy would find the courage to come back with more details. "I'm sorry. I will go away and think it over; see if there is anything, but only out of curiosity. Please don't get your hopes up."

"So we have nothing to hope for." This was not a question. The energy brought first by excitement that Aoife was involved and hope for a miracle and then anger at the police, seemed to evaporate. Mahira flopped, deflated, back to her seat.

"We need something more substantial to work with. We need a motive for their deaths. If there is anything you're not telling me then please, you say you trust me, so tell me."

There was a long silence while Mahira collapsed back on the settee, hiding her face in her hands.

"There may be something." Mahira whispered.

Aoife felt her skin tingle. This was the moment. When everyone had clammed up, scared or ashamed to tell the whole story, it just took one moment of courage. One person to stand up for those who were weaker – or dead. One little beam of light shone in the right direction. Aoife sat slowly back down to give the woman some space, but not wanting to disturb the moment. She realised she was holding her breath.

"Iqra did tell me once that she thought Anwar's father was…" Mahira couldn't look Aoife in the face as a deep blush crept up from her throat to her forehead.

"What did Iqra tell you?"

"Anwar's father was doing things. Disgusting things, that a man should never do to any boy, let alone his own son."

"You mean Anwar was being abused sexually?" She knew it was important to use the right words. To make sure there was no misunderstandings. If Mahira was embarrassed some of the terminology that was banded around by those who knew the depravities that people indulged in could be a step too far.

She nodded her head. "Yes. And she said there were others."

"Other men or other boys?"

"Both. And not just boys."

"Did she say who?"

A shake of the head. "But I did wonder if… Well sometimes …"

"You wondered if Iqra had been abused too."

Mahira's head shot up. "Yes. How did you know?"

Aoife shrugged her shoulders. The truth was that she didn't know. Hadn't even suspected that Anwar might be scared of his father before today. Then her brain, left to its own devices, did what it did best and unscrambled all the pieces and discovered that several of them fitted together. This latest bit of information had pulled the other fragments like magnets, and they had started to fall into place to form the smallest glimpse of a bigger picture. With too many gaps to see what story would eventually be revealed, but never-the-less, this felt like progress.

"Did she say anything specific? Or mention names?"

"No."

She took the young woman's hand in acknowledgement of the effort she had made. Then she stood up.

"Thank you. That is very useful. Do you know which of your neighbours thought they saw Jamal's car that night?"

Mahira gave her the name and address then offered a wan smile. "Thank you. I understand. I know I must seem pathetic. Not able to talk of these things. Stupidly clinging to a man when all the evidence says I am wrong. But I do know my husband." She held out a small hand "Thank you for listening."

Aoife took the woman's proffered hand in her own much larger, stronger grip.

As Mahira closed the front door, Aoife's mind went to

Detective Inspector Cooper. She speculated on how much of this was suspected or even known during the investigation. She closed her eyes as she realised that she should tell him what she had discovered. Something she automatically felt herself cringe away from. She immediately chastised herself. Many things had been said about Aoife over the years, but never had she been called weak.

'The only thing I can do is to look for patterns that might connect unexpected deaths to each other. I will tell him the facts and then it will be up to him to decide whether to take it seriously or let it drop.' She thought.

As Aoife ducked into the driver's seat of her hatchback, she was sure Mahira was watching her movements through the lace curtains. She turned to look out over the rest of the street. It was a modern housing estate lacking in character, not to her taste. Every house in the close was identical except for the colour of the front doors. *'I suppose it's handy if you get home drunk.'* She thought to herself.

CHAPTER 10

GRIFF TOMLIN

Griff Tomlin didn't bother to watch his wife walk down the path as she left their four bedroomed barn conversion. They'd bought it while Janet was pregnant with Keeley, their youngest. Set on the edge of Bristol it had a large garden surrounded by open spaces. It had been marketed as an ideal family house and it had been. Thomas, Harrison, Petra, and Keeley had all enjoyed the freedom to roam while still being on a major bus route to the city and their schools. Now all the children were long gone, and the place felt empty.

The old man nudged the back door closed with his elbow. His normally straight back bent over as he lugged the heavy wicker basket full of dried logs to the large living room where the wood burning stove stood within the red brick chimney breast. He stretched out his back. Only in his early sixties he was not that old, but arthritis had started eating away at his hips. He shuffled back through to the kitchen and touched the teapot. Still warm enough for one more cup. He reached across the wooden table for the Sunday newspaper.

Griff Tomlin liked Sunday mornings. His wife relaxed her normally strict rules about what he should eat to nurture what she called, his "failing heart" and cooked a fry up of mushrooms tomato, egg, and toast. This morning, she had spoiled him with both sausage and bacon. He had wondered when he saw it on his plate if she was warming him up because she wanted something, but there had been no requests from her before she went off to visit Petra, their eldest daughter. Just the reminder to fill the log basket.

Griff hadn't stepped foot in his eldest daughter's house for nearly five years. He wasn't allowed. Still, it didn't upset him. He didn't much like Freddie, his son in law. Too soft for Griff's taste. Since when did men change nappies or cook dinner? And he was always holding his wife's hand and giving her gooey looks. But the old man had to take his hat off to him, Freddie worked hard, brought the money home, and played a decent game of football.

He didn't begrudge Janet the time with her children and grandchildren. He knew she particularly missed Thomas, their eldest child. They hadn't seen him since he scarpered off to Canada going on twelve years ago.

He imagined Janet spending the morning cooing over her grandchildren and drinking coffee with Petra while his son in law went off to kick a football around. Griff had a few hours to himself, every Sunday during the football, season without being nagged. Peaceful seclusion. He never for a moment suspected he was being watched on these occasions. Nor that a careful note had been made of the time Janet Tomlin left the house with a cake tin or basket full of treats in hand for her grandchildren, and the time she returned.

Every Sunday for the last eight weeks she'd left around nine-thirty and had never arrived back before midday. The team had noted that Janet got back just in time to dish up her husband's lunch. The football season was nearly over. They would have to act soon. That was OK. They were ready to make their move.

CHAPTER 11

DI COOPER

The noise generated by the café's clientele, which at this time of day was dominated by mothers with pre-school aged children, and the self-employed holding meetings, was amplified by the hard surfaces and cavernous space. It hit her senses like a barrier as soon as Aoife opened the door. She had suggested the café closer to the police station but had checked it out on a Thursday afternoon not nine-thirty on Monday morning just after school drop off time.

She spotted DI Cooper marching briskly toward her before she had even made it over the threshold. If Aoife appeared as tired as she felt she hoped she wasn't as bad as the detective who looked grey with fatigue and even more dishevelled than at their previous meeting. His unshaven jaw and damp hair adding to the unkempt appearance.

"This was a mistake." He said placing his hands on her shoulders and twisting her around to face back out onto the pavement with a gentle shove.

Slightly taken aback by the physical contact, and unsure what exactly it was that had been a mistake, she shook him off and muttered 'Morning to you too.'

As they reached the edge of the pavement she turned, ready to give him a quick blast about how she didn't appreciate being dismissed in such an offhand manner. Luckily DI Cooper got in first.

"Since when did parents stop teaching their kids to sit down at tables and not shout in public places? A Café is not a playground!"

Aoife felt relief sweep through her and laughed at his obvious distress. "Come on." She turned on her heal and signalled with her head for him to follow. "There's a small place down one of the side streets. I've been there to write when I needed a change of scenery."

"Fine."

They walked the eighty metres in silence which felt only a little bit uncomfortable. Aoife led the way into a small café with no more than ten tables and an assortment of mismatched wooden chairs. One of the walls was lined with books for its customers to read. It was part of a small chain of coffee shops in the Southwest. Not as generic as the mass-produced coffee bars that had sprouted in every shopping mall, every medium sized town and city including this one. A trait of modern living that Aoife hated, believing that it was one more thing killing creativity as much as the featureless houses that mushroomed up everywhere.

She went to the counter and ordered herself a black Americano before turning to her companion "What would you like Inspector?"

"Cappuccino." He still looked grumpy which added to his overall rumpled appearance.

"Go and sit down, I'll get these." She noticed he selected a table that, by dint of the shape of the small shop, was on its own in the far left hand corner. Offering both some privacy and comfortably upholstered chairs. When she eventually joined carrying two glasses of water, he was rubbing his left temple.

"Coffee's on its way. You don't look well Detective Inspector."

"Tension headache. It began to pound in that awful place down the road. And please, call me Ben." He hadn't looked up while he spoke.

Aoife searched in her shoulder bag for a moment and pulled out a packet of painkillers which she chucked casually on the table. "Help yourself. And its Aoife."

He took the tablets gratefully, swallowing them with water from one of the glasses.

He rubbed his forehead with his hands pushing his fingers on up through his hair. "Sorry it's been a long day already."

Aoife looked at her watch. Nine fifteen. "You're in trouble then, unless you finish at lunch time." She sat back and smiled her thanks as the barista slipped around the bar and brought their drinks.

"No such luck. We got called out before five this morning. Drugs raid. I doubt any of us will be home for dinner."

"Really? I'm surprised you're here."

"I've read some of your work."

Thinking this comment didn't logically follow their conversation so far, Aoife stayed quiet. He hadn't offered an opinion so "thankyou" was inappropriate, and she refused to ask what he thought. She sat watching him, her face impassive. Her silence didn't seem to disturb him too much as he calmly poured a paper tube of sugar into his coffee, lifted a spoon, and sluggishly stirred before looking up at her.

"I was impressed."

"Thank you."

"I also noticed that you were based in London. Have you been in Bristol long?"

"No."

He raised his eyebrows, a small grin lifting one side of his mouth. "It must be a lot more convenient for your choice of leisure activities. What with the Mendips on the doorstep and what is it, an hour to Porthcawl from here?"

This caused Aoife's eyebrows to rise a little. She'd never hidden the fact that she enjoyed being near water, particularly the sea and it was a tidbit the media liked to add to flesh out articles about her as they described her and Cameron Connelley's life together. She had taken up surfing eight years ago and it had become her main passion during summer months and quite a few of the winter ones too. Since the recent success of some of her investigations, and popularity of the related articles, there had been pieces in women's and general interest magazines about her personal life. Of particular interest had been her three year relationship with Cameron and the fact that they both liked hiking and water sports.

Having this knowledge did mean that Benedict Cooper had done his homework though. She gave him an old-fashioned look "Someone's been cyber stalking me. Do you surf?" She asked.

"Hardly stalking, just due diligence. And I sail. I have tried surfing but spent most of my time on my back fending off the board from hitting me. My parents love sailing. Got me started at a young age and I caught the bug too."

Aoife noticed that his dark, unbrushed hair fell in unruly locks over his forehead, while bruise-coloured shadows emphasised his dark eyes. The picture of the overworked detective. But his skin was clear and youthful, lightly tanned and no hints of the weather-beaten look of an avid sailor. She was worried that her own skin was starting to hold tell-tale signs of her joy of outside activities despite the high UV protection cream she smothered on her face and body.

"Do you have your own dinghy?"

"Yes, she's parked up at the Chew Valley Sailing Club, about forty minutes from here. I don't get to use it as much as I'd like. But then that's the story of police officers everywhere. Not a career that makes time for hobbies."

"I can see that."

"You must run into the same difficulties. Travelling a lot, long days away from home."

Aoife wasn't sure why Cooper had decided on small talk, but she went along with it. "I try to fit it in. I learned a long time ago that a change of scenery resets my brain. Cutting out exercise doesn't really save me time. Not in the long term anyway. I am fitter, my heads in a better place and more importantly, I'm invigorated after a physical workout, particularly if it involves water. I walk a lot too."

"I guess that's where being self-employed helps. You can arrange your working day to suit. No one but yourself to answer too."

"I still have to work the hours. Stories seldom fit into a nine to five kinda routine."

She knew she sounded tetchy, but it was a subject that had been broached by friends and even colleagues many times. Especially if she had spent a weekday hiking in the Brecon hills or made the most of particularly good waves. The fact that she might have put in sixteen hour days for a couple of weeks beforehand didn't seem to register. She was often up all night following a lead or working to meet a deadline, none of which seemed to come into their consideration. Fear of not being able to pay the mortgage or that she was slacking made her much harder on herself than any boss had ever been.

The detective frowned, obviously a little put out by her sharp tone "I don't doubt it."

"Sorry. Sore subject. And I do like being able to juggle my time. Anyway, you are on the clock, and you didn't come here to discuss water sports." Her smiling friendly face closed down and Benedict was taken aback by the change of attitude.

"No. Obviously not." He felt suddenly irritated by this woman again, and his mood wasn't improved by the fact that he was doing her a favour by taking time out of the office when there was a mountain of other things he could be doing. He pushed away the thought that he had chosen to keep this meeting as a good excuse to get away from the office and get some fresh air in the hope that it might reduce his headache.

"I'm aware you have a pile of work." She smiled.

"You're right, a change of scenery does help bring a fresh perspective to a knotty problem." Despite being dragged out of bed at such an early hour to help with the raid, and being goaded by this woman, he was beginning to feel much better than he had an hour ago sitting at his desk. "You said you might have something that I'd find interesting."

"As I told you on the phone, I met with Mahira."

DI Cooper nodded.

"Do you know if the autopsy on Anwar Patel gave any signs of childhood abuse after you pulled him out of the river?"

81

"I thought Mahira wanted to tell you about Iqra Aziz."

"She did, and part of that story is the close friendship between Iqra and Anwar and the relationship their fathers had."

"Interesting." The policeman looked thoughtful as he rested his elbows on the table." I wasn't on the case, but I flicked through the notes after our last meeting. I don't recall anything being flagged, no. I'm sure I would have remembered. What makes you suspect abuse?"

"Because once Mahira understood that neither you nor I would have any reason to continue investigating unless there was new evidence, she decided to tell me that she had known Anwar as a child. They're not the same age but they went to the same school."

"That's a fairly loose connection. If you think how many children go through a school in any year." He tipped his head to one side and raised his eyebrows in query.

"Anwar spent a lot of time at Iqra's house, even though his father didn't like it and Anwar was scared of him. Mahira eventually told me that she thought Anwar's father was doing 'disgusting things that a man shouldn't do to any boy.'" Aoife quoted.

"Did you say that Mahira's father knew Anwar's father?"

"Yes. Mahira may still not have told us everything, but she didn't show any signs that she was covering up for her father. When she spoke of her father and how close her family were, it seemed genuine. Mahira's father was concerned for Anwar because he was a loner."

"So are you thinking that Anwar and Iqra were both victims of sexual abuse."

"I'm not that far along yet. Mahira believes that Anwar was abused by his father. If Iqra and Anwar were friends, Mahira used the term 'drawn together,' then it's possible that was the connection. We don't know if Iqra had anything to do with Mr Patel though. Anwar always went to Iqra's house, not the other way around."

Benedict sat back and considered what Aoife had brought to him. Then he looked at his watch. "I have to go. What are your plans? Will you keep digging?"

Aoife still looked preoccupied. "Not sure at this moment. I will continue looking for other deaths that have similarities." She gave him her most charming smile "Unless of course you'd like to share?"

He gave a short snort and a sardonic smile.

"Thought not." Aoife shrugged. "But we are on the same side you know. I mean if I hadn't told you about Anwar being abused you would not have gone down that route would you?"

"We might."

"Yeah, at some point in the next thirty years. Another case of historic abuse."

"I'll have another look at the notes, and I will let you know if there is anything relevant comes up from the post-mortem."

"Thank you."

CHAPTER 12

HABIB

The early spring moon had begun to rise long before the team had reached their waiting place, but thick clouds were fighting to keep it hidden. The moonless dark that wrapped around him didn't scare him; it was his friend. He had always found comfort in the invisibility of shadows.

As Gabriel waited crouched amongst the bushes that ran along the small footpath, he felt the anticipation of one who is about to be set free after years of incarceration. A mixture of excitement and fear tingled through his body setting the hair on his arms and neck on end. He slowed his breathing to calm himself. He had to work to keep focused on the task in hand.

He could sense the same feeling from Adam and Gina who were both hunkered down nearby, like an electric charge running between them all. Others were a few steps further down the path, ready to cut off any escape should Habib try to run back the way he came. The trap was set.

Gabriel ran his fingers over his new toy. The tasers had been a gift from a supporter from a previous generation of survivors who had been pimped out while under the supposed protection of nuns and priests. Servants of God. Children raised to believe in a loving all seeing father. Children who had any hope or comfort that they might have found in praying to a higher deity, ripped from them.

The team had originally planned to creep up on their targets and hit them over the head. Gabriel was relieved when they were told this wasn't going to be necessary. The taser was so much less messy than a cosh, with less chance of leaving traces of blood on their clothing and no need to burn everything after. It had the added bonus that the target would remain conscious throughout. He would know what was happening to him. Feel the fear and frustration of the prey as his punishment was inflicted upon him.

The therapist that Gabriel had visited for three years liked to call the children who had suffered abuse "survivors" not victims. Gabriel was not sure if the little boy that he once was had survived, but his body had grown into a young man. He smiled with satisfaction as he realised Habib was never going to be called a survivor.

He tensed as he heard footsteps crunching along the well-trodden footpath. A rustle of twigs and leaves as the team left their hiding places, confirmed that this was their prey. The old football coach was still ignorant of what awaited him, but Gabriel knew that his friends had already closed in behind. They had practised until their actions merged into one coordinated body. Like a pack of wild hunting dogs, they may be smaller but on mass the bulk of the middle-aged man would be no match.

By the time Gabriel allowed himself to be seen, Habib was already on the ground, wrists and feet bound as the team attached him to the surrounding trees and bushes that bordered each side of the path. Gabriel wore the expression of one who feels nothing as he stepped out. The moon momentarily lit the place like the opening scene at a theatre. He stood there for several seconds watching as Habib struggled against his bonds. The words he tried to scream muted by the tape across this monster's mouth were abusive and bluster, but the fear in his eyes was real.

The lower half of Gabriel's face was painted chalk white except for black oversized lips and a single blood red tear drop on one cheek. To Habib's unfocused gaze it looked as if the young man was wearing a green mask with electric blue stars across his eyes, but this too was painted on.

Habib caught sight of the steel of a knife in Gabriel's

gloved hand glinting in the last shards of moonlight before it disappeared behind rain clouds. The old man's body writhed and bucked as Gabriel pointed the knife close in on Habib's groin. He slit the man's trousers, then his underpants and Habib tried to cry out as his drooping penis was exposed to the air.

"Do you recognise me old man?" Gabriel sneered as he pulled Habib's trousers to his ankles.

Habib shook his head but was otherwise frozen in fear as Gabriel, dressed completely in blue coveralls, fixed a mask over his mouth. Gabriel pointed the taser. One prong gripped Habib's lower stomach the other his naked thigh, just missing his genitals. His muscles spasmed, and he gasped in pain. As the tremors subsided one of his companions passed Gabriel a can of spray paint.

There was a hint of amusement in his eyes as Gabriel sprayed the red dye. He stared down at the man who had persecuted so many of his friends for years, now looking pathetic with his trousers around his ankles and the bright red across his penis and thighs.

"This is for all those innocent children trusted to your care who just wanted to play football."

The young man removed a small silver tin from his pocket, breathed deeply to steady himself and bent close to the groaning man who struggled and twitched as he saw the syringe. Gabriel stamped his boot down hard on Habib's fingers and left it there while, with gloved hands, he pushed up the man's sleeve and injected the heroin into the vein. He stood up, a hint of the victor in his smile, but there was no joy in any of the young people's eyes as they quietly turned and walked away.

Anna looked at her watch. "Perfect. Eight minutes. Well done." She said as they jogged away through the trees.

The crew still clad in their blue coveralls moved toward the middle of the woods, still under the cover of the moonless night and the trees. Quickly they spread the first plastic sheet on the ground. Two of them stood on it, stripped off their coveralls and replaced them with waterproof jackets over their jeans and shirts. The other three used a second plastic sheet and did the same. Folding their discarded clothes and the plastic up before stuffing them in dustbin bags and then shoving everything into back packs. The rain began to fall on the leaves overhead and drip to the ground in heavy plops.

The five of them leaped up the hill climbing over fallen trees and avoiding brambles as best they could. Anna made a phone call as they went. They ran quickly and quietly using their arms as much as their legs to propel themselves up the hill over damp leaves, avoiding the paths, hoping to leave no footprints. Then, through the trees they could see the open space of the road ahead and river beyond. They slithered down the slope then all slowed, simultaneously crouching, wary of the exposed expanse in front of them.

A van pulled into the side of the road and waited as they broke cover. Anna threw the mobile phone into the river before bundling into the back of the van with the others which moved off the moment the door clicked shut.

"OK?" asked the driver.

"OK." confirmed Gabriel. "Just as we practiced."

The mood in the van was sombre and no one spoke for several minutes.

"We did it." said Will eventually.

"We did it." Agreed Anna and there was a general releasing of breath and a few chuckles of relief.

"Three more to go." Kiki smiled, a sparkle in her eye.

CHAPTER 13

CRIME SCENE

The drive to the crime scene without daytime traffic was straightforward. Benedict had managed to splash water on his face, get dressed, pour coffee into his thermos cup and still be pulling in behind a marked police car within thirty-five minutes of the phone call.

As he closed his car door and stepped out into the torrential rain, he saw that the normally quiet residential street lined with respectable 1930s semi-detached houses resembled a fair ground. Ambulance, first responder's vehicle and police squad cars lined up along the road and into the mouth of the park. All had lights adding to the illuminations. Further into the woods Cooper could see more bright lights despite the heavy rainfall, enabling the scene of crime officers to do their work.

DC Justin Hyslop was waiting for him at the edge of the police cordon, a thin blue and white barrier taping off the access to the path that ran through the nature reserve. Cooper pulled the collar of his raincoat as tight as he could around his neck to no avail.

"Crap night to be called out sir."

"Have you heard from sergeant Goss?"

"She's on her way." He turned as he spoke and pointed to lights heading their way.

"Looks like her now sir."

Having allowed Goss to catch them up they ducked beneath the tape. Justin led them along the path that after a few metres turned back on itself into the woods.

"What have we got?" asked Cooper.

The DC spoke at speed in an excited, anxious voice. "Asian man in his early sixties. The call came in shortly after two this morning. The doctor pronounced him dead at the scene."

"Who called it in?"

"Young couple. Homeless. They've got a small tent pitched up the top of the hill. Walking back and stumbled across him."

"Why the circus? I take it we're not talking heart attack?"

Justin looked at him with a serious expression, conveying the gravity of the scene. "No sir. It's definitely not natural causes. Someone took their time to get their point across." He took a moment to emphasise the distinct nature of the sight they were about to witness. "It's nothing like anyone here has seen or heard of before. Dr Nick Cartwright is already there and set-up."

DI Cooper trudged along the dirt path. He could feel the wind whipping the rain into his face, water running freely down the back of his neck and soaking his shirt. His torch was almost useless as the light died just inches into the barrage of water that was now torrenting down. The flash river that ran down the bank at the side of the path gushed over the toes of his wellington boots, turning the once dust path into thick mud and taking with it any chance the forensics team might have had of discovering meaningful tracks.

"There is no hope of taking any casts of footprints, and probably any other clues that might have helped reveal whoever was responsible." Said Hyslop. "It's going to be a tough one for forensics."

A clap of thunder joined the cacophony of noise provided by the rain and wind as the police officers approached the makeshift white tent the SOCOs had managed to erect in the futile hope of preserving the crime scene. Thick sheets of rain obscured Cooper's vision and he was relieved to see the bright arc lights illuminating the way ahead. All around the forensic team were battling hard. A canvas roof had been erected, forming an additional shelter on all sides of the main tent, but as he approached, he realised that even with the hastily erected canopies, hope of preserving the integrity of the crime scene was just a dream.

"Do you think our murderer is a weather forecaster?" one of the women clad in white coverall asked as Benedict dipped under the cover of the canopy, making sure he remained on the stepping stones the woman had put down. He hated the idea of taking his raincoat off, and quickly replaced it with a white coverall.

"Possibly." He was soaked and irritable but relieved to be out of the rain.

Benedict took a look at the body while attempting to keep out of the way of the team. "Anything you can tell me?"

"He's definitely dead." Said a grumpy voice from the other side. Ben recognised the voice of Dr Nick Cartwright. "We will probably manage the how, but as to the who or the why, well there's not much left for us to collect as you can imagine. You're going to have your work cut out."

"Is there anything you can tell me?"

"Meet Mr Habib Patel." Nick allowed himself a small smug grin. "Whatever the motive it almost certainly wasn't theft. His wallet, phone, watch, all still here. That ring I would say is worth a pretty penny." The pathologist pointed down to the thick band of gold on the man's ring finger."

"So, we know who he is. I don't suppose you have his address there too do you?"

"He lives just around the corner. In the daylight, and without this weather, you could probably see his house from here."

"Cause of death?"

"Looks like there's been a recent injection into the cephalic vein. Could be cause of death. He was still warm to the touch – just - when we got here despite the rain."

Benedict looked at his watch. "Which means time of death yesterday evening."

"Mmm, night. After 10pm I'd say.

"It's reasonable to assume he was on his way home."

Nick looked at the police officer. "I don't deal in assumptions.

I'll leave that to you. Though you might need to make a few conjectures in this case. Needless to say, any footprints have already been washed away. Don't hold your breath for much else either. He and his clothes have all had a good shower."

"Whoever did this was making a statement." Cooper stared down at the red dye across the man's genitals, then turned to his sergeant "What do you think?"

"Sex offender is the obvious guess. He's well and truly tied up and staked out. Probably too complex for one person to set up on their own. Also has to be someone who knew his routine. A random attack, doesn't look likely." Said Goss.

"Your right. Two or more people with a grudge." Cooper took another look at the dead man. "He looks, what, in his sixties would you say? His weather-beaten skin might suggest someone who's worked outside."

"Sixty two, according tohis driving license. Someone who works with his hands. Builder maybe." Said Goss

Benedict turned to his sergeant "Can you check to see if his wife or family have reported him late home? Then you and I had better get to his house and break the news."

"Already checked it boss. His wife called in at midnight."

"She'll be waiting for us then. I doubt she's missed the show."

"You ought to know, he is a local councillor." Goss hesitated a moment "And Anwar Patel's father."

"Great. We have to break the new f another family member dead." His voice was sarcastic.

The frenzy of the earlier storm had subsided to large lazy drops of water splashing on the branches as sergeant Goss led the way back along the path, cursing as she slipped on the mud and dead leaves.

"Just remember how much you love your job sergeant Goss."

"I love my job sir, I hate rain. I thought this weather was supposed to mean less crime." She moaned. Cooper was only fairing a little better as thick gooey mud curled over his feet and formed heavy clumps that made it difficult even for his rubber boots to find any grip on the steep bank. He put out his right hand to find some balance but too late. Like a drowning man, clutching feebly at the air he windmilled his arms until with a whoomph and a yell he landed on his back side.

"Fuck!"

Goss startled looked round too quickly and tripping over her boss's feet, joined him in the mud on hands and knees.

"Shit! Remind me to keep wellies in the boot will you." The sergeant scrambled to her feet.

"Didn't do me much good. Time I invested in some oil skins." He watched as Goss wiped the worst of the mud from her hands on the damp grass along the bank. "People pay good money to be covered in this stuff."

"Not me Sir." She started to giggle at the ridiculousness of their predicament.

"Nice to see you find it funny." Cooper was struggling to keep his temper. "Come on, I think we both need to get cleaned up a bit before we pay that visit."

CHAPTER 14

THE HABIB FAMILY

T he rain had at least eased as the beginnings of dawn crept over the horizon. Too late to help the investigation but the activity had attracted the inevitable crowds curious to know what was going on, even at this time in the morning. Videoing the action and posting on social media of their choice.

Attired in clean, if not totally dry, clothes Cooper turned his car around and stopped a little behind the blue tape and police cordon. His sergeant slipped into the passenger seat. "How far down do they live?" he asked.

Aida Goss looked again at her telephone to check. "Not far sir, first right then a left. We could walk but probably best to take the car with all these cameras here."

They pulled in behind a marked police car which was parked a few metres away from the house. A uniformed WPC climbed out of the police vehicle and joined them as they walked up the short path to the 1930's semidetached house. Cooper rang the doorbell, hearing it reverberate further inside. Moments later the hall light went on and a short round figure was seen through the glass.

As the door opened an elderly woman of no more than five feet tall was revealed. Her grey hair swept back in an orderly bun, and her pale grey eyes betrayed no sign of stress.

Cooper showed his warrant card and introduced Sergeant Goss behind him, also brandishing her identification, and the uniformed constable who would be staying with the family acting as Liaison.

"Mrs Patel?"

"Yes. Mrs Patel senior. Habib's my son. His wife is indoors." She gestured for them to enter.

Cooper took his time, looking around the entrance hall as he passed through. It was small with wood panelling which continued up the carpeted staircase to the first floor. It held a dark and gloomy feel much in need of an update, but it was clean and the surface of the hall table and many pictures that hung on the wall were dust free.

Mrs Patel led the way through to the living room at the rear of the house and the police officers filed quietly behind her. She turned before entering the main room "Shut the door behind you" she commanded.

A stout, middle-aged woman who had been sitting on the edge of an armchair looked anxiously at the visitors as she stood "Have you found him?" Her voice relayed her anxiety.

"Are you Mr Habib Patel's wife?" DI Cooper asked the younger woman.

"Yes. Yes. I called the police to tell them Habib hadn't come home."

"Please do sit back down Mrs Patel." The woman resumed her position on the edge of her chair. Benedict took the seat opposite even though no one had invited him to sit. He didn't want to tower over her as they spoke. His tone was serious, conveying the gravity of the reason for their visit.

"What is it?" Mrs Patel junior anxiously asked, a worried frown on her brow, tears in her eyes. "It's never good news when a police officer comes to your door at 6am."

"It's never good news when they come in a pack and are so bloody polite." The old woman's voice was clear and flat. "Bushra, this is Detective Inspector Cooper and his colleagues come to see us."

"I'm afraid we have some distressing news for you. The body of a middle-aged man was found tonight in Ropers Woods. I'm sorry to have to tell you that we believe it to be your husband,

and son" He nodded to include the older woman who had taken position behind her daughter-in-law's chair. "Habib Patel." He paused waiting for any exclamations of grief. Both women had their eyes fixed on the Inspector's face. The youngest stricken with horror while Habib's mother remained calm as she waited for more news.

"Who found him?" Asked the older woman.

Benedict looked up at his sergeant who was standing to the side of his chair and nodded. "He was found just after midnight by a young couple walking home from the village." Aida's voice was steady.

"How do you know it's Habib? It could be anyone."

"Don't be silly Bushra, how many middle-aged Pakistani men are going to be lying dead on the ground not a mile from this house?" Her mother-in-law's tone was firm but not unkind. Bushra didn't seem at all perturbed by the older woman's rebuke.

"I'm very sorry Mrs Patel, he was carrying his wallet and identification. We strongly believe it is your husband. Obviously, we need to carry out a formal identification."

"I'll make some tea." Mrs Patel senior said. "Would you and your officers like some?" She looked at the Inspector, but the sweep of her arm took in Aida Goss and the young female PC who was standing by the door.

"Thank you. WPC Dharma can make it if you like." He nodded toward the uniformed officer.

The old woman nodded her consent. "I can come and identify my son." Her voice was steady, and Cooper looked at her wondering at her lack of emotion. Bushra already had a large pile of damp tissues on the floor beside her, while the dead man's mother had managed to maintain her composure, barely appearing ruffled by the news.

"Thank you Mrs Patel. We'll let you know when he is ready."

"How? I mean was it a heart attack? He has been to see the doctor about his blood pressure?" asked the younger woman.

"I'm afraid Mrs Patel, he was murdered."

The wife's pudgy hand flew to her mouth as she gasped, rocking her shoulders slowly back and forth.

PC Dharma arrived with a tray of cups which she handed out.

DI Cooper kept his eyes on the family members. "I know this is an awful time for his family, but do you know if Habib has any enemies? Anyone he has argued with recently or who may have a grudge against him?"

The older woman snorted while Bushra shook her head. "He worked hard in the community, always willing to help. He was a councillor you know. He was respected. No one would want to see him hurt." The younger women's voice was earnest.

The inspector's eyes turned on the mother who said nothing. "What about you Mrs Patel? Would you agree or do you know of anyone your son may have upset?"

"Habib is my son. His father and I brought him up to respect the needs of others, but sadly, he only saw his own needs." This brought a gasp from her daughter-in-law. "You always keep your eyes closed Bushra, but Habib ..." She paused and for the first time she lowered her gaze "He was not a nice man."

The room went silent as the police officers collectively held their breath. Even Bushra paused her whimpering.

"In what way was he not nice?"

"He was selfish and arrogant and a bully."

"How can you say that Mama? That's not true. He raised funds for the Mosque, he organised groups to help the aged members. He did so many kind things."

The old woman looked down dismissively at her daughter-in-law. "He only did things that would be seen by others and might earn him status. Tell me, where is your daughter Bushra? She couldn't wait to leave home. And Anwar?" For the first time Benedict could see tears in the pale grey eyes that softened at the mention of her grandson. "He needed his father's love not his scorn."

"Anwar was always a troubled boy. Habib thought it best to give him boundaries and he sent him to see many people he hoped might help."

From the corner of his eye Benedict saw sergeant Goss stiffen at the last comment. He worked hard at keeping his voice soft and level as he asked. "Do you know who he sent Anwar to see?"

Bushra looked confused. "Um. Why is that important now? Anwar died months ago. He wasn't murdered."

"We will be building a picture of Habib's life. That includes everyone he knows or has done business with."

"Oh, I see. No. No I don't think I do."

"We can look through his papers." Said Mrs Patel senior "But not now."

"Of course not. When you're ready, but the sooner we know the more likely we are to find whoever did this." He looked at his sergeant and gave a slight nod indicating that she should take over the questions.

While Goss checked on Habib's recent movements and basic details of his life Benedict took the opportunity to look around the room. The dark furniture, deeply patterned wallpaper and heavy brocade curtains would have been better suited to a much larger room. Like the hallway, the décor was tired, the only recent addition appeared to be the overstuffed three-piece suite. An enormous ornate mirror hung above the mantlepiece, and the marble topped coffee table stood on a silvery, grey and blue silk carpet. His glance moved quickly across the shelves and walls which, except for two wood carvings of elephants, were curiously impersonal. No holiday mementos, family photographs, or pictures of the children in school uniforms. Not even of their dead son.

"Sorry to interrupt. Did Mr Patel have an office or a desk here, at the house? Somewhere he might have worked from?"

"Yes. The little room off the hall." Again, it was the mother who answered.

"Do you think I could have a quick look?" Ben gave the older lady his most charming smile as he stood up and headed toward the hall. The room was small, tidy, and again no hint of anything personal adorned its walls or shelves.

Goss returned her notebook to her pocket signalling the end

of the interview as her boss walked back in. Cooper asked quickly. "Do you have a picture of your husband we could borrow Mrs Patel?"

If anyone noticed the questioning look that Goss shot her boss at that moment they didn't react.

"Erm." Bushra looked confused "I think his work identity card is on the sideboard in the hall. It is the most recent picture." The group all trailed out through the hall where Bushra handed over her husband's ID.

Goodbyes and condolences were once more uttered, and they left. Once the two police officers were inside the car and the doors shut Goss commented.

"That was interesting."

"You noticed."

"Firstly, I would just like to say that Mrs Patel senior may be in her late seventies or eighties, but she has all her marbles, and she is one very tough lady."

"That's true. The only sign of emotion was when she mentioned her grandson. And secondly?" Cooper asked.

"What does the mother know that she's not telling us?"

"I thought the same. That is something we will have to find out. She might be more forthcoming when her daughter-in-law is not in the room. Can you make sure you're there when she comes in to identify the body?"

"And not a family photo in sight." Finished Goss.

"Their daughter left home as soon as she could, and their son is dead. According to Macarthy, Anwar was friends with Iqra Aziz. No one believes Iqra would leave voluntarily. And Anwar didn't drink or do drugs yet ended up in the Avon with Heroin and alcohol in his system."

"And the mark on Habib Patel's arm could be from a recent injection. You think there's a connection?"

"Aoife is talking to people who claim Anwar, Iqra and Cara Felton were murdered to keep them quiet."

"Cara Felton?"

"Another death by drowning stroke misadventure. There's no doubt Anwar's father was murdered, and you saw how he was laid out. Someone was sending a message. I'd like to know who Habib took his son to see and I want to show the photo to Aoife's contacts. See if they have anything to say about him."

"You think Macarthy is on to something?"

"It's beginning to look that way."

CHAPTER 15

DAISY

A oife sat at her desk staring vacuously out at the view over the city. This view had been the main reason that tipped her decision to buy the house. From the third-floor window she could just see the train line below between the trees, Bristol Cathedral near the city centre, Cabot tower above Brandon Hill, and in the far distance Isambard Kingdom Brunel's famous bridge.

Having been staring at a computer screen since 6a.m. she was struggling to maintain her concentration, and her brain kept wandering in different directions. She had been searching through reports on the internet about the deaths by drowning of anyone under twenty-six years old in the Bristol area, over the last eight years. She'd also traced the murders of anyone under the age of thirty in the same time period, highlighting those involving Asian or Muslim families.

Feeling more and more sleepy, she was just debating between lying on her bed for half an hour, going for a walk to get some fresh air, or making another cup of black coffee. The chime from her doorbell reverberating through the house cut through her revery. Someone had made the decision for her to stand up and take a break from the computer screen.

She closed the file she was reading and tapped on the keypad until the screen saver came up. She wasn't expecting anyone to walk up the two flights of stairs and pry in her study, it was a defensive tactic she had learned while working in a busy newspaper office with a bunch of over curious journalists.

Getting up she made her way quickly down the stairs

and along the hall to the sitting room. Looking through the window she expected to see her neighbour, Phiah, come for a coffee. To her surprise it was Daisy hopping from foot to foot looking over her shoulder and generally appearing uncomfortable.

As she went to open the door, she wondered if Benedict had followed up on what she'd told him about their conversation in the cafe. "Good morning Daisy. This is a surprise. Would you like to come in?"

The girl didn't wait to be asked twice and stepped forward, forcing Aoife to move aside.

"I'm sorry to bother you at home." The girl was still hugging her own body as if she were cold and she looked agitated.

"Don't worry. I'm glad you've come." She walked back along the hall and signalled for the girl to follow. "Come along into the kitchen. Have you remembered something else?"

"Yes, well sort of. Maybe. I don't know."

"Oh, well, that sounds as clear as mud." Aoife laughed "Would you like a coffee? Tea, cold drink?"

"Tea please."

"Grab a seat." Aoife pointed to the big wooden table and chairs that offered diners a view of the small garden. Daisy sank down abruptly as if her legs could not be relied upon to hold her up any longer.

Aoife put the kettle on, got down two mugs from the cupboard then searched in another cupboard for sugar. While she was waiting for the kettle to boil she took the cake Phiah had given her as a thank you for helping her write an article for the school magazine, and put it on a plate. While she was moving around Aoife surreptitiously watched her visitor. She kept her movements calm and deliberate not wanting to fluster the girl any more than she obviously already was, or upset her into losing her nerve and leaving again.

Out of the blue Daisy suddenly announced. "I've had suspicions for a long time, but I wasn't sure, and I didn't want to get anyone into trouble. Or have the police think I was trying to, you know, push in. Become more important than I am."

"If you have something that could help them it might be important. I think they would be very happy to hear from you." Aoife sat down across the table from her guest and keeping her voice as calm as possible asked "Would you like to speak to Inspector Cooper?"

"No!" The response was shot back. She folded her arms across her chest again, as if this stance could deflect any further attempts at persuasion.

"What if it might save lives?"

"I'd rather tell you. Then if you think I should perhaps." She paused keeping her gaze on the table. "Or maybe you could pass it on to the police." Daisy's fingers were twisting the corner of her cardigan so hard Aoife feared for its survival.

"OK. Would you mind if I record our conversation?"

Daisy shot a terrified look at her and for a moment she thought the girl might get up and run after all.

"I do it for all my interviews if I can. It is less intrusive than me scribbling notes and it helps me write a more authentic article at the end of it. It's difficult to get details right from memory.

Aoife waited. There was no answer.

"I promise it will be just for my use. I won't pass any of it on to anyone else without your approval. And I do want to get it right."

To her relief Daisy gave a quick nod. "If you promise. And you can't use my name. In whatever you write. Not yet. If it's what I think it is - what's happening - they wouldn't think twice about doing away with me as well."

Daisy leaned back in her chair and looked up at the ceiling. 'I feel like—' she paused again, drawing breath and pulling at her fringe. 'I feel like you're the kind of person who will listen and maybe find the missing pieces. I'm not safe I know that, but I'm no less safe talking to you than leaving it and seeing what happens.'

Aoife noticed the girl's hand trembling and she stretched

across the table to encase Daisy's fingers in her own. "Try not to worry, you're doing the right thing."

"I don't know how you do it?"

"Do what?"

"Stand up and tell your stories like you do."

"They're not my stories. I help give a voice to those who struggle to find their own voice."

"But you must make enemies?"

"Not everyone appreciates what I do that's for sure." She thought back momentarily to D.I. Cooper then dismissed the thought. He was not the enemy. "The people who hate my work most like to hide in the shadows. I shine a light on them."

"You're very brave."

"So are you."

'I find it easy to talk to you. I don't know why, but it feels like a relief at last. For years I've let fear rule my life. Keep me quiet. You've...." She stopped. Aoife saw she was embarrassed. "I know this sounds daft. You're sort of the key."

"The key?"

"Yeah, that unlocks the door."

"No, I can't take the credit. This is you. It's your strength. It's always been there. You've found your voice because you know it's time. It's the right thing to do. I just happen to be the sounding board."

Aoife could feel a frisson in the air between them. The journalist in her had a gut feeling she knew well and was thrilled by the scent of a story unfolding. Her instinct told her that the real chase was about to begin. Deep down a little voice was telling her she should be encouraging this girl to talk to the police. She tried to ignore it. If she pushed too hard there was every chance Daisy would clam up for good. There was real fear in the girl's eyes. If there was enough trust between them she could write the facts down and perhaps, once the story was out, Daisy might find it less frightening and be willing to repeat it to the police. And Aoife would have got there first.

"So, what is it that you are suspicious about?"

The direct question took the girl by surprise despite her earlier announcement. She floundered for words. She took a gulp of her tea, then placed the mug slowly and carefully down in front of her as if it was something precious that might break. Looking up at Aoife from under her thick, black fringe she blinked twice then began.

"I was coming back on my own from an evening out with the girls from school. Years ago. Cara was still at the care home at the time. It was just before she got taken in by her final foster parents. It was about *half*-past nine. I was in Stokes Croft heading for the bus stop when I saw some people coming out of the pub. Mostly older guys in jeans and shirts, but I looked twice because I noticed a couple of them had their arms around much younger girls, sort of really tight, like they didn't want them to get away. And there were a couple of lads with them too. I thought "Pervs" straight away. Then I realised one of the girls was Cara. The older guys sort of guided them toward a van that was parked on the pavement. They all got in the back. I thought at the time that the younger kids didn't seem too keen."

It was the most Aoife had heard the girl say. It sounded rehearsed, which Aoife knew might be the only way Daisy was able to tell her story out. It could also mean it held some untruths or missing bits.

"Did you mention this to Cara?"

"Yes. She told me it was none of my business."

"Was that the only time you saw her with older men?"

"No. I saw them again a few weeks later. There were Christmas decorations up, but it wasn't Christmas holidays yet. We were still at school. Cara was in her new home with Mr and Mrs Davies a couple of weeks before Christmas and it was before that. I saw something similar except this time three guys seemed to be sort of herding the kids forward." Daisy took another sip of her tea. Aoife kept quiet. This time it seemed to take Daisy a while for her to find the right words or to get her thoughts in order. At last she looked up. "I recognised a couple of the others too. One of them was Anwar."

It was all Aoife could do to stop herself from exploding with all the questions that sprung into her mind. She couldn't hide the sharp intake of breath which made Daisy's eyes wide with fear.

"The boy who drowned down by the harbour?"

"Yes."

"He was being herded along with Cara?"

"Yes." She lowered her head again. Aoife waited in silence, but Daisy seemed to have got stuck, lost in memories that were more powerful than the present moment. Aoife stood up, opened one of the kitchen cabinets and pulled out a small yellow cardboard box. She ripped it open and poured half the contents into a brightly coloured bowl.

Placing it on the table in front of her visitor she said. "I don't often eat chocolate or even puddings but there are times when only a jelly baby hits the spot." She nudged the girl's arm with the bowl and smiled encouragingly as she put one in her own mouth and placed two more beside her hand on the table. "Help yourself."

Daisy lifted her head. Her face was pale, but her cheeks were flushed, feverish. She took a sweet.

"He wasn't from the home though. I recognised him from school. The thing is… I'm not sure but, I think one of the other girls might have been Iqra."

"Did you know Iqra at the time?"

"Not really. But I'd seen her with Anwar. She was holding Anwar's arm. She looked terrified. I thought she was going to start crying. Her face sort of never left me. And then years later I saw her picture in the local paper. She was older in the photo of course. Cara was already dead by then and I'd lost touch with Anwar. But I do think it was her."

"How long ago was this?"

"It was just after CGSE's."

"Did you recognise any of the older men?"

105

"No."

"Is there anything else you want to tell me?"

"No."

"Anything else you think might help identify any of the other young people or the men? The type of van maybe?"

Daisy closed her eyes for a moment. "It was dark blue and had a yellow logo on the side. But I don't remember what. Not sure I ever knew. Just remember seeing a flash of yellow as they drove passed."

Aoife knew she would have to pass this on to the police and wondered if she could get hold of Benedict and ask him to come here now, but she guessed it would be too soon for Daisy who was visibly shaking.

"Do you think that's why they are dead?" Daisy asked.

"I don't know. It doesn't sound good. It's one hell of a coincidence, but as you said, it was a long time ago. We have to tell the police."

"If they find out I've told you isn't that going to put me in danger too?"

"There is no reason why they should find out. The police can keep their sources anonymous. Even if they did know you are talking to me, you were nothing to do with what was going on at the time."

Daisy stared at Aoife. Her mouth had dropped open. "I think I'd better go." She suddenly seemed even more on edge.

"Before you go can I ask you one more question?" Aoife knew there was more. Knew she had hit a nerve with her last comment. Confident that the casual assumption she had made was incorrect.

Daisy sat back down her face was flushed and her eyes unnaturally bright. "Sure."

"You've told me about your friends, and I know bringing up those memories and fears is not easy. Would you like to tell me your own story now?"

"What do you mean?"

"What happened to you when you were a little girl?"

"I've got to get to work."

"OK. When you're ready to tell me I'm a good listener." She smiled remembering the compliment.

"I know." Daisy stood up scooped more sweets from the bowl in her hand and left without looking back.

Aoife went to the door and watched the young woman walk quickly up the hill with her head down. She had been so close to finding the bigger picture. Part of her wanted to throw her own jacket on and run after Daisy, but she knew it would do more harm than good. Daisy had proved that she was willing to talk. That she wanted to get the whole thing off her chest, but it had to be at her own pace.

Aoife closed her front door and went to the kitchen to clear away the mugs. She poured herself another coffee, opened the flowery cake tin that her neighbour had given her and cut herself a slice of lemon drizzle before walking back upstairs to gaze out the window some more.

CHAPTER 16.

DI COOPER

T hey had eventually spoken on the phone the previous evening. Aoife had been surprised to hear from him so late in the day thinking she would be the one pushing for another meeting. She was even more amazed by his obvious affability.

"I'll buy the cake this time." Benedict chuckled.

"Sounds good to me." She smiled broadly. As she put the phone down she wondered if he had found information that corroborated the girls' stories and if he would be willing to share with her. Either way she was relieved that she would have someone to discuss her own findings with.

Aoife had learned to follow leads and track suspects on her own; learned to keep secrets until the story was ready to be released to the world, but this was different. There were people still roaming the streets of Bristol who got pleasure from the torture of young children. What's more, their victims' bodies were turning up in the river.

She was very aware of the mental health issues brought on by childhood trauma. Without help that path could easily lead to self-harm and death, but she now suspected that these young people had not died at their own hand. Cara, Anwar and Iqra had all proved that they were more than their past and stronger than the architects of their misery. Each had discovered a more fulfilling life before they had died or disappeared.

The next morning Aoife made her way to the smaller, more relaxed café they had used before, and sat at the same table Benedict had selected last time. She started to log on to her laptop, prepared for another long wait. She was taken off guard when she looked up to see DI Cooper looking down at her.

"I've ordered my coffee. Left the cake for you to choose this time." She said as she gathered herself.

"That's fine." He gave her a weak smile.

Aoife noticed he seemed less sure of himself. She wondered if he had something he needed to say or just wasn't confident on the choice of cakes, but eventually he went up to the counter. He returned with two chocolate muffins.

"A man after my own stomach. Thank you." She looked at him and there was genuine concern in her voice as she said, "Well I thought you looked washed out last time, but I have to say, you might have topped it today."

"Thanks."

"Seriously, have you thought of getting a full night's sleep?"

"That would be nice, but it seems to elude me."

"Nightmares or work?"

He looked as though the question had taken him by surprise "You could say they're one and the same thing."

"You could have called and said you needed to postpone."

"I would have cancelled if it weren't for the fact that … well we'll get to that. And I needed some time out and a coffee." He gave a half smile that didn't reach his eyes. "Your friend came back I gather."

Motivated by what seemed genuine interest from DI Cooper Aoife opened her mouth to continue only to be stopped by a rather imperious finger wagged in her direction.

"Before we get into that." He smiled at the disgruntled look on her face. "I think there are a couple of things I should tell you."

"Oh?" She braced herself for another disagreement.

"Since our last meeting I have done a little bit of digging." He took a gulp of his coffee while he gathered his thoughts. "Some of what you were talking about could have substance."

Aoife frowned and felt her hackles rise. "Of course it has

substance! Do you honestly think I would be wasting my time eating cake with you if I didn't think it was important? Young lives have been ruined and more children could be in danger."

Cooper stiffened and his face flushed a deep shade of red forcing the shadows under his eyes to turn darker still. For a moment Aoife thought he might shout he looked so put out. Instead, he managed to keep his retort to a low level hiss.

"I meant it might be relevant to another incident we are investigating. The reason we were all wading around in the rain and mud up to our bloody knees before dawn this morning."

Aoife felt her frustration disperse a little. Despite his obvious irritation he seemed more fragile than she had seen him before. Even unsure of himself. An early morning soaking would explain his poor delivery, ruffled look and the dark shadows under his eyes. He was biting into his cake as though it was the first time he'd eaten today, and she wondered if she should point out the moustache of white froth that had settled on his upper lip courtesy of his coffee. The overall effect made it impossible to be angry at him, He looked more like a little boy being taken out for a treat than a Detective Inspector. She couldn't hold back a grin which was wholly inappropriate considering the next thing she said.

"Another body?"

Her sudden switch of moods completely confused him, and he gaped as he asked, "How the hell do you know that?"

"I didn't. But why else would you be wading around in the mud and rain before dawn?" She knew she sounded smug and didn't care.

"Right. Well, yes. The point is it could be connected to what we were discussing."

"Oh no. Not another young victim."

"No. Not this time." He hesitated. "Look, I don't know you very well. It seems my boss is a big fan of your work."

"Nice." She beamed.

He gave her a stern look. "Yes well, but I have done some

background work, spoken to officers you worked with in the Met, and I hope… believe, that you are not out to make a quick headline."

Aoife thought it best to say nothing.

"The Superintendent thinks that if you have information you are willing to share, we should take it seriously, that it could be useful to this investigation."

"Ah ha! Now we get to the point. So ……." she beamed triumphantly.

"So, if I tell you some of the details about the body, I trust you not to let it go any further until we have done a formal identification and questioned the family? And please, stop looking so bloody smug."

"Well, yes. I won't pretend I've not been hoping the flow of information would stop being all one way, but I think I have proven I am willing to share what I have. Unless your body is a politician or high-ranking celebrity the national media won't be interested in a name anyway, and I'm more concerned about finding the story that connects everything together."

"Oh, I think you'll find the nationals will want this one."

Aoife raised her eyebrows "Someone famous?"

"No. not that. Remember, we haven't had a formal identification yet." He removed a pen and notepad from his pocket and wrote. She was aware that despite their distance from the other customers he was being cautious. He handed the notebook to Aoife. She looked at the neat letters then up at him, inclining her head to one side and taking a deep breath in as she felt the excitement build inside her.

"The father?"

He nodded.

"Interesting."

"I thought you might say that." He took the notebook back and placed it in an inside jacket pocket.

"Do you have any ideas as to how or why?"

"Not at the moment, and if we did, I'm not authorised to

tell you. Sorry." He grimaced at the look this last comment garnered. "Before we carry on, would you like another coffee?"

She had barely started her first drink. She looked at his empty cup. "Is it helping?"

"I feel better now than I did an hour ago."

"Yes please then. Same again."

When he had placed their order, he simply said "OK, so, what did you want to tell me."

Aoife pulled out her notes and was about to report everything she had learned the previous day from Daisy. Before she had got past the introductory points, she noticed another flash of irritation cross his face.

He stood up and for a moment Aoife wondered if she had upset him again without even speaking.

"I think we should find somewhere more private to continue this conversation."

"OK." Startled she stuffed the last piece of her muffin in her mouth and gulped down the remains of her first coffee before collecting up her note pad and bag. "I need the loo before we go."

As she returned Aoife noticed the detective slip his phone in his pocket. "There's a room at the station we can use. I've ordered the coffees to go." She felt like a child as she scurried to keep up with him as he marched the three hundred or so metres along the pavement to the modern office block that housed Bristol's most central police station.

CHAPTER 17

THE STATION

Once they had got over the formalities of getting her through security, Aoife found herself far less comfortable in the sparsely furnished room with its hard chairs and plain walls, than she had been in the café earlier. She was pleased they had brought their own coffee having spotted the vending machine as they walked by.

"OK. This is better. From now on we will have to meet here. We can't discuss live cases in a café." He still looked just as tired, but he seemed a bit more relaxed in his home environment.

"I'm sure the police on TV do it all the time. Even amongst themselves down the pub."

He gave her a weary look which simply made her laugh. "Do you want to carry on?"

Benedict Cooper had transferred to the Bristol Police force three years ago to take up his first post as Detective Inspector. His olive skin, thick dark hair and tall, strong build made him a subject of interest amongst the female police officers young and old and several of his male colleagues. He was undeniably attractive, though more with sensitive boyish charm than the classic chiselled chin and bulging muscles. It was his blue eyes that Aoife noticed being an unusual combination with his skin colouring.

Despite their frequent sparring, Aoife felt comfortable in his presence and believed she could enjoy working with him. She just needed to gain his trust. She pulled out her notes and picked up where she left off.

When she had finished relaying everything that Daisy had

told her she sat back and waited.

"So, you're suggesting the ..."

"I'm not suggesting anything." She interrupted "I have tried to repeat what I have been told as accurately as I can."

He leaned forward on the table and tried a different approach. "It would seem from what Mahira said that Anwar had a tough time at home. Possibly abused by his father. That is why you asked me about the pathologist's report. Now we have a possible sighting of both Anwar and Iqra being taken off in a van."

Aoife simply nodded, keen to hear what he thought.

"And we also have Habib Patel murdered. Keeley's version of events suggests that Iqra and Griff Tomlin had some sort of history. Iqra and Anwar were best buddies in their teens, so there is an excellent chance that Iqra knew what was happening to her friend. Do you think that Griff Tomlin was involved with Anwar in some way?" he asked.

"Keeley Tomlin said her dad knew Anwar. It's possible that Iqra thought Griff knew what was happening and she was disappointed that he hadn't stepped in and stopped it."

Cooper sat back with a look of distaste. "Or that Griff was one of the "others" that she mentioned."

"Yes. That is the thought that keeps running through my mind as most probable, given their intense reaction toward each other. It would certainly explain why Iqra didn't want to visit Harrison's family home once she found out who his father was. She could be disgusted by him or scared."

"And Griff Tomlin would be terrified that she would tell her future husband - his son - that his father was a deviant."

"Which would be motive enough to get rid of her." Aoife pointed out.

"And possibly the reason to dispose of Anwar too."

"So, DI Cooper, is this enough for the police to have another look into the deaths of all these young people?" Aoife's eyes were bright, her brain was firing on all cylinders, and she was struggling to remain composed and still in her seat. The fourth cup of strong black coffee of the morning that she had just consumed probably wasn't helping with that either.

"Please, do stop calling me that. Ben is fine." He looked at her and could see that she was fired up like a blood hound on the scent of the prey and desperate to be allowed off the leash. "The trouble is, it's still all hear-say. There's not a shred of proof and all our known or suspected victims are dead."

"What?"

"I don't want you going back to these women and getting them excited about something that might not happen."

"But we have people who have come forward."

"No. We don't. We have people who have said they thought that *others* might have been abused. And the people they are talking about are all dead so we can hardly go back and ask the victims to tell us what happened."

Aoife slumped back in her chair. She knew what he said was true. It didn't discourage her. So far everything had fallen into her lap. She was sure there was a story here, and a case for the police. She would just have to start digging. It's what she did.

"Was there anything in Anwar's postmortem that might indicate abuse?"

"Inconclusive I'm afraid. He had bruises. There was a history of a broken arm, and on another occasion a couple of broken fingers. At the time of his death abuse wasn't considered."

Benedict noticed her body language change. "Look, for what it's worth I think you might be on to something, but the police don't work like that. It would take a great deal of resources to reopen the case and we have a new murder on our hands. We don't know if Iqra is dead or a missing person." He saw the look of disappointment switch to anger on Aoife's face. She looked as though she might jump out of her seat at any minute and shake him. He held up a hand in a placating manner before she was able to get a word out.

"I'm not saying we won't do anything about it. I've already got someone having a look back over the files. Anwar's death was tragic, but it appeared to be a case of a young man with a stomach full of scotch topped up with drugs who slipped and toppled into the water. We see it all the time." He paused and cocked his head briefly to one side. "His father dying in the way that he did just a few months later opens up other possibilities. Now if we can connect the two deaths – beyond the familial relationship - then we have a reason for digging deeper. I'll get someone to look to see if there was ever suspected abuse reported involving Anwar or the other two. We'll look through all autopsy reports for anything that might indicate a connection or long term abuse. If there is, then it might be enough to push out the parameters.

"Surely if something had been reported it would have flashed up on the system when they died?"

"If the deaths weren't considered suspicious then possibly not."

"I intend to keep digging no matter what you decide." She said indignantly.

"Good. I thought you might." He smiled. "You seem to be a magnate that draws witnesses out. For some reason these people trust you. Perhaps you could continue to let me know when you find anything useful." This brought a broader smile to his face. He was pretty sure he was going to be bombarded with information.

"You said there was something we would get to?"

"Sorry?"

"You are busy, and you said you would have cancelled our meeting if it weren't for ....?" Aoife raised a questioning eyebrow. "I assume it's not just that Anwar's father is dead. Is there something in the way he died? You said we would get to that later. This is later."

"I did. Well, I can't tell you all the details yet. Forensics are still processing the site and the autopsy won't take place until later."

"But you seem sure it is Anwar's father?"

"Mrs Patel senior is coming in this afternoon to formally identify the body, but we found items of ID and he looked like the man in the photograph I was given. Unless he has a twin, it's Habib Patel."

"So how did he die? You must have some idea. Shot, strangled, hit over the head?"

"Didn't look like any of those. But that wasn't what caught the eye at first glance. He was staked out with his trousers and underpants pulled down to his ankles."

Aoife stared at him for a moment then looked down at her hand holding her cup as her brain worked on the many implications this offered up. "So, it might mean either Cara, Anwar and Mr Patel were all killed by a third party and we've misunderstood the reason for the young people's deaths. Or possibly....."

"Or it's some sort of revenge killing for Anwar yes. We will have to talk to your three young ladies and find out officially what they know about Iqra and Anwar's history."

Aoife looked unsettled "I can see why you would like to do that. And why you suddenly want to buy me cake."

"You don't look happy. You wanted the police to take them seriously. They have to come forward to the police." It had already been a long day and Benedict was tired. His words came out more snappishly than he had intended.

"I'm not trying to hide them. I would just have liked … No, you're right, it will be for the best. Sorry I'm still digesting what you said and my brains jumping to different connections."

"We know Keeley Tomlin and the Aziz family of course. I'm going to need contact details for Daisy Marston."

"I don't have them I'm afraid. Keeley Tomlin arranged it with her. I spoke to Daisy on Keeley's phone to make the arrangements. After we met I gave her my card and told her to get in touch if she wanted to talk further. She came to my house."

Benedict looked irritated. "Right. Do you normally just sit and wait to see if sources feel like coming to you?"

"Of course not. She just ran off first time. Not much different the second. If she doesn't get in touch I can ask Keeley. And I think I should point out I have given you everything I know. You've just told me Habib Patel is dead which will be in the papers and all over social media by morning. The balance of sharing is pretty one sided."

"And how his body was laid out. "

"True. Thank you."

"If you are willing to help then I've been given the OK to give you relevant information we find on Anwar Patel and Cara Felton. You'll have to sign an agreement."

"And what do you want in return?"

"These women are happy to talk to you. If any of their friends get in touch you keep us informed."

"And if they ask me to promise not to tell the police?"

Cooper's expression was cold. "Why would they do that if they want to get justice?"

"Because they reported abuse before, and nothing was done about it. Worse, they were made to feel irrelevant. Plus, people are still dying, and they're scared."

"What are you implying?"

"Nothing. I can understand their concern and it wouldn't be the first time a police officer has been found to be involved in child abuse."

Benedict looked tense. For a moment Aoife wasn't sure if he was going to kick her out of the office. Their relationship was not well established, they were still feeling their way. She was relieved when he appeared to do a sharp mental about turn.

"Fair enough. I need you to give me your word that you will encourage them to come forward but if they insist on keeping their identity secret, at least for the moment, then I will respect that. I mean you're the press not us." He gave her a mischievous grin "I'd also like you not to publish anything while the case is ongoing without running it passed me first."

"Sorry? I'm obviously onto something and you think you can gag me by offering me the odd tidbit!"

"No. No, not at all, that's not what I mean. Anything you

discover from your own investigations, well, you have to use your own judgement. I'm just referring to information that we might offer you. I didn't think you wrote quick articles for the daily papers anymore. I was under the impression you do your research and put all the pieces together first. Not publish speculation."

"Well, you're wrong. I do sell my work to the national and local media if I get something worthwhile. I've already formed a relationship with the Bristol Post and other locals. But I think I have proved some worth to you. I mean if I hadn't told you about Anwar being abused you would not have made the connection so quickly with his dad's murder. Nor did you make the connection between Mahira or Cara with the Patel's."

"People didn't come forward first time around with information. If they had that would have been useful."

Aoife had to admit that finding this information hadn't so far been down to her hard work and ingenuity either. She'd had the story thrown at her. She let the spark of antagonism that had been building inside quietly fizzle out.

"Or perhaps they did but no one took them seriously." She cocked her head to one side.

Benedict sighed. "Maybe."

CHAPTER 18

GIRLS' NIGHT

Aoife hadn't spoken to Leigh since she had left her at the train station three weeks ago and was pleased to hear her voice on the other end of the telephone, even if it was just as Aoife turned out the kitchen light and was about to make her way to bed.

"Hey girlfriend, what are you doing this weekend?" Leighs bubbly voice was a welcomed distraction from the more sombre thoughts that had filled Aoife's mind for the past few days.

"I was thinking of hitting the hills at some point, but otherwise nothing planned."

"I'm in Reading tomorrow for work. It's halfway to Bristol so I was thinking of just hopping on the train and coming to see you. Friday night drinks or, my treat, I could buy you dinner?"

"That sounds good. I've invited a neighbour round for drinks Friday night, but if you don't mind the extra company then it would be great to see you."

"Male of female?"

Aoife grinned. "Female. Phiah. She's the one that bakes cakes and made me food on my first night here."

"I'm happy if you're happy."

"And bring your walking boots." Aoife laughed.

"I could do with some fresh air. See you about six thirty."

Phiah lived three houses along from Aoife, with her husband and small daughter. The two women had struck up an easy friendship within a few days of becoming neighbours. When the woman with long, lustrous brown hair and skin the colour of dark honey, first approached Aoife to introduce herself, she had been momentarily taken aback by the warm welcome. Aoife had lived in her London flat for three years and had never got past "Good Morning." With any of her neighbours.

Phiah's mother was, she later discovered, from Malaysian descent but her father had been born and brought up in the Welsh valleys as had Phiah, just a few miles from Aoife's family home. University had pulled her to Bristol, then, with her husband she had settled down and started a family of her own.

Despite working fulltime as a biology teacher, on the day that Aoife had moved into her new home, Phiah had presented Aoife with a vegetable stew with dumplings and a vegan chocolate cake. A very welcome gift.

"Wow, that's amazing! Certainly beats the cheese sandwich and a squashed iced bun I was considering for dinner." She laughed.

"I won't keep you from your boxes. I know what it's like, but if you need anything, or just want a break and a chat, knock on the door. I'm just opposite." Phiah pointed to a blue door on the other side of the narrow road.

Within the six weeks since Aoife's arrival, they had met a few times for drinks and coffees in each other's house. On hearing Aoife had a friend arriving from London, Phiah, jumped at the opportunity to go for a night out. It wasn't difficult to persuade Marcel, her husband, to have a father daughter evening with their two-year-old toddler, and took Aoife and Leigh to a wine bar in North Street.

Leigh and Phiah hit it off straight away. Phiah expressed her surprise that neither of the two attractive women she was sharing tapas and a wine with, were not in relationships. "I know it's hard for most people to understand, but I've never felt freer than I have since I married Marcel. There is no clock ticking in the back of my mind, no pressure from my family to find a 'nice man'. I can enjoy being out with my friends or chat to men without being suspected of an ulterior motive. I feel like I can concentrate on getting on with my life."

Leigh almost shouted "It's not from lack of trying! I put myself out there. It's this one who has turned celibate." She hooked a thumb in Aoife's direction and laughed.

Aoife ignored her friend and faced Phiah "No, I get what

you're saying. It wouldn't work for me in the same way. Some days I like shutting the front door and spending the day painting or curled up with a book. I can't always be bothered to cook, and housework is overrated. I live like a pig. It would take an incredibly special person to want to share a house with me."

"I can still do that." Said Phiah "Maybe not the living like a pig bit." She took a sip of her wine to hide her distaste.

"Really? Didn't know you painted." Aoife raised her eyebrows and smirked.

"I don't. But I like pottering in the garden and eating cheese on toast for dinner. I know you like taking off to the hills, but wouldn't it be nice if you had someone to share the views with, or even surprise you with a picnic they'd prepared especially when you got there?"

Aoife paused to let this thought sink in. The whole point of 'taking off to the hills' as Phiah packaged it, was to get away from everyone. She loved the thrill of adventure as she got up early and set off in the car with supplies for the day. Yes, she loved the exercise of walking up the hills with the sun or the wind on her face, but it was so much more than that. The wide open spaces and the absence of conversation and the feeling of opening up such possibilities in her mind excited her. It was where she had formulated some of her best stories; problems got untangled or dissolved, and life made sense. She always came back energised.

She didn't feel the need to explain this to her new friend, so she said "I know. You and Marcel seem really good together. Perhaps I just haven't found the right person to share it with, or perhaps I am better off on my own,"

Aoife was not ready to take on the partnership of marriage and was still smarting from her recent breakup, but marriage had never been mentioned even with Cameron. She may never be ready although she could see that her neighbour was content, and Aoife was happy for her.

Phiah took this conciliatory response as it had been intended.

"You might not be ready to bear your sole, it takes time." Leigh smiled encouragingly at her friend "Doesn't mean you can't sample the menu though. You know, have a little nibble here, a quick taste there."

Aoife spluttered in her wine forcing her to grab some a napkin and mop herself up. "Do you have to put it so graphically?" They all giggled.

"I never really loved anyone enough to think about marrying them. You have to be really sure to make that commitment." Said Leigh.

Phiah frowned. "We may not know what's coming, we can't plan out every part of our lives and we can't predict our futures, life isn't perfect, but we can hope. It's scary to hope, to leave yourself so open but it's better than wrapping yourself in a cocoon that gets hard and brittle with age."

"Are you trying to tell me I'm scared of life or that I'm hard and brittle?" Aoife tipped her head to one side and raised her eyebrow.

"I don't know why you haven't met your prince, but I'm sure he's out there somewhere. It's good that you're never going to settle for second best."

"I'm open to new things. Sometimes, life reminds us that the unexpected things are the best things that ever happen to us. A spur of the moment decision that changes our lives forever in a good way. Like leaving my job and becoming freelance." She raised her glass and the other's followed her lead.

"Or meeting someone new, at work or a local shindig, who becomes a huge and wonderful part of your life." Leigh gave an impish grin and raised her glass. "Here's to a future that's fulfilling and …." She struggled to find the right words.

"And" Aoife emphasised the word "Full of joy."

"Perfect!"

CHAPTER 19

CHARITY FUNDRAISER

T he "Brothers in Business" dinner was not the only event being hosted in the Faregate Manor hotel that evening. The signage in the reception also directed participants to a Women's Institute meeting and a golden wedding anniversary celebration. Members of the Brothers in Business were however, guided to the largest and most opulent of the rooms.

Four enormous crystal chandeliers hung from the ornately decorated pale blue and gold ceiling. Three of the walls were covered with blue, brown, and orange birds perched on golden leafed trees. At the furthest end floor to ceiling French doors were left slightly ajar to let in a cool breeze and the fragrant spring air.

When they arrived, the group were welcomed by staff in white jackets guiding them to round tables each seating eight dark suited gentlemen. The tables were covered with white linen cloths and laden with polished silver cutlery, tall cut glass wine goblets and beautifully folded napkins that matched the wall coverings.

There were no women. Even the serving staff who were calmly topping up glasses and removing general debris from the table while the guests tucked into their desert, were all male.

There were eighty diners, all dressed to show off their wealth and good fortune. The majority of them were middle aged white Anglo-Saxons but there were a good number of different ethnicities represented.

Up on the platform an imposing, white haired gentleman had just finished telling his audience how beneficial their humanitarian support had been to the people of the city in the last twelve months. Food banks had been funded, life-saving equipment had been supplied to the children's hospital, and Christmas hampers had been given to twenty percent more underprivileged households than in the previous year. Everyone duly clapped, cheered and banged hands on tables.

As the noise calmed down the white haired gentleman announced that coffee and port was to be served and now, he would be handing over to a fellow member who would be running the auction for some *'truly fabulous'* items. All proceeds going to the Brothers in Business charitable causes.

At one of the tables Michael Harvey stood between Griff Tomlin and Douglas Thornbeck. A hand on the back of each of their chairs. "Good evening Griff, Douglas." He nodded at the two friends.

"Ah, Mr Harvey. Jolly good dinner as always." Said Griff. The others agreed.

Michael stood up straight and gestured with his chin for them to follow. As he wound through the tables, he tapped the shoulder of a sandy haired man whose cummerbund was working hard to keep his large stomach from bulging over the top of his trousers. He led them a few steps toward the wall where they wouldn't be overheard. Never-the-less he kept his voice soft.

"Tell me, how are things progressing with that other business?" he asked. The other three went silent for a moment. "Times ticking away." Harvey urged. Tomlin and Thornbeck both moved until their backs were to the room.

Griff's face turned dark, and he glared at Harvey. "I don't think this is the place to hold that particular discussion."

"How is your son Griff? Dreadful business. To lose the woman you plan to spend the rest of your life with. Still, it could have been worse. What are the odds? Harrison should pick that little slut as his future wife hmm? Still at least you'd finished with her." Ex-Superintendent Mewse smiled salaciously. "Good job she's no longer around to cause you any embarrassment, but I'm not sure it stops there."

A waiter in a white jacket was pouring coffee at each table. He approached the four conspirators "Can I get you gentlemen a port?"

"Brandy for me please" All four men replied.

"What's the inside story on Habib?" They looked at each other.

"They found him in the woods near his house. All I know is it was a heroin overdose. The gossip is he was pegged out on the ground. It was obviously murder. They've put a cloak over it. My sources can't get details." Said Mewse. The group all went quiet. Hands became clammy and a worried look spread over each of their faces.

"I'm being watched. The police are still asking questions about Iqra and my son. What with Habib and all. It's too risky for me to get involved." Said Griff.

"Something or someone is stirring things up." Said Mewes.

"He's right." Said Thornbeck. "Can't you get your goons to sort it out?" He looked at Harvey. "We can't have any more bodies turning up in the river. It's already starting to raise eyebrows."

"OK. Leave it to me." Glowered Harvey. "Just one more to go. We've removed that sister what's her name? Sophia? Too bloody clever by half. Cut off the head and the others will disappear back into the woodwork."

"One more for now." Griff sneered and turned to make sure the punters at the nearest table were paying attention to the auctioneer.

"For now. Yes." Harvey said quietly. "It would of course have been a lot easier if you had dealt with it at the time." He turned to Douglas who shrugged casually and heaped several spoonsful of sugar from a table nearby, to his coffee, before stirring it briskly.

"Things were different back then." Douglas Thornbeck said unperturbed.

"Don't look so smug, you may have ducked that business eight years ago but not before it made the papers. You're already tainted." Spat Harvey.

"Bloody journalists just like to sling mud and see what happens. It didn't stick."

Tomlin swilled the wine in his glass before slugging it down his throat. "I hear we may have another journalist poking around."

"Oh?"

"Her name's Macarthy. Recently moved to Bristol. She's won awards for her investigative work in the past. Been seen talking to one of the girls. I've had her watched. She went to visit Jamal's wife too." Said Harvey.

"You mean that woman that caught one of your guys with the kid in his arms on the Downs? Bloody slack that was. How could he have let a woman get the better of him?" Thornbeck glared at Michael Harvey.

"Don't worry he's been dealt with. It won't happen again."

"Who's been blabbing to the journalist?" asked Mewse.

"That bloody little freak with the kid. If she thinks there's a story, we're in trouble."

"That weird, scrawny one. Daisy?"

"Does Father Rowan know?"

"Don't know. Doubt it. I was going to catch him later."

"We need to put a stop to it before she gets momentum."

"We can't have any more accidents; it'd be too obvious."

"She's got a family now. We can make the little slut see what's in her best interest. And have a word with the journalist."

"You mean warn her off. How would we do that."

"I think it's time a certain councillor paid back some of the favours he owes."

At that point their conversation was disturbed by the exuberant banter of the auctioneer encouraging them to participate in the bidding.

"You gents standing chatting there. Take your beautiful ladies on a holiday to this wonderful villa with all the luxuries included, and you can gossip on the golf course without being disturbed. The bid stands at the ridiculously cheap price of four thousand five hundred. What do you say six thousand pounds for the two weeks lavish holiday in Portugal?"

CHAPTER 20

DAISY

N ow that Daisy had found her way on her own initiative to Aoife's house there seemed no point in meeting in a café. Given the nature of their conversation sitting in a public place didn't seem sensible. Aoife had encouraged her to come for another chat. They were sitting once more at Aoife's kitchen table, coffees, water, and jelly babies to hand.

Aoife had tried to push the conversation toward the girl's own home life, but Daisy was reluctant.

"I.. I told you. My dad died and I had to look after mum 'till she got better after the accident."

"You stayed at Poppy Hill for a while too didn't you."

"Yeah. Poppy Hill was a dump, but I wasn't there that long." There was a silence.

"So, what happened to you?" Daisy didn't look away she stared straight into Aoife eyes, but Aoife got the impression it was the past the girl was seeing. "You said you could talk to me."

Aoife noticed the girl's eyes flick nervously to the door as if worried someone might walk in, then down to the table. The nails of her right hand dug into her left leaving red marks. Without looking up she blurted "It was Father Rowan."

Aoife let go of the breath she'd been holding. She had meant what she'd said to Daisy. The credit was all hers. She had hidden the memories and horrors deep inside for so long. To open the door to them now was not just scary but painful. Aoife knew there was more locked behind the fortifications of the young woman's mind. Keeping those memories locked away had enabled Daisy to maintain a semblance of normal life. She watched and waited to get the timing right.

"He used to come round to check on mum, first while dad was ill and then when mum got out of hospital. You know – after the accident."

"And where is he now?" Aoife wondered if this Father Rowan was still preying on vulnerable children.

"I don't know. He moved to a different church a few years back."

There was another long pause and despite having the voice recorder on Aoife made a note to make searching out Father Rowan a priority.

Daisy continued. "Dad refused to speak to me if I didn't go and help with the little ones at Sunday school. Said I owed it to the father for all the time and attention he had given to helping me. Dad was ill and I felt awful making him upset."

"Did you ever try to tell them? Explain why you didn't want to go."

"I told them when it first happened. When I was ten years old. They didn't believe me. Repeatedly refused to listen. My dad gave me a beating for having a filthy mind."

"Did you try to tell anyone else?"

Daisy became hostile and stared at her. "I was still at junior school. My dad was ill and died and my mum was upset. I thought you were different, but you have no idea do you?"

Aoife was taken aback by the outburst. She sat very still for a moment before saying in the most conciliatory voice she could manage. "I'm sorry Daisy. I'm not blaming you in any way. I am angry but not with you. Please excuse me for being clumsy. I can have no idea what it was like, but I believe you."

Daisy chewed her nails then her hand slipped to her hair which she wound around and around her fingers. Her breathing slowed and her face lost the flush of colour. "The Father was unwilling to give up control over me even when

I was older. Told me I was complicit. Told me no one would believe me, which was true. I had nowhere to go, so I lied, not able to explain. I begged my mum to allow me to go into town with my friends instead, but she said I was selfish. That was before she was ill." There was a long silence. Daisy stuffed another jelly baby in her mouth and chewed quietly.

"Finally, I went to live with my friend for a few weeks. They took me in to give my mum a break while she was still recovering. My aunty came to look after her for a while. They all saw the bruises on my arms from Father Rowan, but no one said anything.

"Bruises?"

"When he held me down. He'd squeeze and pinch. He liked little breasts. He said it over and over. They only saw the marks on my arms."

"Did you tell them what had been going on?"

"No. I'd learned by then that no one would believe me. I just kept my mouth shut. When I went back home mum never mentioned me going back to church and I slipped out if Father Rowan came to visit. I didn't see him again."

"How old were you then? When it stopped."

"Fourteen."

Aoife made more coffee and checked the voice recorder. She made a few notes by hand just to remind herself to ask the right questions when the time was right without disturbing Daisy's flow. Two glasses of water, several sheets of kitchen towel, and a bowl of jelly babies later, Daisy came to a stop. The abscess had been lanced, the poison and dead tissue had finally been drained. The girl was exhausted.

Aoife's hand was trembling.

"I really need to go now."

"Only if you're ready. If you prefer, I could try and get hold of Detective Inspector Cooper. I know he will be interested." She didn't think she should say anything about a connection between Iqra's disappearance and the deaths of Cara and Anwar. There was a good chance that Daisy already knew.

"No. No police. You can tell him, but you can't mention my name."

"I need to pass on your information on. This Rowan man has to be stopped. It will carry much more weight if it comes from you."

Daisy looked horrified. "You promised!"

"I will not tell anyone that I have your voice on tape, but seriously, think about it. How will you feel if you read in the paper that another young person has been found dead, or that Father Rowan has not changed his ways, when you might have been able to save some young sole from the trauma you've been through?"

"That's not fare! It's not down to me. I had nothing to do with Anwar or Iqra. I don't know what happened to them."

"Nor did I, but between us perhaps we can make a difference."

Daisy hid her face in her hands for several seconds then straightened up raking her fingers through her hair. She looked straight at Aoife. "Would you stay with me? If I talk to him?"

"I would."

"I'll do it. But not now. I've got to get home."

"Let me have your mobile number and I can arrange something." She saw Daisy hesitate. "That way I can come to the police station with you." Aoife wasn't at all sure she would be allowed to sit in while Daisy was being questioned by the police, but that was a problem for a later time. She needed to get the girl their and brief Benedict to be gentle or they'd lose her.

Aoife was worried that the girl's legs might not carry her, nor her mind be sufficiently focused to guide her, so she phoned for a taxi with a female driver to pick Daisy up and get her safely home.

ΔΔΔ

As soon as she had shut the front door behind her guest Aoife picked up her mobile and phoned Benedict.

She tried his mobile but, it went straight to voicemail. She didn't bother to leave a message. She rang the station and asked to speak to Detective Inspector Cooper. After a long wait a young male voice came on the line to explain that D.I. Cooper wasn't available at the moment. A short explanation that she had information useful to an enquiry, and she found herself talking to another young man who introduced himself as P.C. Rahim. As soon as she told him who she was he obviously recognised her name, and his attitude was noticeably cooler. She wondered if they had talked about her at the station or if he had read the Sunday papers. Either way, he didn't seem to have a great deal of respect for the work she did, and his manner became brusque and dismissive as though she was a nuisance caller.

"Thank you, Miss Macarthy, I'll tell D.I. Cooper that you called." The phone line went dead.

"Condescending little squirt!" She threw the mobile across the room – where it landed safely on a cushion.

She doubted if her message would be near the top of his priority list but at least neither D.I. Cooper nor his colleagues could accuse her of trying to keep anything from them. If they wanted to labour on for days to discover information she had to hand right now, well, so be it. Aoife had the basis of a good story and several leads to investigate. More, she suspected, than the police had at this moment.

CHAPTER 21

DAISY

D.I. Cooper had eventually got her message, although Aoife's assumption had been correct, and it hadn't arrived on his desk until the end of the day. When she finally received his call, they arranged to make the most of the sunny weather and meet on a bench in Queens Square for mid-morning coffee the next day.

"So, what did you learn from Miss Marston this time around?"

"Mrs."

"Sorry?"

"It's Mrs Marston. She's married. Got a three-year-old kid."

"What did she have to say?"

"Quite a bit. Though I'm sure there's still more.

"I need to talk to Daisy Marston."

"I agree. Daisy has said she will talk to you."

"Really?"

"She asked me to be with her."

"I don't think so. How do you think it will look if the police start inviting journalists to sit in on interviews?"

"It's not going to be under caution is it? The only thing she's done wrong is not coming forward earlier. And if she had she might have ended up in the river."

"If you're planning on splashing this story all over the papers the police aren't going to be part of it."

"I won't be a journalist while I'm there; I'll be her responsible person."

"She's over eighteen and she isn't a vulnerable adult. She doesn't need a responsible adult with her."

"She's not telling you anything I don't already know. I think she will be more relaxed if I am there."

"She's not being accused of anything she's simply providing us with information that might help us catch her tormentor."

"Look, if you drag her in on her own and surround her with strangers, I think you'll find she'll clam up. And she can't talk in front of her husband either. He gets too upset. You won't get a thing. Why don't I invite her back to the cafe and you join us? If later you think you need to speak to her under caution or record what she says then fine, take it from there."

"Aoife you have been very helpful, but this is a police matter, and you are a civilian." Cooper still looked unsure but despite his words Aoife noticed he sounded less adamant.

"What are you going to do? Drag her into the station, give her the third degree and scare the shit out of her? Why do you think she didn't come forward in the first place?"

Cooper stared at her for a full minute without speaking. She didn't move. 'Yeah, all right,' he sighed "I'll check with the Super. If she has something that is relevant to a case she will be brought in for formal questioning. We need to check she's genuine. And remember you've signed the agreement. You can't write anything that might prejudice an ongoing case."

"I've signed a piece of paper that says I won't print anything I discover from your investigation without your say so. We had the newspaper's lawyers look over it before I signed remember? I've not mentioned the details. I already know everything she's going to tell you. You won't be giving away secrets."

Aoife thought about the diminutive figure of Daisy sitting in one of the formal interview rooms at the station surrounded by uniforms and undergoing an intensive interrogation by D.I. Benedict Cooper and sergeant Goss. The thought had crossed Aoife's mind several times that Daisy might not just be a spectator in this chilling account, and she had been proved right. She could only hope that the young woman's determination to impose retribution against people who had caused so much pain would hold out.

Aoife had sat with Daisy for several hours over the last few weeks, listening to her story, letting her talk at her own pace. She'd watched the tears trickle down Daisy's face as she hugged her knees and rocked backward and forward in her chair. Aoife couldn't help but wonder how well she would hold up in front of the police. Especially a man.

It seemed that DI Cooper was having the same thoughts. 'How did you get her to talk?"

'I listened,' she said.

Cooper shot her a harsh glance. "Fair enough."

She was relieved to see his face soften and a hint of a smile.

"I look forward to reading your article when it's published. Who are you going to sell it to?"

"I don't know yet. The Post is keen of course. I don't even know what the story is or if I have a story. This is all still just flotsam floating around my head. There is no solid core to anchor anything to. The paedophile ring grooming young kids in care would be important but the only name I have is Father Rowan, the rest are all just shadows. Have the police got any suspects?"

"No, not yet. Since Habib Patel's body was found displayed as it was the powers that be are beginning to agree that there is something much bigger going on. The good news is we are looking again at Anwar Patel. Iqra and Anwar were mates. I've run it past my boss who's run it past his, and it appears that Mahira was right; Anwar's dad did know Griff Tomlin which means there's a good chance Iqra could have met him at some point. We're looking into the connection with Cara too."

CHAPTER 22

GRIFF TOMLIN

G riff Tomlin sat comfortably in his armchair reading the Sunday papers, a cup of tea by his side. He planned to walk down to the Star for a couple of pints a bit later. Janet had left him some lunch in the oven and wouldn't be back before two. He was content. The newspaper dropped suddenly, and he could feel himself almost dozing off again.

He'd become an old man he realised. Naps in the chair were unheard of when he was younger. His two eldest children, both boys, had played a sport every weekend and both his girls swam and played tennis at the club. They'd kept Janet busy, and Griff had gone along to watch matches and galas. None of the children lived at home anymore. The eldest had gone to Canada and Petra, his eldest daughter, had left home as soon as she'd finished school. Some part of his consciousness prodded his drowsy mind for a moment. He was aware of a noise in the kitchen but didn't bother to open his eyes. Probably the cat.

He woke with a start blinked and coughed then gave a loud snorting sniff. Something unusual had happened, but he had no idea what it was. His head was heavy and felt like he had cotton wool stuffed inside. He looked up at the ceiling. Somehow he had got to his bedroom. He didn't remember. Was his age really starting to get to him?

"What the!" Griff's voice was dry and rasping. His head hurt and he had lost his glasses. He recalled his wife leaving to see their daughter as she always did on a Sunday morning. All he could remember after that was sitting down in his favourite

137

chair and drinking a cup of tea then wondering what was tapping against the window out the back. Now he opened his eyes and there was this girl dressed in a fancy-dress costume standing over him. He struggled to sit up.

He growled in the back of his throat, like a beast ready to fight, angry and frustrated.

"Help me up will you!" It didn't sound much like a request, but then he was more used to grunting orders than requests.

"I don't think so Papa Zi."

At the sound of that name the man froze. He couldn't see well without his glasses and his thoughts were still spiralling and foggy with sleep. But he knew only one group of people knew him by that title, and no one had used it for almost six years. They had all had false names. Safer than risking the little urchins knowing any true identities.

"Who are you? What do you want?" His voice was dark and coarse, and there was a sharpness to it, as if of surprise or puzzlement.

"Ah. Now how many times have you been asked those questions Papa Zi? Hmm? Can you count them all? Do you see those terrified little faces staring at you as you abused them? Do you hear their cries at night while you try to sleep? Do their cries for their mother keep you awake at night?"

His head was spinning, and he was struggling to focus. He wondered for a moment if he was hallucinating. This infuriating person was wearing a bright red scarf that covered her hair and was tied tightly around the back of her neck. She wore layers of colourful loose shirts over hareem pants. Her chin, cheeks and forehead were chalk white. Across her eyes was a painted mask of deep burgundy with electric blue highlights while her lips were painted black. Griff couldn't take his eyes off her. The way she moved, her voice; she was mesmerising.

As he stared at her something in the woman's right hand caught his attention. He didn't think it had been their earlier when he had first woken up. He'd seen the blue rubber gloves, he was sure he would have noticed a knife, but he hadn't seen her reach for it either. It was white with some sort of pattern in yellow green and red. As she sensed his gaze drawn toward it she stroked its cool enamel covering then slipped it to her fingertips for him to get a better look. It was pretty. A lady's penknife in mother of pearl with decorative birds.

"Would you like your glasses so that you can have a better look? I wouldn't want you to miss anything." Someone in blue coveralls and surgical gloves moved to her side and placed his glasses over his nose, hooking them behind his ears. For a moment he wondered if he was in hospital. He was on a bed.

Then he realised it was his own bed in his own bedroom, surrounded by people in blue coveralls. He tried to pull his hands free, but they were tied to the bedposts as were his feet.

A silver blade sprung to one end of the penknife. The girl smiled as she felt the terror that ran through the old man's body.

"No need to be scared Papa Zi." She cooed as he struggled to stand up only to find the plastic cords that held him pulled tighter cutting off the blood from his hands and feet. "Isn't that what you always used to say? Don't be scared sweetie."

"I don't know you. This is stupid." She could tell he was trying to bring authority to his voice. He was a man that was used to being obeyed.

"Aren't you pleased to see me. You always used to be very excited when you saw me. And today I dressed up especially for you."

"You won't get away with this!"

The tip of her pink tongue ran slowly, thoughtfully, around her top lip, then she laughed. "Who will tell? Not you old man." She leaned forward until her hands touched the material that covered his flaccid penis. Then she slowly brought the sharp knife down.

"Let's see if you're excited to see me today. Would you like me to put my hands around your throat and squeeze? Is that the way you get it up? Or was it the screams of terror that turned you on?" She felt him buck and roll in panic beneath her fingers as the blade closed in on his genitals.

"I would lie still if I were you. It's very sharp." Her voice was soft as if she were reciting a nursery rhyme. She pushed the blade through his trousers and drew the sharp edge toward his belly button cutting through his trouser and then underpants. She heard the sharp intake of breath accompanied by a small whimper, as he braced for the pain. There was none.

"You're not scared of me are you Papa Zi?" Using the tip of the knife she pushed his shirt up then pulled his trousers down to his ankles. She straightened and stared down at the grey wrinkled mass that had been used to hurt so many children. One of the others in blue passed her something and she shook it in her hand, then she took the lid off and sprayed the bright red paint over his belly and genitals down to the top of his thighs.

"No. No!" Griff croaked. "Why are you doing this?"

"Are you saying you don't recognise your own daughter?"

The old man stared aghast. His mouth open, his eyes wide. "Petra?"

"Who else?"

"Where's your mother?" It was the only phrase from all the words that were buzzing in his brain that he could get to his tongue.

"She's looking after her grandchildren."

"She will be upset when she finds out."

Petra laughed. "Oh Papa Zi. You have no idea how much you disgust her, do you? She will celebrate. Who do you think drugged your tea?"

"You're trying to frighten me?"

"No. I'm going to kill you."

The old man managed a strained laugh. This wasn't real. If only he could get his mind to focus. "Don't be silly."

"Is that what you said to Iqra?"

"Iqra?"

"You really shouldn't have killed her. You think Harrison doesn't know? You ruined my life years ago. And now you've ruined your son's life too. Your whole family hates you. You. Are. Poison." The words came out like bullets.

"You were young and robust. I loved you. I didn't ruin your life."

Petra looked down at her father through cold eyes her mouth was set firm as the blade closed in on his genitals. Her father screamed "No!"

"Don't. He's not worth it. Stick to the plan." A male voice came from the corner of the room. Griff looked around as if noticing the four people in blue coveralls for the first time.

"My husband has taught me that I deserve better than you. Thanks to him I know my true self-worth. My children love me, and I love them, and you will not get a chance to ruin their lives too."

"I always loved you best Petra."

"Oh, you know why Papa Zi? You didn't think there would be a price to pay for all that pleasure you stole. Those lives you ruined?"

"Think of your mother. I will look after her I promise."

"Did you ever show *them* compassion and let *them* run to their mothers? I think not."

She carefully replaced the penknife inside her capacious costume and handed back the can of paint.

"You are sick. Is this how you get your kicks?" He spluttered to the others in the room.

For a moment the young woman's face became ugly as a sneer took over her previously calm countenance. She now had a small enamel tin in her hands which she opened and took out a syringe. She heard him breathing hard.

"Don't have a heart attack on us now, you'll miss out on all the fun."

Her movements were calm, as methodical as a doctor who had done this many times before. She rolled up his sleeve. Other hands held him still as she pressed the needle into his cephalic vein.

"Goodbye old man. Enjoy the ride. It will be your last."

"No! You will regret this!"

"You're wrong. I will celebrate this day each year, along with your wife and other children."

She had no more words for him. She put away the needle and the tin disappeared back in the pocket along with the knife. Then she turned with hand outstretched. She high fived her friends. They all quietly left the room without looking back.

They had no need to wait and watch, the heroin would do the rest of the work now. There was no way he could survive such a huge dose.

They went to the kitchen, washed out the teacup that sat on the coffee table and put it away in the cupboard before replacing it with another. Setting the table as if for two they poured a little tea and milk in each cup and headed for the back door. Then they froze as a blue Toyota car pulled onto the driveway at the side of the house.

"Down!" Hissed Peter. They all crouched down. Silent.

The car door slammed, and footsteps could be heard on the gravel as someone walked toward the front door.

"Against the wall. Quick!" Peters voice was urgent, but he managed to stay calm as he pulled Petra around the corner, out of sight from the front door.

The doorbell rang. Then someone knocked loudly on the glass. "Hey Griff. You fallen asleep again?" Silence. "Get your lazy arse out of that chair mate. I need a beer." The footsteps moved from the front around to the side of the house.

"This way!" Petra took two steps along the front hall and opened a door. "In here." The utility room was not built to hold five people, but they all managed to squeeze in. With the door shut behind them they were unable to hear footsteps. The back door rattled. They held their breath. Then they heard a ringtone somewhere nearby.

"Fuck!" whispered Lilly squeezing her eyes closed. "It's on the kitchen table."

For several minutes they all remained still and silent. No one made eye contact. Then a collective release of breath as they heard a car door slam, the engine start. Peter opened the utility room door a crack and peeped around the corner in time to see the car move through the front gate.

"He's gone."

"Let's get out of here before he comes back." Said Lilly. Her voice still low. The scare had shaken them all.

"Keep to the plan." Said Peter as they rushed back toward the kitchen. He turned. Petra wasn't with them.

He looked back into the utility room. Petra was still squeezed into the corner. Peter put his arm out toward her, but she shook him off. "Come on. We have to get out of here."

The girl didn't move, and Peter saw tears rolling down her cheeks. "We're nearly there. Just a few more minutes. A few more steps. Your Petra. The bravest girl I know. You can do this." He took her hand and pulled gently. To his relief she followed.

They ran along the path at the side of the house that was not overlooked by neighbours and led to a garden shed where they jumped over the wall into the trees. They placed a plastic sheet on the ground and removed their coveralls and gloves. The large house was surrounded by gardens and backed onto woodlands. When they reached the other side of the trees Gabriel was waiting for them in an old blue and cream, beat up land rover, number plates replaced.

Gabriel turned the key, started the engine, and drove slowly and quietly with caution along the deserted lane. With shaking fingers Petra pushed forward between the seats and switched the radio up high, she sat back and pulled up her legs hugging them to her chest and let her head hang down until her forehead touched her knees. She sat like that for several minutes, her tears cascading down her cheeks, smudging the remnants of her make-up and making breathing difficult as she gulped for air.

Peter put his arm around her shoulders. "You did well."

Anna turned in her seat at the front, placed a hand on Petra's knee and squeezed. "It's all over. He can't hurt you or your family anymore."

"What can you tell me." Benedict arrived at the Tomlin's large, detached house just after three-thirty, but the detectives had remained outside to allow the forensic team to do their job.

DC Hyslop looked earnest as he reported his findings so far. "As I said on the phone, similar to Habib Patel's murder. So, not much about the body at first glance that you can't see or guess already. Doc's up there now. He might have something for us."

"Well, there's no storm and the body's inside so we should have some evidence." chipped Cooper.

"First glance he thought drugs overdose of some sort. Not been dead long. His wife found the body. She's inside. She left the house at nine thirty to visit her daughter and grand kids, stayed for lunch and arrived back just after two."

Sergeant Goss stepped in "She didn't discover her husband straight away. He'd said he was going to the pub. His mobile was in the house, so she went looking for him. Found him in the bedroom."

DI Cooper looked at his watch. "It's now nearly four. Come on let's see if it's safe for us to go indoors yet.

They walked through the kitchen on steppingstones laid out by the forensics team. Benedict glanced into the living room as he passed and saw Janet Tomlin with a mug of tea in hand and a uniformed PC sitting nearby.

Dr Nick Cartwright acknowledged them as they hovered at the edge of the bedroom.

"If we hadn't seen Habib Patel last week. first glance might have suggested a sex game gone wrong." Said Goss.

The pathologist gave her a strange look "Reallly? What sort of sex life do you have?" He put the palm of his hand up toward her. "Don't tell me I don't want to know."

The sergeant laughed. "Do you think it could be Heroin again?"

"Puncture wound in his right cephalic vein indicative of a syringe, same as Mr Patel."

"At least we're not fighting with the rain washing away all the evidence this time."

"No. That's the good news. The bad news is whoever did this was scrupulous."

"What do you mean?"

"We will keep looking and we've bagged his hands as you can see in case he got a good hold on his attacker. First sweep hasn't given us anything."

"What about wounds to the body, blow to the head? He didn't just walk to the bed and allow them to bind his hand and feet. There must be bruising?"

"Neither blood nor bruising as far as I can see at the moment. I'll know more when I get him on the table but at the moment nothing obvious."

"They must have incapacitated him somehow. Even if he was lying on the bed having a snooze he would have woken up when they entered the room and started man handling him."

"We've done a preliminary search. Found nothing." Nick was obviously as confused as the police officer.

"There has to be something. Hair, DNA on the ties. This is not a small guy. He didn't just lie down and let them tie him up without some sort of physical contact. How did they keep him still?"

"Perhaps he thought he was in for kinky sex. Being tied up was all part of the game." Said Hyslop.

"Or they drugged him first? Put something in his tea maybe?" Suggested Goss. "I saw cups on the table in the living room."

"Drugging is the most obvious possibility at the moment. There were breakfast things on the table. We'll bag them all. They might have taken a glass away with them of course. Again, once I get him back to my office I can do tests and have a closer look." Said Nick.

"No one can get in, tie a big guy like him up and get out again, without leaving some trace." Scoffed Cooper.

"I'm sorry to disappoint but the place is spotless." A woman in a wite coverall and mask was bending down in the hall working on the floor. "We'll check the prints around the house. Plenty of samples from Mr and Mrs Tomlin up here. A few more downstairs. We'll have to eliminate other family members. The only thing they left behind were the cables they used to tie him up."

"Anything special about the ties?"

"Probably not. You can buy them in the thousands as you know. We left them on for you to see. We'll get them bagged and tagged. "

"No DNA, no fingerprints. How can that be?" Goss sighed.

"Nick shrugged his shoulders. At this point your guess is as good as mine. Look around you, what do you see?" He gestured with his arm to take in the SOCO team all dressed in coveralls. "Gloves, boilers suits, hair tied back, shoe covers."

Ben looked aghast. "You don't open your door to a bunch of people dressed like these guys." He turned to the nearest person dressed in white coveralls. As they turned he saw it was a woman "Do we know how they got in yet?"

"No sir. No obvious sign of a break in. No forced locks no fingerprints. But then Mrs Tomlin said they rarely lock the back door during the day."

"Ok Nick. As soon as you get anything let me know. I'm going to really need the autopsy results asap on this one." Cooper sounded grumpy.

"Doesn't everyone?"

"Not everyone has two murders with absolutely no trace left behind." He turned to his sergeant. "Have the neighbours seen anything?"

"You're not going to like this either. No CCTV anywhere nearby that points toward the road. So far only checked with the nearest neighbours. We'll do a wider sweep. But no one close has seen nor heard anything. Doesn't seem he was very popular by the way."

"Great."

Cooper and Goss went back downstairs and were joined by DC Hyslop. When they were in the garden Benedict turned to the others.

"What do we know about Griff Tomlin?"

"Wife Janet. Daughter Petra married to Freddie has produced two grandchildren. Eldest child Thomas moved to Canada twelve years ago. Never been back. Harrison you know about, was engaged to Iqra Aziz, now lost or dead. Youngest daughter Keeley you know about. She was the one to contact Aoife Macarthy. Lives with friends in Bristol. Griff worked as an engineer on British Rail before starting his own engineering company. Built it up from scratch seems to be doing well. Had his drinking buddies down The Star and the Golden Heart. Neighbours don't seem too upset about his death. All said they'd keep an eye out for Janet make sure she's alright. She seems well liked."

"Has he been in any trouble?"

"Got in a bit of a scrap in a few pubs a few years back. Sounds like he gets handy with his fists with alcohol inside him."

"Could be why his kids don't like him Boss. Eldest in Canada, Petra keeps her distance."

"Could be." Justin Hyslop nodded then continued. "Nothing else on record. No skeletons rattling around in the cupboard that we can find at the moment."

"Only what Macarthy has told us. Seems a bit of a coincidence doesn't it? His son's fiancée disappears, Habib Patel's son dies a few months ago. Kids come and talk to Macarthy and now the two fathers have been murdered." Suggested Goss.

"It's not a coincidence. This is planned and coordinated." Benedict Cooper turned to leave.

△△△

The police station, usually almost deserted on a Sunday afternoon, was buzzing as sergeant Goss herded everyone into the briefing room and got things started.

DC Hyslop joined in. "We've knocked on doors. No one noticed any strange cars parked up in the road or in the drive. No CCTV nearby as Aida said. Apparently his drinking buddy a Bill Hollingsworth, knocked on his door at about midday. Got no answer. Said the house seemed empty so he went to the pub and waited for Griff Tomlin there. We picked his car up on the camera's turning off the main road which corroborates the timing. The pub landlord says he served him about twenty five minutes later. That wouldn't give Hollingsworth time to do much more than knock on the door as he said."

Goss turned to the group. "We can widen the search but unless we know what we're looking for, a car or a description it's a bit pointless. It's like chasing a ghost. They walked through walls, didn't touch anything, and disappeared into thin air. Nobody saw or heard a damn thing."

DI Cooper had been leaning against a wall at the side of the room. He now stood forward. "I don't believe in ghosts, whoever did this is out there somewhere. If we don't have forensics lets work with what we do have. Two murders within five days of each other. What else do we have? I want all thoughts. Absolutely everything. Nothing too small or big. Who's going to start?"

A rugged young man with blonde hair stood up just as Benedict's phone rang. He recognised the pathologist's number. "Carry on. Let's get everything on the board." He stepped out of the room.

"Hi Nick. What have you got?"

"Well, nothing to get too excited about, but he was sedated before he was tied up. There was nothing in the teacups that were on the table, but we had a look around the house, one of the cups in the cupboard was still damp. Could have been washed and put away."

"There were two cups on the table weren't there?"

"Yes, and one on the draining board that Mrs Tomlin had used and washed before she left. Also found a couple of fibres in his mouth. Looks like he had a gag at some point to keep him quiet but there is no trace of it in the house.

CHAPTER 23

HIRAN

Hiran Khan was sitting quietly at a corner table when Aoife walked into the large space that served as a café and waiting room for the various theatres. His head was slightly down but his eyes took in everyone as they roamed across the room.

"I have to admit something." The young man, siting opposite Aoife, looked remarkably relaxed. Still a teenager, but his manner made him seem older. He turned his head to look out of the café window and seemed to be watching the passengers dismounting from the yellow river ferry boat. Aoife scanned the boat too, wondering if any of them held any specific interest for him or the story she was putting together. A long silence took over while he gathered himself to look Aoife in the eye once more.

"Yes." Aoife tried to keep her voice neutral.

"It … It was me that told Daisy where you lived."

"How do you know where I live?" Aoife didn't try to hide the surprise in her voice.

"I followed you a few times."

"Oh." This admission sent a chill down Aoife's spine. She wasn't sure if she should be scared, but it went through her mind that she had better keep an eye out for stalkers from now on. New locks on her doors and windows would be a good idea too. Was this one of the down sides of living in a small city? The anonymity London offered was suddenly more attractive than she'd previously given it credit.

"I'd been watching you for a couple of weeks. Keeley told me about you. Said she'd spoken to you. Said you seemed alright.

Said I should talk to you. I needed to..." His voice trailed to silence once more.

Keeley had suggested Aoife listen to Hiran's story. She had said that it wasn't directly related to Iqra or Cara, but he had been caught up in the web spun by those who wanted to make money from children.

Aoife had agreed to meet him in the Watershed Café on the Harbour side.

"Why didn't you introduce yourself earlier?" She was trying not to sound as irritated as she felt.

The young man stared at her; his eyes piercing. "Because I didn't trust you. Daisy told me about you too. She trusts you. I said she was stupid. You want a story. Something you can sensationalise and take the credit for. And the police aren't going to do anything to help us. What's the point?"

Aoife sat quietly. She didn't reach for her cup or move her hands. She waited for him to fill the silence. He had a strong accent, Asian but a bit of Bristolian mingled in. She wondered where he had been born.

"Everyone who's tried reporting this stuff is dead. She was just gonna get herself and the rest of us into trouble." He spat the words out. For a moment Aoife wondered if she had misread his intentions for being here.

"But you're here now."

"I wanted to talk to you. To ask you something. Well, tell you something really." The young man gave a deep sigh as he played with the metal medallion around his neck. "I decided that I need to try to move on with my life. I've been talking to a counsellor, it's what he said I need to do, but I can't. Not while I know they are free to rip lives apart and get away with it." He was angry. Probably not with Aoife, but his anger was close to the surface which made him unpredictable. She strove to keep relaxed and concentrate on his body language and what he was saying.

"You might as well get it off your chest then. I'm listening." Aoife wasn't scared but she was on her guard. It was because of meetings like these that she kept to public places whenever possible. This meeting was in the busy cinema café, which was packed with customers having a drink after work or waiting to go into one of the auditoriums to watch a film.

As the young man looked up Aoife noticed that he looked flustered. From where the pendant chain lay on his collar bone to the roots of his fringe, his dark skin looked moist. "Now I'm here it seems stupid. I can't think what made me..." He gathered up his wallet and mobile and pushed himself up from his seat.

Keeley had been the go between arranging the meeting. She had warned Aoife that Hiran's past had been traumatic, and he was still upset. Now his sister Sophia had disappeared, and he was scared and angry. Quite a cocktail of emotions for a young man barely out of school to handle.

Aoife had felt his aggression when the young man had first approached. She had felt her own anxiety levels rise, and her thoughts became disturbed. She reminded herself that Hiran was little more than a boy and he'd been through a lot in his young life. She needed to process any information he gave her with an open mind. Testing it for faults and weaknesses. Being biased against this man would put a skew on the way she heard things. She raised the level of her voice but didn't stand up as she said.

"You spent two weeks following me, you found the courage to say hello, you might as well give it the final push and say whatever it is that is causing you so much turmoil." She leaned back in her chair so that she could more easily look up as Hiran stood uncomfortably in front of her. She tried to give him more space. "I'm a good listener." She was pleased to see she had his attention. "And, unless someone is in imminent danger, I won't tell anyone where I got my information from if that helps." He pulled out the chair again and slowly sat down. Aoife saw him as an injured animal. Angry and hurt yet desperately wanting what she had to offer; she would listen, and she wouldn't make any judgement.

Hiran shuffled uncomfortably in his chair and then without

introduction dived straight into his account of his short life.

"My family live in rural Pakistan, a small town, where it is difficult for boys to get an education and not acceptable for girls to go to school. Parents have been punished for teaching their daughters. My sister Sophia is four years older than me, and my parents knew from a young age that she was very bright. My father taught her to read and write even though it was dangerous. Eventually Sophia and I were smuggled to England to live with a friend of the family and to get an education.

"How old were you?"

"Sophia was fifteen and I was eleven."

"That's an enormous undertaking for two such young people."

"We didn't want to leave our parents, but part of us was excited. We were promised food and water on the journey, but they fed us tiny amounts of rice, vegetables and bread. We were constantly thirsty. My parents had scrimped and saved for our journey. We travelled mostly in the back of closed lorries with grown-ups who were also fleeing persecution. We were told to keep quiet because if we were found we would be sent back, and our parents would be punished, maybe killed. At first the sun beat down without mercy and there was no air conditioning. Then later we were cold." He took a sip of his drink.

"We were moved from truck to truck and eventually we were loaded into a big shipping container with others we hadn't seen before. There were twelve of us who had started together and thirty-eight by the time we were loaded into the container. It was corrugated metal and very cold. Some of us were seasick and there were no toilet facilities. Sophia was very brave. She looked after me and I clung on to her the whole journey. We were shut in there for four days. Several of the adults started to go a little crazy. I think it was the dark. They said we weren't promised comfort, but we were meant to get food and water. We were being treated worse than animals. Perhaps they were naive to think that the smugglers would care; For them it was all about money, and we were cargo."

He stopped abruptly, lifted his head and looked over his shoulder then out of the windows scanning the faces nearby.

Aoife spoke softly to him "You're doing a good job. It can't be easy talking about it." He glowered back at her then dropped his head. The silence continued. Noticing he had drunk hardly any of his tea which was now cold, Aoife reached across the table and, not wanting him to feel she was holding on to him, gently rested two fingers on his arm. "Would you like a juice, or a soda?"

Hiran looked up "Soda please."

When she returned a few minutes later the young man took a gulp of his drink but made no attempt to continue his story."

"What happened when the container doors were opened?"

"I remember the light seemed very bright after the darkness. We were told to get into another lorry. Sophia pulled me into her and kept her hand over my cheek so that I could only see straight ahead. She told me later that a man and a little girl had died on the ship."

"Did your parents friends come to fetch you?"

"A group of us were taken to a big warehouse and allowed to wash. We were given food. I don't know what happened to the others. Sophia and I changed into clean clothes that we had brought with us. We slept there overnight on mattresses and there was a toilet for the first time. The next day we were taken in a small van to live with Mr and Mrs Bukhari."

Your parents friends?"

"Yes."

"And you went to school?"

"Yes."

Aoife was bewildered. This was a hideous story of fraud and deception, pain, terror and abuse of human rights. Money being taken from desperate families willing to give every penny they could scrape together to provide their children with a better future. And she had no doubt it would have been traumatic for two children ripped from their family and put through an horrific experience like this on their own. It made her angry that people got away with it every day. But this was not the story Keeley, Daisy and Mahira had been leading her towards.

"How long ago was this?"

"It was six years ago. I am seventeen." Aoife was surprised, he came across as a very mature young man. He was very articulate, obviously bright.

She looked across the table into his sad, soft brown eyes. He had talked freely for nearly ten minutes. His anger had subsided as he spoke, and then he had just stopped. Was that the account of his life that he wanted her to know, wanted her to tell the world, or was there another chapter?

She wondered if he was waiting for her to acknowledge that she had understood how the harrowing experience had diverted his and Sophia's life? Did she need to help him find the way in to unravel his feelings before he could attempt to bring any more into the open. Or should she just sit very still and patiently wait for him to speak in his own time?

Then a thought came to her. This story involved parents and family unseen for years; a confused eleven year old boy torn from the life he had thought was his universe to travel halfway around the world in fear for his life; and a sister, Sophia, just four years older than him, who he had clung to and who had cared for him during this traumatic time.

"Where's Sophia?"

"She's dead."

Two simple words that Aoife had half expected, yet she felt her stomach flip and her throat tighten as her own emotions threatened to take over. She was surprised at the change in the young man's face. He spat the words. The fire in his eye, the firm line of his mouth and colour in his cheeks were back. A contrast from the gentle person who had told the story of the scared little boy.

"How did she die?"

"They killed her. They were scared of Sophia, and they took her."

"Why were they scared of her?"

"Because she was smarter than they are."

"Who are 'they'?"

Hiran stiffened. "Thugs hired by the company. They said she still owed them money but that's a lie."

"Do you know any names?"

"They never used names. Sophia and I talked about it. They were just the thugs who got paid for doing a job. Not the ring leaders. The container had an 'H' printed on it." His eyes watered, and his cheeks had turned red. He looked feverish in his torment. "But I didn't see a name."

She decided to move the subject on "OK Hiran. Tell me, you obviously know Daisy and Keeley. Did Sophia know Cara Felton or Anwar Patel?"

"I knew Anwar from football. He was older than me, but I saw him around. His father was the academy coach. You know, for those who show promise. They got extra training. I was never in that group, nor was Anwar. Sophia was in the orchestra with Cara at school. She gave evidence to the police about Cara. That's why they took her."

Bells were ringing madly in her brain. Aoife considered her next move. "You are telling me your sister has been murdered. What do you want to happen now?"

"I want all of them lined up and whipped. Tortured in the way they have tortured, and then shot."

"Well, you may have come to the wrong person, that's not quite my line of work." She smiled, attempting to break the anger she could sense was building in him once more. He looked at her and she thought he was furious at her frivolity. Then to her relief he gave her a weak grin.

"No. I disagree. You may not have a gun, but you can tell our story. Humiliate them in front of the world. Destroy their reputations and their business. That is the damage they dread. And you can stop them ruining more lives."

"Phew Hiran, you don't ask for much do you? You're right, I can write about them. The police might be able to round up a lot of them and hopefully they would be stripped of their assets. With research and a lot of hard work they might be able to find their delivery channels and contacts that brought you to this country. But if done properly, thoroughly, it will take time and manpower."

"But you will do it?"

"I will need to look into it, see what is involved and if I can find people who are willing to talk, I would like to write your story yes. I have to check my facts and be sure of everything before I commit to it."

"I can find you people who will tell you their stories." He said enthusiastically.

She looked at him hard and she talked slowly to make sure he understood the gravity of what she was saying "So, Hiran, we have a choice. I can ask you questions which you can choose to answer or not."

"I will answer all your questions."

"That's good. If we are to deliver even half the outcomes you want I will need to know names. There will be no justice without identities."

"I will give you names when I am sure what your plan is. We have to be careful. If they find out then we will both be in danger."

Aoife nodded. "I understand. We are dealing with murder, and I would like to get a friend of mine involved. A police officer." She had no idea what reaction she would get from this so she did the only thing she could. She watched and waited.

"You mean Detective Inspector Cooper?" Out of all the answers to her suggestion that had flown through her mind that was not one of them. But then, he had been following her.

"How ..."

He laughed. "Daisy and Keeley both told me that he was your friend."

"Oh. Fair enough. Well at least you're not upset by the idea of getting the police involved."

"No. They almost trust him." He frowned "I have already been to the police. I told them that Sophia was missing probably murdered."

"You don't know for sure that she is murdered?" Aoife had assumed his sister would be amongst the bodies pulled out of the river Avon. "When was that? That you went to the police?"

"I haven't spoken to her for ten weeks. I went to look for her in Nottingham. Sophia was in university there."

"And what did they say?"

"They didn't believe me. They said she had probably gone off with a boyfriend and she would show up when she felt like it. But I know my sister. She would never do that."

"O.K. Let's see if we can get some energy into that police search for your sister. I don't promise anything, but we can start by giving that a go. Would it be alright if I make a phone call?"

To Aoife's surprise he hesitated for only a moment "Sure."

"Is it OK to tell DI Cooper that you are with me?"

"Daisy and Keeley trust you and they have spoken to the Inspector. Will you be with me?"

"I'll try."

"Only if you're there." He looked her straight in the eye his face contorted with pain, and in that one look, Aoife saw the scared little boy and the anguish he had suffered. She nodded.

CHAPTER 24

HIRAN

Seventy-five minutes later Hiran was sitting on the opposite side of the table from DI Cooper and Sergeant Goss. Aoife sat slightly to one corner of the table, but still close the Hiran. He looked pale and drawn. The fire had gone from his eyes and his shoulders were hunched. He leaned back in his chair and his arms crossed over his chest, fingers under his armpits in a defensive pose. Distancing himself as far as possible from the officers. Dark shadows had appeared under his eyes and his brow was furrowed. The boy was tense, and he looked ill. Knowing everything he had already suffered and the turmoil that was raging inside, Aoife's heart went out to him.

DC Hyslop placed a cup of tea on the table in front of Hiran and left the room.

Following Aoife's call, sergeant Goss and DC Hyslop had come to collect Hiran and Aoife from the café in an unmarked car. Aoife had made sure that she and the boy, were ready to leave the moment she saw the police officers outside. Despite being in plain clothes, it was obvious, to her anyway, what profession the two were in.

After some negotiation and Hiran's insistence, Aoife had been allowed to sit in. Other officers were behind the glass.

Sergeant Goss was leading the interview with Benedict sitting alongside. As she settled in her seat she gave Aoife a quick nod, turned on the recording equipment and made the introductions.

"Before we start, I want to assure you that we will do all we can to find your sister." Sergeant Goss's voice was calm and her words unhurried. "We have been in touch with Nottingham and asked them to send copies of their files. We will be working closely with them and co-ordinating things from here. To do that we need to know everything that happened leading up to Sophia's disappearance, and since. We have to ask you a few general questions. You might find them difficult, but they are necessary."

Goss paused for a moment, gave a grim smile and asked "Did Sophia's behaviour change recently? Did she seem worried?"

"Yes. She was quieter. Preoccupied perhaps. But I don't know why. She said there was nothing wrong, just pressure of work. She is close to finishing her education and that is very important. It is for everyone, but she feels... we both feel, we must make our parents proud after all they have done for us."

"Do you know if she had any financial concerns? Had she fallen out with a boyfriend? Anything like that?"

Hiran was shaking his head and frowning "No. She doesn't have a boyfriend. She doesn't want the distraction."

"OK. You told Aoife about how you got to the UK. I'd like you to tell me please."

His eyes flicked toward Aoife then down to his hands which were now in his lap. Hiran repeated everything he had said earlier without further prompting until he arrived at the part about the dead father and child in the container. He stumbled over his words and struggled to keep his emotions in check. With gentle encouragement he finished the story of their journey, and the detectives asked their questions.

Then Cooper asked in a matter of fact way "Is there anything else you want to tell us about how you arrived in England?"

Hiran shook his head. "No. Not really." He placed his hands on the table in front of him. Reliving the story for a second time had left him raw. His grief for his sister and loss of his family life, held in for so long had risen to the surface through repeating the memories out loud, and left him feeling sick and vulnerable. His face was pinched, lips closed tight as though he had given everything that was in him and now he was empty. Aoife wouldn't have been surprised to see tears rolling down his cheeks, but he held them back, refusing that final rupture in his soul.

"We need to ask you more questions, especially about your sister. It might help us find her. But perhaps now is a good time to take a break." Cooper stood up, lifting the manilla file and notebook he had brought in with him. PC Davies will stay with you. if there is anything you want just to let him know.

"I miss her." Hiran's words were heartfelt. "I should have looked after her." His voice was so soft everyone on the other side of the glass strained to hear. "She was always there for me. I let her down." The comment cut through the outer defence of everyone who heard them. His quiet voice as potent as a mother's scream for her dead baby.

Cooper glanced around, desperately looking for help, and then, perhaps realising there was no outside help coming, sat back down. Unsure how to offer comfort in an appropriate manner and in front of his colleagues he turned to Aida Goss who had reached her hand across the table, just short of touching Harin's arm.

"You didn't know. There was nothing you could have done."

"She was always going to leave at some point. I knew she had to get away." Hiran sobbed now. His restraint giving way as the words he had held back for so long punched through the walls he had built up around his emotions.

"Did she talk about it, Sophia, did she talk about leaving? Did you discuss where she might go" asked Cooper.

"Yes. But she knew she had to get her degree first. Qualify as a doctor, or it was all pointless. The suffering, the hard work, our parents investing so much in our future. She couldn't let everyone down."

"How much longer did she have at university?"

"She was in her last year. After five years there is no way she would have voluntarily walked away a few months before the end."

162

"Let's take a short break and then we'll talk more about your sister." Said Cooper.

"What will happen now?"

"You mean after today?" asked Goss.

Hiran nodded. His eyes pleading "Will you catch the people who did this? Who killed my sister?"

Cooper knew the young man only wanted one answer. That wasn't how police officers were trained. To give loved ones false hope was something he tried not to do.

"We don't know for sure that she's dead. We will certainly do our best to find her. We think we know some of the lessor players, we need to tie in the ring leaders, or they will simply move business elsewhere and nothing will change."

Hiran drew breath. The young man was still intently focussed on him, searching the Inspector's face and posture. Despite Hiran's look of depletion there was something else, beyond that stare, something more. Cooper couldn't put his finger on it, but it made him uncomfortable.

"I suggest we take a comfort break, have something to drink. We can get you a sandwich if you're hungry. PC Davies will sort you out something to eat." The two police officers stood, and this time made it through the door. Aoife put a hand on Hiran's shoulder and followed them.

CHAPTER 25.

AOIFE

I t was late by the time Aoife left the station and she was hungry. Knowing she had nothing in her fridge at home and not wanting to fall back on junk food she decided a dash to the supermarket was called for.

Luckily there were very few other customers and a quick swoop around the aisles had only taken five minutes. As she walked through the automatic doors to the car park she made herself pull in a few deep breaths of the cool night air. Her conversation with Hiran, making sure she appeared calm and encouraging had been demanding. And listening to the boy's story all over again with the police officers, while not being allowed to say or do anything, had been stressful. Her head was still buzzing and she felt the tension across her shoulders and her breathing was shallow.

At first she didn't recognise the middle-aged man who walked confidently across the near empty supermarket car park toward her, his hand outstretched. She didn't reciprocate, but she did stand still and allow him to approach.

"Aoife Macarthy isn't it?"

"Yes." She frowned sure she didn't know this person. It was 10 p.m. and she had only just managed to scoot to Lidl and grab a few vegetables and some dried pasta to keep her going before the shop closed its doors.

"You do get around don't you." The man continued smoothly "I saw you in the media. Hero of the moment saving that young boy. Very brave of you."

"Oh, right." She felt flustered and blurted out the first thing that came to her lips "And you're catching up with last minute groceries too?"

"Yes. It's usually quieter at this time. I hear you were talking to that strange girl, what's her name? Daisy the other morning. I imagined someone with your intelligence and interests would keep more stimulating company."

Aoife's skin prickled and she was now on full alert. She didn't know this man, although his face seemed familiar, but she was confident his being here and bumping into her was not coincidental. She took in the green wax jacket, gold signet ring and Rolex watch. He didn't look like someone who would do his own shopping let alone at a discount supermarket at ten o'clock at night. A thrill of adrenalin ran through her body making her heart pump faster and she had to fight to keep her breath steady. There were a few people with shopping carts milling around. Still, she kept her knees soft and her arms ready to drop, or throw her shopping if need be.

Words were her bread and butter. She had no problem returning the taunt now her brain was in gear. "I find people of true intelligence who have a wide range of interests, keep an open mind and are more able to see the potential of others, no matter what their background."

As she was speaking it dawned on her where she had seen this man's photograph before. She slipped her hand into her pocket and pressed the button on the small recording device she had used with Hiran earlier. "As a councillor who is entrusted with the care of the community, I'm sure you feel the same."

He cocked his head to one side as his expression became less affable. He kept his eyes firmly on Aoife's face. Perhaps he hadn't expected to be recognised. "Ex-counsellor. A farmer may care for his cattle but that doesn't mean he lies down in the muck with them or eats from the same trough."

"I will remember to quote you in my article."

Aoife allowed herself a smile as she saw her response had found its target. Ex-councillor McVeigh's face darkened as he clenched and unclenched his fists.

"I would suggest you get your copy thoroughly checked by a lawyer before you print anything slanderous Ms Macarthy."

"I only print what I know to be true."

"I think you'll be advised to only print what you can *prove* to be true in a court of law."

"Oh, I can prove it Greg. I am fascinated to know why you have taken an interest in my business with Mrs Marston?" She felt some satisfaction as she saw the use of the abbreviated first name irritate him even more.

He ignored her comment "You have done your homework haven't you? I'm flattered you know my name. I'm not sure what you think you can prove. I've had run ins with Daisy Marston before and she lost. This is just a friendly warning. Be careful who you mix with." His voice was low and threatening and Aoife realised she had probably pushed him as far as she dare. She really wanted to lift her voice recorder from her pocket and show him it was on record, but her survival instinct won trough.

"You wouldn't be here if you weren't worried." She berated herself for allowing the tension she was feeling to enter her voice as she turned to walk away. Her throat had tightened causing the pitch to go up a notch. It took all her determination not to look back over her shoulder as she turned away to find her car.

Having dumped her shopping in the footwell of the passenger side she sat for several moments in the driver's seat conscious that her heart was beating at double its normal speed and her legs were pathetically weak. After the events of the whole evening - meeting with Hiran, her involvement at the police station and now the obvious threat from McVeigh - she felt more as if she had completed a marathon race than a five minute shopping trip.

She spotted the councillor driving away in a silver BMW. Taking a couple of deep breaths and pushing the air from her lungs she clicked the door lock and played back the conversation she had recorded to check the quality. It was muffled and she wasn't sure if anyone would recognise it as the councillor's voice, but most of the words could be understood.

Giving a loud sigh she shrugged her shoulders a couple of times, twisted her neck from side to side and circled her ankles to release the tension. Turning the key in the ignition she set off for home, pleased there would be little traffic at this time.

She slowed for the first roundabout, there were no cars coming. She was about to accelerate away when the force of the impact to the rear snapped her head backwards. The violent bang of metal and glass smashing was deafening, the seatbelt tensioners locked, and her head was momentarily flung forward, hitting the side window as it jerked back again, and air was forced from her lungs. A shot of pain raced up her neck and for a moment she froze waiting to feel if any other damage had been done. As she twisted around in her seat she saw a grey SUV pulling out from behind her and zooming past. Before her confused brain could fully register what had happened the large car turned right at the roundabout and disappeared from view.

Taking a deep breath, she realised she was shaking. She turned stiffly to look through the smashed rear window, at which point she was aware several other cars had stopped, including one forced onto the pavement on the opposite side of the road when the big SUV pushed past it on its way to the roundabout. Two men had run to her car and were trying to force open her door. She jumped in fright, not sure if she should unlock the car or try to race off.

"It's OK luv." A guy in his fifties called to her. He took a couple of steps back seeing the apprehension in her face and pulled his friend back too before lifting his hands palms forward.

Realising there was a small crowd building and that these were probably the good guys she unlocked the door and twisted herself around until her feet hit the ground. Unsure if her legs would support her, she made no attempt to stand.

++*+

As one of the men pushed a blanket around Aoife's shoulders a middle aged woman handed her a small bottle of orange juice. "Here love, the sugar might help."

A few minutes later blue flashing lights announced the arrival of the police and an ambulance. Having checked Aoife did not have any life threatening injuries the uniformed officers cordoned off her car and were now questioning witnesses.

As Aoife thanked the paramedic she was astonished to find D.I. Cooper by her side.

"How did you get here so quickly? In fact, how did you get here at all?"

"The P.C. called me when they verified your name and car registration. He knew you were at the station earlier. Checked to see if the incident was relevant to our investigation."

"Great. And is it?" Aoife didn't sound particularly grateful. She was perched on the back of the ambulance wrapped in a large blanket. A paramedic who had introduced herself as Claire, had examined the bruise on the side of her head, shone a light in each of her eyes, Placed a small plaster over the cut on her cheekbone, and carried out a cursory examination to make sure no ribs were broken from the force of the safety belt or airbag. There was a further run through to make sure all her limbs moved roughly as they should, and no other damage was done, then the medic had given her a smile.

"You tell me. Do you think it is?" Benedict looked serious.

"DI Cooper, this is Claire." Said Aoife without moving her head.

"You're going to ache in the morning. Headache and a stiff neck I imagine. Take some painkillers and don't go rushing around for a couple of days." Said Claire.

After checking she was not badly injured Benedict had been speaking to the uniformed officers but had now returned to her side. "You look tired. Let me get you a ride home."

"You can do that?" Aoife realised her brain was still not functioning at full speed.

"Of course he can," said Claire with a smile.

"One of the uniforms will be more than happy."

"I'm not sure which I want first, something to eat, my bed or a hot shower because, I mean, well just look at me!" She waved her hands to take in her whole body and chuckled.

Ben laughed. As he continued to look at her, he realised her humour was a shield. She was fighting back tears. "You're trembling." He said.

"I'm suddenly really tired."

"It's shock. You need to take her home and make sure she has a hot drink and gets safely tucked up in bed." The paramedic gave Benedict such an eloquent look he found it impossible to mistake her meaning.

Aoife oblivious of the implication in the paramedic's stare. "You're right I just need to get home."

"Do you have someone to stay with you tonight?" asked Claire.

"I'll be fine." Aoife made a brave attempt at being firm. No one was convinced.

"You've had a nasty shock and a bump on the head. Do you want to spend a night in hospital so the nurses can keep an eye on you?" Claire turned and gave Cooper a hard stare.

Ben turned, discomforted by the paramedic's gaze that made him feel like an insensitive child and spoke directly to Aoife. "Tell you what, let's get you all of those things. Then you don't need to worry about anything."

"Don't you have to do policing type stuff?"

"No. Not this time."

"That would be nice then. Not sure how we're gonna manage it, but I'm willing to give it a go."

"Give me two minutes. I just need to take care of a couple of things."

"I've got shopping." She called after him. She noticed everyone had turned and looked at her amused. She looked at the crumpled boot of her car. "It's in the passenger seat. And my handbag." She went to go and get her belongings but found a firm hand on her shoulder.

"You just sit back and make sure he waits on you." Claire winked. Aoife smiled back. Her mind was in lock down and it wasn't until the next day, when she was running through everything in her mind, that she realised the paramedic had for some reason assumed Ben was her boyfriend.

Five minutes later Ben and Aoife, now with Ben's coat wrapped around her, were in the back of a squad car together driving toward the city centre.

"This is ridiculous. You don't really want to be lumbered with me and I don't need babysitting."

Benedict looked at her "It's not babysitting."

When they arrived outside a terrace of attractive yellow stoned, Georgian houses, Aoife smiled and thanked the two uniform police officers. One of whom jumped out and opened the door for her while Benedict rushed around the car to help her out.

"This is very kind of you but really, you must have so much better things to do with your time."

"If I hadn't offered to help, I think Claire would have reported me to the Super." He smiled. "Come on let's do this properly." He placed his arm carefully around her and helped her up the four steps that led to his front door.

"I thought for a moment you were going to carry me over the threshold!" she teased.

"Ha! How about shower first while I get supper ready."

"Look I really am feeling a lot better. I can get a cab back home from here. I won't tell Claire, or your boss. I promise."

He turned to her, and she noticed for the first time that underneath the professional façade and the fatigue DI Benedict Cooper was probably younger than she had first thought.

"You have suffered a shock. I have a spare bed that is clean and made up. The shower is hot and by the time you come back down there will be food on the table." He was smiling at her reassuringly. He led her through to the kitchen at the far end of the house. "I have some ham, cheese, salad, eggs. I can make pasta."

"I'm vegetarian."

"OK. Drop the ham, do you eat cheese and eggs?"

"Yes."

"In that case which would you prefer pasta salad or cheese omelette and salad.?"

"Omelette please. It's very kind of you."

"Let me show you the bathroom and your bed for the night."

He insisted she went up the stairs in front of him, presumably to catch her if she fell. At the top he stepped forward and opened a door which Aoife assumed led to the bathroom. He disappeared inside as he said, "I'll get you fresh towels and I've got some jogging bottoms, T-shirt and sweater that will all be a bit big for you but will keep you warm if you want them. I'll leave them in your room then it's up to you."

Aoife laughed. "You are so masterful."

He came and stood next to her "Sorry, I didn't mean to be bossy."

"Don't worry. It's kind of you and ever so slightly sexy." She gave him a cheeky grin. He turned away obviously embarrassed but not before she saw a slight smile appear on his lips.

By the time she came out of the shower she was feeling stronger, her mind was less scattered, and she regretted flirting with DI Cooper. She had allowed her guard down. It wouldn't happen again. He was a colleague, and she needed a good working relationship with him. She was grateful for his help, and it was reassuring to know he was willing to step up in the absence of her friends. She resolved not to complicate their relationship.

CHAPTER 26.

LIAM

Lilly could see the family sitting down to eat their evening meal together. The room was illuminated by a mixture of wall lights and expensive looking floor lamps. Framing the group in the window in a warm, buttery backdrop like a scene from a film; a perfect tableau of what 'domestic life' should be.

They seemed a happy family comfortable in each other's company. Their plates were piled high with food, as they chatted and laughed. She saw Liam's mother make some comment that made her son smile and his parents briefly joined hands. His parents looked nice, sweet together, and would probably never believe what a monster their sadistic son was. But Lilly knew, so did the rest of the team. Liam had been the youngest of the predators and the most sick in the head. He got his kicks from inflicting pain and hearing children scream. He got high on the smell of fear. His family would certainly miss their eldest son, but the world would be a safer place with him gone.

Lilly had been watching life from the outside for so long she had no idea how to be part of a family group. Nor did she know what it was like to be herself. She had not read much Shakespeare, but she knew the quote *"All the world's a stage, and all the men and women merely players: they have their exits and their entrances;"* That was her life and her family had entered and exited as had numerous foster parents, and each time she had played the part that was most expedient or expected of her. The real Lilly was so well hidden she may never be found.

She was skilled at playing an observer, sneaking around, watching what was going on, never drawing attention to herself. And she liked the most recent role she had been given as the analyst, combining the information the other watchers in the team had gathered and drawing conclusions that would support the crew's decisions.

She had even discovered that she could play the part of the mediator. Fear and tensions had run high in the team. Not surprising with what they were planning to do. When the others became nervous and edgy and tempers frayed Lilly could stay calm, the voice of reason. She adapted so well to whatever was required of her, she had no idea which one was the real her. She suspected none of them. It was all play acting. It was how she had survived those years she now refused to furnish with any detail.

The naïve little girl she had been, the one who thought she would always be safe in her father's arms, who had been sure her mother would take her away once she knew of the horror that had become her life. That little girl was dead.

She had a new family now. Not the traditional kind like she was watching through the window. People who understood where she was coming from. People she could rely on. They had saved her even from herself when she had sat in the deserted car park with the sharp knife and her sleeve pulled up to expose her bare wrist. They had taken her into the group. Talked to her. Listened to her. Believed her.

A strange collection of young adults who on the surface had little in common, yet understood each other's thoughts, emotions and motivation in a way most other people never could. It bound them closer than most blood relatives ever could be.

A clattering from the house next door pulled her from her musings. She pressed quietly against the tall viburnum hedge and into the shadows of the old monkey puzzle tree. The man from next door was hauling a heavy black garbage bin from the alley between the two houses to the end of the high brick wall and left it for the morning collection.

From her hiding place Lilly heard a rustle of branches at her back. She froze. It was too heavy to be a bird. Never fond of wildlife, her imagination conjured up images of rats or even a snake. She turned her head a little to one side and strained to look out the side of wide eyes. Her breath came in short gasps. She jerked forward covering her mouth with a clammy hand to stop a scream escaping as something gently tapped her shoulder. Every muscle in her body wanted to run but she didn't want to break cover and knew she must not draw attention to herself. She heard a gentle rumbling purr in her right ear as a marmalade cat appeared balanced on branches that seemed far too delicate to hold its weight. Lilly felt a bubble of laughter rising in her throat but swallowed it back. Her body, weak from relief leant further into the hedge and turned to see if the neighbour had been alerted by the sound of crunching twigs. He hadn't.

She walked along the pavement that she knew Liam would be taking later, on his way to the pub, and where her friends would be waiting to complete the trial run. Liam would never spot them. There was a good hiding place there at the side of the Chinese restaurant and just a few feet from the back of the football pavilion where Habib and Liam had lured their victims. It would be poetic justice. The daylight was fading fast, but in another few weeks summer would take hold, the early dusk would not be there to conceal them, and it would be much trickier to stay discreet. That didn't matter, they had rehearsed hard, and the game would be complete very soon now.

CHAPTER 27.

AOIFE

Aoife was lying in bed sensing a new day, enjoying the warm comfort of the nest she had made with duvet and pillow. Shadows of dreams wafted past her thoughts but refused to be caught. The anticipation of a new day momentarily filled her with the energy to move and the will to get out of bed.

Even before her eyes flickered open confusion filled her brain as the smell of fresh coffee filtered through. She opened her eyes and started to turn to look at the small clock she kept by her bed. Pain shot up her arm and bounced against the side of her head. She held her limbs still, mentally exploring the source of the discomfort, then she remembered. Thoughts and images of her real world flowed in and out on waves, then crowded in with a vengeance, threatening to keep her pinned to the bed as her brain felt overwhelmed. Bad people had warned her in no uncertain terms that they were watching her and could get to her at any time.

She wondered if she could cling to the blissful ignorance of sleep. Failing she opted instead to follow the smell of the coffee. As she swung her legs over the side of the bed and sat quietly waiting to see if any part of her body was going to complain, she realised that for the first time in weeks Cameron Connery hadn't been her first thought as she woke. Before she had fallen asleep last night, she had craved the safety of his warm touch on her shoulder, the rhythmic sound of his breathing, while she rested her head on his chest. Instead, she had felt the familiar emptiness. Now, she almost froze as the memories of how he had betrayed her so publicly blasted into her mind and she struggled off the bed in an effort to get on with her life and leave the past where it belonged. She heard footsteps and the sound of cutlery being sorted and at last her brain clicked into gear and she was once more in control.

As she entered the kitchen, she saw that Benedict was dressed ready for work. She became suddenly aware that not only was her face bruised and puffy she was wearing his clothes.

If he noticed her discomfort Benedict did a first class job of hiding it "You look heaps better this morning." He smiled. "I've made coffee. How did you sleep?"

She knew she looked a wreck but gave him a ten for effort as she went to grab the coffee jug. Before she reached it he guided her to one of the wooden chairs instead. "Sit down, make the most of being waited on. I will have to go soon. How do you feel about scrambled eggs?"

"Sounds good."

"The breads pretty fresh or you can have toast."

With plates of egg and toast in front of them, it dawned on Aoife that this was the first time for a long time she had sat down to breakfast with anyone other than Leigh. "Thank you for this. Way above and beyond the call of duty. Or is being chivalrous part of the police training nowadays?"

"Gallant, courageous and courteous all essential elements for the budding DCI."

"Hm, and is that what you are? A budding DCI?"

"That's the plan."

"Your mother would be proud of you. Thankyou. I'm sure you could find better ways of starting the morning than waking up to cater for a woman that looks like one of the ugly sisters with a bad hair day."

"Don't be so harsh on yourself. You look beautiful." He grinned unselfconsciously.

Aoife couldn't remember anyone outside her family, calling her "beautiful". And never in a thousand had she imagined that DI Cooper would be the first to have spoken those words to her face, even in jest. She could feel herself blushing but luckily Benedict was already standing up with his back to her, placing his mug and plate in the dishwasher.

"He turned to face her "You can stay here as long as you like, or I can give you a lift home. I'm sorry I woke you so early."

Aoife looked at the large old fashioned wall clock. It was still only 6.30am. She felt fragile and unsure what she should do today.

"Can I have a lift please? I can sort myself out when I get home."

Aoife went back upstairs and collected her few belongings, then followed Benedict to his car and got in.

"You'll have to come into the station at some point and give a statement. Sorry."

"I guessed. When?"

"As soon as possible. If you feel up to it today would be best."

"Sure. I'll come by later."

"I'll tell Sergeant Goss to expect you. Is there anything you need doing before I go?" He asked as they pulled up outside her house. "Would you like me to come in with you?"

She wasn't sure what he had in mind and didn't ask. She hadn't had any worries about walking into her house alone until he mentioned it, and now she looked at her front door suspiciously.

"No, I don't think so. Thank you for everything." It sounded a bit weak considering the effort he had made but she didn't want to embarrass them both by gushing. She gave him as warm a smile as she could manage to make up for it.

"Well, take it easy today. There's no shame in a duvet day and takeaway pizza you know."

She was aware of his eyes on her back as she walked to her door and unlocked it. She turned and waved before she disappeared inside.

She went straight through to the kitchen dropped her bags of shopping from the previous night on to the table and turned on the coffee machine. As she walked back along the hall she called to her smart speaker.

"Play BBC Radio 2." She decided she couldn't face the news stations.

In her bedroom she called the second speaker, glad of the upbeat voices and music rumbling away in the background. She got out of her clothes and wrapped her long pink towelling dressing gown around her before heading back to make a cup of coffee. Then, mug in hand, she walked to her office to turn her laptop on.

She was determined that yesterday's incident was not going to upset her work routine. There was more incentive than ever to push forward with this story. The best plan of defence was attack, and her weapons were words. She intended to get a piece about last night's incident into the Bristol media. She wondered if she had enough yet to prepare a series of articles. She would have a talk with the editor. If she was careful, she wouldn't give anything away that would harm the police investigation, but she would run it past Benedict and whoever else if necessary.

A quick shower and her working day would begin.

CHAPTER 28.

AOIFE

Working for a large and renowned national newspaper has many advantages. The security of a regular wage, the prestige that gets you through doors, and the resources, to name just a few. Aoife had chosen the freedom of working freelance. She knew people she could call on to help with research, at a cost, but at the moment, without guaranteed income, she decided to resist the temptation and knuckle down to it herself.

A morning spent going through reports of death by drowning in the Bristol and Bath area during the last fifteen years, supported Daisy and Keeley's concerns. There were a lot. The majority involved young people in their late teens and early twenties. As many of the coroner's reports mentioned alcohol and drugs, this was not surprising. If Keeley and Daisy were right, it was also a great camouflage for premeditated murders.

Following the web of connections between the victims of drowning and the deaths brought to her attention, had taken most of her morning. She started with Anwar Patel whose body had been brought up by police divers.

"Pathologist Dr Patrick West told the inquest the boy's medical cause of death was drowning but said his alcohol intake was a 'significant contributing factor' to him drowning in the cold water. Coroner Dr Christine Harmon said: "His entering the water was possibly not a deliberate act, and there is no evidence to show any other person was involved."

Mr Patel's body is one of several which have been recovered from the river over the past few months leading to speculation from Bristol residents who fear a serial killer could be pushing young men into the river."

Aoife moved on.

"Cara Felton, aged 23 years old, was found last night in the river near Toll Bridge Road in Bath. She leaves behind a grieving partner Chris Wakefield and their two-year-old son. A spokesperson for the Avon and Somerset Police said: "Cara was reported missing by her partner. We were called at 7.12am the next day by the ambulance service amid concern for someone floating in the water.

Friends close to Cara are shocked. They all knew her to be a strong swimmer.

"I can't believe it's happened, it's not sinking in. It doesn't feel real. Cara was a good swimmer. She often took her little son to the pool." Said one neighbour.

"I saw Cara two or three days ago. Some of my friends saw her playing with her son at the playground the day before she died. She was happy and looking forward to becoming a nurse."

Coroner's Court heard she was three times over the legal drink-drive limit, and it was a "significant contributing factor" in her death. The coroner recorded a conclusion of accidental death."

By the time Aoife had finished she had flagged up seven more accidental deaths where drugs or alcohol had been a 'contributing factor' and a comment by the RLSS UK.

Water safety charity, the Royal Life Saving Society (RLSS UK), issued a warning to young people to be more wary of water in light of the deaths in Bristol. It said it had already targeted the city as an area of concern as there are many waterfront nightclubs dotted along the harbour.

Pacing slowly around her study, then down the stairs to the kitchen and back again, Aoife felt tension building as her mind pieced together a picture of what could be happening.

Having started the morning feeling shaky from her own experience the previous night, then continuing her day by being alone and reading distressing articles about the loss of life, had increased her agitation. She decided it was time for a change of scenery. Half an hour later she had decamped to the Harbourside and had chosen an outside table by the water. The sun was shining, and it was pleasantly warm for April.

She planned to continue working but for the moment she was enjoying sipping her green tea and munching on a panini.

Before she could get her head down and concentrate on her morning's findings, her attention was drawn to a small group of young people that she had seen walking around the area before dressed and painted in outlandish costumes.

A tall, lean young man with golden skin and tightly cropped curls, blew her a kiss as he approached. He was mesmerising. Aoife had never had much of an interest in makeup, but this group made her wish that she had been a little more daring as a teenager.

He wore a mask drawn in burgundy and deep red across his eyes that faded into his hairline. A girl held on to his arm and laughed. Her lips had been painted white with a bright red cupid kiss in the middle. She wore her hair down and her long fringe was held in place with a burgundy and gold braid band that circled her forehead.

Another girl, though painted and dressed almost entirely in monochrome as a Pierrot, was even more fascinating. Her white face was decorated with black tears, eyebrows and lips. Smudges of pink on her eyelids and cheeks being the only trace of colour.

Others had birds, flowers, and fairies on their cheeks and all their garments were exotic and colourful.

Aoife sipped her tea and smiled.

CHAPTER 29.

POLICE BRIEFING

A s he entered the back of the room unnoticed, DI Benedict Cooper looked at the large clock on the far wall. Ten past seven. DS Goss, who was adding details to the crime board, didn't look up. As he moved forward he felt the attention of thirty sets of bleary eyes on him.

Cooper had been called to Superintendent James's office first thing and informed that they were scaling up the investigation. This included calling in detectives from other areas and temporarily promoting Cooper to acting Detective Chief Inspector. The elevation came with both congratulations and a warning. This was becoming a high-profile case, and any mistakes would be in the full glare of the media. The powers that be had decided that a new set of eyes with no connection to the past events was needed. A new DI would be assigned to assist.

Acting DCI Cooper would be in charge of two investigations. The recent murders of the two men and the deaths and disappearance of the teenagers and young adults that included Cara Felton, Anwar Patel, Iqra Aziz and now Sophia Khan. There was almost certainly a connection between the cases. It was down to Cooper and his team to find that connection.

As she became aware that her boss was nearby, Sergeant Goss threw him a bright smile "Morning Boss. Congratulations."

"How do you know?"

"The Super called me in too. If we do well with this case, I get a crack at DI when it's over." She was beaming with excitement.

Cooper patted her on the shoulder. "Good luck. Anything

183

new?"

"Not really. Just making sure we're up to date."

Benedict knew that Aida Goss had not left the station until nearly ten the previous night, the same as him, and she had beaten him in this morning, yet she looked as sharp and healthy as a sixteen year old cheerleader. At thirty-six Cooper suddenly felt old.

He sighed and turned to the room. "OK, Let's get started. You will all have realised by now that our ranks have been swollen with extra bodies pulled in to work on this case. Thank you for coming and welcome. We have a second murder on our hands and reason to believe they may be tied into other deaths previously thought to be suicides or misadventure. He turned around to face the board.

"We also have the recent disappearance of a young female medical student. Information we have received suggest that she too may be connected in some way. It is our job to try and find her alive." He paused to taking a sip of his black coffee.

"As you can see, there are a lot of trails to follow down, a lot of loose ends if our suspicions are correct. We're going to go through what we've got so far. So please ladies and gents, make sure you have coffee, get yourselves comfortable and switch on those brains. Hopefully with all the brilliant minds in this room we can not only get to grips with it but put a stop to whatever the motive is behind it all."

He looked around at the new faces as a general murmur broke out, comments were made, feet shuffled, and everyone settled in. A silence came over the room as Superintendent James stepped up to the board. He'd slid quietly in through the door and had remained leaning against the wall, but his aura had obviously permeated through the group.

Benedict nodded to Goss.

I am DS Aida Goss. That is acting DCI Benedict Cooper. DC Justin Hyslop has been working closely on this too, she nodded towards Justin who gave a sharp nod of his head.

"We have two murders on our hands. A quick look at

the crime scene photos should leave you with no doubt that they are linked. The commonalities are the way the victims are laid out. Spreadeagled with both wrists and ankles tethered. Trouser and underpants cut open and pulled down to their ankles. Red paint sprayed across their genitals and upper thighs. Cause of death is heroin overdose administered to the cephalic vein." She turned to look at her audience. "Disappointingly for us the final similarity is the lack of evidence. No DNA or fibres, no fingerprints, no footprints and no sightings from neighbours or passers-by. Justin, can you take us through what we know about Habib Patel?'

Justin moved to the board. "Habib Patel. Sixty-two years old." He pointed to a photograph of Habib." Married. Lived with his wife Bushra and eighty-two year old mother. They had a daughter and a son. Armeena and Anwar.

The body was found in Ropers Hill Nature Reserve sometime after midnight by a young couple camping in the wood. He was laid out as DS Goss said, pinned to the ground. He had been to a board game club that he belonged to and visited every Tuesday evening. Never missed. So easy enough to find him, lay in wait, and pounce. He left at ten pm. The area is quiet by then and does provide a bit of a short cut. His wallet with bank cards and thirty pounds cash, a heavy gold wedding band and his mobile were all found still on him."

Justin took a step toward his audience. "There was seriously heavy rain that night. Thunder, lightning, the works, so the fact that we found no forensics was not a huge surprise. The body was well washed, the ground turned to mud, and water was pouring down the slope and across the crime scene."

"Right. The daughter, now thirty-one, left home before she was eighteen years old and currently lives in Manchester with her husband and four children. Bushra, Habib's wife, is in phone contact with her daughter and has been to visit a few times when her grandchildren were born, birthdays etc. But Armeena has not been to the family home in Bristol since she left thirteen years ago."

Sergeant Goss cleared her throat, took a couple of steps

toward another set of photographs and pointed to a picture of Anwar. A blue line joined him to his father. "Anwar Patel was found in the Harbour River six months ago. The coroner ruled "death by misadventure" due to the amount of whisky and heroin he had taken onboard. However, his friends all said he never drank alcohol, and he hated the idea of drugs."

"Thank you. Before we move on, any questions?" Benedict was leaning by the door.

"Have we spoken to the daughter?" a sandy haired DC from Portishead who wouldn't look out of place in the second row on a rugby pitch asked.

Justin answered "Our colleagues in Manchester went to the house. Ameena wouldn't be drawn on the subject of her leaving home so young or staying away from her family home. She claimed she knew nothing about her parents' life except the little her mother mentioned in phone calls. Apparently, she didn't seem to care about her father's death. She and her husband both have strong alibi's. We will need to speak to her ourselves and get answers. We would like to know what went so badly wrong that she has not set foot back in the family home but at the moment she doesn't seem a likely suspect."

Justin stepped back to the board and pointed. "Griff Tomlin, sixty-three year old white male, married, four children. The three older ones are all estranged. He was found by his wife tied to his bed using the same style of ties as were found on Habib Patel." Justin glanced across at Cooper who nodded for him to continue.

"His wife Janet left the house at nine-thirty as she did every Sunday morning to go and visit her eldest daughter Petra, and small grandkids. This was another regular event. Petra's husband went and played football, Janet Tomlin would bake a cake or other treats to take with her. She and Petra would drink coffee play with the children, maybe go to the park. The only variable is that Janet usually, but not always, went back to have lunch with her husband. This time she had left Griff a meal in the oven while she stayed and ate with her daughter and son-in-law. She arrived home just after two, and wasn't bothered that her husband wasn't there. Apparently it's not uncommon for him to go to the pub on a Sunday lunchtime. Then she noticed that the lunch hadn't been touched and went to look for Mr Tomlin and eventually found him in the bedroom already dead."

At this point Aida Goss took over. "Thank you Justin. Now the fact that there was no DNA, or any other forensic details left at the scene of Mr Patel's murder was not a great shock due to the downpour of rain. This time," Aida paused and looked at individuals in the room "This time it was indoors, and there were still no tracks, no prints, no DNA, no signs of a break-in, nothing. The house backs on to a small copse that wraps around one side of the garden. The other side are the neighbours and in front there is a lane with a few more houses. All well-spaced out. None of the neighbours saw anything and the few that have CCTV didn't pick up anything remarkable that morning either. Both men show no other significant injuries. No needles or drugs found.

Benedict straightened up and started to pace the front of the room. "OK. We have two murders with the similarities as DC Hyslop pointed out. What we also have are two families where the children have left home at an early age and almost never go back. In Mr Tomlin's case, the eldest son, Thomas, now lives in Canada. Petra the next eldest, doesn't visit as a rule but made an exception to go to a family function when her brother brought his fiancée home to meet his family."

"No one's said the words, but given everything, are you suggesting child abuse Boss?" A short blond haired man with freckles and gold rim glasses called out.

"Hi. Your name is?"

"Richard Elks sir."

"At this moment we are open to anything Richard, abuse of a sexual nature is certainly a possibility given the stylised manor in which the bodies have been laid out. The fact that we have two dysfunctional families could be related but no one has come forward yet to make any accusations against those men in particular. However, by coincidence, if you believe in such

187

things, at the same time, and by that I mean ten days before Habib Patel was murdered, we have been talking to a group of young adults who claim that there was an active paedophile ring in Bristol a decade or more ago. Complaints were made at the time and the children attempted to report it to the police, teachers and clerics, but none of it was taken seriously. More disturbingly, if it was reported to the police" He paused, his face became grave, "there is no record of any of them coming forward."

A chorus of murmurs and exclamations built up from the group.

Benedict put his hands up in a placating manor. "So far, we have had three young people come in willing to talk about their experiences. They are also claiming that others have disappeared. Several more have died and their deaths attributed to misadventure or suicide. We do have those records. I must tell you that at their request we are not using the survivors' real names, at least for the moment. They believe their lives would be in danger if the perpetrators found out that they were talking to the police."

"Where were the children living at the time? Was it a council estate gang?"

Goss stepped forward. "Some lived on the Fordwell Hill estate, yes. The biggest connection we've picked up on so far is Poppy Hill Children's Home. The manager at the time was a Marion Newel. Ex-social worker." She looked at her boss. "We need to track her down and have a word with her as a priority."

CHAPTER 30.

PETRA

"I don't know how you do what you do and stay sane." Said Petra.

"I've had good teachers and I've learned to celebrate the successes, however small." Said Aoife.

"Don't you want to write about happy things instead of delving into everyone's misery?"

"I don't see it like that. I do write about happy things. The fact that you are here talking to me is impressive. All the survivors I've learned about who are not letting their past dictate their future. I think that's something worth celebrating."

"Does it scare you?"

"What do you mean?"

"Knowing that there's so much shit in the world? Does it ever weigh you down?"

"I'm sure if I dwelled on just that. I've also come across some amazing, wonderful inspirational people who fight the odds and win. People who give their life to help make things better. The world can be a beautiful place too."

"Don't you worry that people will try to stop you exposing them?"

"Of course. Every time I start to shine a light on areas others prefer to keep dark someone tries to stop me. It's too easy to let the disappointment and sad things play in your mind. If you can learn from them that's good, but don't let them take over. It's the future and what you do next that truly matters. And yes, some times I get scared."

"Yeah? You've got guts."

"I try not to let anyone push me around. I have three rules I try to stick to."

"Oh? And what are they?"

"I Listen. I try not to judge. And I stick as close to the truth as I see it."

"Have you ever been asked 'What would you like to do? If you could do anything?" The physical resemblance between Petra and her little sister Keeley was pronounced. Both women had sturdy lean bodies, stood about five and a half feet tall, and unlike Daisy, were not afraid to take up their full space. Petra however needed to know what Aoife was made of before she was willing to share her story.

Aoife had been aware of Petra looking her up and down while she bought the drinks, and her steely blue eyes were looking directly at her now. Whatever had happened to this young woman was not going to stand in her way, but getting the conversation started might prove difficult.

Aoife nodded her head. "That sounds like a simple question, but even those on an even keel will struggle to find an honest, no holds barred, answer."

"It was always an easy question for me." She stared at Aoife "I wanted to kill my father." There was no smile, no apology in her voice. It was a statement of fact. 'I thought if he was gone, no, not just gone but obliterated, then I would be free to be me. I spent my childhood not knowing who 'me' was. I'm not sure I do now. I never expected to be happy. I just wanted a firmer footing in life. I ran away when I was sixteen and that was the start of me piecing myself together.."

Petra stared out the window for a long while. It gave Aoife a chance to study her. Like many of the young people she had interviewed over the years, there was a dead look in her eyes. Not because she was stupid. Perhaps because she had lived for so long without hope.

"In the beginning my mother pleaded with me to come home. There was nothing she could say to make me change my mind.

I kept myself out of sight as much as possible. The house I shared with three other girls was close to the hospital where I worked as a clerical assistant. I never told my parents the address, nor did they know where I worked." She took a sip of her water.

"Sometimes the other girls in the house would come into my bedroom and we'd sit on my bed and talk and laugh or do each other's hair and play with make-up. I'd never been on a sleepover as a child, I never dared allow friends home. It made me feel warm inside to have friends I could relax with. People that I didn't need to protect from my father."

Aoife hadn't really expected Keeley's sister to agree to be interviewed. She was sure that for everyone who came forward there were three or more who would forever keep their experiences bottled up. It seemed to Aoife that now the cork was out of the bottle all these young people who had been through so much trauma in their short lives needed to get their story out. She wondered if they hoped it would give some sort of justice to have their persecutors named and shamed where the police had let them down. She would need to do a lot more work, but with so many survivors willing to talk it could shape into something not just the local press would pick up. The police would have to pick up on the story, and to be fair, despite his belligerent attitude, she had faith in Benedict Cooper wanting justice too.

Whatever the outcome, she was also conscious of the fact that having her listen to what they had to say, how their lives had been derailed, how they felt, without making judgement, was cathartic.

Petra continued. "When my flatmates left my room I'd call 'Good night', stand close to the bedroom door as they walked out and turn the lock. I had a habit of pulling the handle twice making sure it wouldn't open, then doing it again when I was in my pyjamas before I got into bed. I'd fetch the chair that was by my desk and lodge it against the doorknob. I used to wonder if the others heard me and made jokes, but they never said anything."

"How did you meet your husband?"

"When I met Freddie, I knew he was attracted to me. I had always discouraged any flirting in the past, but he just used to chat, never made any suggestions or gestures that gave me cause to worry or feel uncomfortable. He is a radiographer and loves his job. After the fourth week of smiling as we passed in the corridor or chatting at my desk when he had some time to spare, he suggested we got a coffee together during our break. He was happy to take things slow. He's very gentle. It turns out men can be tender and strong at the same time."

Aoife smiled but made no attempt to interrupt.

"He asked me if I had a boyfriend and was surprised when I said I'd never been out with a boy. I remember he held my gaze and asked, 'Do you like boys or are you into girls?' I giggled so much I almost choked on the biscuit I'd just stuffed in my mouth."

"How did he take it? That you'd never been close to a boy?"

"He assumed it was a parent thing, that they didn't let boys near me. He asked if my parents were strict and wanted me to marry someone of their choice. Freddie's not religious. I didn't contradict him. It was too embarrassing to explain that I was too paranoid to let any man touch me." Petra stopped again, staring at her empty glass.

"Let me get some more water and coffee. Would you like anything to eat?" She shook her head. Petra had chosen a cafe in Bedminster to meet. It was close to where she lived and convenient to get to after she had dropped the children at school, but far enough away that she was unlikely to bump into other mums.

After Griff Tomlin's death Keeley had spoken to her sister and asked if she would be willing to tell her story. Aoife had explained that she could be kept anonymous, but Petra was adamant that she should stand up and be counted. Not for any celebrity, but so that others would know that they could come forward to talk and get help too.

This time when Aoife settled back in her chair, she didn't have to work at getting Petra started again. The tap had been turned on and the story was going to keep flowing until the tank was empty.

"I worried about my little sister. We had never spoken of it, and I never heard him go to her room at night. I thought 'He's already wrecked my life; I can't let him hurt Keeley." I think he found someone outside the house to go to. In fact, I know he did now. That is why he's dead. The way they found him it has to be a message." She looked up defiantly. "All those nights I dreamt of killing him. If I'd had the chance back then, when I was a kid, I would have stuck a knife in him, not a needle. I would have made him suffer. But I was not brave enough."

"You were a child, and he was your father. You thought of your sister's safety, that is very generous." Aoife wanted to provide some comfort but felt wholly inadequate. "Have you ever spoken to anyone about what happened? Does your mother know?"

"How can she not know? For all those years creeping around the house at night. I used to ask myself. I wanted her to walk in, and also dreaded her walking in. We're friends now. My children have a grandmother, but I can never be close to her. She should have saved me."

"What about counselling?"

"Yes. A few years ago. I went to SARSAS. They're a rape and sexual abuse charity. I wouldn't be here talking to you if I hadn't gone to them. They helped me a lot."

Aoife nodded she had already spoken to SARSAS and The Green House to get some background information about rape and abuse and a few quotes from their staff.

"And your husband?"

"I told Freddie I had been raped, not who by. Freddie knew there was something wrong with my relationship with my father, but I never told him what had gone on, not until Harrison brought Iqra home and everything was so obviously weird in our family. I put two and two together. I knew when he stopped coming to my bedroom he'd turned his attention elsewhere."

Petra wrapped her long fingers around her cup, Aoife wondered if it was because her fingers were shaking. "I spoke to a counsellor on the phone anonymously for nearly two years before I screwed up the courage to meet anyone face to face. It's so much better now. Not perfect. Images of the past haunt me, the smells, the sounds, and I'm returned to my childhood bedroom, though I know I'm in the house I share with Freddie and the children. I feel his breath on my neck, and I want to run, but they taught me ways to ground myself, to come back to the real world."

"Do you have any idea who else he might have abused?"

Petra looked up with a sardonic grin. "No. And even if I did, I wouldn't say. If one of them killed him they have done everyone a favour. They do not need to be punished; they have suffered enough whoever they are."

"It may not have been a survivor; it could have been a parent who found out."

"Same applies. If I thought my children were being hurt I could never forgive myself. In some ways it would be worse." She drained her coffee. "I've got to go. Is that everything you need?"

"Yes. And thank you. You are an amazing woman."

Petra raised her eyebrows. "I don't think so. I had no choice. Perhaps I should have done more. If I had stuck that knife into him fifteen years ago, I might have saved others. Perhaps Iqra would still be alive."

"You were a child. You didn't need to add that nightmare to your memories. No child should have a death on their hands. And it seems he wasn't alone. There were others in the ring. Allowing the world to know your story, that will help far more people."

"Thank you for giving me the opportunity. Let me know when it gets published." She collected her things and left.

Aoife noted that, like her sister and Daisy, she ended the interview abruptly. Petra had said what she wanted to say, then, with few niceties, picked up her stuff and walked out the door.

Aoife rested back in her chair and sipped her coffee for some time. Mulling over what she had learned from Petra. Thinking about the death of the man who had abused his daughter, and probably others, for so many years.

Questioning how she felt about a group of individuals being judge and jury, was a tough one to answer. Did being survivors of abuse give them the right? She could understand their motivation completely, but it was always a difficult line to walk. As she had said to Petra, the blood of Habib and Griff would always be on their executioners' hands adding to their nightmares. As much as they had every right to hate these men, they had denied other survivors from seeing their persecutors in court and locked behind bars.

Aoife had just decided she needed to pull herself away from her meandering mind, get up and walk home, when she felt the vibration of her phone in her pocket. It was DI Cooper.

"Hi. We've managed to get Daisy to come in."

"Great! That's a step in the right direction."

"She won't talk unless you're there."

CHAPTER 31.

LIAM REVENGE

In his heart Peter didn't just want this man dead he wanted him tortured, shattered, destroyed, with nothing left of his existence to be remembered.

He breathed deeply. He reminded himself he wasn't that boy anymore. Had not been for years. Counselling, friends, a decent job, had all helped him move forward. Particularly his friends who understood what he had gone through and had walked with him every step of the way back from the edge. He had a lot to be grateful for, he knew several who hadn't made it this far. Some were dead, some in prison, others spent their lives in and out of hospitals. He was here for them as much as himself and the loathing he felt for this vindictive, pathetic lump of meat in front of him now was not going to derail their plan.

Anwar had shown him the way. Had stayed with him into that roaring inferno of rage that he had kept alive for so long. Anwar had shown him how to control it and reduce it to a tiny spark to be kept to one side ready to light the fire only if it was needed.

This was revenge, but it was also duty. It was his task to finish what Anwar had been unable to complete when the police had turned away from them. Peter had responsibility to protect the next generation; to protect the child Kira carried. The only physical part of Anwar they had left.

He watched in silence as the team, clad in the now familiar blue coveralls, tied the weeping man to the old metal benches that skirted three walls of the changing room. His mouth filled with a sock they had picked up from the floor. As the other blue suits moved a step back Peter leaned forward so that Liam could see his ornately painted face. He leisurely blinked his pink painted eyelids. He pulled the sock from his victim's mouth, wanting to hear him plead.

"What are you doing?" Liam sobbed.

"You can inflict pain, now you'll find out what it's like to be on the receiving end. Are you ready Liam?"

"I don't know what you mean!"

"Oh now, now. No porkies. This is the moment of truth."

"Who are you?"

"It doesn't matter who I am. This is pay back for Anwar and all those other kids whose lives you thought you owned." he held the knife close to Liam's face as he pushed the dirty sock back in his mouth, taking delight in his muffled scream of terror. He gradually lowered the knife to the man's groin and slit unhurriedly through the material of his trousers and underpants. he felt the temptation to pierce the soft skin or even chop off his penis, but they had agreed, they must not leave any traces of their own DNA nor take any traces away with them. He wondered if the musty, mouldy smell accumulated in the changing rooms by decades of sweaty footballers would cling to them when they left.

Liam tried to scream as his trousers were pulled open to expose his genitals. Peter   took his time sneering openly as Liam whimpered. One of the blue suits stepped forward and passed the can of paint.

"Hold still now Liam, this may hurt a little." He sprayed the bright red liquid generously over the monster's lower body. Liam bucked and rolled but his bonds held fast.

"Please! No." But the words were muffled and ineffective.

Bending low in front of his face once more Peter asked "Did you stop when Leo asked? Did you care that Cara couldn't walk for days after you'd all finished with her? Did you or Habib show any mercy? Ever?"

His appearance was more terrifying because of the red and black mask he had painted on his face. Liam saw the devil giving a lopsided smirk as he looked into his face. Eyes bright in anticipation of extinguishing this brute's life and the years of fear that had haunted Anwar and all the other children who had just wanted to play football.

He pulled out the small tin from inside his pocket and removed the syringe. Realisation came to Liam's face followed by horror as Peter took his time, until the needle pierced the exposed skin on the monster's arm.

CHAPTER 32.

LIAM CRIME SCENE

"**G**ood evening Nick." Cooper's voice sounded as grim as the demeanour his whole body portrayed.

"Benedict. We meet again." The pathologist had his back to the police officer, but Benedict could tell he was disgruntled.

"I take it this is more of the same.

"It is."

"Which means there are no traces of hair, fibre or prints on anything." This was not a question.

"We have only just started, but so far..." Martin straightened up to look at the detective "not a thing."

"So, either these murders were perpetrated by ghosts and magicians or people who really went to a great deal of effort to clean up after themselves."

"There is comfort in science Inspector. It brings clarity and a level of order to the turmoil of the average crime scene. This is no average crime scene, and I am no magician. You have probably worked this out yourself, but these murders are not hot headed, spur of the moment attacks. Someone has spent a great deal of time watching and planning and choreographing every move."

"They have to make a mistake at some point." DC Hyslop's comment sounded more like a plea.

"The only difference is the sock stuffed in his mouth to keep him quiet."

"And it's of a type used by every person in the club?"

"It is. I would say it was also improvised. Picked it up off the floor. We found it's partner over under the bench."

"Ugh" Goss grimaced "so DNA will be from some sweaty, muddy fourteen year old who got told off for losing his kit."

"We'll see what we can find. But yes, most probably."

"No fibres, no DNA, no identifiable weapon, no clues." Chimed in Goss.

"Well, that has to be a matter of opinion. I think the perpetrator, more likely perpetrators, have been leaving us one very massive clue." The doctor swept his arm in the direction of the dead man's bright red penis and groin.

"It doesn't take a great imagination to guess what these three men have in common. They may be wicked men, but I would like to find any other potential victims while they are still alive and have them punished in the courts, not on the playing fields and in the woods." Said Cooper.

"I have a feeling you won't be finding a queue of men lining up asking you to save them from the scary murderers" The doctors face was grim. "If it is what it looks like, they won't be getting a lot of sympathy from the general public either."

"You're right, but I don't believe in kangaroo courts. Whoever did this is equally guilty of murder."

"Mm, I wonder if you would feel so strongly if it was your mother or sister who had been raped. And if we are looking at a paedophile ring then potentially much worse than rape too."

"These people, if they are the victims of rape, have been through enough in their lives. They don't need the added trauma of killing someone. If we had done our job properly in the first place these men would be behind bars. As it is, it seems highly probable we are going to end up with the real victims of the whole sorry situation in court, not the really bad guys. Anything you do find will help stop the true casualties from getting into any bigger trouble than they're already in."

"Of course Ben. As soon as we have anything I'll let you

know."

Benedict left his sergeant at the scene and drove back to the station. The morning briefing had been interrupted by the discovery of yet another body and he'd left the team in a subdued mood. They had got to an almost ridiculous stage where they were swimming in information, largely thanks to Aoife and the number of survivors who were coming out of the woodwork to talk to her. The team was processing the historic evidence as quickly as they could. The trouble was, the survivors of the original crime did not seem to know, or were unwilling to supply, names of their persecutors.

If what Daisy, Keeley, Hiran and the others had said was true, asking for help had got them nowhere with the police and several of their friends were dead because they'd spoken out.

When Sergeant Goss arrived back in the station they decided to call the team together for a 6pm progress meeting. Ben realised there was no way he was going to make supper with Aoife. He had just picked his phone up to call her when it rang. He was surprised to see Dr Cartwright's number on the screen.

"Hi, Nick. Please tell me you've got something."

"I thought you'd like to know that I've got our latest body on the table."

"What did you find?" Benedict knew the doctor would not be calling just to tell him he was about to start the autopsy.

"It's difficult to be sure exactly what it is, but I have found a couple of small red marks on his back. It's just possible that our attackers used a taser on him."

"A taser gun? That would be one way to keep him quiet. What sort of marks?"

"Tasers typically leave a signature mark. Small puncture wound from the barbs. I think that might be what we've got here."

"But you didn't find any on Griff Tomlin?"

"I didn't notice any, no. I'll go back now and have another look, but he was drugged so it may not have been necessary."

"And Habib Patel?."

"I'll go over him again too. It could be used at close quarters as a stun gun. It's not much, but it would explain why there are no other injuries. You'll get the full report in the morning."

"Thanks Nick.

CHAPTER 33.

DI COOPER MEETS DAISY

A oife had seen Daisy turn into the café a couple of minutes earlier. She had decided against following her in, choosing instead to wait for Benedict, hoping to gauge his mood. She was worried that Daisy might be frightened away by his surly behaviour and was planning to smooth any sharp edges he might be displaying.

She waited a short distance away from the entrance, and soon saw the detective walking briskly toward her. He had his phone to his ear and raised his other hand in greeting as he stopped several steps away to finish his conversation. He looked clean shaven, and his hair was damp. Aoife wondered if he had been up all night and run home to shower before their meeting. As he came closer she was confident that she had guessed right. The shadows beneath his eyes were pronounced and his eyes were bloodshot with fatigue.

"Hi, she's waiting for us." Aoife nodded toward the café.

"Remind me again why we're not doing this down the station?" His was irritable.

"You know why. She doesn't trust police officers and she won't talk if you try to force her." Aoife saw his frustration "Just be the warm, friendly charming person we all know you are, and you'll have her eating out of your hand." She teased.

"Right. How do you want to play this? I was thinking as she trusts you it might be a good idea if you got us started."

"O.K. I can do that." Aoife was relieved.

"The important thing is to get her talking. From what you've told me she'll almost certainly have to come in and give a statement like it or not. For now, I'll sit quietly and take notes although I will have questions. It would be good if you could back me up if she is reticent about cooperating."

Aoife gave him a harsh stare "Of course." She was annoyed that he thought she would have gone to the trouble of giving him the details of her previous conversation with this girl, persuade Daisy to meet with them both to talk, and then withdraw her help at the final hurdle. He still didn't trust her despite everything she had given him.

Aoife pushed open the door to the café. The interior was light and colourful. At the far right hand corner sat the petite figure she had come to realise held a much stronger character than appearance might suggest.

Daisy was wearing a rust coloured sweater that slipped down over one shoulder to reveal a white sleeveless vest top underneath. Her jeans had the strategically placed rips that had become fashionable years ago and seemed to have stuck. Her dark hair was pushed back behind her ears, but several wisps had escaped to join the heavy fringe that covered half her face. She looked no more than a teenager. Despite being in her mid-twenties, Aoife imagined Daisy would regularly be asked for ID before being allowed entry into bars, clubs or over eighteen movies.

Aoife knew DI Cooper wouldn't like the volume of music in the café, but it reduced the chance of anyone overhearing their conversation. She walked up to the girl while Ben went to the counter to order their drinks.

"Thank you for coming. Are you OK for coffee?" She asked. The girl nodded.

Aoife chose the seat opposite her which would force Benedict to sit to one side. It was better that he wasn't in Daisy's direct line of sight every time she looked up. The place was virtually empty except for the girls behind the counter, but Aoife dropped her voice as she introduced Benedict, knowing that the presence of a police officer would instantly draw attention.

"Would you mind if Ben takes notes?"

She hesitated "This isn't official, or anything is it?" Aoife sensed a slight quiver of alarm go through Benedict, but he kept his voice calm, and his words slow.

"If we need a statement from you, we will invite you to come into the station. For now, if you can repeat what you told Aoife it would help me piece together some of what we think has been happening."

"I don't want to end up like Cara or Anwar." Daisy looked at him through her fringe.

Aoife jumped in. "I know it's scary but what you're doing now could save the torment of a lot of other young people and get you some justice at last. And I won't print names of any of my sources without permission."

"The police won't disclose where the information came from, but it is important to get a conviction. Do you really want one of your tormentors to walk free to ruin more lives?" He paused and looked at her his head to one side. She didn't answer. "So, is it alright if I take notes?"

Eventually Daisy gave a small nod and a mumbled "Fine." The girl leaned forward on her skinny toothpick arms. Her bony hands with long splayed-out fingers on the table in front of her as she had before when she was talking to Aoife.

Benedict was impressed with the way Aoife coaxed and cajoled the girl into recalling everything she had said in the privacy of Aoife's kitchen. Not surprisingly Daisy seemed nervous. The café was almost empty with no one sitting nearby, but she kept looking around and cocking her head to see out the window and down the road. Benedict was half expecting her to turn and run.

When they had finished Benedict thanked her for her help. "What made you decide to come forward after all this time?"

"I've been scared half my life. Then I've been to this group, someone said, 'Don't let fear keep you quiet, you have a voice, so use it.'" That was almost true. Daisy dropped her head to stop herself giving anything away.

Benedict gave her one of his cards and told her to call him

if she thought of anything else. He also confirmed that they would want her to come into the station to give an official statement. To his relief Daisy didn't back away from the idea, even asked if she could do it tomorrow because she wouldn't be working in the morning.

"That will be fine. I'll send an unmarked car to pick you up tomorrow after school drop off. Is that alright?"

Daisy confirmed it was, grabbed her coat and left at speed.

"I don't think she likes my company."

"You can understand why she doesn't want to stick around. Firstly, you're a cop, and secondly, well what do you say after that? Any other form of conversation seems meaningless. Also" Aoife grinned "It's what she does. Like she's Cinderella at midnight." A Frown came over her face "It was much more stilted this time. I hope she doesn't lose her confidence before she gets the official bit over with tomorrow."

"The first time of telling was no doubt liberating. I think speaking about it with a policeman listening in makes what she's doing more real. It's good but making it public can have consequences."

"Like what?"

"Her friends and family will find out. People might treat her differently.

Aoife looked at him with a ghost of a smile on her lips.

"What have I said wrong?"

"Nothing. You are a lot more aware than I expected."

"I'm not sure that's a compliment?" He raised his eyebrows.

Aoife smiled.

CHAPTER 34.

REFUGE MANAGER

The weather had been perfect for an early morning run, and Aoife had made the most of it. A shower and a quick breakfast and she was ready for her first meeting of the day.

The refuge was in a part of the city she hadn't explored yet but she estimated it would take her about forty-five minutes to walk. Standing outside the ornate metal gates she looked at her watch. Forty-three minutes.

The house was made of the local quartzite sandstone, as were so many of the buildings in Bristol, but Aoife noticed several distinguishing features that set this house apart from its neighbours. The high stone walls were topped with spiked metal railings, four lights were focused on the short driveway and main entrance, along with two CCTV cameras. Not, she assumed, to keep the inmates from escaping but to alert the staff to any suspicious characters lurking outside.

She had been warmly welcomed by an exceptionally tall and attractive black woman, dressed smartly in a pale blue shift dress that skimmed her hips and finished just above her knees.

The hallway was designed and furnished as one might expect any family home to be.

"This is a lovely house. It feels very welcoming." Said Aoife as she was led into a small office, off to one side from the staircase.

"Thankyou. The women and children who find their way here need to feel secure and much more besides, if they are to heal."

"Thank you for finding the time to see me Mrs Cushing."

"Isabelle, please. And you're welcome. I understand you have been talking to some of Iqra's friends. We spend our whole lives protecting women here. To have one of our own possibly murdered in this way has hit us hard."

"It must have been a horrible shock."

"Not just a shock. It rocked our foundations."

A young woman with her hair tied in a loose top knot and dragon tattoos on her arm and poking from the top of her t-shirt, walked in with a tray of coffee.

"Thank you Mandy. Ooh, and some carrot cake." Isabelle looked at Aoife "You must try some. Mandy is a talented baker, and her carrot cake usually gets eaten before it makes it to this office."

Aoife smiled. "Carrot cake is my favourite. That's very kind."

When the door was closed, and cake and coffee distributed, Aoife continued. "How long did Iqra work here?"

"She first came here when she was still studying. She did a joint honour in sociology and psychology. Then she came back to us full-time a couple of years later. About five years in total."

"Would you say she was happy in her work?"

"It was what she had always wanted to do. As I said, she volunteered here while she was still studying and then after a bit of experience elsewhere, she chose to come here to work. She knew what she was getting into so she must have liked it here."

"And she was good at her job?"

"She was. She had great empathy. The women got on well with her. Opened up to her."

"Would you say Iqra was an anxious person?"

"No. The opposite. She was very calm. Almost serene in her contact with the families here. The children especially loved her. She had a good understanding of their needs."

"Did you talk much about her life outside work?"

"I'm sure you know Iqra was engaged to be married. That

made her happy. She was very excited. I think she truly loved her fiancée. She was close to her family too. I met her brother a couple of times. He did some lifting and carrying when we needed to move things around. Harrison, her fiancée, also helped out a bit. Checked over some papers for us. As a lawyer that is."

"So you like Harrison? You must have trusted him if you allowed him in?"

"Oh yes. They were similar Harrison and Iqra. And close. It was obvious they liked each other. They were in love, but they were also friends."

"Do you know if her family was proud of the work she did? Or approved even?."

Isabelle eyed her suspiciously. "Her family were certainly proud of her. They supported her wherever they could. They weren't wealthy. They had helped their daughter to get through university. Not all Asian families think it a good investment of time or money to educate their daughters, but Mr and Mrs Aziz encouraged Iqra to follow her dreams. It seems the police don't agree with me however."

Aoife chose not to be distracted by the side comment for the moment. "Did you notice any change in her behaviour or attitude before she disappeared? Looking back did she appear scared or maybe ... she was in turmoil. Not her usual self?"

"She was not scared. She was always very strong. Very brave."

Aoife noticed the other woman's eyes flick to the side, just for a second.

"We can be brave but still have concerns about something while we work out what best to do."

"Maybe." There was another pause. "She might have had something that occupied her mind. I noticed that she seemed a little quiet. She was always a thoughtful woman but perhaps she seemed ... a little distracted."

"Did she give any indication what might have been on her mind? Was there perhaps a subject she spoke about more than usual?" Another pause. Aoife was going to have to work hard to help this woman, who was so used to being discreet, to open up. "Or the opposite even. Was there a subject she avoided?"

"Nothing like that, no." Isabelle sighed deeply "She had been upset before Christmas. She came in one Monday morning, and I could tell she'd been crying. You know, puffy eyes, blotchy skin. Something had upset her, but she didn't want to talk about it. She was quiet for a few days."

"Just a few days?"

"Yes. In fact, I had forgotten about it until you asked."

"Did she say why?"

"No. That wasn't her way. She was warm and friendly but self-contained. Didn't make a song and dance about anything. It's one of the reasons she was so good at this job."

"Is there anything else that you think is worth mentioning?" Aoife didn't really expect anything to come from this question. It was a way of winding down the interview. Isabelle Cushing was a busy lady, and she didn't want to overstay her welcome, so she was surprised when she saw the woman looking earnestly straight at her and her fingers fidgeting.

"There was one thing. I haven't told the police about it because, well it was over a year ago." She took a deep breath. "We had a very generous offer of support from Michael Harvey. I don't know if you know him. He's got several businesses. Mainly in the Southwest. When I asked what sort of business, he said Import and export, that sort of thing. Seems to be a label that covers a lot of things doesn't it?" She gave a grim smile. "Anyway, Iqra saw him leaving this office and seemed quite agitated. When I told her about the generous off of support she said straight away 'Don't touch it'. She was so adamant. It just wasn't like her."

"Did you ask why she felt like that?"

"Of course. I mean he was offering not just money but people to come in and refurbish this place and manage the upkeep." Isabelle sighed. "It does take a lot of looking after. Iqra said his businesses were illegal and immoral and we mustn't be seen to be associated with him. I looked into his business and asked him for details of course. Eventually he withdrew the offer."

"And you've not heard from him since?"

"No."

After a few more pleasantries the meeting was closed.

As Aoife walked through the gates she knew she had made the right decision to walk when she left home. She had a lot to mull over, and the exercise always helped.

She didn't know Michael Harvey, but that was no surprise. It wasn't the first time his name had come up. She would have to find out if he and Griff Tomlin were associated in any way. If Iqra was uncomfortable with him and claimed his business dealings were immoral and Tomlin was connected, that could explain Iqra's reaction to Tomlin. He was well worth looking into. She would pass this information over to Benedict too.

CHAPTER 35.

ASSISTANT SUPERINTENDENT TAYLOR

The meeting with Daisy had been far more straight forward than Aoife had expected. Perhaps it was because the young woman had already downloaded much of her story a few days before. It could be easier the second time around. She hadn't given any details that Aoife hadn't already heard. Some of the palpable tension seemed to have been released when Aoif walked into the room. Daisy gave her a small lopsided smile.

Seargent Goss had pulled Aoife to one side before the interview. "She obviously feels more comfortable with you nearby. Any thoughts on how we help her to tell us all she knows?"

Aoife gave a small snort. "I don't think any of us will ever hear all she knows. It's buried too deep."

"OK. I accept that. But they all open up to you. I just want to help. To do my job."

"Well, the obvious really. No sudden moves or noise. Absolutely no judgement or looks of disgust, no matter what you here. And listen. Actively listen."

"OK. Thank you."

"Oh .. and jelly babies." Aoife smiled at the sergeant's look of confusion. "She likes jelly babies."

"Right." Goss gave a half smile not sure if she was being teased.

As before, Daisy stopped the proceedings abruptly as soon as she felt she had said enough, and despite the police officers asking if she could answer a few more questions, Daisy had refused, gathered her belongings and headed for the door.

As Aoife started to follow a uniformed officer informed her that Assistant superintendent Taylor wanted to see her along with DI Cooper.

Taylor had declined help when Aoife had approached her for information on the historic reports of child abuse at Poppy Hill. The fact that Aoife had then asked a favour, which led to her friends at the Metropolitan police, speaking directly to Taylor's boss, was never going to go down well in this office. And the Assistant Superintendent started the meeting by making her feelings about journalists clear.

Aoife laughed, "Really? You still think my only interest is to get an inside story?" She didn't appreciate being dragged into this office as if she was a naughty schoolgirl and she wasn't scared to show it.

"The only thing every journalist is interested in is making the headlines out of other people's tragedy."

"That's harsh, boss. Macarthy has provided us with some of our best leads."

Taylor shot Benedict a look that made it clear she didn't appreciate being interrupted. "I know you've got D I Cooper here mesmerised by your charms, but it doesn't work on me. Not a word of anything you learn here about this case leaves this building, Macarthy, do you understand?"

"That's a joke. Without me you wouldn't have a case. Shit, you wouldn't even have got off your arse to discover why so many young people were disappearing!"

"If I hear so much as a whisper about any of what has been discussed here, outside this station I will have you up for withholding evidence and perverting the course of justice."

"Withholding evidence?" Aoife shot up out of her chair. "You may get away with that sort of arrogant attitude with your officers, but I will not be intimidated by you. I do not appreciate being spoken to like that. If you want me on your side - and you really do want me on your side - you need to change your approach."

Cooper had never seen anyone stand up to the AS before and was interested to see how she reacted. He stepped forward ready to intervene just in case things got out of hand.

"Do you realise you are standing in my station, and I could have you put into a holding cell?" She reminded Aoife of a bull with her square frame and face dark with emotion, and she was breathing heavily. She just needed to snort, and the picture would be complete.

"This police force ignored all the efforts of victims and survivors to report this torture for over a decade. Everything points to your former colleagues covering up wrongdoing by various officials including senior police officers. You worked the case at the time so either you were ignorant of the fact, or you went along with it. Either way it puts you right in the middle of whatever is going on at the moment."

Taylor was clearly not used to people sweeping aside her threats. "Young lady, you may get away with this behaviour in London, but in Bristol we respect the law, respect the authority of the policeman's badge and if..."

"Police officer." Aoife interrupted. "Police "man" is archaic and sexist."

Taylor was apoplectic "Get out of my office. Get out of my station. I do not want to see you here again." She turned to Benedict "And as for you DI Cooper. I am amazed that you would choose to associate with the press. Please in future keep your sex life and work separate. That's an order."

Aoife refused to be swept to one side. "Are you saying nothing's changed? Are you really more interested in covering your backside than finding the truth and putting culprits in prison?" For a moment Aoife thought she might have to put her first aid training into practice. She wondered if Benedict knew where the defibrillator was kept. The older woman was visibly sweating, and her face went so purple she really did look at risk of a heart attack.

"Who the hell do you think you are to come here and interfere in police business?"

"I simply listened to what these young survivors had to say

and brought them to your attention. I'm not sure how it will look in court when the judge hears that you then put me in a cell. As for my integrity, I have published none of the facts about the way the bodies were arranged– yet – and brought the result of my, rather more rigorous, investigations to the attention of your officers every step of the way. So, embarrass yourself if you like. Meanwhile I will continue doing my job. Please do yours!"

Furious, Aoife turned on her heal and left before the AS had a chance to fully process what she had said. On her way past she shot Ben a look and was surprised to see he had turned his back on his superior officer, ostensibly to watch her leave, in actuality it was an attempt to hide the obvious amusement that was written all over his face. He followed her out.

"Way to win friends and influence lady."

Aoife neither slowed down nor looked at him. She marched straight to the reception desk, removed her lanyard, and signed out. Benedict followed.

"Hey, hang on." He said softly. "I'm on your side remember."

They were outside the glass doors before she turned to look at him. "I know. I'm just steamed up."

"Really? You hide it well." He chuckled.

"How can you find this situation amusing?"

"I don't. You, however, were quite impressive."

Aoife glared at him until her face slowly softened. "I think I might have blown any chance of sitting in on your investigation."

"You think?" They both laughed. "Sorry about that. Are you OK?"

"Why are you sorry? She's an arse from the Jurassic era. Not your fault. Unless you agree with her."

"Of course I don't!" Ben shot back. He took a deep breath. "I'd better get back but If you want to meet up for supper tomorrow I can fill you in."

"Supper tomorrow would be nice. You'd better come to mine

that way it won't matter so much if you're late."

"Thank you. About 8pm unless something comes up."

"Sounds good."

Benedict watched as she turned and walked down the road, wondering if he had underestimated this woman.

CHAPTER 36.

KIKI MENSAH

K iki Mensah BSc (Hons). The letters after her name would proclaim forever that she, a girl from a shanty town in Kumasi, Ghana, had achieved something worthwhile against all the odds. The fact that she had done it on the back of her mother's murder and her father's alcoholism, made her feel proud and gloomy in turns. There was no family back home jumping with joy, shouting to neighbours that their little girl had a certificate from a big university in England no less! She had been given a grant because she was considered a deserving cause. Ticked all the boxes. She had passed all her exams, been top of her year, showed promise and was an orphan.

When their mother had died, leaving eleven and nine year old daughters behind, her father had fallen apart and turned to the bottle for comfort. Zena, just two years older than Kiki, had become the main wage earner, leaving school behind her. Kiki worked before school too, selling water and snacks from a basket she had learned to carry on her head, walking between the cars as they queued at traffic lights on their way to work.

And then they had found support from a well-known international charity sent to support children who were going hungry and struggling to get an education. Children like Zena and Kiki. But it had been too late for Zena.

The nuns from the orphanage had helped Kiki too. They had persuaded her to take the money the charity offered and get away. They had done their best to protect the children whose only home was the street, bringing as many of them as they could into the orphanage, but even they had been duped.

Even these strong women in their blue and white habits, could not hold back every predator who came on the pretext of charitable aid. In the guise of 'Do-Gooders' they were no better than the thugs on the street who preyed on defenceless women and children. Kiki's mother and sister had been raped and killed by such a man. Kiki had managed to keep the memories from taking over her whole life but at night, as she closed her eyes the nightmares tried to creep into her thoughts, and she had to work extra hard to hold them at bay. A compilation of the worst moments of her life. The attack on her mother, the agony and shame in her father's eyes, her sister's body found naked and discarded in the old warehouse. A memoir of despair and darkness. Now it was up to her to write the final pages of her family's life.

BSc (Hons) Wildlife Ecology and Conservation Science. Even with the scholarship she had needed to work to afford the extortionate cost of living in the UK. Everything in this cold grey country was outrageously expensive. She had become a nursing assistant at Bristol Royal Infirmary. The hospital was desperately short of low paid staff like her and were happy to fit working schedules around her lectures, which often meant working overnight. She didn't mind. She didn't understand how her fellow students would throw their money away on booze, clothes and makeup. She was happy to spend her time in the hospital. She enjoyed being part of a team and caring for the people who needed her help.

Some of the students on her course had found jobs in Bristol Zoo, but she figured that would be her life for the next forty years so getting a wider experience was important. She liked her fellow HCAs at the hospital and most of the young junior doctors could be a laugh in the few moments when they weren't run ragged looking after ten or more wards overnight, with only one over worked registrar between them, to call on in an emergency.

Camaraderie and compassion were in abundance. Something that Kiki had greatly missed since her mother's death. Whether they laughed quietly or swore under their breath so as not to disturb the patients, there was no animosity. It was just a way of coping with the world. And she had met Anna, a senior nurse. Perhaps they had recognised each other's suffering. Kiki liked to think it was their resilience. Whatever it was the attraction had been instant and mutual.

The thing Kiki enjoyed most about her life as a student was the library, where she'd spent every minute she wasn't in class or at the hospital. She studied hard but in quieter moments she emersed herself in literature from around the world, certain that she would never be surrounded by such a wealth of knowledge and history again or have the opportunity to read like this for free.

Her hard work had paid off and she was grateful. Her years in the UK had been mostly happy. She loved the food and the freedom, the energy and endless possibilities of the city. She had learned to appreciate the British dry sense of humour, wondered at the architecture and history, and appreciated the beauty of the countryside that was so different to back home. But she had never quite managed to shake off the feelings of guilt and anger. Her sister should have been here with her.

Douglas Thornbeck had visited the school in Kumasi and had quickly spotted Kiki's potential. He'd taken a special interest in her. Promised her a bright future.

The fact that she had gone to university in Bristol, just twenty-two miles from Thornbeck's family home was coincidence. She had started her search for him from the first day she had moved into student halls but had waited until she had finished her degree before she acted upon it. He had ruined lives, and men like him were responsible for her mother's death, now she was ready to wreak havoc on his comfortable, pretentious life.

Now Kiki sat opposite Thornbeck's wife. For three years she had worked on her plan deciding the best approach and this was her opportunity. With the proof in her shoulder bag, she would make sure Miriam Thornbeck knew the kind of man she had married.

CHAPTER 37.

DI COOPER

Since Aoife's run in with the SUV, she had noticed a decided defrosting in DCI Cooper's approach to her. In the station and in front of his colleagues he was all work and professionalism. Outside of the office, even though their meetings were always work related, he was becoming more open, and she caught glimpses of his personality.

Their conversations had also become more relaxed and edged towards the convivial. Following the fracas with AS Taylor, Aoife had been reassured by Benedict's immediate offer to meet up. She took it as a sign of conciliation, or even appreciation. Either way she wanted to run a few things by him and get an update on the investigation, so a working supper was welcome. There had been a new turn of events, although Benedict had not elaborated over the telephone. He had warned that he might be late or not turn up at all. To her relief they were now sitting at the table in Aoife's kitchen just half an hour later than planned.

"Long day." It wasn't a question. Aoife could see it written all over his face as soon as she opened the door. "Wine, beer, water or tea?"

"Wine. I got a lift here and I'll get an Uber home. It'll be another early start in the morning, so I'll have to eat and run. I know that's rude. I'm sorry."

"Don't apologise. I've pulled enough all-nighters over the years. I know what it's like, but you have to eat. "It will be ready in a couple of minutes." Aoife poured two glasses of Australian chardonnay. "So, what was the big news?"

Benedict slumped down in one of the wooden chairs. "Would you mind very much if we talked about something else for a few minutes? I have done nothing but talk and think about this case for the last forty-eight hours. I've not even managed a walk or get any fresh air today."

"Ok." Aoife was surprised. She was eager to find out what had been going on, and also keen to impart her own information. "That's not quite true of course."

Benedict frowned "What do you mean?"

"Didn't AS Taylor and I provide some entertainment to distract you yesterday? You seemed amused."

He laughed "That was entertaining. I thought she was going to leap over the desk at you for a moment. She's known for her temper, and you pushed all the buttons."

"Well, I've come across her sort before. You have to stand your ground."

"You certainly did that. The news spread like wildfire of course. You're now a double hero at the station."

Aoife looked questioningly "I am?"

"Saving young Oliver on the Downs and now refusing to be pushed around by the AS. You're gathering quite a following."

"Oh Ha-ha." Aoife said sardonically.

"I mean it. London's loss is Bristol's gain. That's the saying that's going around."

"I don't think London sees me as much of a loss." Aoife took a large gulp of her wine before turning to serve the kebabs from the grill. Benedict noticed her cheeks had turned pink and he thought he detected a sadness in her voice.

"So running away or running to?" Benedict kept his face neutral.

Aoife didn't turn to face him. She knew instantly what he meant. "A bit of both. You were right when we first met."

"I was?"

"About the water sports. Except it's also the hiking and hopefully the horse riding. And I get to look out my window to that view. You don't get that in London."

"There's a bloody great river running through central London!"

"And apartments with water views have a bloody great price

tag to match!" she scoffed. She placed their plates on the table. Help yourself to rice and peas.

"So that's what you were heading 'to'. I guess the running 'from' hit the front pages of the national newspapers."

There was a long silence as Ben watched the shadows and emotions cross her face in fleeting waves.

Aoife thought back to her last meeting with Cameron Connery. She remembered that awful evening together when she faced him with the rumours. There had been no shouting. Not trusting her voice, the words had been barely a whisper, *"You don't need me,"* but the statement was weighted with sadness. *"You'll be fine. You are fine."* She'd gestured around her. *"You have everything you need."*

She'd taken in the house, the walls, the car they were sitting in. Cameron had always been so proud of his possessions. It represented his success, his status in the world. Growing up in poverty he needed the constant reassurance. She could understand that.

"You can't possibly leave it all behind. WE are good together." He'd looked at her unsure if she was committed to leaving or wanting to be persuaded to stay. He thought he heard a note of derision in her voice. They both knew she was right. Yet he'd thought she had at least reconciled herself with what had happened.

He'd said sorry. He was sorry, but Aoife suspected what he was really sorry about was getting caught, not the act of betrayal.

She'd sighed as she went on. The anger still threatened to bubble up inside her as she thought of the blonde with the long legs and cupid lips the camera had caught getting out of this car with him. "I can't be with someone I can't trust. It just hurts too much."

Their two years together had been fun, easy and relaxed. They had made no promises. Even when they had moved in together there had been no big soul searching conversation. It had seemed the right thing to do. Every night they were both in London was spent in each other's arms and running two houses seemed pointless.

The hurt was still as raw at this moment sitting at her dining table opposite DCI Cooper, nearly a hundred miles away from the cause. No amount of berating herself had lessened her feelings for the man she had imagined spending the rest of her life with. She just couldn't get it into her head that Cameron wasn't that caring, loyal, thoughtful person she had thought she was living with. Their story together had ended just like countless others, and she had to learn to live with it.

She pulled herself back to the present, aware Benedict was watching.

"Sorry. I didn't mean to pressure you." He said softly.

"It's the penalty of living with someone famous."

He leaned forward and poured wine in her empty glass while he changed the subject. "I haven't visited the Wye Valley. In fact, I don't venture over the border to Wales except to watch the rugby. I need to get out of the city more. I haven't even taken the boat out recently."

Happy to follow his lead she said. "I'm more of a cricket fan, but I have been to Twickenham a couple of times. Perhaps when you've cracked this case, we can explore Wales together."

He looked up quickly, a light in his eye. "I'd like that." Despite himself he couldn't crush the feeling of joy that pushed its way forward. By unspoken consent they both moved the conversation back to business.

Aoife noted that Benedict had been right, he had needed a few minutes off from work. He looked brighter and sat more upright.

She updated him on her talk with Isabelle Cushing, Iqra's boss. About her conversation with Petra and the abuse she had suffered and the ongoing mental torment that had continued long after she was away from her father.

Benedict probed deeper about her meeting with Isabelle Cushing, taking particular note of Iqra's tear stained face coinciding with the family party at Harrison's parent's house. Then he told her the basic details about how they had found another body, this time in the football club where Liam had coached the teenagers.

"Tasers are illegal aren't they?"

"Stun guns, tasers, they're weapons capable of discharging an electrical current that can seriously harm, even kill. They're classified as a prohibited firearm."

"Does it help at all? Knowing how they were brought down?"

"Maybe? The better the picture we can form of whoever is doing this, the closer we get to finding them. Nick went back and took another look at the other two. Tomlin was drugged but Habib Patel was tasered. The marks weren't picked up on the first inspection because they'd been masked by the dye used. The other two, it was red paint and could be cleaned off."

"So why use dye for the first one?"

"Not sure. Possibly because they knew there was a storm coming and didn't want their message to be washed away."

There was a pause while Benedict swilled the wine in his glass and thought how to phrase his next comment. "We're going to call all survivors who have come forward. Invite them in for questioning."

Aoife looked astonished. "You don't think Daisy and Keeley are your murderers surely?"

"We can't rule anyone out at the moment. Except Petra. She was with her mum and kids when Griff was killed. She met you, then she went to dinner with her in-laws the night Liam was attacked. We checked. That gives her an alibi for the whole of the estimated time of death. We'd still like to talk to her though. She might know something." He noticed Aoife's worried expression.

"Look, we know there was a paedophile ring operating in Bristol. We know Daisy, Keeley, Hiran, Petra have all seen people who were involved even if they don't know names. That means ...."

"Keeley hasn't said she was abused, and Petra only mentioned her father. And as you said, we know she was with Janet when Griff Tomlin was killed."

"You're right, but they have come forward with information and they want these guys caught and punished. They might well have seen or heard something that might be relevant even if they don't recognise it yet. Right now, they are our only witnesses. Them and you of course."

"Me?"

"Counsellor McVeigh tried to scare you off."

"Well, yes."

Benedict softened his voice "And you? How are you feeling after your run in with McVeigh and the SUV?"

"I'd like to say it's in the past and I've moved on. To be honest McVeigh keeps popping into my thoughts. I need to ask Daisy if she knows him.

"We'll do that. He could have been part of the paedophile ring, or perhaps he's under some sort of coercion. He was always a slippery character."

"He's the right sort of age. He was a councillor at the time. And why else would he have got involved with me?"

"Now that is the big question. He might be in their pay or being blackmailed. Why would he voluntarily step up and show his face to you? He either has a lot to lose if you keep digging or he drew the short straw and was the one chosen to scare you off. He might be being set up to take the fall. He knows people who are involved that's for sure."

"You mean he was blackmailed into confronting me? If you know he is connected then won't he be in danger too? From them, I mean. We know they're not squeamish about killing people."

"You mean perhaps he had a debt to pay off and now he's disposable?"

Aoife nodded, "It's a thought."

"Who does he owe the debt to? That's the big question. We're starting to wonder how wide and deep this thing goes. Chief Superintendent James is looking at pulling in even more reinforcements.

CHAPTER 38.

FOUND OUT

M iriam Thornton watched from bed as her husband brushed imaginary specks of dust from his trousers, smoothed back his thick head of hair with gel and straightened his tie. He had been invited to give a speech at a fund-raising dinner for a consortium of charities that worked with deprived and sick children in the Southwest of England. The invitation had included his wife but on this occasion she had declined, complaining of a sore throat and headache.

Douglas looked across at his wife and smiled. "Are you sure you don't want to come along? It might do you good to get out and about." He was still a good looking man with his high cheekbones and full head of hair now mostly turned to white. Years spent in hot climates had given his skin a leathery, permanently suntanned look under his closely trimmed beard.

"No. I really don't feel great and the last thing you want is to be worrying about me when you should be concentrating on charming a bunch of suits. Anyway, they're not going to want me spreading my germs."

He sat on the edge of the bed and took her hand in his. He had to admit she did look febrile. Her eyes were distant and her cheeks bright red. She had not been her normal self for a few days. "OK." He brushed her hand with his lips. "Have you got everything you want?"

"Of course I have." She lifted her book with her other hand. "And I'm not an invalid, just feeling a bit pathetic. I'll have a shower when you're gone, get into my PJs and snuggle up with

Dobson." She ran her fingers through the soft, sandy hair of their shaggy mongrel.

"Alright". Doug's voice was troubled. "If you're sure." He was aware that the start of her illness coincided with the discovery of Griff Tomlin's body, and it made him uneasy. Rumours about the way his friend had been murdered were rife amongst their community and it had upset a lot of people. Miriam had become subdued in the few days since his death, and he caught her eyes on him when she thought he wasn't looking.

Miriam didn't watch as he left the room, concentrating instead on Dobson. The dog licked her hand and sighed happily. As the front door clunked shut Miriam slipped from the bed and moved to the window. Watching her husband through the lace curtains as he drove off through the gates in the navy blue BMW. She turned and, with Dobson at her heals, went downstairs to the kitchen where she took a bottle of white Rioja from the fridge and poured herself a large glass.

Leaving the half empty glass on the kitchen table she walked slowly along the hall to the elegantly decorated room Doug had taken over as his office. Two walls were furnished with floor to ceiling dark oak bookshelves. A third wall had French windows leading out to the garden, while the fourth boasted a beautiful Victorian fireplace with two high backed armed chairs stationed either side. A modest but elegant walnut desk faced out from one corner.

In the early days of their marriage Miriam would come and sit in this room with a book or some knitting, after her children were safely snuggled in bed. She enjoyed sitting quietly while Douglas worked, both relishing the close proximity of the other. That habit had stopped many years ago when Douglas had started travelling so frequently, often staying away for a month at a time. Miriam had taken on the responsibility for their family and the house alone.

The death of John, her son-in-law and the subsequent bankruptcy procedure against his estate had devastated his wife, Miriam and Doug's eldest daughter Elizabeth, who came back to her parental home with her own two children,

Molly and Charlotte. Miriam had taken them under her wing and cared for them as best she could. Elizabeth was not a strong woman. The strain of her husband's suicide, the stories of fraud and lies that followed, and the loss of every penny of their money became too much, even with her parents' support. Eventually Elizabeth had been admitted to a psychiatric hospital that ultimately became her home. Molly and Charlotte, who were raised by their grandparents, had both left home when they finished their education, and now shared a flat in Bristol. Since then, there had been just Miriam and Doug in the large Victorian house overlooking the Sea in Weston-Super-Mare.

Miriam looked around the room. It was cosy and uncluttered. The desk was clear except for an antique pencil holder and a bronze desk lamp. Neat piles of folders representing the projects that Doug Thornton was currently working on or interested in, lay on the coffee table between the armchairs. She felt anxious but determined to overcome her apprehension. Ever since she had heard of the manner in which Griff Tomlin had died she had felt an unease and she needed to know.

Griff and Janet Tomlin, Michael and Diana Harvey and their children had been regular visitors to the house in Weston-Super-Mare, especially when it was clear that Elizabeth was no longer capable of caring for her children. Molly and Charlotte had both played with Petra and Keeley Tomlin. They had all participated in family picnics and games on the beach together and been the best of friends. Was it possible that Griff could be guilty of the things that he was now being accused of without Miriam realising? Without Doug knowing? Everyone had been talking about it for days, except Doug who had kept uncharacteristically quiet on the subject.

Now young Liam, who had always been hanging around, was also dead and rumours were that he had been found laid out in the same hideous way as Tomlin and that football coach and was being called a nonce. A child molester. A predator. Janet felt her stomach churn as she thought about all the children that parents had entrusted to his care as football coach over the years.

She felt her hands turn sweaty as she started opening the desk draws. None of them were locked. She turned to the piles of folders and then moved her attention to the bookshelves. To her relief she found nothing. She hurried out of the room and went in search of her glass. Slugging the remaining wine down in a couple of gulps she topped it back up with the bottle from the fridge and carried it back to the study where she flopped down in one of the comfortable armchairs.

As she sipped, she looked around the room. She went back to the desk and once more opened each of the drawers, this time smoothing her hand under the roof of each drawer and under its base. Still nothing unusual. Moving her glass to one of the bookshelves she rolled up her sleeves and pushed both the big armchairs and the coffee table to the side of the room, got to her knees and started rolling the edge of the beautiful silk rug until it reached the desk. Swivelling around she inspected the bare floorboards she had just uncovered, pushing and poking for any loose edges. When she had finished she unfurled the carpet replacing the furniture. She took another large gulp of wine and stood by the desk. It was substantial but nowhere near as big as she remembered her father's oak desk when she was a child.

At sixty-nine years old Miriam had lost a lot of muscle, but she was not pathetic, and she was determined. Putting her hands under the rim of one side she lifted the desk and pulled an inch or two shuffling it toward the edge of the rug, then going to the other side she did the same. She repeated this process until the desk was no longer standing on the rug. This time she didn't bother to roll the carpet and just picked up the corner flap to fold it back.

It wasn't difficult to find what she had been looking for. Two floorboards were loose. Her hands were trembling as she levered them up with a ruler she'd taken from Doug's desk. She looked inside the cavity and found a manila envelope, a green painted wooden box, and a small camera. She pulled them out. She knelt on the floorboards for several minutes before replacing the rug and the furniture. She gave a quick glance around the room to make sure everything was back in its place before she quickly grabbed her glass and took the stash to the kitchen suddenly not wanting to spend a minute longer in the office.

She threw her finds on to the kitchen table and turned her back to them. Her wine glass in one hand she leaned her other on the worksurface for support as she let her eyes stare out at the garden she had nurtured and adored. Her mind searching for some comfort, some normality, from the world she knew she was about to leave. She desperately wanted to pour herself another glass of wine, but she knew she had to keep her wits about her.

She opened the box. Inside were DVDs in plain white covers all standing on edge. She pushed the box to one side and reached for the envelope. Her hands were trembling violently as she tipped the contents out in front of her. She felt her chest tighten as air escaped her lungs in a gasp, tears blurred her eyes and in an instant the comfortable life she had known disappeared to something from a distant life as she stared at the pictures in front of her.

She pushed the photographs around until several of them were displayed in a loose pile. She brushed away tears from her damp cheeks, but they kept coming. For a moment she thought the wine she had gulped down to steady herself was going to push its way back up, but she straightened herself and refused to allow this sign of weakness to overtake her. Picking up her mobile phone she called her granddaughter Molly.

Twenty minutes later she was standing in her garden. The place she had always come to allow her soul to breath. She knew every plant, every nook. It was her haven and her hideaway, and she breathed in the fresh salt air in an attempt to sooth her aching heart. She was wearing her warm jacket. An overnight bag was on the doorstep behind her. It would take her granddaughters about forty minutes to get here from Bristol, but she couldn't bear to stay in the house a moment longer.

She had scribbled a quick note to her husband and left it on the kitchen table. She couldn't face him, nor could she put the truth in words. She needed time to get her mind around the enormity of his crimes. It was too much to think about in one sitting, so she had lied, saying that their granddaughters had called in and were worried how poorly she looked. They had taken her back to Bristol with them for a few days.

With one hand on her knee for support she bent and caressed the golden head of a daffodil, as she stood, her fingers trailed the purple lilac, and she inhaled its scent. Looking at her watch, she clipped the leash to Dobson's collar, picked up her suitcase and walked briskly out of the gate and, without a backward glance, carried on down to the promenade to meet Molly and Charlotte.

CHAPTER 39.

DAISY

Saturday morning, the streets around the old Corn Exchange were filled with delights. The second-hand bookstalls were her biggest magnet. Always on the lookout for a bargain she loved the thought of these books once being held by a Victorian gentleman drinking a glass of port and reclining in his wing backed armchair by the fire to read, or a young woman perched on a park bench in the sunshine being thrilled by the latest Charles Dickens novel.

Aoife had always liked markets. Whenever she holidayed or worked abroad, she had sought out the souks and street food stalls. She had learned to pop into Bristol's St Nicholas's covered market whenever she was passing to pick up fresh fruit or treat herself to a humous and vegetable wrap from Matina's.

Slowly mooching from inspecting handmade jewellery, to fresh farm produce or bric-a-brac, Aoife was enjoying herself. She'd already tucked some particularly smelly blue cheese in her bag and was bending to inspect some silver jewellery when there was a tap on her left shoulder. She swung around to see Daisy, her arm through that of a tall, gangly man with warm brown eyes and a thick mop of curly brown hair.

"Hey. Didn't expect to see you."

Aoife smiled. "Daisy, hi."

"Aoife, this is my husband Ryan. Ryan this is Aoife." Daisy was beaming with pride.

Aoife shook the young man's hand, amused at the excitement in Daisy's eyes. Pleased to show off her man, and, Aoife was fairly sure, pleased to show off Aoife to Ryan.

Ryan held out his hand. "We don't usually come here. Daisy said you told her it was a good place to hang out on a Saturday morning. Apparently we have to buy a wrap from Matina's." Ryan rolled his eyes and gave a grimace before breaking into a chuckle. Daisy punched his arm.

"You won't regret it. Just make sure you don't leave it too late, or the queue will be halfway through the market." She lowered her gaze to take in a small dark-haired girl of about three years old holding Daisy's other hand.

The little girl toddled forward and wrapped her arms around her mother's leg. Her dark curly hair was adorned with a yellow ribbon. Dressed in yellow tights with bright red flowers, a denim dress and red jacket, she was unmistakably her mother's daughter.

"This is Flora." Daisy swept her daughter up in her arms. "Flora this is Aoife. She's a very clever lady."

"Thank you. Hello Flora." Aoife gave the little girls hand a shake. "I don't usually get introduced in such a flattering way."

"Well, you are. That's obvious. And I don't want Flora to grow up thinking that being pretty is the only thing a woman can aspire to. That's lovely." Daisy nodded toward the vintage silver pendant Aoife was holding.

"I'm looking for a birthday present for a friend. Do you like it?

"Wow. I'd be made up if I got that for my birthday."

"You're right. I think I'll get it."

"We're off to buy our lunch then. "

"Nice to meet you." Said Ryan.

Aoife smiled. Despite the height difference, they seemed well matched. "Enjoy." She called after them.

As she paid the stall holder and placed the pendant in her backpack Aoife felt pleased with herself for haggling a few pounds from the price.

The air was scented with the smell of warm bread, pungent cheese, sweet, iced buns and an abundance of farm fresh vegetables. A busker was also doing a good trade as customers threw money in his open guitar case. It was such a little thing but bumping into a friendly face in this city she hardly knew had made her smile.

She continued to nose happily through the goods on another antique jewellery stall until, from the corner of her eye, she became aware of being watched. There was something about the utter nonchalance of the man resting against the stone pillar of the old Commercial Rooms, just a few feet in front and to her right. He seemed to be staring at nothing in particular, no mobile occupying his attention, no focus on any of the market sellers, just idly waiting.

Aoife moved to her right lured by the second-hand books on display, trying not to look directly at the man but conscious of his presence. She was aware that he wore pale chinos and a dark waterproof jacket. She picked up a small copy of Mill on the Floss, appreciating the feel of the soft leather cover in her hands. She was conscious the clear sky overhead was swiftly being pushed to one side by a grey bank of gloomy clouds and the first spit of a rain drop on her face. The walk between The St Nicholas covered market and Totterdown would take most adults around half an hour. She figured that she could cut at least seven minutes off that if she pushed it and wondered if she ought to go and queue for her lunch too if she didn't want a soaking.

As she turned to leave the man caught her eye and was almost smiling a welcome as if it were Aoife he had been waiting to meet. Then he turned and weaved his way through the crowds of people with their bags, and a group of teenagers munching on fresh cut slices of pizza; working his way to the entrance of Exchange Street where he disappeared around the corner.

Nothing had been said and no move had been made toward her, but Aoife felt ill at ease. Her first thought was to try and shake it off as no more than an echo from her incident with the white SUV. Then suddenly a chill ran down her spine and she looked around for Daisy and Ryan. There was no sight of them. She turned and ran as fast as she could back the way she had come. The man had taken one of the routes on the edge of the covered market, Aoife headed for the tiny All Saints Lane in the middle. Dodging and turning to avoid the crowds as best she could, she felt her adrenalin surging. A group enjoying drinks in the spring warmth at the Cocktail Bar were spread across the narrow passage. She pushed herself close to the far wall and edged sideways, frustrated at the holdup but it was nothing compared to the logjam as she turned left into the food isle. It was lunch time and the queues for pies, noodles, handmade cakes, crepes and cakes filled the alleyway.

From her height she could see above most people's heads. There was no sight of the scary man, but nor could she see Daisy and Ryan. Aware that she might be making a fool of herself but still unable to calm her beating heart, she managed to edge toward the queue for the wrap stall they were going to. Then to her relief she spotted Ryan's mop of hair as he bought cakes from an amazing display of sweet treats. She slowed and wondered if she should just leave them alone. She would feel silly explaining her mad dash to find them. Catching her breath, she started to turn, then she looked back. Ryan was standing on his own. She looked around for Daisy but didn't see her. And felt a shiver of horror run down her spine.

"You following us?" Ryan laughed as Aoife walked toward him.

"Where's Daisy?"

"I left her buying some cards from one of the shops inside. Don't know where she's got to she's been ages." He noticed the anxious expression on Aoife's face. "Why?"

Aoife turned and hurried into the main hall. It was busy but not as much as the food hall. Even with Aoife's height she realised it was not going to be easy to spot the five feet two inch Daisy. She started to move amongst women looking for bargains, the men looking at tools and racing bicycles, the lovers with arms around each other. Her eyes darted wildly, a fear encroaching over her good mood with every passing second.

She rushed to the first of the two card shops, then toward

the second. There was no sign of the woman and little girl. She told herself she was being stupid, just hypersensitive after her own strange incident with Councillor McVeigh. She turned and headed back to where she had left Ryan. Relief rushed through her as she saw the couple standing at the entrance. She laughed at her own stupidity, wondering how long she was going to be on high alert.

Then as Aoife approached them she realised something was terribly wrong. Daisy was frantically screaming and tugging at Ryan's jacket. Ryan scanned the crowd as Daisy spotted Aoife she waved her hand, her eyes wet with tears.

"Flora's gone!" The girl blurted out before Aoife had a chance to say anything. "She was stooping down looking at the toys. When I turned around and she wasn't there." She sobbed.

"How long ago?"

"Not more than a minute."

Aoife jumped into action. "I'll go to the Corn Street entrance. You stay here Daisy. Ryan work your way through. See if you can spot her. Tell as many people as possible you're looking for a little girl." She turned and pushed her way to the main entrance. Scared she was too late she ran outside and looked both ways up and down the street but could see nothing resembling either her strange man or the little girl. She went back to the large archway that led into the covered area and stationed herself two steps in, constantly combing the area with her eyes. She could hear Daisy and Ryan calling their daughters name and she noticed that several other people had joined in the search.

She looked at her watch. Three minutes must have passed since Daisy had last seen her daughter. It must be every parent's nightmare. To lose a child when you knew it was your responsibility to keep them close by and safe.

She became aware of a disturbance to her left. A small crowd were forming and talking excitedly then a man raised his hand and yelled at the top of his voice "She's here!"

Someone else called out "We've got her!"

Aoife raced over and pushed through just as Ryan arrived, knelt down and pulled his daughter so closely to his chest they could have been one. The crowd moved aside to allow the small, frantic figure of Daisy to reach for her family. The audience gradually dispersed as the three of them knelt down and hugged each other as though they would never let go. Aoife saw tears escape Ryan's tightly closed eyes.

Eventually Ryan stood and turned to Aoife. "Thank you for your help."

Aoife put a hand on his arm "One of them was here."

"Who?" asked Ryan.

"I know." Said Daisy.

"Who!" Ryan's voice echoed all the stress and frustration brought on by the last few minutes.

Daisy put a hand to her husband's cheek "I don't know. I didn't recognise him. He knew who I was. He asked if I wanted to go party with his friends."

"What made you think he knew you?"

"He said my name. Said it could be just like old times".

As Aoife scanned the crowd she knew who she was looking for and ran through the description to Daisy.

"Yes. How do you know."

"Because I saw him too. He wanted me to know he was watching me."

"Shit!" shouted Ryan. Flora jumped and her face crumpled. "I'm sorry darling. I was scared. Daddy was scared when I couldn't find you."

"Are you OK sweetie?" The little girl, now secure in her mother's arms, nodded.

"Where did you go Flora. When you lost mummy. Were you scared?"

The girl shook her head and then buried her face in her mummy's shoulder. Daisy pulled her to sit up again and said quietly. "It's ok. Were you here by the hats all the time?" Aoife looked around and realised they were standing between a hat stall and another selling brightly coloured jumpers and scarves.

"What's that on her back?" Her father put his hand up to reach for a small bright envelope pinned to Flora's jacket.

"No!" Aoife's sharp voice brought his hand to a sudden stop and made several heads turn their way. "Don't touch it."

"What?" Daisy's voice was frantic. She couldn't see her child's back.

"It's a note," said Ryan.

"There might be prints." Explained Aoife as she pulled her phone from her pocket. Ten minutes later DS Goss and two uniformed officers were walking toward them.

CHAPTER 40.

MORNING WALK

I t was too early for the full dawn chorus, though nearby she could hear a wren's repetitive chirrup trying to get things started. Somewhere in the predawn darkness a small creature scurried through the tall grass as in the distance a dog gave a lack lustre bark, more out of habit than agitation.

Aoife breathed in the crisp salt filled air. Her steps lengthened as she marched briskly up the hill, until she was aware of the thumping of her heart. In the distance she could hear a dustcart rumble as it travelled between pubs and restaurants collecting the debris from the previous night's trade. Soon the early morning traffic making its way to and from the city and nearby M4 motorway would become a constant background hum even at this distance. Urban life at full blast.

She had risen early from a disturbed night's sleep. For a short while she had slept deeply, exhausted by the intensity of her work the day before. The words from all the interviews she had been part of crashing around her brain so rapidly and with such force, she could think of nothing else until they found escape on the blank page. Flowing through her fingertips and appearing on the screen in front of her.

She had crawled into bed at midnight and fallen asleep almost instantly. Then, with a start, she had woken up as her mind came alive once more without her bidding. Looking at her phone revealed she had been asleep for less than five hours. This time the conversation with the Inspector was the subject disturbing her rest, The words thrumming through her head insisting on being examined and defined.

His words from a few days ago, so perceptive, had unconsciously triggered thoughts that she had considered safely locked away. "So, running away or running to?"

The truth was she had never thought of her actions as 'running'. She delighted in her separateness. It wasn't isolation. She wasn't a hermit, just detached. She believed she did her best work without the distractions of friends, lovers or colleagues demanding pieces of her. There was energy in solitude and while she would hardly describe her life as troubled, she threw herself into work and avoided comforts and distractions while she was in the middle of an assignment.

Remote walks and evenings spent brooding were all founts of creativity. There was also the fact that she was not good company at these times. Even at school and university she had shut herself away to study for weeks before crucial exams. She avoided others for the purely selfish reason of not wanting to feel guilty about turning down invitations, or her brusque manner if she accepted. There was legitimacy in the thought that "inspiration was born of adversity".

She suspected that DCI Cooper had asked the question because he recognised her need. Because he'd experienced it in his own way. Solving an important case required not just his concentration but his passion and the full weight of his obsessive character. For him finding the truth was all consuming and demanded every ounce of his attention. Yet his asking had disturbed her. Required her to examine her motives.

She pushed the thought aside as the picture of Daisy and Ryan hugging their daughter filled her mind. It wasn't the first time that her work had brought threats and real danger to both herself and others as she closed in on the truth. Evil worked best in the dark and those involved wanted to extinguish the light that she shone on the harm done to others.

When Benedict had called to say that Daisy and her family had been taken by the police to stay with Ryan's aunt in Cornwall until it was deemed safe to return, Aoife had been relieved.

He had also informed her that there had been another attack on a potential child molester. This time in a village near Minehead. An ex-policeman.

CHAPTER 41.

AINSLEY MEWSE

Sergeant Goss stared at the man in front of her. She had known his father, Superintendent Andrew Mewse. Known the man's reputation as a misogynist and a man with a temper that had scared the station into compliance with his extreme methods. And now the ex-police officer was in hospital close to death. She wondered how many people would mourn him if he didn't make it.

Luckily for her, he had been moved to another job a few months after Goss had transferred to Bristol. She couldn't imagine what it must have been like being his son. To share a house with such a man. To grow-up with his shadow looming over you.

She was sitting in the interview room with her boss by her side, Ainsley Mewse, now aged thirty-one, sat opposite with his solicitor, a neat young brunette of similar age to her client.

The news that ex-superintendent Mewse had been found in his garden had reverberated around the station at high speed, but no one seemed sad. It appeared that it hadn't caused his family much distress either.

"The officers who visited you this morning said you did not seem surprised when they broke the news of your father's assault. And now, well, you don't look particularly upset." Said Goss.

Ainsley Mewse sat still, his head cocked to one side, as if contemplating the situation.

"I'm not."

"Oh? Why's that?"

"I watch the news. I've read the headlines on social media. There have been a lot of old men being put down recently. I'm not surprised my father is one of them."

"Put down? That's an unusual turn of phrase." Said Cooper.

"It's what you do with rabid dogs. It seems appropriate."

Benedict took his time phrasing his next question, but the young man was quicker and took his turn to ask a question. "Now you look surprised detective. Did you know my father?"

"No. I was still in London when Superintendent Mewse was in charge."

"Well, lucky you, because I'm sure you would have been the sort of young lad he would have been attracted to."

"Are you trying to say..."

"I'm not trying to say anything. I am simply confirming the fact. My father was not only a beast but a sadistic, evil, domineering psychopath. And yes, his colleagues in the force, even those who didn't partake of young flesh themselves, chose to look the other way."

"The other way from what?"

"Buggery, paedophilia, sadism, misogyny. He played the full hand."

Despite their investigations and the stylised manner in which the man had been found, both Cooper and Goss were surprised by the intensity of the verbal attack. To hear the words out loud to describe a former police officer - that was shocking.

"You mean you knew. Did you report him?"

"No. Sadly I didn't have the courage. I knew what would happen to me if I did and I was trapped under the same roof as him. There was no escape for me. Others tried to do the right thing but fared no better."

"Someone did report him?"

"Yes. Maria Stephens. She was fifteen years old when they pulled her out of the river a few days later. Then there was Matthew, I can't remember his surname. He disappeared. Reported to have run away."

"And no one got suspicious about so many reports of abuse that weren't followed up?"

"You tell me. Although I doubt you'll find any reports of abuse at all. Not when the priest, the councillors and the police all took such a special interest in the poor, unfortunate children who found themselves in need of comfort, away from their families." He sneered.

"You didn't spend any time at Poppy Hill yourself?"

"No. Some of the children from the home were in my year at school. They thought they would try taking their hate for my father out on me for a while. Eventually we all realised we were in the same boat, along with Councillor McVeigh's daughters who were in the years above and below me."

Cooper tried his best to keep his face neutral. He felt Goss wriggle in her seat next to him as she said, "You mean all those children were being abused?"

"We were a few of the children who lived with the monsters whose gross sexual appetite was sanctioned by so many in authority."

"And Councillor McVeigh, he was one of them?"

"He knew what was going on. His own daughters were part of it, but he turned a blind eye!" Ainsley's fist crashed down on the table.

Both police officers took a pause as they tried to compose their thoughts and steady their voices.

Eventually Cooper managed to ask, "And did McVeigh ever abuse you or any of the children?"

"I don't think so. He just pimped out his daughters."

"Did you try telling anyone else. Another family member or a teacher?"

"Yes. And yes, my mother did know before you ask. I don't blame her though. She probably got it worse than I did."

"Do you know the other children who were dragged into

this?"

"Some. I don't know names other than those I went to school with."

"Do you know where they came from?"

"I don't know. I assume there were years before me and years that followed on. I know of eight, plus the two I mentioned."

"Maria and Matthew? They would have died fifteen years ago?"

"Sixteen now."

"What did you mean when you said your mother got it worse than you?" asked Goss.

Ainsley put his head down, his right hand rubbing his eyes, and for the first time Benedict saw the young man struggling to keep his emotions in control.

"I saw him use his belt on her more than once." Now it was Benedict's turn to struggle to keep himself under control.

"He beat his wife?"

"My mother's was just one of the many lives he took pleasure in destroying." He glared at the camera in the corner of the room "I did not do this to my father, but I will raise a glass tonight to those who did. And if I had known it was going to happen, I would happily have held him down while they cut his bollocks off with a blunt knife." The young man's face was dark, and tears now streamed down his face. His solicitor placed her hand on his arm and spoke quietly in his ear.

"Perhaps I should remind you that you have no alibi for the time of the attack on your father. You are talking yourself into our prime suspect." Said Cooper.

Ainsley lifted his tear-streaked face "I am self-employed. I was in the workshop all day until about eight in the evening. It's a small light industrial estate. I know there are CCTV camera's outside, and I imagine there will be others on my walk home. I walk past several shops and a couple of large houses." He had calmed down now although Cooper noticed his fingers were twitching and restless.

"Do you know who else might wish your father harm?" asked Goss.

Ainsley laughed derisively. "Really?" He shook his head dismissively. "I should think half the people in this station! There are dozens of people who will breathe easier tonight. Probably hundreds." He turned to the darkened window behind which sat several officers. He waved his arm in their direction. "Ask them. Some of them knew what he was. They did nothing about it, but they knew. He is a kiddie fiddler and a sadist. You should start by asking those who worked with him."

As they walked back to the office together Benedict paused and turned to his sergeant. "How well did you know Superintendent Mewse?"

"Not well I'm pleased to say. I know he was universally hated."

Cooper raised his eyebrows "Go on."

"We only overlapped by a few months. He had a reputation as a chauvinist, and he certainly had a temper. Everyone was scared of him. Staff turnover was high. It was not a happy place to work."

"Did you hear of any reports against him? Any rumours?"

"You mean of a sexual type?"

Benedict nodded.

"Plenty of rumours of wandering hands and I don't just mean patting bottoms either. A couple of women refused to go unaccompanied to his office. Women did not work late, not on their own. It wasn't just the women; the men didn't like him much either."

"I thought that sort of thing died out with the old millennium."

"Mm. That's because you're a man." Goss turned sharply away and started to walk on.

He called after her "This is important. Tell me. Is it still happening?"

Aida Goss's face softened. She knew her boss would not tolerate discrimination of any sort. "Not here Sir, not anymore as far as I know. I mean most of the male officers could do with a lesson in how to work with women, but isn't that the same everywhere?" She sighed deeply "Mewse got transferred to Portishead eight years ago and retired three years later. He was just fifty-eight when he retired, and I don't think he left voluntarily."

As they walked into the office, DC Hyslop joined them along with two other officers who'd been watching the interview on a screen.

"Do you think he did it Boss? Kill Tomlin and Patel?"

Benedict blew out his cheeks. "What do you think Aida?"

"He certainly seems to have enough motive, and we can't write him off until we check out the CCTV. But no, it doesn't feel right. He's still in pain and there was no sign of either gloating or fear."

"I agree. Justin, any news from the hospital?"

The DC gave a grim smile. "Apparently it's touch and go. He's not regained consciousness" Hyslop looked down at his notepad. 'Mr Mewse is critical but stable' is how they are describing him."

"Have we heard from SOCO yet?"

"Yes. There's a message for you to call Amelia Delaney. She confirms our suspicions. This looks like a different crew. No spray paint and several cuts to the groin area. The injection was not so expertly administered, went straight through the vein."

"No paint involved. Serious wounds inflicted and a non-lethal dose." Said Cooper.

"And sounds like it was much sloppier. Possibly a spur of the moment attack whereas the others had to have been planned." Added Hyslop.

"Copycat?" asked Goss.

"That's the thinking, yes."

"OK." Benedict looked at his watch. 6pm. Get everyone into

the briefing room. We need an update."

A young DC approached them. "Sir, Superintendent James has asked for you. He's in his office Sir."

"Thank you Paula. Aida can I leave you to get everyone together?"

"Yes sir."

CHAPTER 42.

SUPERINTENDENT JAMES

"I hear we have a breakthrough."

"Yes Sir, possibly."

"Oh? Why the doubt?" James questioned "I heard they'd got sloppy, left DNA and fingerprints behind."

"Apparently so yes."

"So why the sullen face."

"Because it doesn't feel right. No spray paint. They cut their victim and he's still alive."

"Could have been disturbed. Didn't the neighbour find him?"

"Yes. As you said it's sloppy and it's out of the area."

"You're thinking copycat?"

"We are, yes sir. Everything they did could have come from the media coverage. As you know we've never mentioned the spray paint, and everyone's held back from printing the details."

"By everyone you mean Macarthy. She's the only person who knows outside the force I take it?"

"No sir, the witnesses who found the bodies, they know too of course."

"Yes of course. So, you think it's a coincidence that it's Mewse. He no longer lives in Bristol after all."

"It's perfectly possible that one of his young victims have moved to the same area. Minehead's not far from here and isn't a big place. They could have recognised him. It looks very much like a revenge attack, just not the same gang."

"God forbid this becomes widespread."

"Yes sir."

Superintendent James stared at Cooper. "I know there are people who think these men have got what they deserve, but these attacks are a crime. When we catch the people responsible they will go in front of a court of law. Something they've denied their victims."

Cooper clenched his fist. "Yes sir. Is that all sir? We have a briefing about to start."

"Yes. Go. Keep me updated. As soon as you get the forensics let me know."

CHAPTER 43.

AOIFE

Aoife felt tired after the meeting with Ainsley. He was a troubled person and she felt she needed the walk home to rid herself of the tension that had transmitted from ex-Super Intendant Mewse's son and planted itself firmly into Aoife's weary body and mind.

She walked up the steep slope of Union Street, crossed over Wine Street and onto the short path of Castle Park that ran toward the river and Bristol Bridge.

The sound of footsteps moving quickly somewhere behind her sent a warning tingle through her spine. The sun had disappeared below the horizon almost an hour earlier, but it is never pitch black in the streets of Bristol. This is a city like all others where light pollution blots out the stars, so as she turned she saw the guy in a hoodie some six steps behind her. Aoife had no time to turn and run as he raised his right arm and lunged forward. She grabbed the attacker's wrist and pulled him using his own momentum to hasten him forward. The assailant was unprepared for Aoife's defensive move, fell to the floor hitting the ground hard on his cheek bone.

Aoife felt the air knocked from her lungs and a pain shoot up through her leg as she stumbled against the wall of the bridge. Her biggest enemy right now was her own fear. She had learned karate. She had won her brown belt, but still the best tactic was not to get entangled with a guy with a thirty percent weight advantage. She turned to run but he was already on his feet. She placed her right hand over her left wrist closed around the watch she always wore when out on her own at night and fumbled to pull the alarm. It caught on the sleeve of her coat, and nothing happened.

"Shit!" There was no time to look to see why it didn't work.

Breathe she heard her sensei's voice in in her head. *Breathe and watch closely.* She tried to focus on her assailant's chest and arms not his eyes. Her attacker was arrogant. He'd made assumptions about her which had given her the advantage. She couldn't rely on that happening twice.

"You just won't listen will you?" He growled as he got back to his feet.

"I'm sorry I think you've got the wrong person."

"I know exactly who you are. I thought journalists were supposed to be bright. Someone with your reputation and you still refuse to learn. It's very disappointing."

"Sorry?"

"The hero of the Downs." He was trying to distract her while circling around, looking for a way in.

"Again. Wrong person."

"Don't play coy with me. You've been stirring up trouble. It's not good for people's health. You need to stay away from the little runts unless you want someone to get seriously hurt."

"Is that a threat?"

"If anyone gets hurt it'll be on your head. Agitating them until they don't know what's best for them anymore."

Aoife decided answering back was not going to do her any good. She wanted to run but turning her back would be a mistake. Going through him was not an option. She took a step as if to move past him but found his bulk still blocking her path.

She refused to step back knowing that such a move would give the man a psychological advantage. Nor did she look around for help. Keeping her gaze focused on him she listened for any voice or noise that would indicate the presence of others and possible help, but there was nothing.

She'd figured out a long time ago that it was better to talk to the other guy and try to fix things with words instead of fists. She tried to kick her brain into action. She was good with words so why weren't they coming to her when she needed them?

Without taking her eyes off her antagonist she weighed up her chances. If he decided to keep this physical she would not be able to fend him off for long. He was probably only an inch taller than her but a good twenty kilos heavier. His bulk was almost certainly made up of more fat than muscle, even so most men are much stronger than women. If she got the chance to run, she would back herself on speed. She took a quick look behind him. There was no-one in sight.

"What exactly are you doing? I don't know you and have nothing against you. Why get yourself into trouble?" She heard her voice sounded high pitched and scared as her throat tightened. He moved toward her, she shifted to the balls of her feet, preparing herself to dodge the full force of any blow. There were shouts from behind her, but she ignored them as she concentrated solely on this man who appeared to want her dead.

She saw his right arm hammering towards her just in time to partially deflect it, but she still felt a pain shoot through the side of her head at the glancing blow. He tried to follow it with a left punch to her stomach but luckily he was not a skilled fighter. Bringing her right elbow down hard on his wrist she moved in closer and kneed him in the groin. As he doubled over her right elbow connected with his nose which instantly spurted a fountain of blood. Stunned, he staggered backward.

Breathing hard Aoife jumped back tripped and landed awkwardly. She cried out in panic as she lost her footing and landed on her backside. Was she going to be the next headline in tomorrow's media? She brought her right hand back to her left wrist and this time managed to pull the pin. 140db loud, incessant, siren emanated from the personal attack security alarm. It was difficult to tell if the noise designed to significantly disorient anyone nearby worked on her assailant as his hands still cupped his groin in pain.

Then she heard feet running and more bodies came into

view. She slung herself back against the stone wall to face whatever was coming but the group of young men and women ran straight past her. Aoife turned her head back to where her assailant had been doubled over, only to see him hobbling across the grass. Someone rugby tackled him, and he fell with a thud.

The students turned to look at Aoife who was leaning against the bridge but still upright.

Like a pack of wolves, the students piled on top of him, sitting on arms and legs to keep him pinned down. Blood flowed from her assailant's broken nose as he slumped backwards. And that seemed to be the end of the scuffle.

She switched off the alarm and the silence poured in on her "So you're the one they send after women and children." She glared at man on the floor. You'd better let him roll on his side. I think he can't breathe."

She felt blood trickling down the side of her face and her head hurt. She felt strong hands hold under her arms and pull her backwards as she pushed herself unsteadily toward her assailant. She yelled a loud guttural noise as she tried to twist away.

"It's alright. Not going to hurt you." For the second time in just ten days a man was helping her to stand up, trying to reassure her.

The hands let go and she stepped several paces away ready to sprint as fast as she could. As she turned to look around she realised the performance had attracted attention and a small crowd had gathered.

Two men in their late thirties were asking her if she was alright. She pointed to her assailant who was trying to struggle to his feet. Another man, presumably the one who had supported her, was checking him over to make sure the students hadn't squeezed all the breath from him while holding him down. Aoife was still breathing heavily as she pulled out her phone, took two quick photos making sure she got his face in the picture.

"Thanks," said Aoife, too shaken to do more than lean back

against the wall.

"The police are on their way. I 've already called them." A woman a bit younger than Aoife was by her side.

As she stood unable to gather her thoughts, another woman came up to her and handed her a bunch of tissues.

"Here, you've got blood on your cheek love." She said pointing to her own face to show where to dab the tissues. "Are you OK. Would you like to sit down?"

"Thank you. No, I'm fine." Adrenaline was thumping through her body telling her to move.

"You don't look fine."

Aoife gave a weak smile. She realised her legs were feeling wobbly. As she held the tissues to her cheek she saw more blood on her left arm. Closer inspection showed a shallow cut on the side of her forearm. Lightly pressing her index finger and thumb against the centre of the cut she closed the edges of skin.

"My names Laetitia." A slender, hard-faced woman with curly blonde hair, of about the same age as Aoife introduced herself. "It's best to sit down before you fall down. The adrenalin will run out in a minute." The words were spoken as a statement of fact. There was no smile on her face, but she encouraged Aoife toward a communication cabinet, placed her own sweatshirt on the ground and gently pushed Aoife into a sitting position.

Her gaze naturally turned to the man who had caused all this turbulence. He was no longer clutching his groin. His hands were tied together with something, and a group of men now stood around guarding him.

The adrenalin had not run out and Aoife could feel the pulse at the base of her throat beating sickeningly fast, conscious of her fingers and legs twitching. The pain in the side of her head threatened to take over and she raised her fingers to tentatively feel for damage only to find a hand grasp her wrist.

"Best not to touch. Your hands are none too clean. It's starting to swell, which is normal, and you've got a bit of a cut but not too bad." Laetitia was crouching on her haunches at her side. She made no other attempt at conversation. Gave no reassuring look. Aoife liked her

$$\triangle\triangle\triangle$$

In the next few minutes sights and sounds flashed past. Paramedics, an ambulance, A&E, wide entrance with automatic sliding glass doors, ambulances lined up outside, paramedics wheeling in patients on trollies. Later she remembered that one was a child in a neck brace, another child screaming in the corridors, doctors running - not to her.

"I wish all women would go to self-defence classes. It should be on the curriculum in schools as far as I'm concerned. If you hadn't, it could have been so much worse." Benedict Cooper was hovering at the end of her bed.

"What are you talking about?"

"The officer who took the witness statements said you knew self-defence."

Aoife gave a dismissing laugh "No. I'm afraid I learned everything I know about self-defence from Miss Congeniality."

Ben looked confused.

"You know S.I.N.G., solar plexus, instep, nose, groin." She looked at him surprised. "You don't know it? I'd give you a quick demonstration except I'm a bit tied up right now." Her face cracked into a broad smile of amusement as she watched the detective flounder for words obviously perplexed.

Unable to hold it in anymore her eyes twinkled and she allowed a burst of laughter to escape.

Looking abashed he attempted a smile. "That was a joke, right?"

"Yes. That was a joke."

"You're obviously feeling better. Pleased I can keep you amused."

"Thank you, I'm not feeling so pathetic. Not sure if it's your company or the drugs." She had been aware that he had not been the usual self-assured DCI Cooper she had become accustomed to since he had walked into the cubicle with her.

"Don't tell me you of all people are doubting your competency. I'm sure you are an extremely useful person to have around."

Through her haze of medication, she saw a sadness in his eyes. Ever since he had arrived and found Aoife stretched out on the bed, her arm bandaged, her face bruised and swollen and two fresh stitches above her left brow he had looked deflated. She'd seen him tired before, and he no doubt had a lot on his mind, but this was different.

"Of course not." Aoife looked embarrassed "Although I am feeling shaken." She tried to give him her most reassuring smile. "I took karate classes at uni. There had been a bunch of attacks on female students, so it seemed like a good idea. I kept it up in London for a while too."

"Did you do your grades?"

"Got to brown belt. Flunked out before the final hurdle. And it's not the same out of the dojo. No referee to stop one side or the other being beaten to a pulp."

"Brown belt sounds pretty good to me. It could be what saved you tonight."

"Yeah, well. As you say. It comes in useful." She waited to see if he had something else to say. He shuffled from foot to foot embarrassed.

"Are you busy at the moment?" She asked.

"Yes, of course, I should go. Let you rest." He took her question as a dismissal.

"Oh, that's a shame."

He looked at her bewildered. "Is there something you need?"

"Well, there is, but I don't want to pull you away from work."

"I can spare a minute. What would you like?"

"Actually, I was wondering if you could hang around for a while. Grab a cup of tea or something and just talk to me." She gave a shy grin. "I hadn't included being assaulted in my calculations when I moved to a new city where I know not a soul." She could feel tears prick the back of her eyes and she fought to blink them away. Benedict looked like a rabbit in headlights.

"Look I'm sorry. Just pathetic. You go please. Stupid of me." Aoife realised he would rather be anywhere other than at her bedside.

"Would you like a tea?"

"I hate vending machine tea, but hot chocolate would be nice."

"Of course. I'll be right back." He shot out of the cubicle obviously relieved to get away. Aoife decided a woman threatening tears was well outside his comfort zone.

On his return he placed two cups on the cabinet by the bed. Removed his coat and manoeuvred a small table until it was comfortably over Aoife's lap.

"Here, I put extra sugar in it. Careful it is hot." He placed the cup in front of her. Before taking the visitors chair and sitting down.

"Thank you." Aoife noticed some of his vigour had returned. Amazing what a difference feeling useful can make she thought idly.

"You were right. The two young men who drowned in the water twelve years ago. Both of them used to play youth football. Both of them had tried to report Patel. Nothing was done."

"Habib was their coach?"

"Yes. I've got DC Hyslop contacting the club to get all the contact details of kids and other coaches from Habib's time there. Superintendent James is talking with his bosses and relevant charities in the area about setting up an incident room and helpline for anyone who wants to come forward."

"It's a big club. There could be dozens of children affected over the fourteen years he and Liam were there."

"I know. We're preparing for people who were affected at Poppy Hill too."

"It's hard to believe they got away with it for as long as they did."

"A mixture of threats, complicity, shame and general disbelief from people with a duty of care who should know better."

"I guess late is better than never. But shit!" Aoife yawned.

"Tired?"

"I've got a pleasant cocktail of drugs pumping through me helping me to relax."

"What's the plan? Are you being discharged tonight?"

"I wish. They're worried about concussion. It wasn't even my head that got hit." She said holding up her bandaged arm.

Benedict looked pointedly at the stitches above her eyebrow. "Those drugs really are strong if you've forgotten that gash and the very large bruise on the side of your head."

She put a tentative finger up to prod the cut. "That's not really my head more my cheek, and it was only a glancing blow."

"I'd offer you a bed at mine, but I've got to get back to work."

Aoife smiled "I'll be fine here. I am so tired it won't much matter where I am. Anyway, twice in two weeks and people will start to talk."

His smile was gentle. "Is there anything else I can get you?"

"No. I'll be fine. You get off. I think I need to sleep."

She heard his voice as he walked away. Talking to one of the nurses perhaps. As she closed her eyes tears ran down her cheeks. To Aoife's surprise she felt someone squeeze her hand. Her eyes shot open. And she saw Benedict standing back by her bed.

"We all have bad days," he said softly. "The key is to have a better day, tomorrow." She watched him as he picked up his coat and left the ward.

CHAPTER 44.

RECUPERATION

Armed with pain killers and a fresh dressing for her wound, Aoife had caught a taxi home from the hospital. Carefully shrugging off her coat, she took a deep breath and looked out of the picture window.

She was tired as she trudged up the wooden staircase to the third floor. To her retreat. Swinging around the final balustrade she headed to the nearest Dorma window and turning the lever up, she pushed it open. The air was cool, and she felt herself shiver but didn't move away. She looked out across the roof tops across Bristol, her own small garden far below and felt comforted.

This was not the first time she had investigated people who wished her harm. It was not the first time she had been threatened. It made her determined not intimidated. She was concerned for Keeley, Daisy, Mahira and Hiran. They had trusted her, and she would not let them down. She had committed to supporting the young people who had been so atrociously pushed to one side and ignored for the benefit of middle aged men. Not telling their story would be the worst crime.

Aoife liked to take care of herself. She portrayed the image as a capable confident woman and she liked it, but as she trudged back downstairs to turn the kettle on she thought how nice it would be to have someone make her a cup of tea and care for her while she curled up in a chair with a book or the remote control.

When Leigh had visited, her friend had managed to refrain

from spouting the actual words, but they both knew they had been in Leigh's thoughts. Knew the question had been implied. It was a question many had asked in different ways over the years. Why did she not have a man by her side? The presumption that an able, intelligent and single female must be in search of a man to give her existence meaning felt to Aoife like a Charlotte Bronte novel. To others it was a simple fact of life.

Following a life filled with adventure, hardships and hope. The creation and extraction of value. Aoife felt she had barely begun to scratch the surface of her own story. Perhaps one day it would be worth the telling in its own right. To do it justice would mean opening up and baring her soul. Something she wasn't sure she'd ever be prepared to do. She had not found the one person with whom she could share such intimacies, to lay her soul bare for others to dissect was an impossible prospect. More important to Aoife would be to look back at a life well lived.

She took her tea upstairs and read through the notes she had written up so far. She tried typing up a report on last night's incident, but her arm soon ached, so she chose a notebook and a couple of pencils and went back downstairs to the settee and wrote her thoughts the old fashioned way.

At some point she fell asleep because she woke with a start and realised she was cold. She put a match to the fire already set in the wood burning stove and settled down once more with a blanket over her knees. She felt cosy and enclosed in the warm glow of the corner lamp and looked forward to spending the evening reading a book. She was wondering what she should do about supper and had just shoved her feet into her old, furry slippers to go and see what she could find in the kitchen, when her phone rang again. Aoife noticed she was pleased to hear Ben's voice. So much for enjoying her own company.

"I just wanted to check you are O.K."

"Yep. All fine here."

"I hope you've managed to get some rest and that take away pizza."

She could hear the smile in his voice. "Rest yes. Soup and ice cream though not pizza. Have you made any progress with the thug?"

"Yes. Quite a bit. Look if you've not made any arrangements for supper yet, I could bring something over and give you a quick update. Unless of course you've stuffed so much ice cream your full up."

Aoife hesitated a moment. She was curled under a furry blanket, wearing leggings and an old hoody. She had bathed but hadn't managed to wash her hair because of the stitches in her forehead and the bandage on her arm. It made her feel vulnerable and she wasn't sure her relationship with the Detective Inspector was on that sort of footing. He picked up on the silence and guessed what was going through her mind.

"And when I get there I expect to find you in your most comfy old sweater and wrapped in a duvet."

"You won't be disappointed on that front. I haven't worked out how to wash my hair with one hand while avoiding the gash on my head."

"Don't worry about anything, we've all been there. Which would you prefer pizza or noodles?"

"I think pizza lends itself to curling up on the sofa best."

"I'll be about an hour if that's alright?"

"Sounds good. And thank you."

"It's purely for selfish reasons. A fresh brain. You might think of something we've missed. Plus, it gets me away from here and any excuse for eating pizza."

When Aoife awoke the next morning she was aware that she looked a mess. Tired from a poor night's sleep in the hospital the night before and her body's need to mend, she had fallen asleep within minutes of her head hitting the pillow. However, the left side of her face was bruised and swollen, and her bandaged arm tender. Each time she rolled over in her sleep she was pulled sharply awake by a shooting pain or aching limb. Aoife was young, fit and healthy and the doctors were sure her body would heal quickly. But right now, her head felt stuffed with cotton wool, and she was conscious that every muscle was complaining as her body strove to mend the damage.

Having wriggled into a full length kimono she padded to the kitchen where Benedict was preparing breakfast. He had brought pizza the night before as promised and Aoife had opened a bottle of wine which they had consumed while sitting in comfortable chairs in the front room. Half a bottle of wine into the evening Benedict claimed he had drunk too much to drive home, which was true, but she knew that this was a contrived excuse. The thought that he was worried about her being left alone on her first night out of hospital brought a smile to her lips.

As much as she appreciated his concern, she was not looking forward to facing him in her kitchen first thing, while she was feeling so rough. Aoife walked downstairs holding the banister as she went. The smell of coffee and the thought of painkillers pulling her on. Too late she realised her hair was unbrushed and there was only a thin piece of cotton between her naked body and the rest of the world.

He turned to her as she entered. "I heard you moving around. I'm sorry if I disturbed you."

"No. I was drifting in and out of sleep." She said distractedly.

"I made breakfast. Cheese omelette and toast. I hope that's OK?" He pulled slices of toast onto two plates. "I do have a larger repertoire, but I knew you ate omelettes and cheese."

"Thank you. You didn't have to." She hugged her arms over her chest.

"Yes I did. I'm hungry." He laughed. "Not much chance of a proper lunch break. Anyway, you need to eat."

"You're very kind. I've been in hospital twice in the last ten years. Both times you've been in attendance."

"Are you saying I'm a bringer of bad luck?"

"I'm saying I'm normally good at looking after myself."

"I'm sure you are." He had made a sandwich out of his omelette and was busy wrapping it in paper towel.

"But it's nice getting my breakfast cooked, and it's very kind of you to look after me."

"I only stayed because I have no food in my house." He teased.

"Breakfast to go?"

"Sorry, yes." He picked up his coffee and leaning his back against the work surface, studied Aoife.

"What?" she said "I look a mess. You're making me feel embarrassed."

"I had a phone call before you got up."

"And?"

"A body's been washed up on Kilve Beach. Female. Asian. She's been in the water a long time, so we'll have to wait for the post-mortem to identify her."

"You think it's Iqra Aziz."

"Too soon to tell, but there's a strong possibility."

"Shit!" Aoife closed her eyes. Perhaps in an attempt to shut the world out. She had never met the woman, but she felt as though she had got to know her."

"I thought you'd want to know."

"Thank you. Strange that it should appear after all this time."

"Apparently it was wrapped in several layers of plastic and oil cloth. Looks as though it was weighted down. It wasn't supposed to be discovered but somehow it broke free."

"Are you going to tell Harrison Tomlin?"

"Not yet. No point in upsetting him until we're sure. By the way, we have stationed a police car outside to keep an eye on things here."

"Here?" Aoife looked shocked. "You think they're going to try again?"

"Probably not, but it would be better if you didn't go anywhere today."

"Don't worry, I don't think my body would allow me to go anywhere. I can keep myself amused and fed without leaving the house."

Benedict smiled. "OK I'm off." He collected up his wallet, keys and mobile from the table. and with the briefest of ceremony, was gone.

Aoife locked the door behind him. As she walked back along the hallway, unable to move with any elegance, she hobbled back to the kitchen to pour more coffee. Her muscles would eventually start to warm up and relax. Recuperation from the extreme emotional turmoil was not going to be so straight forward.

Aoife ran herself a hot bath, partly to ease some of her aching muscles and because a shower was out of the question while she had bandages covering open wounds on her arm and head. She poured in a handful of bath salts and took pleasure in watching the bubbles build. It reminded her of her childhood.

Lying in the hot, steamy water she closed her eyes and allowed her mind to wander, letting the warmth and fragrance do their work. She thought back to the large bath she had shared with Cameron Connery. Their clandestine meetings as they tried to get to know each other without the intrusion of the press had involved staying indoors, mainly at his house. Both being fundamentally private people, this restriction hadn't bothered either of them. They had found plenty of ways to amuse themselves and keeping their relationship a secret gave an added frisson of excitement.

Aoife remembered the day they had walked down the road together for the first time. It was a Sunday morning in early Autumn as they strolled beneath ice blue skies through the streets of West London. A sharp breeze whisked up golden leaves and grit from the pavement and grass bank causing them to keep their heads down, leaning into each other for support, as they walked into the wind. Aoife remembered the warmth of his skin as his hand enfolded hers. The comfort of his body leaning into her as they sauntered along, and the sheer joy of just being together.

They had browsed a second-hand bookshop which was to become a regular place for them to search for treasures on a Sunday morning. Aoife had been excited by bookshops from a little girl, enthralled by the infinite worlds waiting to be discovered. The simple smell of old books made her happy.

"You know, I don't think I could be with a man that didn't like books" she said.

Cameron had stroked the back of her hand. She remembered how her skin had tingled its response. "We have nothing to worry about there. I've been known to spend a whole weekend by myself caught in the magic of a book." They had always left the shop with at least one book each, sometimes an armful.

As she lay alone in her bath Aoife found herself close to tears. The memories bitter-sweet and totally pointless, had a sneaky habit of creeping in when she was vulnerable. She was feeling sorry for herself. The attack had left her feeling shakier than she had anticipated. Pulling the plug from the bath she called to her smart speaker to turn on BBC Radio Two and forced her mind to travel to more productive thoughts.

Feeling better, with clean body and fresh clothes, she made her way to her desk.

She liked the well-ordered office she had assembled in the attic room. Surrounded by bookcases, a printer sat on top of a black metal filing cabinet, and her desk was placed in front of the window to get the best view. Normally she found the quiet of the house coupled with the serenity of the view aided her thinking. Her brain filled the silence and her mind whirred comfortably from one thought to the next with her fingers flying over the keyboard trying to keep pace. She never felt lonely as the days rushed past.

She sat down in the expensive ergonomic desk chair she had invested in, opened her laptop and let her gaze wander across the distant view. She found little joy in the scene in front of her. She looked higher over the grey sky that threatened rain. Like a tongue pushing at a sore tooth her mind wandered inevitably back to the attack and the violence that had ensued. She had escaped remarkably lightly. She had been lucky. Her injuries were not serious, and her bath, coupled with the pain killers that were coursing through her system, had eased her muscles to the point where the pain didn't distract her. She knew that not all the damage could be healed with stiches or pain killers and there was no doubt in her mind that being stopped in the street by a lout almost twice her size was emotionally traumatic. She had been in Bristol for less than two months and had already made enemies. She was also concerned that if Hiran and Daisy had found their way to her door then others could too.

As she relived those terrifying moments she felt a familiar tension in her muscles and a tightening of her stomach. Her body preparing to fight whatever it was that was coming her way. Or was it a symptom of being on her own?

She had friends. Leigh had called for a chat yesterday and it had taken all Aoife's powers of persuasion to stop her immediately hopping on a train to Bristol. She managed to put her off by convincing Leigh that she had enough supplies to last a couple of days and really just wanted to sleep. It would be a waste of a precious weekend. A visit in a week's time would be much more rewarding for both of them.

Perhaps she should have accepted Leigh's offer to visit. She looked at her watch. Not yet seven. Too early to call. This time on a Saturday morning most people would be fast asleep, their limbs entwined with lovers, enveloped in the warmth of bed and the comfort of naivety.

She restlessly left the desk and walked back to her bedroom. She looked across to her own bed. The duvet still formed the shape of a nest. She pulled off her shirt and trousers and snuggled back in. She was tired. Perhaps some more sleep would help her reset her brain. Benedict was right, there was no shame in spoiling herself for a day.

When she had first woken up in hospital, still tired and sore, she had been forced to question her decision to move to a city a hundred miles from the people she knew. The anxiety introduced to her system the night before had not completely drained away and the thought of no one on hand to care for her or cheer her up sent a tremor right through her and she had struggled to keep tears from falling yet again.

She'd forced herself to think back to the reasoning behind her decision to move. For twelve years she had loved the hum and urgency of her life in London. A drink with colleagues in the wine bar after work. The thrill of the London theatres or catching the latest film releases. Even the great monoliths of concrete that hid her from the real world by day, had their attraction. And at night, as she walked along the Southbank or stood on Waterloo Bridge, London was undeniably, breathtakingly, impressively beautiful in its own way. So many twinkling lights. So much amazing architecture and history.

As she'd grown older, or perhaps grown up, she'd relied on her weekends surfing or hiking to get her through the week. She'd spent more time looking up to the sky to let her know that the world was not just shades of grey. She gravitated more and more to the many parks that London is blessed with.

Then she forced herself to look at the life she had forged and the restrictions she had accepted. To most eyes she had a dream life, but to her own, it had become an intolerable treadmill. People around her constantly wanted more 'things' only to throw them away a year or two later without considering the waste or the damage they were doing to the world. Aoife found it distasteful and had longed for open spaces and a simpler life.

The discovery that Cameron had been unfaithful gave her the final nudge she'd needed to escape. It was not practical for her to live in the middle of nowhere so in the end she had settled for Bristol. A much smaller, cleaner city surrounded by stunning countryside. And a hundred miles away from Cameron Connery.

Thinking back induced the old feelings of frustration and resentment which were brimming to the surface. Giving the lie to her belief that she'd put it all behind her. It was still there, deep down. The gaping hole in her heart that had not healed. However much she had tried to fool herself that it was in the past didn't matter, she knew it was untrue.

Behind her tough exterior she had always been too quick to love and slow to judge. In some ways this sensitive side had helped her writing, enabled her to see beyond the façade others raised to hide their true story. It also attracted her to people who were damaged and dangerous to know.

In the beginning she had been the classic 'other woman'. Swept up in the warmth of his enthusiasm to see her. The phone calls at all times of day and night, the urgent sex when they did meet and the weekends away or the trips abroad. She had been keen to be part of his life and eventually she had fallen in love.

And then she found out that she wasn't to be the only 'other woman' in Cameron's life. He chose to ignore the devastation he caused others as he stomped through their lives. Aoife forced herself to see that he was not the kind and caring man she had imagined. He was shallow and careless, and, in the end it hadn't been difficult to pack her bags and close the relationship down.

Now here she was exhausted and still very much alone, trying to figure out her place in the world.

Despite that hard lesson she was still willing to walk the extra mile for people in need of help. She realised it kept her apart from her friends, but she would rather be comfortable with who she was, than mould herself into the vision others wanted of her.

Two hours and another sleep later she got out of bed feeling less troubled. She spent the rest of the day on the settee, reading and watching undemanding films. Occasionally she went to the kitchen for snacks and cups of tea, but she didn't cook anything challenging. As she stood in her kitchen nibbling on a piece of orange her phone rang. She looked at the screen as she picked it up.

"Mum!"

"Hello baby girl. I hear you've been in the wars." Eva Macarthy's voice was both gentle and strong, resetting Aoife's mind back to its childhood self.

"How do you know?"

"Luckily you have friends who are more communicative than you. I'm just walking along your road. Thought I'd better call ahead to give you time to hide anything you'd rather I didn't see." Aoife recognised the teasing jollity in her mother's voice.

"You're here? In Bristol?"

"Less than two minutes away – unless you'd prefer it if I did a turn around the block?"

Aoife laughed. "No. The place is a mess but nothing you're not used to." She walked to her front door and opened it, looking eagerly down the road. She could just make out the tall, upright figure of her mother.

CHAPTER 45.

DIANA HARVEY

Diana Harvey stood in the centre of her small garden, secateurs in hand, and did a full three-sixty. At this point it would be very easy to go back indoors and make herself a cup of coffee, and she was tempted.

She'd got up this morning with fresh determination and donned her old jeans and sweatshirt, shoved her feet in her walking boots and was now trying to envision being surrounded by a beautiful oasis of flowers, grass and trees with a soft breeze filled with the scent of honeysuckle and lavender.

Having decided to start with the many overgrown Buddleia, she took a deep breath and pushed her way to the far wall through what once, presumably, had been a vegetable patch. This was the best time of year to cut it back and still get a reasonable show in the summer of beautiful purple blooms that would attract butterflies. Meanwhile her little dog, Tangle, busied himself happily exploring amongst the overgrown bushes and chasing down the thrilling scent of wild animals.

She moved on from the buddleia to climbing roses, which she knew should be clipped back in autumn, but needs must. After two hours of cutting and trimming she fetched a spade and fork and set to work on the vegetable garden, digging and turning the soil until her back started to complain and her water bottle, from which she had taken many large gulps, was empty. She stood up and wiped the sweat that covered her face on the back of her sleeve. Looking around once more she smiled. The garden was still a wild, rambling chaos, but it was hers and she loved it.

Diana had been relieved and amazed that Michael had agreed to the idea of a divorce. Married for twenty-five years she had become used to his bombastic, arrogant and controlling ways, learning to simply keep her head down and avoid arguments. He had always been on his best behaviour around the people in power and his co-workers. He relished his image as a formidable man, benevolent to his family, giving expensive presents and providing a lavish lifestyle. He had chosen and paid for extravagant holidays, and he had required Diana to wear the exquisite jewellery he supplied when they went out with friends, but the rest was all a façade.

It made life easier to go along with it, and she'd had their two children to think of too. Now the children had both left home. Dominic, their youngest and at university, was still dependant on hand outs from his father. Daniella, much to her father's disgust, had gone her own way, and having completed an art course, was enjoying life working as a receptionist in an art gallery in London. She was struggling to get by but refused to bow to her father's demands that she train to become a lawyer or accountant or something else he could brag about to his golf buddies.

It had taken Diana almost two decades to realise that the man who had appeared to be caring and concerned was in fact controlling and patronising. Continually eating away at her confidence and crippling her own personality until only a whisper of her old ambitions and desires remained. Even then, so low was her self-esteem that without Miriam Thornbeck's support and encouragement, she might not have found the courage to move from her husband's shadow.

This garden was the first project of her own since her early twenties, and she was determined it was going to be as far removed as possible from the well behaved flower beds and regimented shrubs bordering a lawn resembling Lords cricket ground, that her husband insisted upon in their marital home. There had been no enjoyment in her husband's design, no fun to be had from it by young children too scared to kick a football around in case they damage the daffodils. Its sole purpose was to show off Michael Harvey's wealth. Dogs and cats were out of the question in that manicured showhouse, no matter how much the children and their mother had pleaded.

Diana went indoors, made herself a cup of coffee and cut a large chunk of apple cake. A few minutes later, sitting at the small garden table she tried to concentrate on the pleasure of tired muscles from a job well done. She had to admit that in its current state the gardens unruliness was too extreme for comfort. More of a pandemonium than a consort of colour. But she wanted to keep some of its natural state. As she sat quietly enjoying the early Spring sunshine, she was aware of the postman pulling up outside her gate and Tangle rushed barking excitedly to defend his property.

Annoyingly she found her mind wandering back to a note that had appeared through her letterbox eight months ago. A plain brown envelope, her name written with a child's felt tip pen, the only marking on the outside. It must have been delivered by hand. At first she had thought it was from a friend of one of her children, although they were unlikely to have friends who wrote in such a childish style.

She had slit the envelope open and unfolded the single sheet of unlined paper. Before she had absorbed the meaning she knew there was something wrong. She was conscious of her stomach doing a flip. Slowly she made her eyes focus on the printed words.

DO YOU KNOW YOUR HUSBAND IS A PAEDOPHILE?

HE LIKES THEM VERY YOUNG

AND HE DOESN'T CARE WHAT DAMAGE HE CREATES.

She had stared down at the note for a long time. For some reason she could not grasp the implication, she was not shocked, although the content was as shocking a piece of news as she had ever received. She was horrified that she should have obtained, and be holding, such an appalling missive in her hands, but the content was only an affirmation of something, deep in the back of her thoughts, perhaps she already knew.

A moment later she felt a cold wave of revulsion and she had to resist the temptation to shove the paper back into the envelope and burn it. Her husband was controlling and manipulative. A bully with the ability to drain every drop of fun and goodwill out of any situation. She had disliked him for years, but had she known that he was a beast that prayed on children? She wasn't doubting the note for one second so surely that answered her question. In the back of her mind somewhere she had suspected.

She had been aware that her hands were shaking and wondered what best to do. Her thoughts fled to her children. She must keep them safe no matter what. At that point she realised she felt quite calm, and her plan became clear. She had to leave her husband and file for divorce. She was a relatively young woman still and she didn't want to squander any more precious time in a marriage that she had been too scared to admit had died fifteen years ago.

She must keep this letter a secret for now. If she showed it to Michael he would become aggressive and insist she tear it up. No, she would make good her escape and then she would think what to do with it.

Now in a home of her own and the children safely out of reach she decided that this was the time. She tipped her head back to allow her face to absorb the warmth from the sun. Her body relaxed and she felt remarkably calm in the knowledge that not only would this serve as a small revenge, it was, undoubtedly, the right thing to do. She remembered her mother's words many years ago after Diana had witnessed a friend bullying a younger child. "Darling, follow your conscience; however difficult it may be. No one can ask more of you."

She would take the letter to the police. It would be difficult explaining why she had waited so long but hopefully they would understand when they realised what sort of man she had been married too. Whatever happened next, she would not be that scared, subservient woman anymore and she was prepared for the consequences.

CHAPTER 46.

MIRIAM AND PETRA

When Petra Tomlin had received the call from Miriam Thornbeck it had taken her a moment to check her emotions. She had not seen Miriam or her family for almost a decade. When they were kids Petra, Keeley and Harrison had visited the Thornbeck's in their seaside house and spent afternoons on the beach with Molly and Charlotte, Douglas and Miriam's granddaughters, playing ball, making sandcastles and jumping waves just like thousands of other kids.

No one had ever commented on the photographs that were taken of the girls as they stripped off their sandy swimming costumes, or later when they prepared to jump in the bath. The hugs and the kisses as they sat on Griff and Mr Thornbeck's knee were accepted as fatherly love. As the girls got a little older they felt uncomfortable being naked in front of the men, but their requests for the men to leave went unheeded, and the touching became more personal. Then her father started to visit Petra in her bedroom at night and slide under the covers, telling her how much he loved her.

The morning following Miriam's phone call she had grabbed a shower, dressed in jeans and a soft brown sweater, left her children with their father, and caught the bus to the centre. Miriam had asked to meet Petra in one of the busy cafes on the Harbourside. She felt uneasy about the meeting, but another part of her was curious. Miriam had been a close friend of her mother for many years.

Miriam Thornbeck was already seated at a corner table at the back with a cup of coffee in front of her. She was wearing jeans and a dark blazer over a white cotton shirt. Her short white hair was soft and framed her face well. She looked tense as she raised a hand to beckon Petra.

"Petra, lovely to see you after all these years. You have grown into a beautiful young woman." Miriam stood to welcome her young friend. "Let me get you a coffee."

When she returned and had placed the cup in front of Petra she sat down and spent a moment shuffling in her seat to get comfortable. Petra decided to break the silence.

"I was surprised to hear from you after all this time. Are you still in Weston?"

"Yes. Sort of. Look it's difficult to find the words for what I have to say, so it seems false to mouth pleasantries. If you don't mind I'd rather just come out with it."

Petra took a sip of coffee "Right. If that's what you want." She gave Miriam a hard stare trying to brace herself for what she felt sure was coming next.

Miriam noticed the young woman's hand was shaking. "I know this won't be easy for you to hear but to cut a long story short and to start at the end, well the end for me anyway ...." She pulled out a manilla envelope and placed it on the table. "I found photographs in Doug's study. After Griff and Habib Patel were found dead, in the way they were, and with the rumours and everything, well my mind started pointing out things I had been uncomfortable about but had never really acknowledged. I don't know how else to put it.

Petra had frozen. Her gaze fixed on the brown envelope that lay on the table between them. She said nothing but in the few seconds of silence she raised her eyes to the white-haired woman's face. She wanted to slap it. This woman could have stopped what had happened to her. She should have protected her. Neither woman moved.

Eventually Miriam continued "Things started to slot into place. Small things that I remembered but had dismissed previously. But when you start to put all the dots together they aren't so little after all. It's enormous. I started looking when Doug was out. I found them under floorboards in his study." She looked at Petra's tense expression "You know what they are don't you?"

Petra realised she had been holding her breath and gasped at last to take in air. She looked down at the package and back up at her mother's friend and nodded. "Have you shown them to Molly and Charlotte?"

"Yes." Miriam felt suddenly exhausted. The adrenalin that had pumped through her veins to get her here had now deserted her, and she slumped back in her chair. "There is nothing I can say. I mean, I can say sorry. I am sorry, and appalled and shocked and sick and angry. I should have known at the time." Tears were starting to trickle down her old face. The two women sat in silence for what seemed like minutes.

At last Petra said, "I can't look at them."

"No. Of course not."

"But I'd like to take them."

"Of course. If you want to take them to the police I understand. I think you should. I almost did but I wanted you to know first." Miriam had gained some control over her voice and the tears had stopped. "There are others. Other pictures I mean. And other children. Did you know?"

Petra nodded "Yes."

"And your father, Griff? He was involved too?"

Another nod.

Miriam gasped, and her hand flew to her mouth as she looked on in horror. "Oh you poor child. Poor children. There are photos of black children too. From his work in Africa I guess. He was always so popular. Everyone loved him. Praised him for the wonderful work he did. I didn't look beyond." The tears started to flow again.

"No one did. It was a perfect cover. Those who tried to complain were bribed or threatened. Made to shut up." Petra placed the envelope in her shoulder bag and stood up. Her coffee was untouched.

Miriam automatically rose too. "Anything you want. Anything I can do, I will. I will go to the police if you would like me to."

Petra's voice was low and soft. "Miriam, there are a lot of victims in this. Most of them were children. And there are a lot of people to blame for letting this happen. The police, the church, the staff at the children's home, even doctors. I don't think you are one of them" She turned and walked quickly between the tables to the glass doors and the stairs beyond. She didn't say good-bye. She didn't turn back and wave.

Miriam waited five minutes then she left too.

CHAPTER 47.

MICHAEL HARVEY

On a sunny Saturday, a few days after Aoife's meeting with Isabelle at the refuge, a sixty-one-year-old businessman sat alone at one of the cafe's pavement tables overlooking the river on Bristol's refurbished harbourside. This man oozed confidence. He had the swagger of someone who gets his own way by fair means or foul. His hair was cut short and so blond that at a distance he looked bald. His shirt sleeves were rolled up to show thick forearms. A red and black tattoo of flames on his left arm. A small patch of sweat on his broad chest had seeped through to his pale blue shirt but he looked comfortable sitting in the midmorning sun.

As he stirred his coffee a group of wildly dressed youngsters walked along the covered paving. Students no doubt. He appreciated their commitment to their appearance. A tall black man dressed in deep burgundy baggy trousers and waistcoat, and another young man dressed like a musketeer each with their faces painted in vivid blues and deep reds. Two girls followed arm in arm, their faces painted white and decorated with oriental birds. At the rear were what looked like two Pierrots in black and white costumes.

Michael smiled. He had enjoyed living in Bristol and the energy the students brought. He looked out over the water while smugly reviewing his life and contemplating his upcoming retirement.

He liked people to think of him as a self-made man. To

some extent he was. Michael Harvey had started his business importing and exporting from scratch. He acknowledged that an expensive education at one of Britain's leading public schools had given him the advantage of the contacts he had found so useful throughout his career. His parents had left a reasonable inheritance to be split between him and his sister. His accountant had made sure that his tax bill had never been too burdensome. But the business had been all him.

He pulled out his iPhone to look again at the pictures of the villa on the Algarve, with sea views, that he was in the process of buying.

His had been a good life so far, and he planned for many more just as comfortable years to come. Buying the cottage in Devon for his wife had been a bargain. He had been lucky. She either had no idea of his true worth or had lost the motivation to fight him in the courts to get her hands on a larger share of his wealth. Or perhaps, she realised it was best to cut her losses and retire to the country without fuss.

Their children, now both grown and in careers of their own, would never be short of money, he'd see to that. He would also make sure that the other two, that neither of his legitimate children nor their mother knew about, would be looked after. Not because he was particularly fond of them, more that he didn't want them causing any problems, It was easier to pay them a relatively small amount than have them causing a public fuss or dig into his true situation.

All in all, he thought, life was pleasant. He considered himself to be fit, healthy and good looking. He'd got several years still in front of him and a lot to look forward to.

He had no idea that the young man and women sitting just a few metres away from him had no intention of letting him enjoy a long and happy retirement. They too appeared to be enjoying the sunshine as they sipped their coffee at one of the tables at a different café further along the river. They had both been children when Michael had last seen them, and now, ten years on, they were confident he wouldn't recognise either of them. Just to make sure the girl wore a short blond wig over her own darker locks, and the young man sported a close-cropped beard and a jaunty cap. Both sported dark glasses.

They watched on as Michael picked up his phone and answered the call they knew he would be receiving. They paid for their drinks and walked calmly arm in arm along the walkway past Michael's table and headed toward the car park where Michael had left his BMW. As they turned the corner they noticed the big man had lost a little of his "cool" and smiled as he irritably slugged down his coffee and collected sunglasses and keys from the table.

The business had really taken off when he had been approached by another "company" to use Michael's part empty containers that travelled back and forth across continents. It made economic sense to work with full capacity and the amount of money he had been offered came with at least one more "zero" on the end than he had been expecting, along with the unspoken expectation that no questions would be asked. Of course, he had heard of the 'Trojan Horse' method of smuggling goods and even people, to prevent anything looking unusual, provoking less question from customs and inspectors.

When Michael had expanded this import export business UK border inspection staff levels had been reduced by nearly 30% between 2010 and 2015, and although officer numbers were increasing again they were still insufficient to check all the cargo that passed through British ports. Preventing migrant smuggling by sea requires states to work together. With staff levels so low, efforts were channelled on intelligence led tip offs, and selected containers are searched based on this information and routing patterns. The timing had worked in his favour, but Michael was pleased to be getting out now while the going was good.

Michael Harvey had left the café and his pleasant mood, to drive the six miles to the Port of Bristol. He paid people to look after the mechanics of the business. Sorting out paperwork or whatever the problem was, definitely came under the remit of Jim Wainwright, his cargo manager. The phone call from one of Jim's underlings telling him that their boss had not turned up for work, and was not answering calls, was unusual. A first in fact. Jim had not answered Michael's call either. The hapless team did not understand the paperwork and, not wanting the responsibility if a mistake were made, insisted that he really had to see the problem for himself. Michael had made other plans for the day and sorting out someone else's balls-up would mean he would be late for his lunch date.

He knew his way around the port. In the early days he had felt a thrill when the first deliveries had arrived. While he never had any real need to be there and inspect the goods himself anymore, he had often found time to visit. This morning he was far from thrilled as he marched toward the containers in question. It was Sunday and the place was almost deserted. He turned the corner where he came face to face with two workers in full coveralls and face masks. He was suddenly aware of his muscles cramping and his legs gave way. His whole body seemed to spasm and then seize up. The first thought that went through his mind was "stroke!"

Michael fell, his mind tumbling through the darkness like a lump of clay, too startled to be truly scared. Before he could think any further he was aware of something soft clamped over is mouth and the world went away.

When he opened his eyes he was staring up at a face he didn't recognise. He was in some sort of dream. A whitened face, black diamonds dripping black and red tear drops over her eyes and blush-pink painted cheeks. Bright red lipstick in the shape of a heart. Her clothes were a loose white blouse with large buttons and wide white pantaloons. She pushed back the large white hood from her head to reveal a black skullcap concealing her hair.

He felt a chill shake his body although he was fairly sure it had been a sunny day, warm for the time of year. He moved to stretch his back. The surface beneath his shoulder blades and hips was hard and unforgiving. He struggled to move, to sit up, but found he couldn't move either his hands or feet as plastic bindings dug painfully into his wrists and ankles at each tug.

Tipping her head to one side in a robotic movement the

Pierrot whispered "Can you smell it? Death? This is the site of your latest murders. It's so humdrum - and cruel and totally abhorrent. We thought leaving you here was appropriate. You should feel right at home with the ghosts of the men, women and babies whose lives you have stolen."

"I haven't murdered anyone."

Anna tilted her head slightly to one side. Even through the make-up he saw the look of repugnance. If she was looking for a sign of remorse, a niche for weakness, well she was going to be disappointed. He wasn't going to give them that satisfaction. Who did they think he was? He regretted nothing.

Harvey had misread her. Her gaze was not from someone searching for remorse. She knew that was pointless. She was sure in another life he would do it all again. He was without compassion. The real purpose behind her stare was to see what sort of monster thought the acceptable price for the latest BMW was the enslavement and torture of young children. The devastation he had caused to countless numbers of people fleeing from one hell to find themselves in another paid for his membership at the Wentworth Golf Club.

"Oh, but you have." She said knowingly in a sing-song vice. "One man, two women, a six year old child and a baby all died from cold and starvation in this very container." She uncurled her fingers as she counted off the victims. "But don't worry. You will pay for your weaknesses and the appetites you indulged."

She looked back over her shoulder and outlandish looking people clad from head to toe in blue suits, painted faces and masks stepped into view. "You know everyone here – intimately." She laughed. Her voice shrill. "People claimed we'd get over it. They said we were only young. Things will get better over time. It's not true you know. But I think maybe today is the day that just might help the healing."

"I don't know what you're talking about. You're past has nothing to do with me." His voice remained strong, although in the back of his mind something was telling him that perhaps his own past was about to catch up with him.

"We all know that's not true Michael don't we? The police will know too, and you will lose everything."

"You will not get away with this. You are not clever enough. Then it will be you who will be sent back to whichever sewer you crept out from."

"Such cliches. I really expected better from you Mr Harvey. Do you think I am afraid? I have nothing to lose." Her voice was eerily soft and child-like. "As for being clever, well, several of your colleagues have already been brought down because they underestimated us."

They watched as some of the fight left Michael's face and fear took over. "I don't know who you mean."

"Griff Tomlin, Habib Patel, Liam Knapp. Ring any bells? Even the mighty Douglas Thornbeck, although he doesn't know it yet. And then there was the bonus of the ex-superintendent Mewse. Nothing to do with us, but nice."

One of the young men joined in "You thought it was so easy to bully children. You call yourself a businessman? You forgot to plan for the future. We are not little children anymore. We have planned for this day for the whole of our adult lives."

"Do make yourself comfortable Michael. You will be waiting here a while." A girls voice nearby joined in.

"What for? What am I waiting for?"

"The police." The Pierott paused, cocked her head to one side, a finger to her lips as if to think "Or death, whichever comes sooner." She smiled at the look of horror on his face.

"Oh, I almost forgot." The young woman pulled a knife from her pocket, leant down and pushed the point into the older man's groin, just far enough to pierce the delicate flesh.

"No! Please no." Then he screamed in pain and fear as blood spread across his trousers. One of the blue suits stuffed a dirty smelling rag in his mouth.

"Oops. Did that hurt?" The Pierott withdrew the blade from his balls and slit through the expensive material of his trousers and underpants with ease as he squirmed in pain and frustration.

The blue suits tugged at the material and with his trousers

and pants around his ankles he noticed a blue suited young woman shake a can of spray paint. It was offered to the Pierott who hovered smiling above him for a moment before she shook her head and said,

"You may have the honour."

The red liquid sprayed liberally over his thighs and stomach, not bothering to avoid the cut inflicted on his balls. Blood mixed with red paint on the floor.

"Now all you have to do is wait. Maybe hope the police get here before it's too late. Gets cold enough to kill people in these things. The thirst will probably be worst though."

The Pierott leant down and removed the rag from Harvey's mouth. "Anything you would like to say before we leave?" she smiled.

"You can't leave me here to die." He tried to hang on to his usual authority, but his voice betrayed him. "You'll be done for murder."

Anna smiled down at him "I was waiting for death most of my life. It would have been preferable to the hell you put me through. And then I found a reason for living. Revenge may not be everything, but I feel a lot better knowing that you will suffer. Not as you made so many young lives suffer of course, but it will be fun to watch everything stripped from you. Your friends, your family, home, money and your precious reputation. Most of all your life. You will know what it is like to have your freedom taken from you while you are still living. You are going to jail for a very, very, *very* long time. And the world will know you for the scum you are."

"You won't get away with this. No one will believe you!" He shouted at their backs as his jailors started to leave.

"Oh, I think they will." Said a male blue suit. He unzipped his coverall and pulled a small package from inside." Opening the envelope, he removed a series of photographs and held them, one after the other, for Harvey to see before giving them to one of his colleagues. Each was a black and white picture of young children and teenagers, naked. Some were sitting on a man's knee, also naked. Several were performing disgusting acts. Many of them had caught the tattoo on the man's left arm. Flames of red and black.

The colour from Harvey's face drained. "It means nothing."

The next photo clearly showed the blonde hair and profile of Michael Harvey as he fondled a young girl's undeveloped breast.

Each of the pictures were stuck to the walls of the crate with blue tack. No more words were said. The remainder of Douglas Thornbeck's private collection were scattered on the floor.

One of the men pinched Harvey's nose and stuffed the old rag back into his mouth before they all turned, closed the container and quickly walked away, leaving Michael Harvey, in darkness to contemplate his future.

The team had always planned to leave Michael to live, which is why they had left him until last. There was a chance that he would recognise one of them or provide some detail to the police that would give them away, but they doubted it. Michael had never dirtied his hands with sourcing the children, he simply paid for his pleasure and this team had been chosen because they had not run up against Michael Harvey for many years. It was unlikely that he had ever known any names or where they came from.

It was even less likely that anyone else would come forward with that information to help the police with their prosecution or his defence. To do so would be to admit knowledge and compliance. The children that had known Michael Harvey though, did not forget him. This man. who had stolen their childhood. He had been vicious and destructive and profited financially from their pain. They had decided that for him death would be too easy. Watching everything around him crumble and to undergo the shame would be far more fitting.

CHAPTER 49.

DAISY

The sea had been chilly, but the sky was blue, and a bright spring sun was encouraging the white blossoms on the blackthorn bushes, yellow cowslips and dandelions and startling bluebells to open.

It was Monday morning but the Porthcawl beach was starting to fill with families making the most of the Easter holiday, and the surf school began their lessons. Time for the serious surfers to leave. Aoife was securing her surfboard to the roof of her car, her short hair wet and her cheeks glowing after two hours in the water, when her mobile rang. She checked the caller ID.

"Hi Daisy. How ..."

Daisy's panicked voice cut her short. "Aoife. You have to get DCI Cooper to the port now. There's something going on and it's bad."

"Aoife got into the driving seat of her car "Why? What's happening?"

"I got a phone call. They've trapped Michael Harvey in a cargo container. I tried to get Cooper, but they put me through to a woman. She said she'd take care of it. Told me not to tell you. She didn't want the press involved."

"OK. Fair enough. I'm not popular with a lot of officers."

"No!" Daisy almost screamed. "You have to tell Cooper and Sergeant Goss. They have to be there."

"I don't understand."

"I recognised her voice. The policewoman on the phone. She's one of them! You've got to stop her. She's on their side."

Aoife didn't know exactly what Daisy was trying to say but she had a good idea. Adrenalin started pumping as she turned on the car engine and switched the call to hands free.

"OK Daisy. I need you to tell me what you know and where you told her to go."

Five minutes later Aoife still hadn't got through to Benedict, but she had left a voice message on his mobile telling him what had happened. She'd also spoken to a highly irritated Aida Goss.

Assistant Superintendent Taylor had told Sergeant Goss to stay put and await further instructions, then left the office with a small group of uniformed police officers. No one at the station knew where she'd gone or why. Aoife filled in the gaps.

"Shit! Shit!" Was Goss's first reaction as her own mind buzzed into action. "How sure is Daisy that she recognised Taylor's voice?"

"Enough to set her into a blind panic when she heard it. And why has Taylor gone off and left you behind?"

"OK. Leave it with me."

"And where's Benedict?"

"He's on his way back from some remote village in The Chiltern's."

"Morning off?"

There was a moments silence while Goss considered telling Aoife about Father Rowan. "We had another body."

Aoife gasped "In the Chiltern's?"

"Yeah. An adult. Could be another copycat."

Aoife gave a sigh of relief "If Daisy's right and it sounds as though she could be, someone needs to get to the docks before the evidence is gone."

"Leave it with me." Goss started running out of the office "You sound as though you're in your car. I hope you're not thinking of going there."

"Well, I did think of it, but I am in Porthcawl."

"Good. Stay there. Got to go." The line went dead.

CHAPTER 50.

THE PORT

A ssistant Superintendent Alison Taylor had been to Avonmouth Docks a couple of times before but was pleased to see one of Harvey's men waiting for her as the two police cars pulled up to the gates. Two thousand six hundred acres of storage and warehousing was a lot of land to get lost in. One of them waved her through the other jumped into the back seat of her black 4x4 as soon as she slowed down.

She parked close by the container that her guide pointed out. She checked It's ISO code against the one she had written down from Daisy's message.

As the men opened it up it took Taylor a moment to control her features. A body was prostrate on the floor surrounded by a large pool of red. Whoever it was, had obviously defecated and the smell hit her as soon as she stepped inside. Michael Harvey stared at her through dazed eyes. Over forty hours to contemplate his future had had an effect. Fear and then embarrassment covered his face.

He disgusted her at the best of times and right now she couldn't look at him. "Get him out as quick as you can." She snapped. She looked down at his naked groin. "And cover him up for fuck's sake. I take it that is paint not blood."

She put her forearm over her nose and mouth to try and filter the smell of sweat and faeces as she walked to the far end of the container. Someone had stuck photographs on the walls.

Harvey, now standing with a blanket wrapped around him,

had regained a smidgen of dignity, and was fuming. "I will get each of those cock arsed little fuckers and make them wish they'd chucked themselves in the canal years ago. "

Most of the pictures were of naked children posing in lewd positions or teenagers touching each other. Some had pictures of men in them doing things with the children that made the hardened police officer feel physically sick.

She turned round to the men her face dark with rage and marched up to Harvey. He never saw it coming so took the full force of the punch that landed on his nose. AS Taylor was a stocky woman and did not mess around with girly slaps. Harvey stumbled backwards, his head hitting the metal wall with a thud.

"You deserve everything you get and more after what you've done. You disgust me. All of you. I should lock the door and leave you all here for Cooper to find."

For once Michael Harvey was speechless. No one spoke to him like that. Ever.

"I assume you've arranged a bolt hole overseas and your passport is up to date" She spat.

He nodded. "I have clothes in the car."

"Then just get out. Don't stop to pack. Don't go back to your house, don't say goodbye to anyone just get some new pants and trousers and get out of here. Get on the next aeroplane – or better still, ship. Don't leave the docks."

The man who had guided them through the port took Harvey's arm and started to lead him out. Harvey shook the man off and turned around to face Taylor. "I will not let this go unpunished."

Taylor walked up to him and standing toe to toe she said calmly and firmly. "You will. You will get your arse off my patch, and you will let these kids go. Do I make myself clear?" She spat in his face and turned to her officers. "Get this place cleared up as best you can. We need to get out of here."

∆∆∆

The convoy of three marked cars, a plain car and a van tore along the A4 Portway road toward the docks, lights and sirens blazing. Aida Goss, who had passed her car advanced driving with flying colours, drove the unmarked BMW.

As they neared the port the instruction was given to kill the sirens. Two cars and the officers remained just inside the barrier blocking any other vehicles from entering or leaving. A heavy man in overalls and high viz vest jumped into the lead vehicle and guided the remaining group through the maze of containers to the destination that Daisy had given.

A marked police car could be seen parked. A little further on a light blue container was open. Armed uniformed officers spilled out of the van and one of the cars, keeping low as they ran to points of cover around the open container.

AS Taylor strode out, head held high "What the fucks going on?" she yelled.

"We brought some back up. Thought you could do with some help." Answered Goss.

"I told you to stay put." The older woman's face was puce with rage. Her voice set to intimidate. "What the hell do you think you're doing dragging half the force out on the whim of a misguided slut?"

"You forgot to mention it to forensics. They're on their way." Goss remained cool but didn't move further forward.

"They're on their way 'Mam!' The Assistant Superintendent strutted menacingly forward "Have you lost the plot Goss."

"No. Just doing my job. Giving you assistance."

As she spoke the armed officers had crept behind her and into the container. Their voices could now be heard yelling instructions "On your belly! Hands behind you head! Now! Move!"

"What the ...?" The AS turned and started to run toward the noise.

"Leave it Alison." A deep voice from one of the marked cars stopped her in her tracks and Superintendent James stepped out stretching straight backed to his full height. They are acting on my instructions." He nodded to Goss who, with the unarmed officers close by, walked to the edge of the container.

"He's not here gov." She called out.

"Where is he?" Asked James calmly as he approached his second in command.

"We missed him. Only just by the look of things." Said Tayor as her boss passed her to enter the container. "I warn you, it's not pretty in there."

"They were trying to clear up but definite red paint on the floor." Said Goss. She held up something in a gloved hand. "And photos of children. Not the sort their parents would display on the living room mantlepiece." She glared at Taylor.

"This doesn't look good for you Alison, don't make it worse. Where is Michael Harvey." Said James. Taylor didn't answer.

Dr Nick Cartwright got out of the van that had pulled up while they were talking. "Do you have a body for me?"

"Do we?" James asked the AS. Calmly.

She shrugged. "Not seen one."

He turned to the tall blond detective seconded from Portishead "Caution her, cuff her and put her in the van."

"Yes sir."

Twenty minutes later with all of Taylor's team cuffed and in the van Superintendent James stood next to Aida Goss.

"This is a sad day Sergeant Goss."

"Yes Sir."

"But that doesn't take away from the fact that you did a good job. You're quick thinking and determination means we've got some of these monsters locked up."

"Thank you sir. It's also thanks to Daisy Marston. If she hadn't recognised AS Taylor's voice they'd have got away."

"You're right. But that doesn't take away from the part you played. It's not easy to question the decisions of a higher ranking officer."

A car pulled up behind and they both turned to see Benedict get out.

"Acting DCI Cooper. Welcome to the party, although I think we've pretty much wrapped things up except for the forensics."

"Sir." Smiled Cooper.

"We missed Michael Harvey though. We've got a BOLO and all ports out for him and his car. He can't have got far.

Cooper's smile widened. "He didn't make it out of the Port. The uniforms you left on the gate spotted him and were chasing him down as I arrived."

"Ha!" shouted James. "Today just got better."

"He wasn't going far in his car anyway. Someone slashed all his tyres."

CHAPTER 51.

DIANA

Diana smoothed her hair as she stepped through the glass doors. For all the world she appeared the calm, sophisticated, lady with poise. Inside her stomach flipped as she hesitated, took a deep breath and straightened her back.

DC Hyslop arrived to greet her. His self-assurance irritated many women, and he made it worse by not noticing their disapproval. Diana instantly felt defensive as he put his hand out to greet her, holding back for a second, wondering if she had made a mistake by coming. Together they entered a small, simply furnished meeting room. Left alone, she did not sit, but checked her lipstick and hair in a small mirror, returning it to her handbag in time to turn and walk toward the two detectives as they entered the room. Her hand outstretched as she welcomed them.

Small actions, but all part of the power play she had learned by watching her husband over the years.

"Mrs Harvey." Benedict smiled warmly as he held out his hand.

"Diana, please. And you are DI Cooper."

"Diana, this is DS Goss and Aoife Macarthy. Aoife won't be sitting in with us this afternoon, but I wanted to introduce you. You may know her as a journalist, but she has been working with some of the young survivors. She has also been instrumental in bringing a lot of the information that has been useful to our investigation."

Aoife smiled from the other side of the table "At some point it would be good to have a conversation with you Mrs Harvey. I would like to reassure you that everything you say will be treated with discretion and I will respect anything said off the record."

Diana held her gaze just long enough to make the others in the room start to feel awkward. At the point when Benedict drew breath to comment she interceded.

"It's nice to meet you Aoife. You have done good work. I hope you can help bring some closure for the young souls who have suffered."

Aoife thanked her, handed her a card and left the room.

A young man brought in a tray of tea. Aida Goss explained that the conversation would be recorded and made the introductions for the tape.

"Thank you for coming in to talk to us Diana. Can you start by telling us what you know about your ex-husband's activities?"

Benedict noticed Diana's eyes drift past him to the plain green wall. For several seconds they sat in silence. In a quiet voice she said "Michael always had a predilection for youthful blondes. Skinny, long legs. Let's face it, I was one of them at one time. I got old, filled out. There's been a whole string of them passing through his bed since our wedding."

"You knew about this?"

"Don't look so shocked Sergeant Goss. Michael and I started out on the same page. I thought we did, anyway. Over time circumstances can change. I got pregnant; we had the children. I became a mother. He no longer saw me as the girl I once was. I found I wasn't married to the person I thought he was. These things happen. I don't know if he changed or if I had simply been so in love I hadn't seen the real man. I'm not the first wife to discover this. We either make do and compromise or..." Diana looked down at her naked fingers where years of wearing a wedding band had left a pale mark.

"Or what?" Aida Goss asked, genuinely interested and not just regarding the case.

"You… we, accept one another for who we are and allow each the freedom they need, or we go our separate ways. And after twenty five years of marriage, that is a scary prospect." Diana spoke the last with an air of submission that turned to disgust.

"How did you know he was sleeping with other women?"

"He kept a flat in Clifton which was an open secret. He freely confessed one day and to be honest, it was a sort of relief. It gave me the freedom to carry on with my life."

"And you were willing to turn a blind eye while he tortured young children?" Goss's voice was sharp, but Diana matched it.

"I accepted my husband's infidelity, not his depravity!"

"You didn't have any doubts about what was going on, even after the allegations against his friends ten years ago?" Cooper's voice was even.

Diana stared at her accuser, but she remained impassive, seemingly impervious to his allegations. "You must think me very callous indeed Detective Inspector. The truth is ……." she paused and closed her eyes for a moment. "The truth is I was well trained. I allowed myself to become that well behaved daughter who never questioned her parents, that obedient wife, that mouse who accepted that women stay at home and look after the house and the children and don't upset the apple cart. And I was tired. It takes a lot of energy supressing your true personality."

"So why did you leave?"

"Because I had no reason to stay."

"You just said you didn't believe in upsetting the apple cart."

"I said I had been trained not to upset the apple cart. Then I discovered that I could leave my prison and the view from the outside was exciting."

"You are saying you never had any idea of your husband's predilections or the company he kept?"

"I knew some of the men he mixed with. I didn't always like them and eventually they stopped coming to the house. We didn't throw dinner parties any more Michael preferred his golf club and fancy restaurants. I never knew… I mean I don't understand how men ….." Diana couldn't get the words to form in her mouth and for the first time tears flowed from her eyes and her face crumpled.

"Can you give us the names of the men you referred to? The ones who came to your house that perhaps you suspected."

"I didn't suspect. Not at the time. But yes. Griff Tomlin, Douglas Thornbeck, Andrew Mewse – Superintendent that is. There was a Father someone, gosh I can't remember his name. Rowan! That was it."

"You said Douglas Thornbeck. Do you mean the philanthropist?"

"Yes. That's him. He lives by the sea in Weston-Super-Mare."

Thirty minutes later DC Hyslop escorted Diana Harvey to the reception. As the officers walked back to their desks Goss asked. "Do you believe her?"

"I think so yes. It's easy for men like Harvey to live a separate life." He looked at his sergeant "And you?"

"I can't imagine living with a monster like that and not knowing. But then so many men search for something outside their marriage. I don't understand that either."

"Not just men." Cooper corrected. "Perhaps it is the illicit nature that thrills them." It is so often a thrill that encourages men to visit hookers when they have a wife or girlfriend at home. And there are plenty of married women who have affairs. But children. I have no explanation."

CHAPTER 52.

BENEDICT

Benedict woke in his own bed, as weary as he had been when he pulled the duvet over himself six hours earlier. It was still barely light outside. He sat up, rubbed his eyes and looked around the sparsely furnished room. It was a far cry from the overstuffed home he had been raised in with his younger brother and two sisters.

He had chosen to live in the city centre because the ease of walking from his front door to the Central Bristol Police Station in Bridewell Street was a novelty as well as a stress reducer compared to the commute across London he had suffered for eight years working in The Met.

A quick glance at the clock told him it was shortly after six a.m. He rolled off the edge of the bed and walked to the window. Throwing it open, the early morning air and the call of seagulls looking for their breakfast floated in immediately. He let the cool breeze roll over him until he felt a shiver run down his neck and he made his way to the bathroom.

The stiffness all over his body from days spent without proper exercise, followed by another poor night's sleep tossing and turning in bed did not help his mood. The hot water from the shower pounding on his muscles helped. There were other reasons for his low spirits, of course. He couldn't shake the feeling of responsibility for the attack on Aoife even though she was back up and about. He didn't want to dwell on why he should feel like this. He had gone over and over in his mind searching for any failure on his part. It wasn't his style to get involved too closely with colleagues and Aoife was a capable journalist used to working on difficult cases.

As he shovelled a bowl of cereal down his throat as quickly as possible, he could feel himself sliding toward a slump of depression which he knew was at least partly down to utter exhaustion. Despite having Michael Harvey under lock and key, he was disappointed with Assistant Superintendent Taylor and her apparent involvement. He had never particularly liked her, but he had respected her as a good cop. She had proved him wrong. He had thought himself to be a good judge of character and now he had doubts.

If Ainsley, Keeley and the others were telling the truth, and he believed that they were, his predecessors had missed the opportunity to get these creatures off the streets. Worse still, they were covering up, or even participating in the abuse and pimping out dozens of teenagers and young children for at least a decade.

The team had been far less enthusiastic about finding whoever murdered Habib Patel, Griff Tomlin and Liam Knapp, believing the men had got what was coming to them. They all felt keenly the humiliation for the police's mishandling of the case starting fifteen or twenty years earlier, leaving the children to suffer, and to make it worse, being snubbed and disparaged by those who should have helped. Knowing that members of their own force had been actively working against them had caused a big slump in morale. There was bound to be an internal investigation. Meanwhile Superintendent James promised to take a more active role in the case.

Ben hoped that reopening the cases would lead to the arrest of those who had colluded with the paedophiles, as well as putting the beasts who had tortured the children in prison for the rest of their lives.

His mind was still wandering over these thoughts when he left the house and walked along Rupert Street to the Station, and he didn't hear Aida Goss as she caught up with him.

"I remember now why Douglas Thornbeck's name sounded familiar," Aida said as she trotted to catch up.

Benedict had been miles away in a hodgepodge of confusing

thoughts, "Well he may not be a mainstream celebrity, but his name does pop up on the news from time to time."

"Yes, well, I've never paid much attention. I wasn't thinking of that. There was a complaint made against him a few years ago, from a young girl. He'd helped her family get a home together when they'd been living in separate B&B's for over a year. She said he'd kissed her and touched her inappropriately."

"I remember now. Didn't the community team interview him? But then the accusation was withdrawn?"

"Something like that. I believe Mewse put a block on the investigation. The story was turned around into a misunderstanding by an overexcited little girl."

Benedict gave a derisive snort. "Can you find the family? Have another word with them."

"I'll make it a priority. This rather changes things, doesn't it? Do you think there could be a connection with Thornbeck and Habib Patel?"

"Not obvious drinking buddies. I wouldn't think they move in the same circles but that doesn't necessarily mean anything, Thornbeck and Harvey were friends according to Diana Harvey. I think there's little doubt that whoever killed Patel and Tomlin were flagging them as sex offenders. If we pull Thornbeck into that group who knows where else it might reach."

"Or it could have nothing whatever to do with it," Goss said. "Anyway, we have to add him to the list of suspects."

"Any luck tracking down the staff from Poppy Hill?"

"Still working on it. Needless to say, records have got mislaid, memories are short and to be honest I smell a cover-up. We've found Marion Newel, the manager at the time. She's moved around a bit, but I'll send someone to pull her in for questioning. At least there'll be no shortage of volunteers for that job."

Before the team had gone home the previous night, Superintendent James had called them together and told all of them that no stone could be left unturned.

"There will be an internal investigation into what happened a decade ago, and sadly, probably longer. Michael Harvey will remain in custody. There is no doubt that it is him in some of the photographs we recovered in the freight container earlier. We have multiple witnesses to the atrocities committed. The problem is most of the children never knew the identities of their assailants. Michael Harvey does know who was involved, and as soon as the doctors give us the all-clear he will be questioned." He paused and looked several members of the team in the eye.

In a calmer voice he continued. "Meanwhile we have to stop this series of abductions and murders. There's little doubt that whoever is killing these men were either victims of abuse or people who knew what went on. We've failed them as a police force once already. We can't fail them again. The best way to do that is to get the paedophiles off the street." He pointed to the pictures pinned to the board in front of the room. "But remember, anyone who is found responsible of physical assault or murder must be arrested regardless of the circumstances."

Pacing backwards and forwards in front of his audience he increased the volume of his voice. "You must turn your frustration and anger with past events into renewed vigour and do your utmost to ensure that it will be this police force that brings them to face justice, not a group of vigilantes. We all have sympathy for the young people who have suffered in the past. We did not do a good job before. We can't let that happen again and we can't let them add guilt and murder to their turmoil."

CHAPTER 53.

SUPPER

Aoife knew from her own experience what it was like to receive a midweek invitation for supper when a work project was kicking off. All hands were expected on deck, but no one could work a solid fourteen hour shift and still deliver their peak performance on an empty belly. Plus, Aoife wanted to know how the meeting with Diana Harvey had played out. Not to mention how they were handling having their Assistant Superintendent locked up.

She had decided to play it safe and go for a simple casserole. She prepared it beforehand to reduce any panic on her side. It was almost impossible to burn as leaving it to sit in the oven on a low heat for hours would only improve the flavour. If for some reason, which was highly probable, Benedict decided to cancel, she could bag it up in portions and put it in the freezer. No one need feel frustrated or guilty.

Benedict had suggested 8pm. He arrived on Aoife's doorstep at ten past, brandishing a tub of cookie dough ice cream and a broad smile.

As she opened the door to him she guessed his day had been demanding but possibly fruitful. He looked exhausted, his shoulders sagging, and his eyes told the tale of lack of sleep, but there was also an underlying sparkle of purpose.

"I hope I'm not too late."

"You're not and I have all bases covered just in case. Dinner is a casserole so lots of leeway." She smiled warmly determined not to add to the load he was carrying from a day that had almost certainly been tough going. "Anyway, anyone who brings ice cream gets a considerable number of Brownie Points added to their account. Come in."

She walked him through to the kitchen where glasses, plates, cutlery and a water jug were already waiting on the table. A delicious smell escaped into the room as Aoife opened the oven door.

"That smells amazing."

"Good. It should taste ok." She placed the heavy metal casserole pot onto the table where a heat resistant board was waiting, switched the oven off and placed a loaf inside to warm up,

"I thought you were vegetarian. This smells like gravy."

"I am. It has vegetarian chorizo and seitan as well as lots of vegetables and the gravy is more of a sauce. Has no meat extracts. I hope you like it."

"Right!" said Benedict a little over enthusiastically.

Aoife chuckled. "Try it and if you don't like there are lots of vegetables and I can always put some pasta on."

"No, no, I am always looking to try new things."

"But not necessarily at the end of a shitty day when you're starving." She laughed. "Beer or wine?"

"Beer please."

"Help yourself, it's in the fridge. I just need to check the bread." After a moment she turned leaning her back against the workbench.

Benedict noticed that her expression was serious as she thought about what she was going to say. "Go on, spit it out. I think I'd better warn you though. I am really hungry and if I end up having to storm out in a grumpy mood I am taking my plate of food with me." It pleased him to see he'd made her laugh.

"I'll get a doggy bag ready! But you're OK. I just wanted to say thank you."

"Thank you?"

"I know it can't be easy having a journalist in the mix, and you've coped with me tagging along and sticking my nose in much better than I could have hoped."

"Ha. And there was me thinking you were one of the intelligent ones."

"And what's changed your mind?" she grinned.

"Well one." He lifted a thumb "You keep feeding me. Not only is it the way to a man's heart, I've not eaten this well for months and I will keep coming back. Two" he said raising an index finger. "I can't believe you haven't noticed that you're doing half my work for me so why on earth would I push you away. And three," another finger, "my boss thinks you are pretty amazing and wants you onside. So I'm not going to upset him, and I've got a gold star for forging a working relationship and keeping you onside." He beamed at her like a schoolboy who just knew he'd aced his exams. He didn't add that he didn't usually relax with people he didn't know well, and he found Aoife very easy company.

"Well, put like that," she laughed "dinner's on you when all this is over."

"If we put away a team of paedophiles I think dinner will be on Superintendent James. And I've got news. Nottingham raided several houses and warehouse this morning. They've found Sophia, Hiran's sister. She was in one of the cleaning teams."

"Cleaning teams?"

"Cheap labour basically. They sleep in dormitories, fed as little as possible and clean offices for twelve hours a day."

"That's fantastic. Have you told Hiran?"

"Yes. They spoke on the phone."

Aoife sat down opposite her guest and poured herself some wine. Five minutes later. She was pleased to see that the pile of food that she had placed on his plate was rapidly disappearing. Benedict reached for a chunk of warm bread which he tore into pieces and used to wipe around his plate. "This is delicious." He had cheered considerably from when he first appeared. Aoife was aware that his enthusiasm for her cooking made her feel stupidly pleased.

After a few minutes he looked up, shamefaced. "Sorry. I hadn't realised how hungry I was. How is your article coming along?"

"It's very satisfying to see people enjoy my cooking." Aoife was beaming. "And the writing is going well."

He ladled more casserole and vegetables onto his plate before reaching for another chunk of bread. "That's something I suppose." Benedict managed, before scooping another fork full of food in his mouth and chewing rapidly.

"Why do you say that? You're getting results."

"We're picking up paedophiles, dead and alive. I'd like to have had the opportunity to get to them all alive. And we have no suspects for their murder, besides the obvious; the ones who have come to you. They all have alibis of course. Did you get any names from Keeley or Petra? Do they know who might be involved?"

"No. Only those Keeley has pointed us to already. And she made it clear that even if she did, she wouldn't say."

Benedict lowered his knife and fork and lifted an eyebrow in question. "Not a surprise. Any hints?"

Aoife shrugged her shoulders "Petra had wished her father dead. She certainly wasn't going to provide names to police because whoever it was, had already endured enough. Her words. She would have preferred someone to have stuck a knife in him and made sure he had a slow death."

A frown came over his face. "Mob rule hmm? It's difficult. I can't condone people who think they can take the place of the law." He rested his hands on the table while he rolled this latest information over in his mind. "Petra has an alibi so we can rule her out. I can't imagine the hell those kids have gone through." He looked across to Aoife "Do you agree with her?"

"I'd like to say I didn't, but if I'd been abused for years by my own father. I'm pretty sure I'd feel the same way." She watched to see how her thoughts had gone down. Benedict busied himself with his food and didn't meet her eyes.

Aoife prepared herself for an argument so was surprised when he looked up and said, "I know what you mean. There are too many broken children walking around in grown bodies. It must be a hell of a struggle to put one foot in front of the other some days, let alone learn to be an adult."

"There is another reason I wanted to talk to you."

Benedict had his fork halfway to his mouth but just managed an "Oh?" before he put a large piece of potato covered in sauce into his mouth.

"Does it all seem a bit strange to you? These women searching me out and willing to talk about things they have kept secret for over a decade. And all just before bodies start turning up, each with a very obvious message."

"Yes." Benedict placed his cutlery on his plate and leaned back in his chair.

"Yes? Just Yes?"

"Well, I'd have to be a bit stupid if it hadn't occurred to me. It is my job to be suspicious." He placed his fists on the table and looked across at her. "In fact, not just me, we've discussed it in the morning briefings."

"Why didn't you mention it?"

"Because we didn't want to put you off, or have you change your attitude toward them. Whatever these people's motive, you are their chosen conduit. They could have come to the police directly, but they didn't. They trust you. I trust you. It seems to work pretty well."

For a moment Aoife couldn't decide if she was angry or flattered. But then she remembered that she had been tossing this question over in her mind for more than a week and she'd come to pretty much the same conclusion. She hadn't said anything either.

"And during your briefing did you come to any conclusions as to why me? Why now? What's the connection with the dead bodies?" She couldn't keep the edge from her voice.

"We came up with a few plausible ideas but nothing concrete."

"Share."

He took a swig of water and folded his arms. His concentration now fully on the topic. "Cara, Anwar and Iqra all died relatively recently. Until today we thought Sophia was in that bunch too. This disturbed Keeley, Daisy and Hiran forcing them to act. No matter what else has happened that we don't know about, I think these two issues are connected."

"You mean if those four had been killed what's to say Daisy and her friends aren't next?"

"Possibly. Or they might be genuinely outraged and want justice."

"They were abused and raped for years and weren't sufficiently outraged to say anything."

"Sadly, not necessarily true." He noted Aoife sit to attention "Obviously we have been going back through our records and while, if what we've been told is true, some reports never even made the light of day, we have discovered a handful of complaints about Poppy Hill. Even the foster parents became anxious about their wards disappearing overnight and coming back bruised and upset. Mewse and his friends were making sure nothing made the light of day."

"What!"

Benedict put his hand up "I know. It was before the Jimmy Savile scandal in 2012 and officers were not trained to pick up the signals. As often as not children were not believed."

"How the hell do you dismiss kids out all night coming home with bruises?"

"Broken homes, troublemakers, getting into fights. They were labelled before they ever got to senior school. Some of them had been in trouble with the police before. Petty thieving, joy riding. I'm sure you know the sort of thing" He saw Aoife face growing darker and realised he had to divert her before the storm broke. "Hideous, unbelievable whatever you want to call it, but the good news is we do all now get trained. It's still far from perfect and there are a few officers who remain blinkered, but their number is reducing. It is a lot better."

"Arrogance and criminal that's what I'd call it!" She was shouting and didn't care. "Anwar and Cara might still be here. They had turned their lives around! That takes an enormous amount of strength. Think what they could have contributed to the world! And Cara's son would not have lost his mother." The anger and adrenalin rushed through her body with such force she jumped to her feet and started clearing the table with unnecessary gusto.

Benedict stood up and removed the plates from her hands. "Um, shall I do that before you break something?"

Aoife threw him a furious look before plumping back down on her chair. "So what's the connection between the kids and the bodies?" she spat.

"That's a little more difficult. We can guess of course, but I hope they're not responsible. There are no clues left at the crime scenes. No DNA, fingerprints, footprints. No one's seen anything unusual, and no CCTV footage has picked anything up that seems relevant to any of the sites as far as we can tell."

He leaned against his chair "We know it is well planned. Someone has taken a lot of trouble checking out venues, CCTV, and the habits of their targets. To get into Griff Tomlin's house, do the deed and out again before his wife came back home, requires close to military precision." He frowned "Not to mention nerves of steel. Taking a life is not easy. People might think they want someone dead, that's very different to actually killing a person at close quarters. Even trained soldiers will tell you that."

"Nerves of steel and a serious motivation." Said Aoife "If Griff, Habib and Liam had put these kids through hell for years, and just as they were starting to get their lives together they're friends are getting bumped off one-by-one, they might think it is kill or be killed."

"You think it is the survivors who are murdering their abusers?"

Aoife took a pause. "I'm not sure. As you say it takes a

lot to kill someone, especially up close and personal. And whoever did this got very personal. Hiran certainly looked angry enough when he was talking, but I'm not sure about the others."

"He might have been angry enough to kill in the heat of the moment. That's not what would be required from whoever killed Patel, Tomlin and Liam Knapp. And Hiran has alibis. As do they all."

"I can see that. It would also take several people to get the job done. I could probably go up behind someone and hit them over the head which would incapacitate them at least for a while. Getting them in the right place and tying them up would require strength. Laying the bodies out and displaying them is a lot of work. If it's the work of one person they must be strong, quick and a really cool character."

"So a team must be involved. That's the conclusion we came to."

"Well, we have met four women if you include Petra and Mahira. None of them are very big or look particularly strong. Mewse's son and Hiran are both resentful enough. Do you think there are more of them in the group they're not telling us about?"

"Possibly. If the paedophile ring was active for ten years or more then there has to be a regular turnover. Kids don't stay kids forever. And both Daisy and Hiran mentioned a van the kids were transported in. We could be talking about dozens of youngsters involved who are now in their twenties or older."

"Do you think they would have kept in touch?" Aoife suggested. "A network maybe? It makes sense, having people who understand what you've been through supporting you in your blackest moments."

"I don't know. It must be tempting to turn your back on the past and slam the door firmly shut."

"Not something your counsellor would recommend." She smiled "And it doesn't have to be your whole network in one throw."

"But why would they contact you and be happy to tell the police, if they're planning to kill the culprits? I mean, they've made it clear what the link between the dead men is. We could have taken ages to stumble across a connection without them."

"Could be two different groups who have both decided to take action. If you say the provocation is the death of some of the victims."

"You mean that both groups got angry or scared or whatever and decided something needed to be done. Some sort of retaliation."

"Or a means to stop more people being killed." Aoife saw his sardonic look. "OK, to stop more of their friends or fellow survivors being killed. As you said, kill or be killed."

Benedict rested his chin on his hand, covering his mouth with his fist and closed his eyes. Aoife sat back in her chair swilling the wine in her glass, letting her mind work over the facts. They both sat quietly lost in their own thoughts.

Aoife sipped her wine and leaned forward on the table. "Penny for them. Or have you fallen asleep?"

He smiled then opened his eyes. "Perhaps that's why Petra was so keen to leave. She'd said her piece. Gave you the facts she wanted passed on, and then got out before she tripped up and said something she wasn't meant to."

"You mean it's all a scripted act? Not just a group of young people who have found strength in Keeley coming forward."

"That's along the lines of what I was thinking, yes. They are feeding us just enough information to keep us interested and make sure we're looking in the right direction."

"You think there's a mastermind behind all this? One person pulling the strings?"

"Coordinating the action. It's a possibility."

"It's certainly a thought, but a bit farfetched. Orchestrating the murders and the scripts. That would require a seriously organised brain. Sounds a bit too 'Spooks'." Aoife went back into her revery for a moment. She looked up through her eyelashes and frowned.

"Is that what you're doing with me? Pulling the strings? Feeding me just enough information to keep me moving forward in the direction you're sending me?" She emptied her glass then reached across for the bottle.

Benedict jerked his head back as if she'd slapped him. "Really? You think your being played?"

"Possibly. It's all a bit easy."

"Well you're not. Not by me anyway. I wouldn't dare. As I thought I made clear earlier, you're too valuable." He smirked. "Nor do I think you're that gullible."

Aoife studied his face, his body language. It was possible that the police were happy to keep her dangling in the stream attracting the different parts of the puzzle to take the bait. She took another sip of her wine. "No. you're probably not. I don't think you're a good enough actor to keep it up for this long."

"Thanks." He grimaced.

"Welcome. Ice cream?"

"That would be nice, and then I need to go. A few hours sleep and it's another early start tomorrow."

They spent the rest of the evening talking about things to see and places to visit in Bristol. Aoife had binged on her sightseeing when she first arrived but had done little since the weekend Leigh had visited. She admitted that what she really wanted to do was get her walking boots on and get out in the hills.

Ice cream eaten, Aoife cleared the bowls and offered coffee.

"No. I really must go. Thankyou."

Aoife walked him to the door and in the narrow passage there was a disconcerting moment as Benedict lent forward as if to kiss her cheek before checking himself and offering a hand instead.

Aoife, partly from embarrassment, blurted out a laugh causing him to turn on his heel and leave. She thought it best not to wait at the door to wave him goodbye.

CHAPTER 54.

DAISY

D aisy had put a lot of effort into decorating the nursery during her pregnancy, and it was now her favourite place in the whole house. She'd painted the walls canary yellow and had sewn green curtains with flowers and birds on, making sure the thick linings would hold back the early morning sunshine.

She loved their little home. It gave her a glimpse of a possible future. She envisaged patchwork quilts and homemade bread, flowers growing in the tiny front garden and a vegetable patch at the back. She saw Ryan sitting on the floor in front of the bright flames of the wood burning stove, playing with Flora. And them all cuddled on the settee together watching Beauty and The Beast on their little TV.

Michael Harvey was behind bars, Mewse was dead and several other police officers were suspended under investigation. For the first time for as long as she could remember she felt set free.

Today smelt of Spring and rebirth and for the first time there was a chance to put all the bad things behind her.

The sun was out, Flora was upstairs having her afternoon nap, and Daisy had made the most of the nice weather to plant out some carrots and peas in the garden. She straightened and listened for a moment. Flora rarely climbed over the side of her cot but that wasn't what had disturbed Daisy. She heard through the open kitchen window someone much heavier than her toddler, moving around in her home. She squinted toward the house and got a glimpse of a large shadow crossing through her kitchen. She ducked down. She wanted to run, but she knew she couldn't. Her little girl was curled innocently asleep in her cot.

These people had stolen so much of her life that she could never get back. She had been trying to focus on the future with her family. She was strong. Two years of counselling and a close knit group of friends, who understood and supported her every step, had got her this far and she was willing to fight to keep what had been so hard won.

Her heart was racing, and her breath came in ragged gulps as she pulled out her mobile and dialled the only policeman she had ever trusted. Then she ran to the side of the shed and pulled out the small axe where Ryan had left it stuck in the chopping block Quietly, she moved toward the house.

She had learned to be silent; learned to be unnoticed while she watched others. She crept in the back door, keeping close to the wall. The man was walking toward the little front room but turned at the last minute, putting his hand out to grab her not bothering to look down. His hand was on her throat, and he pressed hard. Daisy knew he was going to kill her; take her from her daughter. She couldn't let that happen. She kicked him and bit him and with all the strength she never knew she had she swung her right arm and brought the sharp axe biting into the man's calf.

He yelled, his hand moving to clutch the wound. As he bent forward Daisy brought the axe down again. She heard a sickening crunch as it made contact with the man's skull. A second set of footsteps were running down the stairs and without thinking she threw herself against the wall by the doorway leaning against it for support, her legs felt weak, and she dropped to a crouch, sweat cold on her forehead. As the second shape came through the door she swung the axe again with every ounce of strength she had left, catching the man just below his hip. He fell instantly and Daisy shot passed him up the stairs to the nursery. To her baby.

When the police arrived five minutes later the first thing that hit them was the smell like an abattoir. Blood and faeces at the bottom of the stairs was the cause. Lying in a lake of blood was a heavily built man with his head split open and another, more slightly built clutching his left leg trying and failing to staunch the red fountain flowing from his left thigh.

Leaving the paramedics to deal with that chaos Cooper avoided as much of the mess as possible and leapt up the stairs. Pushing first a door to his left which held a double bed then he entered the door to his right and felt a huge relief sweep over his body.

Daisy felt so tired she didn't think she could stand up even when she heard the sirens approaching, or the heavy footsteps and shouting of the police officers downstairs. She sat on the floor of the bright yellow bedroom with the green curtains and pretty birds, and hugged Flora close to her chest, rocking backwards and forwards cooing and singing to her little girl, shutting out the horror of a lifetime.

CHAPTER 55.

MARION NEWEL

I t was 2.30 in the afternoon and Marion was sitting on the couch counting the stash of twenty pound notes she had pulled from behind the loose brick in the old fireplace. She always kept used twenties. They took up less space than fives or tens but didn't raise eyebrows when you handed them over in a shop or railway station. Using credit cards was out of the question.

She'd had a good run. Ten years as a social worker which had been crap pay and hard, depressing work. Then twenty years at Poppy Hill Children's home where she'd swapped horses and started to earn real money. Promoted to director her salary had improved but was never going to give her the lifestyle she craved. Then counsellor McVeigh and Superintendent Mewse had pointed out the unlimited resource she had under her control. Children with hopeless futures in front of them and no family - or family who didn't care.

Marion had hesitated at first. Not because she was squeamish about the proposition but because she knew what would happen if she got caught. Then she realised that Father Rowan and even Doctor Gosford had an appetite for adolescents. If what McVeigh had told her was true, and their customers included MPs and judges, all avenues were covered. She threw herself into the project wholeheartedly.

A while back she'd bought herself a small apartment in Biarritz. No one knew she owned it, not even her close friend and lover Greg McVeigh. It turned out that he did not share his friends taste for young boys. Marion had to admit, he was an accomplished and surprisingly generous man in bed.

She secreted the bundles of money within the many hidden pockets of her especially adapted coat, leaving enough in her wallet for her immediate needs. She checked her passport, and Eurotunnel ticket and gave her rented apartment one final check before she walked to the door for the last time. She would never be back. She was going to disappear and enjoy the rewards she had earned.

The death of Griff Tomlin and the rumours about how his body had been left had spooked her and her first instinct had been to drop everything and run. Then she convinced herself that the police would find nothing to tie her with Griff's past and she needed time to close bank accounts, secure loose ends and plan her departure. Panicking would be her downfall.

Anyway, there were too many barriers for the police to break through between her and a conviction. She was well connected. She knew too many people in high places whose careers and lives would be ruined if she talked.

She made her way to the front door and clicked it firmly behind her. With no remorse, she walked down the stairs and turned her back on her past life. She was still a relatively fit woman. This was going to be a new beginning. The last and most enjoyable third of her life.

She caught the bus that would take her to Bristol Temple Mead Station. She didn't want to leave any trail of hired car or taxis. She looked out the window as they travelled past the open spaces of Durdham Downs, then through the high price tagged Clifton village and on down Park Road to the Hippodrome Theatre and the City Centre. She looked left as the Bristol Police Station came into view. She smiled and breathed a small sigh of relief as she left it behind.

Marion collected her suitcase from the rack as the double decker bus turned left into the grandiose station designed by Isambard Brunel almost two hundred years earlier. A marked police car on the far side of the car park gave her a moment's hesitation and she felt a stirring of disquiet. Then she told herself not to be silly. No one knew she was on this bus, nor of her plans to catch the fast train to Paddington. In two hours, she would be arriving in London Waterloo and boarding her train to the centre of Paris. She queued impatiently with other passengers waiting for the doors to open. Stepping down from the bus she looked around warily as she kept moving.

"Hello Marion. We thought we'd come to meet you." The formidable frame of Sergeant Goss blocked her path. Two uniformed officers closed in on either side.

The blood drained from Marion's face but only for a moment. She had contacts. They might drag her down the station, but she would be out again and with a bit of luck, on the evening train to Paris. She gave a derisive smile.

"I think you've got the wrong woman love."

Goss returned the smile. "I don't think so '*love*'. I take it you know we've been hosting Father Rowan at the station. It's amazing how a couple of nights in the cells will loosen a man's tongue."

"You fucking bastard." Marion's face was white. Fear now in her eyes.

"Good job you've packed." Marion hadn't noticed DC Hyslop until he removed the suitcase from Marion's grip. "I think between the priest and the statements we've got from those children you failed to look after; you'll be spending a long time away from home."

"Not that you'll be needing all the things you've stashed in here. Uniforms will be provided where you're going." Joined in Goss with a smile.

"Oh, and in case you're thinking of calling a friend, we can save you the bother. We have counsellor McVeigh and Doctor Gosford too. It seems when it comes to choosing between a cosy police cell or being staked out with their trousers around their ankles, the cell doesn't seem so bad."

"Read her rights DC Hyslop." Said Goss.

CHAPTER 56.

DOUGLAS THORNBECK

D ouglas Thornbeck relaxed back in his big armchair and swirled the whisky in his glass. The sound of the ice chink, the fragrance achieved from decades in an oak cask, this was how a day should close. His wife had always told people it was his one vice and for years she had believed it to be true. In later years, after their daughter had been sectioned, he sensed even she had her doubts.

Pushing those thoughts away he brought the glass to his lips; savoured the smell once more and poured a little of the liquid on to his tongue and the back of his throat, leaving it in his mouth a while before swallowing. He pressed the button on the remote control and closed his eyes allowing the music to drift through him.

He imagined Miriam sitting opposite him in an identical chair as she had on so many evenings during their early years together. Her eyes were the same golden colour as the liquid in the glass. He thought back to when they first met. The day he had got on one knee and proposed. Placing the ring on her finger he told her it was a token that his love would always be hers, wherever in the world he travelled. And it always had been. The sparkle of joy it had brought to those beautiful amber eyes. It had been the most precious moment in his life.

She had been so proud of him and the work he had done across the world helping children who had lost everything. In the early days she had visited some of the projects with him until their own children were born and she had thrown herself into motherhood. Even now she was with their

319

granddaughters.

He closed his eyes and let his mind drift with Verdi's famous Chorus of the Hebrew Slaves. The glass was in his left hand with his right gently conducting the ebb and flow of a hundred voices. The dusk fell and soft shadows played against the lattice windows. The silky darkness of the room comforted him like a velvet blanket.

He did not hear the gentle click as the key was turned in the back door. Nor was he aware of the door to his study being pushed quietly open. The whisky dulled his senses as he drifted along on the music. There was no warning. He didn't hear her approach as she crept across the wooden floor onto the beautiful old rug he was so proud of. Nor did he get the opportunity to admire the sharp cutting edge of the antique knife that morphed so beautifully into the smooth ornate, mother of pearl handle. His face was vacant with confusion at the first touch, his brain unable to register what was happening. His glass crashed to the floor and its contents mingled instantly with splatters of blood into the carpet.

As his head dropped and his body slumped his executioner dropped the knife deliberately onto his lap where the river of blood was already pooling.

She unzipped the front of her suit with her gloved hands just enough to remove an envelope which she opened. She removed the contents and spread the photographs on the floor where the blood was unlikely to reach. The children in the pictures were mainly black. She had not included any of herself, but Douglas Thornbeck could easily be identified in them.

Then she stiffened, listening. Even above the music she heard a key in the front door. With one last glance at her victim, she pressed back into the shadows. No one was supposed to be here. Her heart thumping, Kiki glanced to her right, the front of the house. She checked that her shoe covers were clean as she moved quickly back down the hall, glancing over her shoulder as she ran through the kitchen and out the back door. She pulled it to, didn't shut it firmly, not wanting to alert whoever else was in the house to her presence. She ran lightly down the concrete steps and across the lawn keeping on her toes. The back gate was still open as she had left it.

Once in the relative security of Weston Woods that butted up behind the house she unzipped her blue coveralls and rolled them up with her mask and gloves tossing them quickly into a plastic bag and shoving the lot into her backpack. Pulling on a grey wool hat and dark hoodie she stepped into walking boots two sizes too big for her feet lacing them tight.

Slipping her hands into grey mittens she pushed her arms into the backpack straps and jogged through the dark woods to Kewstoke Road. In practice it had taken her just fourteen minutes. In Kiki's mind she had lived a lifetime in those few minutes but the lump she had carried in her chest for over a decade had shrunk, just a little. All the years this man had haunted her dreams while being venerated by his country and even adorned with honours by his government, could now start to dissolve.

As she approached the far edge of the woods she slowed, looked at her watch, then crouched. The sound of the aging black Ford Fiesta decelerating was close by. Kiki broke cover opened the car door and threw her backpack in the back seat before jumping in. She smiled at the white haired lady in the driver's seat.

Miriam Thornton turned with grim face to the young girl "All done?"

Kiki Mensah nodded. "All done."

Miriam squeezed the girl's arm, put the ancient car with the false number plates in gear and drove off.

Despite her protests Kiki had refused Anna's assistance on this mission. Douglas Thornbeck had talked his way out of trouble before and she had to be sure it wouldn't happen again.

When they had met she had not been shocked at the depth of Miriam's loathing for her husband but had been surprised when the older lady had contrived the method of his murder. She had even wanted to be the one to wield the knife and didn't care about being caught and punished for her crime. It had taken a while to persuade her that Kiki should carry out the punishment.

Kiki wound down the window and took a deep breath of the salty air and smiled. She felt free. A feeling of elation ran through her body. Her actions weren't a show of cruelty. This was revenge and justice combined.

CHAPTER 57.

MOLLY, CHARLOTTE & MIRIAM

When the police had called late the previous evening to break the news and warn them of a potential media storm that might break on their doorstep, Molly had looked across at her sister Charlotte and seen the same shock plastered to her face that was making her own heart thump violently against her ribs.

They both knew their Grandpa Thornbeck was sometimes on the TV and radio. He had made a name for himself as the voice for those who could not be heard, shining a light on the problems of the hungry and the sick. Not just of the Third World, but his own doorstep too.

He had worked hard during the decades before it became fashionable to champion the less well off, and more recently had been praised for his consistent good works. Visiting remote towns and war torn cities that were home to millions of starving and overlooked families in countries others were too scared to set foot in, and governments chose to ignore. Children whose lives had been smashed beyond recognition because someone more powerful wanted to boost their own status and feed their craving for power.

Douglas Thornbeck was applauded for his work with displaced children in parts of the U.K. too. Raising money and awareness of the hell defenceless boys and girls were going through. While parents avoided landlords and lived in fear of loan sharks they had no hope of ever paying back.

This Douglas Thornbeck, the trailblazer, hero, protector of the disinherited, was not how Molly and Charlotte thought of their grandfather. They knew him for what he was, but they did not know of his death until the police arrived.

The officer's wanted to make sure that the young women would not be shocked by anything they might see in the media, or the manner in which but they had not expected his sudden death he had died. The implications explained to them by police was no surprise.

They were not shocked by his suspected duplicity. Children with no homes and parents who were so grateful to this man who they worshipped as a hero, were even more defenceless than Molly and Charlotte had been. Thornbeck had dozens of young lives to deplete. They lay out in front of him like a smorgasbord without fear of his wife or daughter discovering his loathsome appetites. But they had not expected his sudden death and their shock was real.

As agreed, the sisters had not known who was on the original list of four, but their grandfather's death was number seven. They had heard about an ex-police officer and a priest. These three all unplanned.

Goss had returned with Cooper to the granddaughter's home, early the next morning. Their grandmother was staying with them and, all three women now sat quietly in the large lounge of the ground floor Georgian apartment owned by the sisters. Backs straight ankles crossed, hands on their laps.

"You have no idea who did this to him?" Molly asked.

"We're looking at several possibilities, but it's early days." Sergeant Goss looked at the younger women who were sitting on the edge of the settee, hands clasped on their laps but knees touching, giving each other support.

"I don't think you have any reason to be scared. We don't believe you are a target." Confirmed Cooper.

"Unless there is something you are not telling us." Added Goss.

Molly turned her head to look directly into the sergeant's eyes. "Fear has its purpose. It propels us to take action against danger. It can make us faster and stronger when we need it the most. We've done with running."

Both police officers worked hard to keep their faces neutral.

"We aren't worried detective, just relieved that it's over." Explained Charlotte.

"Over?"

"Don't look so shocked. I know it might be difficult for you to understand. Whoever killed him did us all a good service." Charlotte gave him a little smile.

"He can't hurt anyone else." Said Molly.

"I know this must be distressing for you, but we have to ask. Did you ever suspect that he might be capable of hurting anyone?"

"We both knew exactly what he was capable of."

Benedict left a beat before he next spoke and kept his voice soft "Did he hurt you?"

Goss noticed their grandmother almost imperceptibly flinch at the question.

"He made our lives hell. He was a tyrant. An evil disgusting, arrogant, bastard." Molly's face was deep red as she spat the words out.

"My sister is being very polite; she doesn't usually hold back." Charlotte smiled in such a genuine way neither Cooper nor Goss could hold back a grin.

Molly wondered "Does he still have the photographs he took of the girls while they were naked?" Goss and Cooper looked at each other, unsure for the moment how to answer.

Charlotte took over "He had asked us to pose in positions that were sick. Insisting we touch each other's breast or thigh. Occasionally he had fondled us himself."

"You mean you are the little girls in the photos?" asked Goss.

"Probably. Two of them anyway. If you show them to us we might be able to name a few others." Said Molly matter of factly.

"He never hurt us physically. There were no marks for our

mother or grandmother to find. And he was very clever with the black mail."

"So no one knew?"

"I'm not sure. We think mother probably did. But then she was his daughter. Who knows what hell he put her through? No one would have believed her. It's probably why she's in a care home now."

Sergeant Goss gasped as her mind opened up to the reality. Douglas Thornbeck's reputation had been his invisibility cloak. He was so famous, so venerated, that no one saw beyond the façade. The smiling face and the unassuming comments about how he was only doing what little he could to help those most in need. It had even been hinted that he would be mentioned in the New Year's Honour list.

The sisters had left the family home in Weston-Super-Mare at the same time. Molly had gone to university in Bristol and was now teaching Math at a secondary school. While Charlotte had gone to art college. Now they shared a flat in a pleasant area of Clifton. They hadn't seen their grandfather since that time, although their grandmother was a frequent visitor. The police officers knew that she was staying with them now. Had been in Bristol on the night her husband had been killed.

Thornbeck's body had been discovered in his large Georgian home on the hill, overlooking the sea, by the cleaning lady the evening before. She had explained to police officers that she always did some shopping for Mr Thornbeck when she went to the supermarket if his wife wasn't home, because he had far more important things to do than worry about what was in the fridge.

"You and your mother lived in the house in Weston-Super-Mare with him and your grandmother?"

"Yes. And before you ask we did try telling mum, but she ignored us. Pretended it hadn't happened." Said Charlotte.

"She was either too traumatised herself, or she was willing to sacrifice us for the sake of a roof over her head. Our father committed suicide when we were still toddlers. Lost all his money. Completely bankrupt. Couldn't face the shame so he left mum to face it on her own."

"And you Mrs Thornbeck? Did you never suspect?"

Miriam Thornbeck shook her head. In a quiet voice she said "All those years I watched my husband play with the children and their friends and thought how lucky that the girls had a strong father figure in their lives. Their own father died under terrible circumstances. I'm ashamed to say it never occurred to me." Her voice was quiet as she spoke the truth. She had not known. Not then. And all the time she spoke now tears threatened to spill down her cheeks.

"Did you ever tell anyone else about what happened? When you were older maybe?"

"By the time we left home and out of his reach Douglas Thornbeck was a hero. Invincible. There had been a couple of complaints made about him over the years, I'm sure you've heard about them?" Molly looked questioningly and Benedict nodded. "Both reports were withdrawn. Probably bribed to keep their mouths shut."

"Or threatened." Charlotte added.

Molly nodded agreement. "There might have been others, but the police didn't want to know."

"You probably ask why we didn't say anything at the time. Try harder. I often ask myself. You have to remember we were very young. We'd lost our father. Our mother was ill. We were scared. If our own mother didn't believe us why would we think the police might?"

"And then we were out from under his roof and have never seen him since. We didn't want to talk about it."

Beneath their composed façade both girls were struggling to keep their emotions under control. What those emotions were was less obvious. Goss could see out the corner of her eye that Benedict was concerned, probably thinking he was causing them further distress by talking about their grandfather's misdemeanours and death.

During her visit the previous night Goss had detected the immediate relief in both their young faces when she had broken the news that one of their closest remaining relatives had died. In different circumstances she might have assumed the thought of a large inheritance was feeding an ugly greed. In this case she suspected what they really wanted to know was that their grandfather did not go "easy to his grave." They would like to think that he suffered, punished for the misery that he had spread. They would like to think that he felt the same fear and pain that he had inflicted, had seen at least a glimpse of the shadow that he had cast over everything during their young lives.

"If there is anything you remember however small, please call me." Benedict removed a card from his wallet and left it on the coffee table between them. "Thank you for your time."

"It's a long time since we had any contact with him or went near the house. And if we did suspect someone I doubt we would tell you." Charlotte's smile was warm, almost playful in contrast to her sister who looked solemn.

"When you do find out who finally accomplished some sort of justice for all those children he has tortured, I will give them a pat on the back. Thank them." Said Molly.

As they closed the garden gate Cooper looked at his sergeant "What did you make of that?"

"Two young women who have had a truly shitty life." Goss spat back. Both officers looked back at the ground floor window wondering how Molly and Charlotte would be dealing with the latest turn in events.

"Their father screws up big time and instead of dealing with it, deserts them in the worst possible way, commits suicide and dumps everything on mum. Grandmother becomes seriously ill with cancer and is in hospital soon after. Grandfather who should be a father figure molests them throughout their childhood, and mum loses her marbles and doesn't even recognise them anymore."

"I don't think it's over either."

"What do you mean?" Goss looked shocked.

"When the media gets hold of the story, "major do gooder abuses children", they won't respect the girl's privacy. And Molly's a schoolteacher. How is that going to go down?"

Goss grimaced. "Perhaps they'll show some compassion."

"The family all certainly have strong feelings about Douglas Thornbeck. Do you think they told us everything?"

"I don't know. I mean, their life story would fill a book, we were only there for half an hour. They might have deliberately held information back or it could just all be too much to process. And the police have let them down in the past. Why should they help us now?"

Goss wondered if Aoife would get any more details from the sisters than the police might glean. Barriers were always in place as soon as a police officer revealed their warrant card. She liked the little she knew of Aoife and admired the way the young woman worked with the victims. She had seen how Daisy, Keeley and even Hiran had all relaxed in Aoife's company and chatted about their experiences as if to a friend. She decided to float her idea passed her boss.

"Perhaps if Aoife gets her story out first it will ease the pressure from the rest of the media."

"Maybe. I wouldn't put money on it."

"And she could find out more than their willing to share with us. She seems pretty good at gaining people's trust."

Cooper turned in his seat to face his sergeant. "I thought you didn't like her?"

"I never didn't like her. I was pissed that she was poking around in a crime investigation." She gave him a sardonic smile "And was getting more information out of witnesses than we were."

Cooper chuckled. "Fair enough."

"Should we introduce her to Molly and Charlotte?"

"I don't think that will be necessary. They'll find their own way to her quite soon, I'm sure."

CHAPTER 58.

TWO MONTHS LATER.

Aoife had spent the hours just after dawn that morning enjoying the surf and the almost deserted beach at Porthcawl. So much had happened following the capture of Marion Newell and Michael Harvey that she'd hardly had the time to run in the local park let alone manage an excursion to South Wales.

Aoife had successfully sold the story to both local and national media, keeping her own name out of the mix and taking credit only as the author. Nevertheless, following Michael Harvey's arrest the national media had picked up on the role she had played in the investigation, resulting in an old photograph of her leaving the Connaught in London with Cameron's arm around her shoulders appearing just below the headlines.

Aoife's neighbour, Phiah, had teasingly expressed excitement about knowing such a famous celebrity, and had increased the number of cakes she had baked and left as presents. And Marcus, Phia's husband had insisted on inviting Aoife for drinks on Sunday afternoons in the garden whenever the sun was out.

Superintendent James gave a statement.

"It appears that several institutions, including the police, have repeatedly failed to deal with allegations of child sexual abuse, from turning a blind eye to corruption, actively shielding abusers. It is also clear that there has been a widespread failure to put the needs of children first. An inquiry is to be set up and no stone will be left unturned."

That afternoon, Aoife was back in Bristol looking out over the river.

The small group that gathered in the last of the summer sun below her, at the Ferry stop platform by The Princes Bridge, were solemn but not downhearted. A mixed bunch dressed in bright colours and everyday clothes. They stood close together as one unit. Mostly in their twenties, a few a bit older. A handful of young children sensing the mood of the adults held tightly on to their parent's hand or sat quietly in their father's arms.

Poems were read, words of love and memories were uttered, tears fell. Then as each name of the dead or missing was called out by a different person a flower was tossed into the water. Each a different type and colour, representing the many children and adults who had died because no one had stood up for them.

Sweet sorrow, and silent anguish. An attempt at closure, but everyone who had lived through the pain and terror knew there could be no cessation to the hurt and emptiness.

Aoife stood a little way back, feeling like an intruder, trespassing on their grief. She had been surprised and appreciative of the invitation and it needed to be documented as a fitting end to the account she had reported. She doubted it would be the end of the story.

She noted that Kira looked postnatal with red cheeks and glassy eyes, which was no surprise. The baby she cradled in her arms had only arrived two days ago. She and her tiny son had attracted many hugs and kisses when they had arrived. Now Peter stood with a protective arm around the new mother's shoulders, and Kira seemed happy to lean upon his strength.

Aoife didn't recognise the woman standing close to Hiran. She assumed it was Sophia. The police in Nottingham had eventually pulled together and found several traces of not just child prostitution but also women kept in a warehouse and made to work long hours as cleaning crew for industrial and retail units. Hiran's sister, Sophia had been one of them.

Another group of men were locked up in farm buildings at night and bussed out as slave labour on building sites and farms during the day.

She took a couple of photographs with her phone. As she placed it back in her shoulder bag she was aware of a shadow nearby and turned sharply.

"Sorry, I didn't mean to scare you." Benedict gave an apologetic smile.

"Hi. I didn't think you were coming."

"I thought I should. I needed some fresh air anyway. It's a bigger gathering than I expected."

"Yes. I think there's a few friends and partners."

"I thought you'd like to know that we've moved Daisy and her family somewhere safe.

Aoife had noticed that Daisy was not present. Nor were Flora or Ryan. "She's not being kept in custody then?"

"They're out of the county until after the trial, just to be on the safe side."

"Then what will happen to her?"

"I don't know. She will give evidence against Father Rowan, Michael Harvey and some of the others. Her history and the fact that she was in her own home defending her child is a strong argument for self-defence. Wherever they go they will be offered new identities. Harvey may be locked up, but he will still have a long reach. This network has been active for decades by all accounts."

"What are the chances of you tracing everyone involved?"

A soft snort was the only reply he gave.

They stood quietly for a while watching the proceedings below them and enjoying the summer sun.

Aoife didn't move her gaze from the gathering as she said softly "You think we've been played?"

"Yep."

They both remained still as Peter strummed a guitar and Charlotte's sweet voice rose to pierce their hearts as she sang Hallelujah.

"You still on for Saturday?" asked Benedict.

"Sure. I'll pick you up at seven if that's not too early?"

Benedict and Aoife had already made one excursion to the lake where Benedict kept his dinghy. They had arranged to make the most of the good weather and explore the Wye Valley together at the weekend.

One afternoon, just before the gathering on Princes Bridge,

Benedict had joined Aoife, Phiah and her husband for a BBQ and the four had chatted and laughed while Phiah's daughter played in a paddling pool and drew butterflies in her sketch book. And for the first time in months Aoife realised that she felt completely at home and relaxed in her surroundings.

She knew that Phiah had been thrilled that Benedict had joined them. Her neighbour ignored Aoife's protest that they were just friends and that's how it would stay. Phiah insisted she'd seen something in the way Ben had looked at Aoife, but Aoife had brushed the thought aside with a chuckle.

"He's going to be out of town for some time. There are still a lot of this gang operating in other parts of the country."

"Surely they have other detectives capable of handling it?"

"I'm sure they do, but Ben and Aida have the experience of how they work. It's their case."

"It'll look good on his CV I'm sure." But Aoife knew her friend still had hopes for a romantic relationship blossoming.

Cameron had betrayed her trust, and the pain was still sharp if she let herself dwell on it. She still thought of Cameron of course; caught his soft voice in her head, heard his music on the radio. When she went into a book shop and smelt that familiar odour painful memories flooded back, but he was no longer the first thing she thought of as she lay in bed of a morning.

Aoife had been brought up to be a self-sufficient woman and she was enjoying her independence. There were no plans to change that in the foreseeable future.

Dedication

This is dedicated to all of you who didn't have a great start to life.

Especially those who have found the strength to push through and make their life their own.

Sometimes you just have to jump out the window and grow wings on the way down.

Printed in Great Britain
by Amazon

55404268R00185